Marcel Viau

Griffintown in Turmoil

A Silas Robinson Investigation

ISBN: 978-2-925072-10-2

Reviewer: Sylvie Gagnon

Proofreader: Hélène Lecours

Cover Design: Created by OpenAI

CHAPTER 1

Friday, March 17

On March 17th, Montreal lit up to celebrate Saint Patrick, the patron saint of Ireland. In 1865, the festival marked its 40th anniversary with exceptional splendour. A grand parade wound its way through the city's streets, a religious and national display in character.

From Wellington Street, at the heart of Griffintown, to Place d'Armes, where the event began, the entire city was adorned for the occasion. Balconies sagged under the weight of banners, predominantly green—the emblematic colour of Ireland—while the streetlamps twinkled with garlands. In some places, flowered arches formed festive gateways, turning the streets into open-air theatre. A fine layer of snow lingering on rooftops and window ledges added a crystalline brilliance to the scene. It was the renowned "Saint Patrick's Day Parade," though the clergy, ever eager to add a pious tone to the event, stubbornly referred to it as a "procession." What had once united Catholic and Protestant Irish in a shared display of pride had gradually become a predominantly Catholic event, much to the chagrin of Protestants who now avoided the celebration.

Cheerful crowds bustled under a biting breeze along the sidewalks, though occasionally warmed by bursts of sunlight that made frozen puddles glimmer here and there. In Canada, March was a pivotal month, poised between the harshness of winter and the tentative awakening of spring. While winter still held its grip, with occasional snow showers serving as a reminder of its persistence, the first spring rains would sometimes appear, transforming the landscape. These showers, melting the accumulated snow, hinted at the promise of a new season, even though the lingering cold continued to assert that winter had not yet relinquished its hold.

In this frigid morning atmosphere, men, women, and children from various Irish neighbourhoods crowded together to catch a glimpse of the parade. The men, bundled in thick coats, some already tipsy, sang traditional tunes, their hoarse voices blending with the crystalline laughter of the women, who clapped their gloved hands to the rhythm. The children devoured the shimmering uniforms with curious eyes and jostled each other, their bubbling excitement erupting into innocent scuffles. Their boots, muddied and wet with melting snow, bore the marks of the soggy ground. Among them, coarse, worn, and ill-fitting woollen garments revealed the origin of most spectators: Griffintown, the working-class stronghold and beating heart of Montreal's Irish community.

At Place d'Armes, the tumult of a large gathering was palpable. A colourful, noisy crowd jostled in festive chaos. The various participant groups struggled to find their places under the watchful eyes of their leaders. Soldiers in uniform, wearing their pristine bicorne hats, struggled to calm their nervous horses, which stamped anxiously in the face of the commotion. The hot steam from the horses' nostrils mingled with the cold air. More disciplined were the men dressed in saffron kilts—that distinctive golden yellow—who marched into formation with assured steps. Their movements were synchronized with the rhythmic pounding of the drums they carried proudly, while others adjusted their Scottish bagpipes, preferred over the more demanding Irish Uilleann Pipes.

The procession finally began at the signal of the drums and flutes, stretching through the streets like a majestic serpent. Men in black coats and bowler hats, wearing long green scarves adorned with shamrocks, led the march. At its center, a massive banner floated, emblazoned with the image of Erin playing the Celtic harp, a vibrant symbol of their homeland. Further back, distinctive banners identified various groups: the St. Ann's Society, St. Patrick Benevolent Society, Young Irishmen's Literary and Benefit Association, and many more. Alongside them, children from a school run by the Christian Brothers timidly marched, their solemn faces contrasting with the lively surroundings. Finally, priests in long black coats covering their cassocks mingled with the crowd, their hems occasionally dragging through the melting snow—a detail the Sulpician clergy seemed oblivious to.

When the procession reached St. Lawrence Hall, the temporary residence of the Governor General, Sir James Monk, the parade came to a solemn halt. A fine snow swirled in the biting breeze, but it did not prevent the crowd from turning their eyes to the balcony, where the governor appeared, wrapped in a heavy dark coat with a fur collar. He greeted the crowd with a measured gesture before addressing them:

"My dear fellow citizens! It is an honour to see you gathered here on this festive day. At this moment, my Irish heritage, a precious legacy from my parents, resonates in harmony with you all. I pay tribute to your unwavering loyalty to the country's institutions and your allegiance to our sovereign, Queen Victoria."

Polite applause followed these words, soon giving way to a rousing rendition of "God Save the Queen" from a portion of the crowd, encouraged by local dignitaries. Yet a faint murmur rippled through the ranks: some faces remained closed, marked by a quiet tension. Men, clutching their scarves against the freezing wind, exchanged heavy glances of disapproval.

Monk concluded his speech on a sharper note:

"I have no doubt that the Irish of this country will ignore the seditious calls of those rebels who sow only chaos and destruction. Long live the British Empire, and long live the Queen!"

The drums thundered once more, drowning out the scattered applause, and the parade resumed its path toward Victoria Square, where other speakers awaited their turn to address the crowd. Burned up in a thick coat but visibly uncomfortable in the cold, Mayor Beaudry delivered a speech in halting English, eliciting a few stifled chuckles from the spectators.

Next, it was Thomas D'Arcy McGee's turn to take the stage. Irish-born McGee had made Canada his home for a decade. A prominent figure in the political scene, he stirred passions as much with his eloquence as with his unflattering appearance. Some did not shy away from calling him outright ugly: his sallow face, lined with age and wrinkles, was framed by a mix of gray and black hair, always slightly dishevelled. Heavy with fatigue, his eyes shone with a sharp, almost intimidating intelligence. Draped in a worn coat but clutching a finely carved cane, he climbed the rickety steps of the makeshift platform, each step resonating like the prelude to a much-anticipated speech.

True to form, D'Arcy McGee paused at the top, scanning the crowd silently. This calculated pause worked like a charm: the murmurs and gossip gradually faded, leaving a hum of anticipation in the cold air. His deep, resonant voice cut through the wind's rustle when he finally spoke.

"I look upon the future of my adopted country with hope, though not without concern," he began, his words landing like hammers on the anvil of collective attention. "I see in the distance a great nation, united, like Achilles' shield, by the blue edge of the ocean. I see it divided into many communities, each managing its own internal affairs, yet all bound together by free bonds, institutions, relations, and trade."

A shiver ran through the crowd, perhaps heightened by the cold seeping into the thinner coats. Captivated by the grandeur of his vision, the audience held its breath. Galvanized, McGee continued, raising his voice slightly:

"Within that shield, I see the peaks of the Western mountains and the crests of the Eastern waves: the winding Assiniboine, the five Great Lakes, the St. Lawrence, the Ottawa, the Saguenay, the Saint John, and the Minas Basin. In each of these fertile valleys, in the cities along these rivers, I see a generation of industrious, contented, moral men, free in name and in fact. Men capable of upholding a Constitution worthy of such a country in peace as in war."

Despite the man's undeniable eloquence, part of the audience remained cold. Nothing had touched on Irish pride or the nationalist cause dear to many. While his vision of Confederation drew some applause, it was quickly drowned out by scattered boos. A furious voice pierced through the din:

"Traitor!"

McGee paused briefly, pulling his coat tighter against the icy wind, but said nothing. He fixed the crowd with an intense gaze before descending from the platform, his boots sinking slightly into the slushy snow with each step.

The parade resumed its course, slowly climbing the slope of Beaver Hall. The marchers trudged onward, leaving deep impressions in the slush and mud. Clouds of vapour rose from their breaths, a testament to the crisp March air. Upon reaching the summit, the procession turned right onto Dorchester Street, where the imposing St. Patrick's Church stood on a hill overlooking the St. Lawrence River. The wind, sharper at this altitude, whipped the green banners carried proudly by some despite their fingers numbed beneath woollen gloves. Since its construction, this neo-Gothic masterpiece had become the central gathering place for the Catholic Irish working-class community, hailing from poor neighbourhoods such as Griffintown, Goose Village, and Pointe-Saint-Charles.

The church itself was a breathtaking sight. Measuring 230 feet long and 100 feet wide, it stood as a monument of faith and pride. Its tallest spire, soaring 225 feet into the sky, was flanked by two smaller ones, giving the impression of a protective father standing guard over his children. Three massive oak doors, lightly dusted with frost, opened to a solemn interior, while a brilliant rose window reflected the nearly spring-like winter sunlight. The church's ten bells, including the famous Old Charlotte, rang out in jubilant peals. Their echoes resonated through the surrounding neighbourhoods, blending with the rustling wind that quivered the bare branches of nearby trees.

The procession halted before the esplanade, a vast clearing bordered by trees whose bare branches had yet to bud in the cold but promising March air. The marchers, their shoulders draped in thick coats sometimes adorned with green embroidery, ascended the portico steps to the crowd's cheers.

On the threshold stood Bernard Devlin, president of the St. Patrick's Society, his coat collar turned up against the breeze. His commanding stature and baritone voice, clear despite the wind, demanded attention.

"How great is the Irish race!" he declared solemnly. "It knows how to defend itself. It knows how to fight. That is why you are a strong and proud people. And this, my friends, is possible because you remain faithful to our mother: Ireland."

A ripple of pride swept through the crowd. Devlin's stirring words momentarily ease the effects of the biting wind.

"Your unwavering loyalty to Ireland has allowed you to overcome every obstacle and survive. Continue to honour your roots!"

A thunderous round of applause greeted his speech, far warmer than the reception given to McGee, whose forward-looking ideas, though brilliant, failed to move those still living in the shadow of their past. Cheers echoed in the cold air, mingling with the chime of the bells and the crunch of boots on the last remnants of packed snow.

The procession, now impeccably arranged in orderly rows, entered the church with disciplined solemnity. Once inside, the faithful were struck by a sense of vastness far exceeding what the exterior facade had suggested. Long and majestic central nave stretched out before them, flanked by two rows of wooden pews, their surfaces polished smooth by time and the silent prayers of thousands of worshippers. The side aisles, also furnished with pews, added to the impression of a sacred expanse. A dozen massive colonnades, draped with banners and crowned by finely carved capitals, supported a vaulted ceiling of breathtaking height. Large green and white banners, suspended from wrought-iron chandeliers, cascaded down to the capitals, bathing the space in a luminous solemnity.

The apse stood at the end of the nave, a true masterpiece of neo-Gothic architecture. Its centrepiece was a carved stone altarpiece that captured and reflected the glow of the candles. The walls were adorned with 150 portraits of saints, each encased in finely painted Gothic panels. Their expressions varied between benevolence and solemnity as they gazed upon the congregation.

Gradually, the church filled, the muted murmurs of latecomers mingling with the soft rustling of fabric as people settled into their places. Outside on the square, those unable to enter crowded together in resigned yet respectful anticipation. Once the church was filled to capacity, a profound silence fell, so deep that the faintest flutter of a wing might have been heard. After a moment's pause, the organ burst with a grand melody, flooding the space and resonating into every corner of the vast church.

A group of ten priests, resplendent in liturgical vestments dominated by green—the colour of hope and faith—entered in a solemn procession. They were followed by altar servers and a choir of young boys whose red cassocks contrasted sharply with their crisp white surplices.

The first part of the Mass unfolded in the unchanging order of the Catholic liturgy, conducted entirely in Latin. Omnipresent incense coiled in visible prayers toward the lofty ceiling while the aspergillum generously sprinkled holy water over the congregation, occasionally drawing amused smiles from the children.

Father Patrick Dowd, the day's celebrant, was a figure of great respect, nearly venerated within the Irish Catholic community. A Sulpician priest and the director of St. Patrick's Church since its inauguration in 1847, he was admired for his religious fervour and his compassion toward his flock. His imposing figure, accentuated by his black cassock, ascended slowly to the pulpit at the heart of the nave. When he spoke, his deep voice resonated through the assembly:

"My dearest children. How joyful I am to see you gathered here in such numbers within this sacred place. You are a people apart, a chosen race, called by God to bear His light to the world. You are the defenders of the faith, the protectors of our Holy Father, the Pope, who is besieged on all sides."

The priest's words, filled with power and authority, found their mark in the hearts of the faithful. Approving nods spread throughout the congregation, and soft murmurs of assent rippled through the assembly.

"The Irish have paid a heavy price for their fidelity to God. You have endured persecution in your homeland. You have suffered famine and disease. And yet, here you stand. You have risen again, and that proves that God is with you, my friends."

In the pews, shoulders trembled, and faces were hidden behind handkerchiefs. Silent tears fell from some, a testament to their profound faith and deep sorrow.

"Never forget the words of Saint Matthew: "I have come for the poor and the sick." God will never abandon you. But you, my children, remain steadfast in your faith and obedience to His commandments."

Father Dowd descended slowly from the pulpit, his kind gaze sweeping over the congregation before returning to the apse to continue the Mass. Despite the relative warmth of the crowded church, a faint chill seemed to ripple through the assembly, a reminder of the biting cold outside. The heavy wooden doors, left slightly ajar, occasionally allowed in a draft with the acrid scent of melting snow and muddy streets.

The communion ceremony took considerable time, and the church was packed. The faithful, wrapped in their winter coats and scarves, moved forward in a tight single file toward the altar rail. There, they knelt humbly, their thick garments absorbing the marble's cold, to receive the host on their tongues, distributed with solemnity by the priests. The gentle rumble of the organ accompanied every movement, filling the air with a sacred gravity, mingled with faint vapour rising from the gathered crowd.

When the Mass ended, the thunderous sound of the grand organ and the triumphant peal of the church bells burst forth, marking the faithful's departure. As they stepped through the heavy doors, they were met by a biting wind that whipped up swirls of powdery snow across the damp cobblestones. The joyous and serene crowd slowly dispersed under the curious gazes of onlookers who had remained outside, some pulling their hats lower or tightening their coats against the stinging cold.

While some headed toward Saint-Laurent Street, where the muddy sidewalks bore the marks of a hesitant sun, the majority carefully made their way down Beaver Hall Hill, their boots crunching over patches of snow mingled with slush. They returned to the modest yet familiar streets of Griffintown, their steps tentative as they navigated the treacherous ground, ever watchful to avoid slipping on the slippery terrain.

***

Émile Leclerc, one of the four detectives of the city of Montreal, walked along Wellington Street in Griffintown, his arms full of parcels. Despite his thick coat and the scarf tightly wrapped around his neck, the biting wind found its way through, stinging his skin. He lived near the railway tracks, on a newly opened street called Sébastopol Row. These tiny row houses, their roofs still dusted with a fine layer of snow, had been built by the Grand Trunk Railway to house its managerial staff. As a police officer, Leclerc had been granted special permission to reside there with his mother. However, for the past few years, he had lived alone, his mother having passed away after a long illness.

Leclerc had a fondness for Griffintown, which greatly puzzled his fellow officers. "As a French Canadian, you must feel awfully out of place," they would say. And indeed, it wasn't entirely untrue. Griffintown was a neighbourhood composed of nearly 80% Irish, most of whom had settled there following the Great Famines in Ireland from 1845 to 1852. Many arrived sick, and numerous others perished soon after. Near one of the piers of the Victoria Bridge lay a cemetery—a mass grave, in reality—buried under the winter snow, holding no fewer than six thousand bodies: men, women, and children.

A few of these Irish immigrants had chosen to scatter into the countryside, but the vast majority stayed in the city, mainly because of the work they were offered. Many families crowded into makeshift homes built haphazardly by companies employing them to dig the Lachine Canal. The poorly insulated roofs of these shanties often let smoke from cooking fires seep through, forming wisps in the frigid air. Many newcomers were illiterate, and some spoke only Gaelic or had a rudimentary grasp of English.

Griffintown was considered the most wretched district in Montreal. Due to an inadequate sewage system, the stench became unbearable during heavy rains, as the outhouses in the courtyards of the shacks overflowed into the dirt streets, now sodden and muddy from melting snow. Hemmed between the Lachine Canal and the railway tracks, the neighbourhood was overcrowded with Irish whose reputation preceded them. "Loud and unruly" and "drunken and brawling" were the most common descriptions. Outsiders rarely ventured into the area's narrow streets, which were deemed dangerous, especially at night.

Yet Leclerc was fond of the district. He had a soft spot for these "hardheaded Irish," as he affectionately called them. He had even formed bonds with local families and was occasionally invited to dine with them. In turn, they respected him. His only flaw in their eyes? He was a policeman. Most of the neighbourhood's Irish residents viewed the constabulary force with suspicion. Paradoxically, most of the police were Irish themselves. No matter! They were all considered traitors. Admittedly, the arrest rate in Griffintown, where narrow streets were still lined with mounds of dirty snow, was the highest in all of Montreal.

On this St. Patrick's Day, Leclerc had decided to run his errands, hoping to avoid the usual crowds jostling in the shops. Just as he stepped out of a general store with his bags of provisions, a tide of men, women, and children poured onto Wellington Street, spilling onto the sidewalks and the road, their joyous cries and laughter echoing in the brisk air. The thick clothing of the passersby, dulled by winter's wear, stood out against their faces, flushed red from the cold. The melted snow on the dirt road had turned into slushy mud, and drivers struggled to calm their horses. The animals' ears lay flat against their heads, and their nostrils flared at the unexpected commotion. Clouds of steam rose from the horses' flanks as they tossed their heads, their hooves occasionally slipping on the treacherous ground.

Initially startled, Leclerc quickly realized that these Irish were returning from the parade. He proceeded cautiously along the worn wooden sidewalk, slightly elevated above the street. Though slippery in places, it offered a welcome refuge from the mud and slush that dominated the roadway. With each step, his boots struck the planks with a sharp, rhythmic sound, contrasting with the splashes from the puddles below.

He kept his head down, the brim of his felt hat shielding his face from the occasional biting gusts of wind, hoping to pass unnoticed. But fate was not on his side. A group of young Irish lads spotted him, their mischievous smiles quickly becoming more menacing. One of them recognized him and shouted to the others, "Hey! That's a bloody hound, rotten through! I know him!" Things escalated quickly. Leclerc dropped his bags and tried to defend himself. His heavy coat, while practical for the cold, hindered his movements. Of course, he hadn't thought to bring his revolver. With his slight build, narrow face, and glasses, he looked more like a notary than a police officer.

First, they shoved him, then one of them struck him in the ribs. Leclerc fell backward into the muddy street, the cold snow quickly soaking through his clothes. The youths began to pummel him with fists and kicks. He shielded his face as best he could, but it was useless. A crowd started to gather. Women screamed for the boys to stop while children cried in fear.

Then, a towering man emerged from the store where Leclerc had just been shopping, holding a large stick in his hand. This wasn't the first time he had dealt with such a situation. He moved quickly, his boots striking the frozen ground with purpose, and delivered a decisive blow to one of the youths, who collapsed with a cry of pain. At the exact moment, a constable on patrol rushed over from across the street. Having witnessed the scene, he drew his truncheon and struck another boy, who doubled over in pain. Seeing this, the remaining four boys scrambled to retreat, forcing their way through the jeering crowd.

The constable knelt beside the injured man and exclaimed in surprise, "It's Detective Leclerc of the Montreal Police!" The constable hailed the driver of a horse-drawn cart that had stopped to watch the commotion. He commandeered the cart and asked the towering man to help load Leclerc. Poor Leclerc was in bad shape. His face was swollen and bloodied, his head was bleeding, and one of his arms hung at an odd angle. He had lost consciousness. The cart set off, its wheels crunching over the remnants of compacted snow, led by the constable who cleared the way ahead.

***

The parade and St. Patrick's Day High Mass had concluded in an almost solemn calm, but as night fell, the real celebration began. Finally free of restraint, the Irish dispersed to the city's hotels and taverns, determined to end the festive day in spectacular fashion.

In Griffintown, the focus was on one establishment in particular: Kate Scanlon's tavern. This shrewd widow had taken over her late husband's business and, over the years, transformed it into a thriving enterprise. Located on Wellington Street, the tavern had grown significantly through strategic investments. Kate had purchased the neighbouring building and converted an old backyard stable into a functional space for travellers. Patrons could feed their horses, enjoy a low-cost meal, and spend the night in one of the modest rooms upstairs. Yet the tavern itself, capable of accommodating nearly a hundred people, was the heart of her business and the key to its success.

Tonight, the tavern was packed to the brim. The atmosphere was stifling, overheated by a glowing cast-iron stove in one corner. The air buzzed with energy, heavy with beer, whiskey, and wood smoke scents. Every nook and cranny was filled, laughter and shouts blending with the clinking of mugs and the creak of chairs on the wooden floor. Tom, a hulking red-haired man serving as doorman, turned away the curious who tried to slip in. "No room," he growled, sending away a pair of prostitutes. One tried a flirtatious smile, but Tom was unmoved. "Not worth it," the owner had warned earlier. "Tonight, we let in only the best-paying customers."

The mood was cheerful, almost euphoric, at the start of the evening. Tables overflowed with Guinness and Irish whiskey, served by a bartender darting between the counter and impatient customers. A fiddler set the tone in one corner of the room with traditional tunes, accompanied by a tin flute player. Occasionally, a man in a faded cap stepped forward to sing old Irish ballads with a deep, haunting voice, melodies steeped in nostalgia and melancholy. But the lively jigs and Buck and Wing dances indeed thrilled the crowd. The men stomped their feet with vigour while the women swayed in their chairs, their bodies instinctively following the energetic rhythms. Occasionally, someone would leap up to perform a few dance steps, met with applause and enthusiastic cheers.

Kate moved tirelessly between the tables, ensuring everyone was served. Despite the chaos, she kept a sharp eye on her bartender, who struggled to keep up with the ever-increasing orders.

As the evening wore on, the atmosphere grew more feverish. Alcohol amplified the voices: people spoke loudly, laughed boisterously, and some shouted to one another across the room. The baritone's songs were soon lost in the general clamour, drowned out by mugs banging on tables to summon a server.

Suddenly, an unusual commotion drew attention. A table toppled over with a crash, spilling beer and bottles onto the floor. Shouts erupted: two men, visibly drunk, had grabbed each other by the collars and were wrestling on the ground in a chaotic brawl, resisting every attempt to separate them. A woman, frantic, screamed at the top of her lungs:

— Stop it! Stop it! You're going to kill each other!

Kate, unfazed, exchanged a knowing glance with Tom, who was still stationed by the door.

— Out, you drunkards! Tom bellowed, his voice booming over the din.

Tom moved forward, his imposing frame slicing through the crowd like a steamship through rough waters. Without ceremony, he reached the two men and grabbed them by the collars. Despite their squirming and protests, the giant lifted them effortlessly, holding them upright as their feet barely brushed the floor. A distraught woman trailed after him, crying and pleading, "Please, no! Let them go!" Her desperate pleas were met with cold indifference.

The door groaned as Tom pushed it open, unceremoniously throwing the men onto the icy, muddy road with a heavy thud. They landed in an undignified heap, their curses muffled by the cacophony spilling out of the tavern. The woman followed them, clutching two coats under her arm, still shouting as her boots clattered on the wooden sidewalk. But Tom paid her no mind and calmly returned to his post.

After this brief altercation, the festivities resumed as if nothing had happened, the patrons indifferent to the drama about to unfold outside the tavern.

CHAPTER 2

Friday, March 17

The man lay on his side, curled up like a wounded animal. The hard-packed earth of the alley, frozen by the lingering chill of March nights, was littered with traces of melting snow mixed with mud. It had not yet absorbed all the blood that seeped from him, forming a dark pool, almost black under the gray morning light. Faint wisps of steam rose from the puddle, starkly contrasting with the biting cold. His eyes, wide open, seemed locked in an expression of astonishment as if he had not had the time to comprehend what had struck him down. A little farther away, his cap, soiled with dirt and marked by scattered snowflakes, had rolled into a corner, abandoned like a silent witness.

A makeshift cordon, hastily erected at the entrance to the alley, blocked access to a secluded stable tucked at the back of the courtyard. Its weathered wooden façade, coated in a light frost, bore the silent scars of a past marked by hard labour. Before its entrance, two constables stood as rigid as posts, guarding the scene. One tapped nervously at the handle of his truncheon with gloved hands, while the other, visibly fatigued, blew into his palms in a vain attempt to banish the biting cold despite his woollen gloves. Their jerky movements, one foot stomping the ground after the other, betrayed their battle against the icy wind.

Their navy-blue tunics, double-breasted at the front, were adorned with large, gold metal buttons aligned with military precision. A sturdy belt with a polished metal buckle cinched the coat at the waist. Functional pouches and neatly arranged holsters at their belts completed the uniform. Atop their heads, cylindrical flat-topped kepis with rigid visors added a finishing touch to this imposing and formal appearance, starkly contrasting the harshness of their winter surroundings.

A black police cab, austere and sombre, stood in the shadows. The horse that had drawn it, draped in a thick blanket to ward off the cold, appeared indifferent to the nearby human tragedy. Its attention was fixed on a sack of oats it chewed methodically while snowflakes fell softly upon its neck.

Near the corpse, a tall, broad-shouldered man crouched, observing the scene with the meticulous attention of a veteran accustomed to such grim spectacles. Jack Kelly, a detective with the Montreal police, was a familiar figure in the neighbourhood. Wrapped in a heavy wool coat worn thin by the years, he cut a commanding and pragmatic figure. The extended cut of his jacket, reaching well below his knees, gave him a structured silhouette that conveyed authority and professionalism. The wide lapel collar, slightly turned up against the biting wind, bore traces of snow and mud, souvenirs of the slushy streets of Griffintown.

His sturdy boots, scuffed and weathered, spoke of countless hours spent treading the streets of Montreal. Between his calloused hands, reddened by the cold after he had removed his wool gloves, he idly turned his bowler hat. This accessory, which had become a personal hallmark, stood in stark contrast to the grim atmosphere of the alley.

Kelly's imposing stature—nearly six feet tall, with broad shoulders and a weathered face blending ruggedness with a certain warmth—lent him an air of quiet authority. His chestnut-brown hair, short and slightly wavy, framed piercing blue eyes, ever vigilant, like those of a hunting dog ready to spring. Wisps of his warm breath mingled with the frigid air, adding to the weighty atmosphere of this late-winter morning.

The day was still young, barely 9 a.m., yet already heavy with echoes of the night before. St. Patrick's Day, with its parade of excess, had kept the police on high alert: brawls breaking out on icy streets, opportunistic petty thefts, drunken revellers hauled from the snow and escorted to the station. A turbulent night, to be sure, but not unusual for this working-class neighbourhood where misery and exuberance lived side by side. Nothing, that is, except for this corpse lying motionless on the frozen ground, shattering the brutal rhythm of the festivities.

Still crouched, Kelly glanced occasionally toward the alley's entrance, expecting someone. The cold wind swept between the buildings, stirring small flurries of melting snow mixed with mud, but he seemed barely to notice.

At last, a familiar figure emerged from behind the makeshift cordon. The constables, bundled up in deep blue coats, straightened in unison and saluted the newcomer respectfully. He approached confidently, ducked under the cordon, and strolled toward the corpse, his sturdy boots crunching lightly against the soft snow beneath his feet. Kelly rose to greet him, brushing off a few stray snowflakes clinging absentmindedly to his coat.

Silas Robinson, chief investigator, commanded attention with a natural elegance, further enhanced by his impeccable attire. A good inch or two taller than his deputy, he seemed to dominate the space effortlessly, impervious to the biting cold that numbed the less hardy. Draped in a thick wool coat with a flawless cut, its buttons glinting faintly under a delicate layer of frost, he exuded mastery and refinement. The coat, carefully tailored yet left open, revealed a woollen scarf cascading in loose folds around his neck.

Beneath, a perfectly fitted brown waistcoat emphasized the symmetry of his frame, complemented by matching trousers that harmonized flawlessly. A discreet gold chain, catching subtle glimmers under the cold morning light, linked a pocket watch tucked securely into the pocket of his dark vest. Every detail of his attire, from the heavy fabric to the precision of his accessories, spoke of a man for whom appearance was not merely an art but a declaration of authority and control.

Beneath a bowler hat, flawlessly perched and dusted only lightly with snow, his face seemed almost sculptural in its precision. He was clean-shaven save for a neatly waxed mustache, which maintained its shape even against the whims of winter. His hazel-brown eyes, unremarkable in colour, were nonetheless captivating, framed by thick brows and imbued with an intense gleam. His gaze, sharp as a blade, seemed to pierce into the soul of things and men alike. When Robinson fixed his eyes on someone, one had the uncanny sense he could see beyond the surface, ferreting truths hidden behind the veil of the visible.

Robinson studied the corpse with a cold detachment, arms crossed over his coat, without bending his knees. The oppressive silence of the alley was broken only by the crunch of Kelly's boots against the uneven ground, where snow and mud mingled in a formless mosaic, a grim reflection of the discomforts of late-season Montreal winters.

"Good morning, Chief. I've been expecting you," Kelly called out.

"Morning, Kelly," Robinson replied briefly but cordially.

"Where were you?" Kelly inquired.

"Since it was on my way, I stopped by to see Leclerc at the General Hospital," Robinson said, his gaze drifting toward the pool of congealed blood.

"How's he doing? Those Irish bastards didn't go easy on him," Kelly muttered, the bitterness of an Irishman too familiar with the excesses of his own kind evident in his tone.

"Not great. His head's bandaged up like a mummy, one arm in a cast, and his chest wrapped tight. His face? A mess— swollen eye, broken nose. We'll need to patch him up as soon as we can."

Kelly let out a low whistle, shaking his head.

"Poor Leclerc. Winning hearts wasn't exactly his strong suit if you ask me. Did you manage to speak with him?" Kelly continued, his tone more serious.

"Yes. He was weak but conscious. His mind's intact, though it's taken quite a beating."

"And? What did he tell you?"

"Not much. He was attacked by some young men. No apparent reason."

"Where?"

"On Wellington Street, not far from here."

A silence settled over them—heavy, yet not uncomfortable. Both men stared at the corpse as if waiting for it to speak. Finally, Kelly broke the stillness.

"Will he be able to return to work? We need him."

"There's no question we need him. But not just yet. We'll have to consider a temporary replacement. Leclerc is indispensable for research and archiving."

"Ah, yes, a true library rat, our dear Émile," Kelly said, emphasizing the name with a smile that was part fond, part teasing.

Robinson didn't respond. Instead, he slowly leaned toward the corpse, carefully removing his woollen gloves. His movements were meticulous, almost surgical. He observed every detail, every fold of the clothing, every glint of light on the dried blood.

"Help me turn him over," he finally said to Kelly.

Together, they carefully shifted the body, not disturbing the scene. The neck and jaw were stiff beneath their fingers.

"Rigor mortis is well advanced," Robinson noted. "He's been dead for over three hours, likely in the middle of the night."

"That seems about right," Kelly agreed, straightening with a sigh.

Robinson then examined the gaping wound in the abdomen, where multiple knife strikes had pierced the flesh. The precision of his inspection revealed years of experience.

"This is what killed him," he said calmly, his tone almost instructional. "He bled out."

He gestured to the pool of blood surrounding the body. Kelly nodded.

"Looks like a settling of scores between Irishmen. It is not the first time in this neighbourhood. Maybe a sailor?"

"No. Look at his clothing," Robinson replied, pointing to the sturdy boots and trousers worn thin at the knees.

"Then a canal worker from Lachine or someone from the Grand Trunk. Most men around here work for one or the other."

"Perhaps. But he could also be a stranger."

"A stranger?" Kelly frowned. "No, Chief. A fight has gone wrong between two Irishmen. I'd bet my hand on it. The celebration last night… one wrong look, one word too many, and it escalates quickly."

"Perhaps," Robinson said pensively.

"It'll be an easy case, trust me."

Robinson slowly turned his head toward his deputy, a doubtful expression on his face.

"What, Chief? It's obvious. Two Irishmen. A fight. A knife. That's it."

Kelly mimed stabbing motions, his gestures overly dramatic.

"Perhaps," Robinson repeated for the third time. "But not every fight between Irishmen ends in bloodshed."

Kelly shrugged, then conceded, "You're right, Chief. In truth, it's rare."

Robinson straightened up, adjusting his coat methodically.

"Who found the body?"

"One of those two at the entrance," Kelly replied, nodding toward the constable's standing guard.

The two detectives walked toward the mouth of the alley, their boots leaving tracks in the uneven snow. Robinson fixed his gaze on the designated constable and addressed him directly:

"Was it you who found the body?"

The young man, nervous, nodded and stiffened awkwardly into a salute.

"Yes, sir!" he blurted, rigid as a post.

"At ease, soldier," Robinson said, a flicker of irony in his eyes. "What's your name?"

"Kelly, sir," the constable answered somewhat hesitantly.

At the mention of the name, Robinson raised an eyebrow, glanced at his deputy, then back at the constable, his amusement barely concealed.

"Don't look at me like that, Chief," Kelly growled, crossing his arms. "There's more than one dog named Fido! No, he's not related to me. Besides, half the Irish are named Kelly."

"Well then, Kelly," Robinson said, turning back to the constable, "you're the one who found the body?"

"Yes, sir. I was on patrol last night."

The constable stopped there as if that simple statement sufficed. An awkward silence followed, and the detectives clearly expected more. Robinson folded his arms while Kelly rolled his eyes.

"And…?" Robinson prompted, patient.

"Well, I was walking along the street here. There wasn't much about, just a few drunks stumbling their way home, clinging to walls."

He fell silent again, seemingly satisfied with his sparse account. This time, Kelly lost patience.

"But do go on, you fool!" he barked, his voice tinged with irritation.

The constable lowered his gaze like a scolded child.

"Well, as I passed the alley, I glanced in like always. I saw a shape on the ground near the stable door. At first, I thought it was a vagrant who'd found a spot to sleep. I got closer and gave him a little nudge with my foot to wake him... That's when I saw the blood."

Silence returned, heavy with tension. The detectives studied the young man without speaking. Finally, uncomfortable under their piercing gazes, the constable continued:

"I blew my whistle like mad," he said, indicating the whistle dangling from his uniform on a chain. "Pat came running, and we 'secured the scene.' That's the term, right?"

"You stayed here to guard the scene?"

"Yes, sir. Pat went to fetch you with the police cab."

"And no one else came to have a look? No intruders?"

"There were a few curious folks this morning, but I sent them away immediately, sir."

"You didn't touch anything else?" Kelly pressed.

"Other than the little nudge... nothing at all. I did what I was taught: secure the scene and wait for the authorities."

"You didn't see anything that could've been a weapon? No knife, for instance?"

"No, sir. Nothing that looked like a weapon."

Robinson nodded, satisfied.

"Very well. Go fetch a stretcher from the police cab. You'll take the body to McGill College. You know where that is?"

"Yes, sir. I've been there before."

"Good. Ask for Dr. Campbell, the dean of the Faculty of Medicine. Tell him you're there on my behalf and that it's urgent. He'll understand."

The constable nodded quickly, almost relieved to have a straightforward task. As he hurried off, Robinson turned to Kelly.

"Your namesake has potential, but he needs to learn to speak. It'll take forever if we drag every word out of him."

"We'll do what we can, Chief. At least he knows where McGill is."

As the constables busied themselves, their breath forming small clouds in the frigid air, Robinson and Kelly ventured back into the alley, their boots sinking slightly into a mix of melting snow and mud. The pallid morning light, filtering through the low-hanging clouds and reflecting off the damp brick walls, deepened the sombre atmosphere of the place. Thin patches of frost still clung to the coldest shadows, casting scattered glimmers under the investigators' keen scrutiny. The wind, threading its way between the buildings, added a note of desolation to the already bleak scene, making every corner feel more hostile and elusive.

Kelly stopped before the stable door, a heavy wooden structure reinforced with worn iron fittings. He pushed it with his foot, but it didn't budge.

"Locked," he said with a shrug.

Robinson stepped closer, studying the frame with a calculating gaze.

"Who owns this stable?" he asked, his hands clasped behind his back.

"It belongs to Kate Scanlan's tavern," Kelly replied, standing a bit straighter.

Robinson raised an eyebrow, intrigued.

"You know the tavern?"

Kelly raised his hands in mock protest.

"Chief, what do you take me for? I keep tabs on every corner of this city's underbelly."

A faint smile flickered across Robinson's usually impassive face. Encouraged, Kelly continued:

"It's probably the most popular tavern in Griffintown. Always packed to the rafters. Kate Scanlan is a force to be reckoned with—a real dragon behind the bar, but she knows how to run her business."

Robinson nodded, absorbing the information.

"Do you think our corpse might have come from there?"

Kelly scratched his chin thoughtfully.

"Very likely. Last night, the tavern was overflowing. You could hear the singing and shouting clear out in the street. It was quite the racket."

"Then we'll need to have a word with this, Mrs. Scanlan," Robinson concluded.

Kelly hesitated an unusual occurrence for him. He dropped his gaze slightly as if weighing his words.

"Of course… but…"

Robinson, already attentive, gave him a pointed look.

"What? What is it?"

Kelly shrugged with feigned nonchalance.

"Well, Chief… Kate Scanlan isn't exactly easygoing. She's Irish through and through. And she hates anyone who isn't Irish."

"And?"

"Chief, need I remind you that you're a British bastard?" Kelly said, his eyes sparkling with mischief.

Robinson responded with a faint, almost imperceptible smile.

"True. But you know my secret weapon with the Irish."

"Yeah, your Gaelic is flawless. Fìor Èireannach. You could pass for a proper Irishman."

Indeed, Robinson had spent his youth in Limerick, where he had mastered Gaelic so thoroughly that he could blend seamlessly with the Irish community. His accent, his intonation—everything was impeccable. It had gotten him out of a tight spot with the Irish.

Kelly hesitated again before adding:

"There's something else. Rumour has it Kate's tavern is a Fenian stronghold."

"Ah! That does complicate matters," Robinson admitted.

"You know as well as I do that those Irish radicals despise the Queen and anyone in a redcoat. They won't hesitate to turn violent."

"I'm well aware. But it doesn't change anything. We have a job to do."

He turned to his deputy, his expression resolute.

"Let's go meet Mrs. Scanlan," he said, striding firmly toward the mouth of the alley.

CHAPTER 3

Saturday Morning, March 18

Upon pushing through the heavy door of Kate Scanlan's tavern, Robinson and Kelly were instantly enveloped in a thick wave of heat, a brutal shock after the biting cold that reigned outside. The air, laden with the mingled scents of tobacco, tepid beer, and burning wood, felt oppressively heavy, a sharp contrast to the icy wind that had crept into every corner of their coats. The melted snow on their boots formed small puddles at their feet, reflecting the dancing shadows cast by the crackling fire in the hearth. Their cheeks, reddened and numbed by the cold, slowly regained their natural hue under the soothing warmth.

Never quick to lighten the mood, Kelly swept off his bowler hat with a fluid motion and unwound his woollen scarf. His gaze roamed the room, a smile curling at the corner of his lips.

"Nothing like the warmth of a tavern to forget a Montreal winter," he murmured, winking at Robinson.

"Well, well! Look who's here—the bloody hounds!"

The voice, tinged with mockery, rose from the nearly empty room, drawing immediate attention. Robinson and

Kelly, long accustomed to such greetings, remained unruffled, though Kelly shot a brief dark look in the speaker's direction.

Kate Scanlan's tavern, more significant than most similar establishments Kelly had frequented (and Lord knew he'd frequented many), almost resembled a ballroom—if one could overlook the disorderly tables and chairs. The faint traces of a recently demolished adjoining wall, still visible despite a hasty plastering and a slapdash coat of paint, bore witness to a recent expansion.

The place still bore the heavy air of last night's revelry at this early hour. A hulking red-haired man, wielding a broom far too short for his stature, paced the sawdust-covered floor, attempting—without much success—to erase the evidence of the previous evening: sticky pools of beer, shards of glass, and splatters of vomit. His dark gaze settled on the detectives, laden with barely concealed hostility.

Kelly, wary, kept an eye on him from the corner of his vision while Robinson, unfazed, strode confidently toward the bar. Behind the counter, a tall, broad-shouldered woman was vigorously wiping glasses, her movements almost aggressive. Her dishevelled chestnut hair framed a ruddy face, permanently set in a scowl.

"Kate Scanlan?" Robinson's firm voice cut through the silence.

"Who's asking?" she retorted, narrowing her eyes suspiciously.

Robinson and Kelly, moving in perfect unison, produced their badges and held them out. Robinson added bluntly:

"Silas Robinson, Chief Detective of the Montreal Police."

Scanlan, far from being impressed, did not pause in her vigorous scrubbing of the glass, her movements bordering on the absurd. She cast a sidelong glance at Robinson and declared sharply:

"And what's that supposed to mean to me? I don't talk to bloody hounds."

Robinson leaned slightly over the counter, his voice calm and chilling as he replied in Gaelic:

"Oh, you'll talk to me. Believe me."

Scanlan's reaction was immediate. The surprise broke through her mask of hostility. She had clearly identified Robinson's British accent, but a man like him speaking Gaelic was an entirely different matter, one that deeply unsettled her.

"Well, well, a British who speaks Gaelic," she said, her tone laced with suspicion.

"And a British who'll make your life miserable if you don't answer my questions," Robinson replied, still in Gaelic, his voice lower, almost menacing.

Behind him, Kelly watched the exchange with barely contained amusement, a mischievous grin tugging at the corner of his mouth. Robinson had clearly seized control of the situation, and Kelly wouldn't have missed the show for anything.

The conversation resumed in English, the tension thick in the air.

"Well? What do you want?" Kate asked, crossing her arms to shield herself from an unwelcome intrusion.

"You know there's a dead man in the alley just outside?"

"Oh really? That's news to me."

"Indeed, my dear," Kelly interjected. "A dead man. And don't pretend you don't recognize me."

A flash of something crossed Kate's eyes, quickly replaced by a cutting irony.

"Oh yes. Kelly, the pain in my arse. Been a while since you've come to bother me. What brings you here now?"

"Still a policeman. And you, still a Fenian?"

Kelly's mocking remark landed like a spark on dry tinder: the red-haired giant halted his sweeping. The man, a towering figure of brute strength, was now watching the scene with the alertness of a guard dog, his massive hands tightening around the broom handle.

"Hey there! What are you on about? I don't know these fellows," Scanlan shot back, defiantly planting her hands on her hips.

Kelly responded with a disdainful chuckle and a short "Pffft." The heavy silence that followed stretched long enough for undeterred Robinson to reclaim the moment.

"Mrs. Scanlan, I'll repeat my question one last time and expect a clear answer. Are you aware there's a corpse in your alley? Because it is your alley, isn't it? The one leading to your stable?"

The words cracked like a whip, sparking unease in Kate's eyes. She crossed her arms and replied, her tone more measured but still laced with irritation:

"Certainly. It's my alley, and it's my stable. But listen, when I arrived this morning with Tom"—she gestured casually toward the red-haired giant, still poised on alert—"I saw the two constables and their blasted cordon blocking the entrance."

"And it didn't occur to you to ask what was happening?"

"I don't like bloody hounds and keep my distance from them. You should know that by now. But tell me... is there really a body?"

"Oh yes, my dear. A fine, fresh corpse," Kelly replied with a sly grin, clearly savouring the effect of his words.

"And how the devil do you suppose it got there?"

"That's precisely what we'd like to find out," Robinson responded.

"I haven't the faintest idea!" she shot back, exasperated. "What do you think? That I spend my nights keeping watch over the alley?"

"Would this man have come out of your establishment last night, by any chance?"

"Out of here? How should I know?"

"What time did you close last night?"

Kate hesitated, searching her memory before answering:

"As usual, two o'clock... No, wait. There was a celebration yesterday. We kept the doors open until three. Yes, that's right. Tom and I locked up at three. Isn't that so, Tom?"

The giant nodded slowly and heavily, his massive shoulders rising and falling like the boughs of an ancient oak swaying in the wind.

"There must have been a crowd," Robinson pressed.

"Of course! It was St. Patrick's Day! This place is always packed to the rafters for St. Patrick's. A real feast, I tell you! Tom and I were dead tired by the end of the night. Weren't we, Tom?"

True to form, Tom nodded again, silent but formidable.

"Of course," Kelly sighed, his tone half-sarcastic, half-paternalistic. "St. Patrick's Day: lots of work, but also lots of money in the till. Poor little dear, I feel so sorry for you..."

Kate shot him a frosty glare, her fingers tightening on the counter's edge, her knuckles whitening under the strain.

"At least some Irishmen know how to enjoy themselves without making a nuisance of others," she retorted sharply.

"Were they regulars?" Robinson asked.

"For the most part, yes."

"And everything went smoothly last night? No fights, no unusual trouble?"

"No, everything went as usual. I had friends come to play music and sing. Folks were cheerful. It was a celebration."

"I'd be surprised!" Kelly muttered with a wry smile. "Those blasted Irish—give them half a chance; they drink themselves senseless and start brawling."

"You'd know all about that, wouldn't you, Kelly?" Scanlan shot back.

"I'd be shocked if there wasn't at least one fight last night. Shocked," Kelly added with a chuckle.

A tense silence stretched through the room before Scanlan broke it, her tone edged with a hint of defensiveness:

"There was a little scuffle at the end of the night. Nothing serious."

"What do you mean by 'scuffle'?" Robinson asked.

"Oh, just a couple of fellows getting hot-headed over nonsense. Happens all the time. When that happens, Tom steps in and tosses them out."

"And who were these fellows?"

"With the crowd we had here last night, do you really think I can remember everyone?" she replied, crossing her arms in a defensive posture.

"You said they were regulars."

"For the most part… yes."

Something in her stance hinted that she was holding something back. Her words seemed calculated and deliberate, a detail that didn't escape the notice of the two men.

Kelly stepped forward slightly, a wry smile tugging at the corner of his lips.

"Listen, my dear," he began with a mock tenderness as false as a counterfeit penny. "Stop trying to give us the runaround. There's a corpse in your yard, you get that? Maybe you're responsible for it, after all. Eh? Maybe we'll have to arrest you. What do you think, Chief?"

He turned to Robinson with a taunting look, but the effect on Scanlan was immediate. Her expression froze into a mask of cold fury, her eyes blazing with restrained anger. It was as if she were trying to strike Kelly down with her glare, each word he spoke stoking a latent fire.

"Let's start over, Mrs. Scanlan," Robinson interjected. "There was a fight in your tavern. Can you describe exactly what happened?"

"Well, it was one of our regulars: Michael Murphy. He'd come to celebrate with his wife. He's a good man, Murphy, but… let's say he's got a quick temper when he's had a few."

"And then?" Robinson pressed, his tone sharpening as he fixed his gaze on her.

Scanlan pursed her lips before continuing, clearly irritated at having to recount the incident.

"Well, I gather he accused another man of... ogling his wife. They started trading words, shoving, yelling. It turned into a real mess: tables overturned, chairs knocked about, and then they started throwing punches like a pair of fighting cocks. It was chaos. Thankfully, Tom stepped in. He threw them out, and things returned to normal."

"And the other man, who was he?" Kelly asked.

"Aidan Walsh. Another regular."

"And you're saying Tom threw them both out simultaneously?"

"Of course. My Tom's as strong as an ox."

The two detectives turned their gaze toward the red-haired giant, still planted in a corner, his broom carelessly leaning against a table. He seemed like a marble statue—massive and silent—but his eyes burned with a restrained intensity.

"Your Tom's indeed quite the sturdy fellow," Kelly remarked. "Looking at those arms, he could knock a man out with a single punch. Maybe even kill him with a knife, don't you think?"

At these words, the giant stepped forward, his gaze blazing angrily. The floorboards creaked under his weight, and the entire room seemed to hold its breath. Kelly slowly pivoted to face him, his smile morphing into an expression of defiance, his eyes locking with Tom's like two adversaries sizing each other up before a duel.

The moment was tense, the air heavy with unspoken words and simmering fury.

"Enough. Calm yourselves," Robinson intervened.

Robinson's authority had the effect of a bucket of cold water. Tom straightened, his fists still clenched, but he slowly retreated, fixing Kelly with a glare that promised future retribution. For his part, the detective took a step back with a nonchalant shrug, though an amused glint lingered in his eyes.

"Now, Mrs. Scanlan, let us return to the matter. Did these two men know each other?"

Scanlan tore her attention away from the threatening standoff between Kelly and Tom, raising her chin slightly as she answered in a weary tone:

"Yes, they knew each other. But they never came here together."

"And after the fight? Can you tell us more about what happened?"

Scanlan shrugged as though recounting a scene she'd witnessed a thousand times.

"But… as I told you, Tom grabbed them by the scruff and tossed them outside. What more is there to say?"

"I'd like more details," Robinson pressed.

"He grabbed them by the scruff, lifted them off the ground like straw, and dragged them to the door. Isn't that right, Tom?"

The red-haired giant, weighed down by a heavy silence, slowly nodded. Yet his gaze remained fixed on Kelly, charged with palpable tension.

"There must have been shouting, a commotion around the two men?"

"A few, yes… but mostly the woman."

"The woman?" Robinson raised an eyebrow.

"Murphy's wife," she clarified, impatience cutting through her voice. "She was screaming at the top of her lungs, telling them to stop their foolishness. And when Tom grabbed them, she turned on him instead. She yelled at him to let her man go, said it wasn't his fault."

"And then?"

"You mean after Tom threw them out?"

"Yes," Robinson said calmly. "What happened after that?"

"Well, Tom came back in like nothing had happened. And Murphy's wife, she shoved him on her way out."

"She went out right after them, then?"

"Exactly."

"Do you remember the time?"

A slight silence settled as Scanlan fidgeted nervously with the fabric of her apron, briefly avoiding Robinson's piercing gaze.

"I'm not too sure. It was near the end of the evening."

"Be more precise."

Scanlan furrowed her brow, clearly searching her memory.

"Well... we closed an hour later. Must've been around 2 a.m."

The Chief exchanged a quick glance with Kelly, who gave the faintest shrug. The case began taking shape, but essential elements were still missing.

Robinson turned to Tom, who had not uttered a word since arriving at the tavern. Standing as straight as a post, the giant seemed as unyielding as a boulder in a rushing stream, his gaze fixed on an unfathomable void.

"Is that how it happened, Tom?" Robinson asked.

"Yup," Tom replied without so much as blinking.

"And after throwing the two men out, did you stay outside for a while?"

"Not long," he said with a slight shrug as though the question carried no weight.

"What happened outside? Did they keep fighting?"

"Not a chance. They were too drunk for that," he said in a neutral tone. "They were just trying to get back on their feet."

"And the woman? Was she there too?"

"No. She came out as I was going back in. After that, I don't know."

Robinson narrowed his eyes slightly, thoughtful, his gaze shifting between Tom and Scanlan.

"And these two men—where can we find them?"

"Murphy lives nearby. I'll write down the address for you. But Walsh…"

She hesitated, pausing mid-sentence, her gaze faltering briefly before settling on Robinson.

"Him, I don't know."

She grabbed a scrap of paper and scribbled a few words with quick, angular strokes before handing the note to Robinson.

"Murphy's not a bad man," she added, her tone softening, almost compassionate. "A good Catholic, always willing to help at St. Patrick's parish. But when he drinks… well, he gets a little… unruly, let's say."

Robinson slipped the paper into his inner pocket and slightly nodded to thank Scanlan and Tom. They watched him silently until the door closed behind them and Kelly.

Outside, the icy air struck them like a slap, sweeping away the stifling warmth of the tavern that had seeped into their coats. The biting wind, laden with swirling snowflakes, found its way into every gap in their clothing, defying tightly wrapped scarves and thick overcoats.

"Good Lord, you never get used to this cold," grumbled Kelly, his hands buried deep in his pockets.

Robinson, impassive, nodded silently, his gaze sweeping over the uneven sidewalks where a mixture of slush and frozen mud created treacherous footing. With each step, their boots sank slightly, producing a dull crunch. The wooden planks of the sidewalks, warped by moisture and weather, made their progress even more precarious.

"We walk," Robinson declared.

Kelly raised an eyebrow, glancing around in the vain hope of spotting a cab. But the freezing air discouraged the coachmen as much as the passersby.

"Of course, Chief. Nothing like a brisk walk to warm the blood."

The two men moved forward, their breath rising in vapour clouds into the still air. Each step echoed in the quiet morning, starkly contrasting the lively atmosphere of the tavern they had just left. The pale daylight pierced through a veil of clouds, illuminating the slick cobblestones and the heaps of gray snow piled against the walls of the buildings.

The cold clung to them like a second skin and reddened their faces by the wind, but neither man slowed his pace. They walked briskly toward the Bonsecours Market police station, their boots tapping against the damp planks of the sidewalk. Every movement seemed measured and driven by purpose, as though the biting cold was another obstacle to overcome in this investigation.

"What do you think, chief?" Kelly asked after a few moments.

Robinson remained silent, his gaze fixed straight ahead, his boots crunching against the frozen snow. For a moment, the wind seemed to be their only companion, swirling around them with a nearly mocking insistence.

"I regret letting the body go too soon," he finally said in a calm but frustrated tone. "Scanlan could have identified it. That was a mistake."

Kelly shrugged, pulling his scarf tighter against the biting wind.

"We can still ask her to come to the morgue," he suggested.

"Yes, but it wastes time," Robinson replied, his tone firming. "And time is precious, especially in a murder case."

Kelly sighed, a puff of vapour rising into the frosty air.

"In any case, it is a straightforward matter. Two men fighting over a woman, it gets out of hand... Nothing too original in that."

"Perhaps. But something doesn't add up. The man died around 3 a.m., according to our initial estimates. We'll have to wait for the autopsy to be sure."

"The two men were thrown out around that time, weren't they?"

"Not exactly," Robinson corrected, shaking his head slightly. "And there's the woman. She followed them."

"Precisely. Maybe they kept fighting over her outside."

"Maybe. It's a possibility. But I want to hear what Murphy has to say."

"And the other, Walsh?"

Robinson exhaled deeply, his breath becoming a fleeting cloud in the cold air.

"We'll need to find his address. I know you won't like what I'm about to say, but Leclerc would've already tracked it down."

Kelly let out a hearty laugh, ringing in the nearly deserted streets.

"That's exactly why we need him. Desk work isn't for me."

"True, but Leclerc couldn't do what you do."

"Well, at least I wouldn't have let those little punks rough me up."

"That's for sure. They'd have ended up in the hospital."

They burst into laughter together, their mirth mingling with the sound of the wind, an unexpected echo in the city's frosty stillness. Their good humour was short-lived, and after a moment of silence, Kelly suddenly stopped, fixing Robinson with a serious look.

"If you'll allow it, chief, I'll stop by the hospital to see Leclerc."

Robinson nodded without hesitation.

"Go ahead. He'll appreciate it."

Kelly tipped his head slightly before striding off, his boots tapping sharply against the frozen wood of the sidewalk. Robinson remained still for a moment, watching his colleague disappear into the distance, before continuing his solitary march toward the police station through the icy streets.

CHAPTER 4

Saturday afternoon, March 18

The door to the detectives' office flew open with such force that it rattled the frame. A young woman stormed into the room like a gust of wind, her steps echoing sharply on the wooden floor, her cheeks flushed from the cold March air.

"This imbecile at the desk nearly blocked my way!" she exclaimed, her eyes blazing with indignation.

She was tall, taller than most women, with an arresting presence. With a swift motion, she removed her black felt hat adorned with a simple ribbon trim. Her gloved hands then attacked the buttons of her thick, anthracite wool coat, its collar trimmed with dark fur. With a sharp motion, she shrugged it off her shoulders and hung it on a wall rack, tossing her gloves into the hat, which she placed on another hook, all with a theatrical determination.

Inspired by American fashions, her cherry-red satin gown glimmered in the dim light of the office like an unexpected flame in the night. The perfectly fitted corset accentuated her slender waist, while the heart-shaped neckline and puffed sleeves lent her an air of dramatic elegance. The full skirt brushed the floor and barely concealed her refined black boots. Velvet bows adorned the dress, and black accents—a belt at the waist, a broad hemline, and a lace neckpiece—underscored her bold style.

But it wasn't just her attire that commanded attention. Her face, framed by a meticulously braided chignon, radiated striking beauty. Her regular features were enhanced by sharp, penetrating blue-green eyes, almost untamed. Though young, there was no trace of girlish naivety or softness in her expressions; this woman carried the assurance of unyielding determination.

"Thérèse!" Kelly suddenly exclaimed, springing to his feet.

The detective's surprise seemed genuine, though it paled in comparison to Robert Morin's expression. Still a novice on Robinson's team, the latter stood frozen as though the young woman were an apparition. Robinson watched the scene with an inscrutable calm, though a fleeting satisfaction flickered in his eyes.

"Hello, Kelly," Thérèse said with a sly smile.

"But... what are you doing here?" Kelly stammered, visibly disoriented.

She shrugged lightly, an air of nonchalance and confidence about her.

"I'm here to help you. Haven't you told them, Silas?"

Robinson, still impassive, gave a slight nod but did not reply immediately. Kelly, casting a nervous glance at his superior, pressed further:

"Chief, what's going on exactly?"

Robinson merely posed a laconic question:

"You know her, don't you?"

"Of course!" Kelly replied, still in shock. "The last time I saw her was two or three years ago?"

"Two years," Thérèse corrected, crossing her arms with a mischievous smile. "You came to gorge yourself at the surprise dinner Mother organized for Silas's birthday."

Kelly burst out laughing at the memory.

"That's right! Two years already. Well, I'll be damned; you look like you've grown even more since then!"

"What can I say?" she replied, raising an eyebrow. "I'm like a weed."

The remark sent Kelly into another fit of laughter, eliciting Robinson's faint smile but left Morin unmoving, as if carved from stone.

"Well, Silas, where's my desk?" Thérèse demanded with a mix of challenge and measured insolence.

"You'll take Leclerc's desk," Robinson said with a curt gesture. "And get to work, Thérèse: you'll address me formally and call me Chief."

"At your orders, Chief!" she responded with a mock military salute and a mischievous smile.

Morin, finally shaken from his stupor, frowned before asking:

"But Chief, what's going on exactly? And... who is this woman?"

Robinson raised a brow slightly as if amused by his young detective's discomfort.

"Ah yes, that's right: you don't know her yet. Thérèse is my stepdaughter."

"Well... all right. But with all due respect, Chief, what is she doing here?"

"Good question. I should have given you some warning. You both know that Leclerc will be recovering for a long while. We can't count on him for several weeks."

"Poor Leclerc..." Morin said with a note of sadness. "I went to see him yesterday. He's in a bad way."

"Indeed," Robinson agreed. "And you're also aware that his skills are irreplaceable: he built our filing system from scratch, not to mention his deep knowledge of the law and unparalleled research talent. Furthermore, he set up our darkroom for developing photographs, which is vital for our investigations."

"Of course, we know all that," Morin replied. "It's obvious someone needs to replace him."

A silence settled over the room, during which Robinson fixed Thérèse with a calm but meaningful gaze. His demeanour seemed to finally strike Morin.

"You're joking, Chief," Kelly stammered, his eyes widening. "She's... she's a woman! And still just a girl!"

"A girl, am I?" Thérèse retorted, raising an eyebrow with a biting tone. She stepped forward confidently, turning her heel completely, allowing her voluminous dress to swirl lightly around her. "Do I truly look like a little girl to you?"

"Well... no... that's not what I meant," Kelly stuttered, clearly caught off guard. "But... working in a police station, surrounded by all these men—not to mention the criminals coming and going—it's not serious, Chief!"

"You're not the first to make such remarks, Kelly," Robinson replied evenly. "The chief of police, the mayor, and even the attorney general, Cartier, have asked me the same questions."

"Cartier? Georges-Étienne Cartier?" Kelly exclaimed, astonished.

"The very same," Robinson confirmed in an unruffled tone. "I've known him since the investigation in Quebec City—the one involving the wife of my former colleague O'Connell."

"The Faubourg Saint-Louis case?" Morin murmured.

"Yes. We've maintained a good relationship since then. And he's placed a certain trust in me as a policeman. Given his notable influence in Montreal…"

"Notable? You're modest, Chief," Morin interjected with a smile. "You always find a way to surprise us."

Another silence fell. In the meantime, Thérèse approached Leclerc's desk and examined it briefly. As always, everything was in perfect order. With precise movements, she opened her bag. She removed a few items: notebooks, pencils, two framed photographs, which she placed carefully on the desk, and finally, a small carved statuette. She brought it gently to her lips and murmured:

"My good-luck charm."

***

During the lively Saint Patrick's Day festivities, everything had begun the evening before.

Robinson, as was his custom, was seated at home for supper. His wife Rosalie had prepared a hearty meal, and Thérèse, his stepdaughter, joined them at the table. It had been a decade since Robinson had married Rosalie Cadrin-Dupuis, a woman of strong character and forthright gaze. Widowed at a young age, she had already been a mother of two when they met. Their story began during one of Robinson's investigations at Madame Dupuis' Asylum, an institution she managed with a rare blend of compassion and pragmatism. The asylum, which offered shelter to "unwed mothers," carried within it a quiet revolution: it was Rosalie who had popularized this term, replacing the cruel "fallen women" still too often used.

Rosalie had inherited a considerable fortune upon the death of her visionary husband, one of the first prominent French Canadian businessmen in Montreal. But as a woman in a man's world, she could not directly manage the enterprise. Instead, she chose to sell her shares and devote her energy to providing refuge for these women, transforming her family's manor into a sanctuary.

When Robinson and Rosalie married, she entrusted the asylum to the Sisters of Mercy and moved in with her husband in an elegant Terrace House in the Saint-Antoine district. This home had been their tranquil haven for several years until Thérèse, newly graduated from the boarding school of the Sisters of the Congregation of Notre Dame, returned to settle there.

With her customary liveliness, Rosalie did not take long to tease her daughter:

"You know how much we love you, my dear, but surely you don't mean to spend your finest years under your mother's skirts. Surely, some fine young men are waiting for your word."

Thérèse, unperturbed, would raise a foot and show off her well-laced boots.

"I've yet to find a shoe that fits," she would reply.

Robinson, amused, would add:

"Leave her be, Rosalie. You know she can keep a man miserable his whole life."

Thérèse invariably responded by miming a punch to her stepfather's shoulder:

"That's only because there aren't many men like you who could endure a woman like my mother!"

Such lighthearted and affectionate exchanges were a staple of their household. But that evening, during Saint Patrick's Day, a shadow hung over their table. Silas Robinson wore a grim expression, his gaze fixed on a plate he seemed not to see. This was unusual for a man typically impassive, whose stoic calm had weathered many storms.

Rosalie, ever observant, immediately sensed something was amiss. She had a rare talent for coaxing words from even the most taciturn, but tonight, the shadow on her husband's face seemed heavier than usual.

"What's troubling you, Silas?" she asked gently, her tone blending softness and firmness.

He raised his eyes, a forced smile flickering across his lips before vanishing as quickly as it appeared.

"It's nothing, Rosalie. Just matters at the office, nothing more."

She was not one to relent, leaning forward on the table, her gaze unwavering.

"Come now, Silas. Since when have we not shared everything?"

A heavy silence fell. Thérèse, watchful, studied her stepfather with a mix of curiosity and concern while Rosalie waited patiently, her instincts telling her this was not merely office business.

In truth, Rosalie was much more than a wife to Robinson: she had become his confidante. Since their marriage, he had not hesitated to share the secrets of his investigations with her, fully aware of the value of her sharp mind. Her excellent education with the Sisters of the Congregation and her unfailing intuition often allowed her to shed light on matters he might not have considered.

After a moment, he finally said:

"Something's happened to Leclerc."

Rosalie raised her head sharply, alarmed.

"Leclerc? What is it?"

"He was attacked in the street by a gang of young ruffians."

"Good heavens!" she exclaimed, her face pale. "And how is he?"

"Not well. I stopped by to see him before coming home. He's badly beaten."

"How dreadful! But why did they attack him?"

"For no apparent reason... Probably because he's a policeman."

Thérèse, silent until then, nearly sprang from her chair.

"What do you mean, 'because he's a policeman'?!"

"He lives in Griffintown," Robinson replied with a shrug. "It's an Irish district, rather rough. Policemen are rarely welcome there."

"It's madness," Thérèse muttered, clenching her fists. "The good are slaughtered while the wicked roam the streets with impunity."

"Ah, well," Robinson said with a hint of weariness. "You must understand them a little. The Irish in Griffintown are among the poorest in Canada. They've faced hardships you can't imagine—famine, disease, and forced exile from a land they loved. Those who survived did so by learning to fight like demons."

"You're being awfully generous toward those brutes," Thérèse countered, crossing her arms.

"I don't excuse their violence," Robinson clarified, "but I can understand what drives them to act as they do. And there's something you might not know, Thérèse: I'm a bit Irish myself."

"You? A British stiff of the worst kind?"

"Yes, indeed. I spent my childhood in Limerick, Ireland, where my father was an Anglican pastor in the heart of a Catholic community."

"An Anglican among Catholics," Thérèse said, shaking her head. "That can't have been easy."

"That's putting it mildly. My father worked hard to earn their trust but constantly ran against their suspicion. Finally, he returned to London at the end of his resources and patience."

"Was it really that bad?"

"Bad? And yet, it was nothing compared to what was happening in Ulster, the north of Ireland. There, it was outright war—Catholics and Protestants killing each other. Sometimes, quite literally."

A heavy silence descended on the room, laden with the weight of his words. Robinson straightened slightly, his deep voice still resonating:

"Conflicts like those… they're fratricidal wars. And they persist today, in different forms."

Rosalie exchanged a glance with Thérèse. These long sentences, this tone laden with unusual gravity… Silas Robinson was not a man who gave lengthy speeches. Clearly, what had happened to Leclerc affected him far more deeply than he wished to admit. A heavy silence descended over the table like words had been struck mute. Even the clatter of cutlery faded, leaving only the crackle of the wood in the hearth to fill the space. The conversation tentatively resumed when Rosalie brought dessert—a fragrant tarte à la farlouche, a traditional French Canadian pastry made with molasses and toasted flour.

"Leclerc won't be back on his feet anytime soon, I suppose?" Rosalie finally asked, breaking the silence, her gaze searching her husband's face.

Robinson sighed deeply, his shoulders sagging slightly under the weight of his concern.

"It'll be weeks... maybe longer," he replied gravely. "He may never return at all."

"He's your closest deputy," she said softly.

"Tell me about it!" Robinson exclaimed, his voice tinged with restrained bitterness. "Together, we built the Montreal police detective bureau. Before that, he was my assistant when I was still a private detective. What am I going to do without him?"

Silence fell again, heavy as a leaden veil. Then, in a measured tone, Thérèse spoke.

"You'll have to find him a replacement."

"Easier said than done. Leclerc is irreplaceable."

Thérèse crossed her arms, a glint of defiance in her eyes.

"The cemeteries are full of irreplaceable people," she retorted hesitantly.

"Perhaps," he conceded. "But who?"

"Why not me?"

Rosalie and Robinson turned to her as though she had uttered a blasphemy.

"You?" Rosalie gasped.

"Yes, me!" Thérèse replied, a mischievous glint in her eyes. "What do you think, Silas?"

Robinson was momentarily speechless, searching for the right words. He had never wanted Rosalie's children to call him "Papa." "You have only one father," he often told them. But in that moment, he felt the weight of an authority he would have preferred not to exercise.

"Come now, dear," he said at last, in a tone meant to soothe. "You're capable of many things, no doubt about it. But a policeman... that's no job for a woman."

Thérèse gave a wry smile.

"I don't want to be a policeman. Leclerc wasn't a policeman either; he was a lawyer. And you, for that matter, were a private detective before they recruited you."

"True, but I had been a policeman in London before that."

"Leclerc wasn't," Thérèse countered swiftly. "You've often praised his work—his impeccable note-taking, meticulous research, and photography. You've never said he confronted bandits or fought on the streets."

Robinson pondered for a moment, idly toying with the blade of his knife.

"Indeed," he conceded. "Leclerc had his strengths and weaknesses. Fieldwork wasn't his forte. Kelly and Morin handled that well enough. Most of the time, Leclerc stayed in the background. That's precisely why he couldn't defend himself properly when he was attacked. He wasn't accustomed to situations like that. Kelly would have reacted differently."

"And so, I return to my proposal," Thérèse said, straightening slightly. "Listen, Silas, I'm resourceful. I was one of the best students at the college. Just ask the Sisters."

"That, I know well. But you lack the training."

"You know, I wanted to be a lawyer when I left college. I even began studying the law to prepare myself. But a woman can't become a lawyer, can she, Mother? Wasn't that your dream, too, in your day?"

Rosalie, observing the exchange closely, spoke in a melancholic tone.

"It's true," she admitted. "I, too, once considered becoming a lawyer, like your grandfather."

"And yet, you encouraged me to study law," Thérèse insisted, "just as you did with Aimé."

"Yes, that's true," Rosalie conceded, her gaze drifting into the distance. "But the times are not yet ripe for us, for women. And it pains me deeply."

"I would have made an excellent lawyer. At college, we held rhetorical debates, and I always won. I love to read and study, and I'm naturally curious. In composition, I was always at the top of my class. Why not me, Silas?"

Robinson listened intently to Rosalie and Thérèse's conversation, his elbows resting on the table, his fingers interlaced beneath his chin. His eyes moved from one to the other as though weighing their arguments in a court of law. At last, he broke his silence.

"You indeed possess undeniable talents for documentary research," he said, nodding slowly.

"Exactly! You know, in class, I was often asked to give presentations. The Sisters always praised my diligence. And, I could argue like a lawyer.

Clearing the plates, Rosalie turned toward her daughter with an affectionate smile.

"I can vouch for that," Rosalie replied with a laugh. "I've lost count of our endless discussions on every possible topic. Rarely did I manage to get the last word with you."

"You're exaggerating, Mother. I'm a good little girl, after all. Besides, everyone knows my parents are always right," Thérèse added with feigned modesty, a sly smile on her lips.

This remark sparked a burst of laughter, breaking the lingering tension. With dessert finished, Rosalie returned to her chores while Robinson, still deep in thought, broke the silence again.

"Tell me, Thérèse, are you serious about your proposal?"

"Yes, Silas. I'm free to act as I please and ready to step in immediately."

"And your job with the photographer? Perrault, isn't it?"

"Perrault," she confirmed with a shrug. "Oh, he'll manage without me. By the way, Silas, did you mention that Leclerc was the police's official photographer? Well, I can do that too."

Robinson furrowed his brow slightly, clearly deep in thought. It was then that Rosalie, setting a tray on the sideboard, spoke with a mix of gentleness and firmness:

"My poor girl, working for the police isn't the same as taking wedding photographs. I assure you, you'll be surrounded by men who won't give you any quarter."

Thérèse, undaunted, raised her fists playfully with a wry smile.

"I can hold my own, believe me!"

"That, I don't doubt. But the job is still dangerous."

"Certainly. I agree. But, Silas, didn't you say that Leclerc always avoided dangerous situations?"

"Indeed," Robinson admitted, his fingers drumming lightly on the table. "We made sure to keep him far from criminals. With his build, he wouldn't have stood a chance anyway."

"Well then," Thérèse continued, undeterred. "I could stick to office work. As you've said, research is more about spending time in a library than on the streets."

Robinson nodded, though his expression remained cautious.

"That's true. However, as a photographer, you'll have to examine corpses. And let me warn you: our corpses are not pleasant to look at."

Thérèse, far from intimidated, lifted her chin, a gleam of defiance in her eyes.

"I'm no fainting lily, you know that! So, what do you think, Silas?"

A long silence settled over the room. Robinson lowered his head, his hands clasped tightly before him, visibly torn between reason and Thérèse's audacity. At last, he raised his eyes and replied in a measured tone:

"I'll think about it."

"Seriously?" Thérèse asked, a triumphant smile threatening to break through.

"Seriously," Robinson confirmed as he slowly rose from his chair. "But let me sleep on it."

Though his voice was grave, there was a flicker of consideration in his tone. Thérèse was satisfied that she had planted a seed in her stepfather's mind, rose as well, and had a discreet smile on her lips. Rosalie, meanwhile, watched the scene with a hint of apprehension, but also with a pride she made no effort to conceal.

CHAPTER 5

Saturday afternoon, March 18

"Not a moment to settle in, Dupuis! You're coming with me."

Robinson's curt voice rang out in the small room, barely warmed by a sputtering wood stove. The detective had already donned his thick wool coat. Outside, a mix of snow and rain lashed against the windowpanes and seeped through the gaps in the poorly sealed frames.

Still overwhelmed by the enormity of her new position, Miss Dupuis straightened with wide eyes. Her gaze met that of the other team members, who remained stunned by the chief's decision to replace Leclerc with this young woman.

"Yes, Chief!" she replied, her voice clear but tinged with apprehension. "What are we doing?"

"Grab your notebooks and the camera. We're heading to the 'house of the dead.' There's a corpse waiting for us to photograph."

The announcement sent a collective shiver through the room. The body, discovered earlier that morning in the alley behind Kate Scanlan's tavern, had been transported to McGill College. Doctor George Campbell, dean of the Faculty of Medicine, awaited them for an autopsy there.

With his austere presence and razor-sharp mind, Campbell enjoyed a reputation as cutting as his scalpel. Students feared him as much as they admired him. His lectures on forensic medicine, a discipline still in its infancy in Canada, drew enormous audiences despite the suffocating stench of acrid alcohol that filled the dissection hall.

As students had nicknamed it, the "house of the dead" was a dim room with an atmosphere heavy with dampness and alcohol. The floor, strewn with sawdust, muffled footsteps but did little to mask the persistent odour from the vats below.

While Miss Dupuis slipped away to fetch the equipment from the darkroom Leclerc had set up, Kelly and Morin intercepted Robinson.

"Chief, you can't be serious!" Kelly exclaimed, his brows furrowed. "You're really taking the girl with you?"

"Miss Dupuis, Kelly. She's your colleague now," Robinson shot back, fixing the inspector with a steely gaze. "You'll call her Miss Dupuis or Dupuis. Is that clear?"

"Yes, yes, Miss Dupuis. But still… You're going to show her a corpse? A young woman like that?" Kelly pressed, placing deliberate emphasis on the word Miss.

"She has to start somewhere," Robinson retorted, unfazed.

"Chief, a woman is delicate," Morin interjected with a shrug. "She'll burst into tears or faint the moment she sees a body."

"Delicate, is she?" Robinson replied, locking eyes with Morin. "Have you ever washed a cholera victim's corpse, as countless women in this country have? Of course not. Have you ever cradled a child dead from dysentery, as so many mothers and wives have had to do?"

Morin opened his mouth, but no words came out.

"It's not the same…" he muttered at last.

"And how, exactly, is it different?"

Morin faltered, searching for an answer, but Robinson cut him off.

"Enough whining. Back to work. Kelly, did you mention something about the Bank of Montreal?"

"Yes. Thieves broke in and made off with a considerable sum. They were armed with pistols," Kelly said gravely.

"That doesn't often happen around here," Morin remarked, frowning.

"It's a trend from the United States," Robinson explained, adjusting his heavy overcoat against the cold. "Down there, bandits roam northern towns robbing banks. They say that's how the Confederates are funding their war against the North."

Morin shook his head, clearly unconvinced.

"You two handle that," Robinson ordered. "I'm heading to the house of the dead with Thér... Dupuis."

At that precise moment, Miss Dupuis appeared in the room, her cheeks slightly flushed, betraying recent exertion within the building. Her anthracite wool coat bore traces of dust, and a few strands of hair had escaped from her black felt hat, tousled from her efforts. Her arms were full: she carried a rectangular wooden box of evident weight in one hand and a bundle of rods meant to form a tripod in the other.

"A Dubroni... can you believe it, Chief?" she exclaimed with barely contained enthusiasm. "A Dubroni! It's the very latest in photographic technology. Leclerc was truly ahead of his time."

"If you say so," Robinson replied distractedly, raising an eyebrow.

"I really ought to return home and change," she continued, glancing down at her attire.

She was still wearing her cherry-red satin walking dress, which was elegant but unsuitable for the rough work she was about to undertake.

"No time!" Robinson retorted firmly. "The first thing to understand in this line of work is that time always works against us—and in favour of murderers."

Miss Dupuis pressed her lips together in resignation.

"Very well, if you insist. But this is a walking dress, not a work dress…"

"And?" Robinson replied impassively.

She sighed but said nothing more.

"Fine, fine… it's all right," she finally muttered, readjusting the items in her arms.

Turning on her heels, she strode briskly toward the staircase. Her boots' rhythmic clatter echoed through the grand stairwell's damp, cold air. Robinson, casting one last glance at Kelly and Morin, followed her, pulling his bowler hat firmly onto his head to shield himself from the biting wind.

At the entrance of the Bonsecours building, a police cab awaited under the delicate, silent snowfall that was transforming the uneven cobblestones into a pale mosaic.

Robinson had chosen the cab over his usual police chaise, which was far too cramped for himself, Miss Dupuis, and her photographic equipment. Moreover, with its meagre roof, the chaise would have offered little protection from the weather.

"At least it's snowing," Robinson remarked, helping Miss Dupuis in the carriage. "I detest the rain."

"For a Londoner, you must have had your fair share—and probably a second helping!" she replied, lifting the hem of her coat to sit without crushing her dress.

"And why do you think I immigrated to Canada?" he retorted as he settled beside her.

The black cab was a rudimentary version of a police vehicle, with "Police" painted in bold white letters on its sides. It resembled a small stagecoach—sturdy yet austere. At the front, the constable driver was bundled in a thick wool coat, his hat pulled low against the falling snow, while a makeshift wooden roof shielded his head. Behind him, the enclosed cabin featured two simple benches along the walls, allowing six passengers to sit face-to-face.

The interior was far from comfortable. The oversized wooden-spoked rear wheels provided stability, but the lack of suspension meant every pothole or stone jarred the entire compartment. And in Montreal, the streets were rife with both.

The journey felt interminable. The horse, its dark coat glistening under the melting snow, slipped repeatedly on the slick cobblestones or sank into the thawing mud of the roads. Jostled like a sack of potatoes, Robinson used the time to brief Miss Dupuis.

"The man we'll see was at Scanlan's tavern last night. A brawl broke out, and he didn't leave alive."

Miss Dupuis listened intently, holding her breath each time the cab jolted violently. Her hands clutched tightly to the precious box containing the Dubroni.

At last, they reached McGill University, still commonly referred to as McGill College. The institution stood majestically on the former estate of a wealthy Scottish merchant, a fur-trading empire transformed into an academic legacy. Austere yet imposing buildings presided over what had once been farmland.

A dirt road flanked by a neatly maintained walkway at the entrance led to two massive carved wooden doors. Always open, the doors were fixed to stone pillars adorned with grotesque carvings of figures reminiscent of the Commedia dell'Arte.

Robinson and Miss Dupuis stepped into the dissection hall. The room, barely warmed by a cast-iron stove relegated to a corner, exuded a solemn silence.

At its center stood a massive wooden table, worn by time and countless dissections. Besides, it was a smooth, functional metal table reserved for autopsies. Along the back wall, a row of steel cisterns housed bodies awaiting examination; regularly replaced ice preserved the human remains in a chilling stillness.

Wrapped tightly in her coat, Miss Dupuis clutched her equipment close, visibly unnerved by the morbid atmosphere. Robinson, unperturbed, cast a critical eye around the room before speaking in his clipped tone:

"Right, let's get to work."

Dr. Campbell awaited his visitors in a stark room, its lime-washed walls still bearing the telltale marks of persistent dampness. A sharp odour of disinfectant lingered in the air, mingling with the heavier stench of decaying human flesh. Beside him stood a young man dressed with almost excessive precision: a well-fitted charcoal-grey jacket and a poorly knotted cravat. There was no doubt he was one of Campbell's students.

"Dr. Campbell," Robinson greeted, extending a firm hand.

"Robinson."

The two men's brisk, businesslike handshake resembled more of an exchange between merchants than a colleague greeting. A few steps away, Miss Dupuis had approached discreetly. Robinson turned toward her and made the introductions.

"Thérèse Dupuis, my assistant."

The looks cast her way to the doctor, and his student might as well have been directed at an exotic creature escaping from a menagerie. Their incredulity was plain.

"What is she doing here?" Dr. Campbell exclaimed, his tone laced with cold disapproval.

"She's assisting me with note-taking, and she'll photograph the body," Robinson replied calmly and unflinchingly.

Dr. Campbell's eyes widened as though he'd just heard the most preposterous claim.

"You must be joking, Robinson! A woman?!"

"Last I checked, she is indeed a woman," Robinson replied, his voice tinged with irony.

Miss Dupuis, unperturbed, offered a gracious, perfectly composed smile. She had anticipated this kind of reaction and knew that her composure and confidence were her best weapons against such attitudes. Meanwhile, the young student could not tear his gaze from her, his mouth agape. He seemed both captivated by her refined beauty and astonished by the audacity she represented.

Irritated, Dr. Campbell spun on his heel brusquely, and the group followed in silence. They crossed the room to its far end, where a corpse lay on a dissection table. The table, a peculiar piece of furniture, featured a raised metal slab mounted on collapsible legs. A simple oil lamp cast a flickering light, creating unsettling shadows that danced across the walls. The table, worn with age, bore dark stains left by past dissections.

"I must warn you, miss," Campbell said as they stopped before the body. "The man is unclothed."

Miss Dupuis, far from flustered, responded in an even voice:

"Our father Adam was, too, in the Garden of Eden... before the Fall, of course."

Caught off guard by her retort, Campbell merely furrowed his brows before pressing on:

"Have you ever seen a corpse before today?"

"A few," she lied effortlessly.

Sensing the heavy conversation, Robinson interjected to steer it back on course.

"So, Doctor, what can you tell us about our client?"

Campbell shrugged slightly, his hands clasped behind his back.

"The cause of death is no mystery. He was stabbed four times. The man bled out within about fifteen minutes."

"And the time of death?" Robinson pressed.

"When I examined him this morning, rigor mortis wasn't fully set—it hadn't reached his legs yet. I'd estimate he died between two and four o'clock this morning."

"You can't narrow it down further?" Robinson asked, a trace of impatience in his tone.

"You know I cannot. If I were to hazard a guess, I'd say three o'clock. But I am a scientist, sir, not a fortune-teller."

Robinson, accustomed to such constraints, pressed on regardless.

"And the livor mortis? Was the body moved?"

"You found him curled on his side?" the doctor asked, raising an eyebrow.

"That's correct."

"Then he died that way. The body wasn't moved."

As the two men continued their low-toned discussion, Miss Dupuis wasted no time. She retrieved a notebook and pencil from Robinson's satchel, her nimble fingers racing across the page to capture every word. Then, with determined steps, she approached the corpse lying on the table. The cold wind seeped through the gaps in the windows, adding another layer of chill to the already sombre atmosphere.

Leaning over the pallid face, her sharp gaze traced every contour in detail.

"Do not touch the body, Miss!" Dr. Campbell barked abruptly, his voice hoarse with irritation.

Miss Dupuis raised an eyebrow but didn't bother lifting her head. Turning slightly toward Robinson, she declared in a crisp tone:

"Chief, there are no bruises on his face. Don't you find that strange? You said he'd been in a fight at the tavern. Shouldn't there be some marks?"

Her fingers hovered in the air above the corpse, never entirely contacting the skin. Methodically, she worked her way down, scrutinizing every detail of the bare chest and limbs, her eyes alight with a near-scientific curiosity.

"No bruising on the chest or anywhere else," she murmured. "This man wasn't struck. He was only stabbed."

Robinson folded his arms, a thoughtful crease forming at the corner of his mouth.

"Good observation, Dupuis. Record all of that carefully."

Satisfied, she straightened and quickly jotted notes in her notebook. Meanwhile, the doctor glowered at her, his bushy brows deepening his dour expression.

"We'll take photographs," Robinson said firmly. "Dupuis, get ready."

Miss Dupuis swept the room with a calculating gaze, her jaw slightly clenched, before declaring:

"No, this won't work."

"What's the matter, Miss?" the doctor asked mockingly. "The setting not to your taste? Not pastoral enough for you?"

"Not enough light," she snapped, ignoring his sarcasm.

She issued a series of instructions to the three men. Under her authoritative supervision, the body and the heavy table were moved closer to a window where pale light filtered through. The biting cold intensified each time a draft swept through the room, but none of the men protested. The corpse was securely strapped upright with thick leather straps, and the supporting bars were fastened with sturdy pins.

"Perfect," she said at last, satisfied.

With a skill that compelled admiration, she unfolded the wooden tripod and meticulously mounted the Dubroni camera. She screwed each component into place with precision, her expression focused, unaffected by the silent stares of the men watching her. Once everything was ready, she poured liquid from a small burette, gently tilted the camera, and announced:

"I'm ready."

She pressed her eye to the lens, adjusted the framing, and, after a moment's pause:

"It's done. We can pack up now."

Dr. Campbell grumbled, exasperated:

"All that effort for this?"

Miss Dupuis, a disarming smile curling at the corner of her lips, responded without hesitation:

"Taking photographs, Doctor is like certain encounters: the quicker it's over, the better."

Dumbfounded, Campbell opened his mouth, but no words came out. For his part, Robinson turned his head to hide an amused smile.

In silence, punctuated only by the creaking of the floorboards, the three men busied themselves repositioning the body. The table was lowered again and pushed back to the center of the room while Miss Dupuis, unperturbed, dismantled her equipment. Her movements were quick, precise and almost mechanical.

Still grumbling, Campbell addressed his student without looking up at Miss Dupuis:

"Tell the lowly staff to return the body to one of the cisterns."

Robinson and Dr. Campbell left the room with brisk steps, conversing in low voices. The student hesitated briefly before approaching Miss Dupuis. His hands, still faintly stained with antiseptic powder, fidgeted as he cleared his throat and spoke in French:

"We haven't been introduced. My name is Jean-Baptiste Turmel."

He extended his hand, which she shook briefly, her gaze studying him with polite neutrality.

"I'd like to apologize for my superior's behaviour," he added, lowering his eyes slightly.

"Thank you," she replied simply, her tone neutral but not hostile.

Turmel offered a timid smile as though seeking reassurance that he hadn't offended her.

"Don't worry about it," he continued. "He's unpleasant with everyone, especially his students."

Miss Dupuis didn't reply, focusing instead on securing the case for her camera. As she prepared to lift the box in one hand and the tripod in the other, Turmel stepped forward quickly to assist.

"Allow me," he said, reaching for the tripod.

"I can manage on my own," she replied, raising an eyebrow.

"I don't doubt it for a moment," he said with a bright smile. "But I'd be glad to lend a hand."

Miss Dupuis hesitated before relinquishing the tripod with visible reluctance. They began walking toward the exit, their footsteps echoing off the cold stone floor, punctuated by the creak of old hinges as a window closed with a gust of wind.

"Have you worked for the police long?" he asked, eager to prolong the conversation.

"I started today," she replied curtly.

"Yet it seems as though you've been doing this your whole life," he said with admiration and sincerity. "You have a remarkable composure, Miss."

She acknowledged his remark with a slight nod. After a short pause, perhaps out of politeness, she asked:

"And you? Have you been studying medicine for long?"

"Not really," he admitted. "I wasn't meant for this line of work. My father wanted me to take over our family business. But I always wanted to be a doctor."

He paused, his gaze momentarily distant as if lost in memories.

"I don't know how he managed it, but he found the money to send me here to study."

Miss Dupuis observed him silently, a flicker of interest crossing her face.

"And do you enjoy it?"

"Yes… very much. I enjoy the training. The environment, a little less so."

"Why is that?"

"Very few French Canadians study medicine here, and I haven't made many friends among my peers."

They stepped out of the building. An uncomfortable silence settled between them, punctuated by the rhythmic clatter of their footsteps on the frozen ground. The snow had stopped, leaving a bone-chilling dampness seeping into the marrow. Turmel pulled his coat tightly around himself, but Miss Dupuis seemed unaffected by the cold, bundled in a thick jacket and a dark scarf.

Upon reaching the cab, she placed her box inside, where Robinson sat waiting on a bench, patient as an old bear. She extended her hand toward the tripod that Turmel was still holding.

"Thank you for your help, Mr. Turmel," she said, her tone professional once more.

"It was a pleasure to meet you, Miss Dupuis," he replied, extending his hand again.

She took it, but he didn't let go immediately this time.

"Do you think it might be possible to see you again?" he asked, hope evident in his voice.

Miss Dupuis responded with a genuine and reserved smile. She withdrew her hand, climbed into the cab gracefully, held her coat and skirt with both hands and closed the door in silence, still smiling.

Robinson, who had been observing the scene with amusement, ordered the coachman to return to the station.

"Looks like Cupid's arrow has struck!"

"What are you talking about, Silas?" she asked, surprised by his light tone.

"Don't tell me you didn't notice how that young man looked at you. Don't you think he's charming?"

"Silas, we're at work," she replied sharply.

"Even so," he murmured with a sly grin.

They let the conversation drop. The rest of the journey passed in silence, broken only by the sound of hooves on the wet pavement.

CHAPTER 6

March 19, Sunday noon

After receiving Dr. Campbell's autopsy report on that cold Saturday morning, Robinson and Miss Dupuis returned to the police station. Snow fell in a fine powder, swirling under the force of a biting wind. Later, after having a frugal dinner at home and trading her cherry-red outing dress for more practical attire, Miss Dupuis set to work. Developing photographs demanded meticulous patience; soon, the acrid smell of chemicals would fill the small closet she used as a darkroom.

Meanwhile, Kelly spent his morning traversing Griffintown, trying to extract information from his few contacts in the area. The Irish quarter remained a bastion of distrust toward the police, and the frigid air seemed to weigh down the uneasy silences of those he questioned. There was not an address for Walsh, not even a hint.

"Some of them know him, I'm sure of it, but it's as if they're afraid to talk to me about him," he growled when he found Robinson back at the station.

The latter frowned. The leads were drying up. Determined to question Murphy, who had become the prime suspect, Robinson sent a constable to fetch him. The man returned empty-handed: the house was empty, with no sign of Murphy or his wife.

Frustration mounted. The information about the two individuals involved in the brawl at Kate Scanlan's tavern was far too sparse. Robinson resolved to pursue the remaining lead: the tavern keeper mentioned that Murphy volunteered at Saint Patrick's parish. Could he be found there?

***

The following day, after high mass and the Sunday meal, Robinson and Morin set out in the police chaise, driven steadily by the Chief's firm hand. The old black horse advanced at a measured pace, its hooves striking the ground where melting snow and mud reflected a dull, grey light. The houses lining the streets seemed frozen in the cold, their windows fogged by interior warmth contrasting with the biting air outside. Robinson, his shoulders hunched beneath a thick coat, was well acquainted with Father Dowd's initiatives. For years, the priest had gathered clothing for the needy in the vaulted basement of the parish. If Murphy was anywhere that day, it would likely be there.

"Well, Morin, how is your bank robbery case coming along?" Robinson asked gruffly, pulling up the collar of his coat against the stinging wind.

"We know there were two of them. They wore masks and were armed. It'll be difficult to identify them."

"Did they rough up the staff?" Robinson continued.

"No need. You obey without argument when you've got a pistol at your temple."

"And how much money did they take?"

"The manager isn't sure yet. He's still working on the inventory."

Robinson nodded, his gaze lost in the white mist rising from nearby chimneys.

"What's your take on it, you and Kelly?"

Morin shrugged, his expression dark.

"From the witnesses' accounts, these fellows aren't novices. They know their trade."

"Any descriptions? Their height, the colour of their eyes? Did they speak French or English?"

"They were cautious. Not a word. They wrote their demands on a scrap of paper."

"You've got the paper?"

"No, Chief. They took it back before leaving."

Robinson growled, his jaw tightening.

"Damn! Those two aren't amateurs. Could they be Americans?"

"No, I don't think so. They knew the place. Witnesses believe they'd been to the bank several times before. I've no doubt about it. Young, agile, slim. But nothing unusual for their build."

Robinson paused to think for a moment, his boots crunching against a patch of ice on the carriage floor.

"We should search the archives. We've already nabbed thieves using the same methods.

"It's not impossible, but I'd be surprised. This kind of robbery is rare here," Morin replied.

The wind carried their words down the deserted Sunday street, mingling their voices with the murmurs of the slumbering city.

The chaise stopped before Saint Patrick's Church, its towering spires piercing a grey sky laden with heavy clouds. Morin disembarked first, the collar of his wool coat turned up against the icy wind gusting between the buildings. He tied the reins of the black horse to a post near the entrance, briefly patting the animal's muzzle to calm its restlessness. The streets, mired in a mix of slush and patches of ice, reflected a pale, diffuse light.

Robinson, wrapped in a thick coat and wearing his ever-present bowler hat, stepped down after adjusting his leather gloves. The two men descended a short flight of steps to the side entrance, then entered the church's basement, where the atmosphere starkly contrasted with the bitter cold outside. A modest warmth, mingled with the smell of worn clothing and damp wood, filled the dimly lit room.

A few men and women busied themselves sorting garments around long tables arranged in rows, exchanging words in hushed tones. Robinson immediately spotted Father Dowd, a tall black cassock figure folding a shirt. Despite his austere appearance, he moved among the volunteers with disarming simplicity.

"Good afternoon, Father Dowd," Robinson said as he approached, removing his hat respectfully. "Robinson, chief detective of the Montreal police."

The priest looked up, a polite smile briefly lighting his weathered face.

"Ah, yes, I recognize you. You're quite the celebrity in Montreal," he replied with a touch of humour.

"And so are you," Robinson said with a faint grin.

"To what do I owe the honour of your visit?" the priest asked, carefully placing the garment on a pile.

Though nearing fifty, Patrick Dowd retained an imposing presence, standing nearly as tall as Robinson. His short, salt-and-pepper hair and sharply arched eyebrows lent him an air of natural authority, further heightened by an expression reminiscent of a stern disciplinarian prefect.

"You do fine work here helping the poor," Robinson remarked, glancing at the tables cluttered with clothing.

"It's a necessity above all," Father Dowd replied, crossing his arms over his chest. "You know the wretched conditions in which our Irish labourers live. Entire families depend on us to clothe themselves decently. Today, it's clothing; other times, it's baskets of provisions."

Robinson nodded thoughtfully.

"The Irish in Montreal are indeed the poorest labourers in Canada," he added.

The priest fixed his dark eyes on the detective, scrutinizing him.

"You're British, I presume?"

"Canadian. But I was born in Britain," Robinson answered calmly.

A brief silence followed, laden with unspoken implications that Robinson did not miss.

"We're looking to learn more about one of your parishioners, Michael Murphy. Do you know him?"

"Certainly. Michael and his wife, Margaret, volunteer here. What's this about?" the priest asked, his interest piqued.

"We only wish to speak with him," Robinson assured. "Is he here this afternoon?"

"Usually, he's always here, but he told us last Sunday that he needed to visit his parents in Saint-Colomban, up north."

"Is that where he's from?"

"Yes. His father works in the lumber trade and seldom comes to town, so Michael makes the trip."

"And he's been gone long?"

"He should be back this evening. Michael wouldn't miss a day of work, especially not this time of year."

"He works for the Grand Trunk?"

"No, on the Lachine Canal," Father Dowd clarified. "Even though the activity there isn't as bustling as it once was, several hundred workers are still employed in its maintenance. Michael is a hard worker, a fine young man."

"And his wife, Margaret?"

"An exemplary woman. She laments being unable to give him children, but she remains steadfast. I married them two years ago."

"How old would you say he is?"

"I'd guess 22 or 23," the priest replied after reflection. "But why all these questions? And more importantly, why would the chief detective of the Montreal police personally come to ask them?"

Robinson always disliked revealing his hand to those he interrogated. It deprived him of the strategic advantage he preferred to maintain in conversation. But this time, he had no choice.

"We believe Murphy is a key witness in a murder investigation," he said, fixing his gaze on the priest.

Father Dowd flinched slightly, one hand instinctively clutching his cassock.

"Murder!? Michael? Who would he have killed?"

"We're not accusing him of killing anyone, Father. At least not yet."

The priest slowly shook his head, visibly unsettled.

"Michael, a murderer! That's simply impossible. You must be mistaken."

"That's why we must speak with him—to clarify the situation. The circumstances of this murder make him a critical witness."

Father Dowd furrowed his brow, crossing his arms.

"The circumstances of the murder...?"

Robinson straightened slightly, choosing his words carefully.

"On the evening of Saint Patrick's Day, Michael fought with another patron. The scuffle escalated, and they were both thrown out of the tavern."

"And so? Michael's a good lad. He enjoys celebrating, that's true. Sometimes, he can get quarrelsome after too many drinks, but that's rare. Margaret keeps him straight and narrow. That doesn't make him a murderer. If we locked up everyone who fought while drunk, half of Montreal would be behind bars!" Father Dowd exclaimed, a sad smile tugging at the corner of his lips.

"You're right, Father. But when a brawl turns into murder, it's cause for concern," Robinson replied calmly. "We found a corpse in the alley behind the tavern where Murphy had his fight."

Father Dowd's face grew slightly more severe.

"That doesn't prove Michael had anything to do with it. A simple coincidence, perhaps."

"A coincidence? In our work, Father, we don't put much stock in coincidences," Robinson retorted.

The priest averted his gaze briefly as though lost in thought.

"And who, according to you, would Michael have killed?"

"We're not yet certain of the victim's identity. But we know he fought that night with a man named Aidan Walsh. We suspect it's him who was killed."

Father Dowd let out a bitter chuckle.

"Walsh… Well, it wouldn't be surprising if someone had killed him."

"You know him?" Robinson asked, intrigued.

"Not personally, but his reputation precedes him. Walsh is a petty thug, the leader of a gang of young Irish lads in Griffintown. A bad seed, if you ask me."

"You don't seem fond of him."

"It's not a matter of fondness, Chief Detective. That boy, young as he may be, is a hardened sinner. I've never seen him set foot in a confessional. And my parishioners have enough troubles without enduring the misdeeds of someone like him."

Robinson remained thoughtful for a moment before speaking again.

"Do you think Michael could have killed Walsh?"

"I don't know," Father Dowd replied, "but if he did, it would surely have been in self-defence. Michael isn't a gentleman, but he's no killer, either. Walsh, on the other hand…"

Robinson leaned forward slightly.

"What do you mean by that, Father?"

Father Dowd hesitated, then murmured:

"Walsh... That man could have killed someone. He's capable of it."

"Do you have proof to support that claim?"

"No, of course not. But if you asked me to choose between Michael and Walsh as the murderer, I wouldn't hesitate for a second. Are you certain Walsh is the one who was killed?"

Robinson frowned.

"Why do you ask that, Father?"

"You don't know the body's identity yet, do you?"

"Not yet. We're working on identifying it."

Father Dowd let out a deep sigh, his expression hardening.

"Then it could be Walsh... but just as easily be Michael."

"Murphy?" Robinson said, surprised. "Didn't you say he was supposed to return today?"

"In truth," the priest admitted, "I haven't heard from him since last Sunday."

Robinson fell silent, allowing a heavy pause to settle over the room. His gaze drifted to the concrete floor, cracked in places where dried mud marked the passage of volunteers delivering clothing. The air hums with the tension left by their conversation. At last, he raised his head, his expression once again impassive.

"You've been very helpful, Father. We won't take up any more of your time," he said gravely but politely.

Father Dowd inclined his head slightly, his hands clasped before him, a worried crease still visible on his brow. Morin, who had been silent until now, tucked his leather notebook and worn pencil into the canvas satchel slung across his shoulder. Throughout the interview, he took meticulous notes, his sharp eyes constantly moving between his notebook and the speakers.

This habit of recording every detail had no effect, but Robinson insisted. He had lived through times when promising investigations had crumbled due to a lack of documentation, with officers relying on fallible memory and the often vague accounts of witnesses. From the beginning of his tenure as chief detective, he had imposed a strict rule: every investigation must be thoroughly recorded. This attention to detail had saved him more than once, and he was not a man to risk an avoidable mistake.

The Chief adjusted the collar of his thick wool coat, bracing himself once more for the biting wind swirling outside, and firmly anchored his bowler hat on his head. The daylight pierced through the high windows of the basement, casting long shadows over the piles of clothing and cluttered tables. Robinson looked around as though imprinting the scene in his memory before heading for the exit, with Morin following close behind.

The two detectives left the church, their boots crunching against the packed snow mixed with slush. The icy March wind funnelled between the buildings, making Morin shiver despite his heavy coat. The horse, tethered near the entrance, seemed restless, stamping its hooves and exhaling steam plumes into the frigid air. Robinson gently patted the animal's neck before taking the reins and climbing into the carriage.

Morin, bundled up to his ears in his coat, settled beside him, his shoulders slightly hunched. Once the horse was trotting, he turned to Robinson.

"So, Chief, are we any further ahead?"

Robinson, his hands firmly on the reins, frowned.

"I'm not sure, Morin. Not sure at all," he replied after a pause. "Our main suspect is still Murphy... but after what Father Dowd said, I'm having doubts."

"Because he doesn't believe Murphy's guilty?" Morin asked, intrigued.

"Not just that," Robinson replied, his gaze drifting to the streets where the bare branches of a few trees swayed in the wind.

"Oh no?" Morin prompted, sitting up slightly.

"Father Dowd speaks of Walsh as if he's a petty criminal, the sort capable of murder. What if we've got the wrong suspect? After all, we haven't identified the victim yet. We don't even know where Murphy and Walsh are."

Morin nodded, his brow furrowing.

"So, Walsh might not be the victim?" he ventured.

"Perhaps not," Robinson said pensively.

"And what if the victim is Murphy?" Morin added after a moment.

"It's a possibility," Robinson admitted. "A third possibility is that the victim has nothing to do with either Murphy or Walsh."

Morin mulled this over before suggesting, "Perhaps we should revisit Kelly's lead, then. Remember, he talked about an Irish vendetta."

"That's not exactly what he said," Robinson corrected, shaking his head slightly. "Kelly thought our man's death had nothing to do with the tavern brawl."

Morin crossed his arms to shield himself from the biting cold.

"We're not making much progress, Chief. It's becoming urgent that we identify the body."

Robinson sighed, his eyes fixed on the road ahead.

"I'd have liked to see the photograph Miss Dupuis took at the morgue."

"That's true. Why don't we have it yet?" Morin asked, his brow furrowed.

"She had trouble with her equipment," Robinson explained. "She was short on chemicals, and since the shop that supplies her is closed on Sundays, she couldn't get what she needed today. We should have the photograph by tomorrow."

Morin nodded, looking doubtful.

"So, Chief, what do you make of all this?"

Robinson glanced at him, his expression grave.

"I don't know. I haven't formed an opinion yet. But you know me, Morin—I don't believe in tunnel vision."

A faint smile played on Morin's lips.

"Yes, Chief. You've taught us that focusing on a single hypothesis in an investigation is dangerous, like a horse with blinders."

Robinson nodded slowly.

"Still, I don't like letting go of this lead. Too many coincidences: a fight in a tavern, and then, one or two hours later, a corpse was found in the adjacent alley. No, I don't like it."

Morin, thinking it over, raised an eyebrow.

"So, what do we do?"

"Until we have other leads, we'll keep digging into this. We need to find those two fellows... assuming they're still alive. Based on what Father Dowd told us, Murphy should return home tonight. Take a constable with you and bring him in. If you find him, bring him straight to the station."

"So he'll spend the night in a cell?" Morin asked, a hint of hesitation in his voice.

Robinson turned a determined gaze toward him.

"We don't have much choice. If he's a murderer, he could flee."

"And Walsh?" Morin asked, his tone a mix of curiosity and impatience.

Robinson smirked faintly, adjusting his hat slightly to shield himself from the wind seeping into the carriage.

"We need to keep looking for him. And, believe it or not, I have an idea... one that you gave me, Morin."

Morin raised his eyebrows in surprise.

"Me? Is that so?" he said, sitting up straighter in his seat.

"Yes," Robinson continued. "When you mentioned the two bank robbers earlier and suggested looking into similar past cases, it gave me an idea: we could apply the same method to our friend Walsh. If he's really a petty crook, chances are he's left traces—thefts, brawls, arrests. We should be able to find something about him in the archives."

Morin nodded, considering this.

"Good idea."

"I can't imagine someone like Walsh has never been convicted of anything," Robinson said, his eyes fixed on the street rolling past. "With some luck, his file will give us his address."

Morin frowned slightly.

"His address? You might find his old one, but no guarantee he still lives there."

Robinson turned to him, a confident smile spreading across his face.

"Not with this kind of lowlife. These petty criminals think they're untouchable. They don't change their habits easily. I'd wager that he'll still be there if I find his address."

The horse slowed, its hooves echoing against the damp cobblestones where slush and melting snow had settled into the cracks as they approached Bonsecours Market. The waning light of day touched the imposing yet austere façades of the grey stone buildings. A biting wind whistled through the deserted streets, lifting occasional patches of melting snow. The carriage stopped before the grand edifice, its wheels clattering faintly on the slick stones before halting. Robinson disembarked quickly, tightening his coat against the numbing cold that stiffened his movements.

A constable, clad in a thick coat and wearing a round felt hat dusted with a thin layer of snow, approached to take the reins with gloved hands.

"Take the carriage and the horse back to the stable," Morin instructed calmly as he stepped down from the vehicle.

The two detectives exchanged a knowing glance.

"Until tomorrow," Robinson said, snuffling his scarf around his neck.

"Until tomorrow, Chief," Morin replied, walking off briskly, shoulders hunched in his coat against the gusts.

Robinson, meanwhile, headed toward the police station, his boots making a dull sound against the wet ground. He crossed the threshold and entered the modest warmth of the interior. Without delay, he went to the archives room, where the air was thick with the scent of aged paper and dust—a testament to the many years of secrets and crimes recorded within the files.

CHAPTER 7

Monday Morning, March 20

March was particularly erratic this year, marked by icy gusts and streets alternately blanketed with snow or churned into muddy ruts. For the detectives of the Montreal police, the workweek officially began on Monday. Yet few adhered strictly to that schedule. Every man on the force lent a hand over those days, logging extra hours without complaint. In this brigade, duty came above all else.

Chief Robinson was preparing to open the weekly meeting when a commotion outside the office drew his attention. Frowning, he rose from his chair and stepped out. The chaotic echoes of an argument reverberated against the gray stone walls.

Heading toward the first-floor entryway, he found the station clerk and a constable grappling with a furious woman. Stray wisps of unkempt hair escaped from beneath a faded woollen bonnet, and her coarse wool coat, ill-fitting and threadbare, slipped down over a plaid dress worn thin with age. She was shouting in a hoarse, despairing voice:

"Where is he? Where is he? I want to see him!"

Her tiny but determined fists pounded the arms of the men who struggled to calm her with little success.

"Mrs. Murphy?" Robinson called, his voice calm, almost gentle, but laced with authority.

The woman froze, her gaze fixed on him like a cornered animal.

"Who are you?" she spat.

"Detective Chief Robinson, madam," he replied with a slight nod. "We need to question your husband."

"Why? What's he done?"

"We're not entirely sure yet."

Her expression shifted in an instant—shock giving way to pure fury.

"What do you mean you're not sure? You barge into our home, almost in the dead of night, haul my husband off like some common criminal, toss him into a cell, and then you tell me you don't know why?"

Robinson remained unruffled, but his tone grew firmer.

"Your husband is an important witness in a murder investigation."

The word struck like a slap; her eyes widened, and her mouth fell slightly open before her indignation returned to full force.

"A murder? Have you lost your mind? My man's got nothing to do with a murder! He's an honest working man, that's all."

"Be that as it may, Mrs. Murphy, we need to question him. You're welcome to wait here if you'd like."

She planted her hands on her hips, glaring defiantly at the detective chief.

"Of course, I'm going to wait. And mark my words, I'll leave here with him this morning—no later."

Robinson, without replying, gave a brief nod before turning on his heel. His heavy, deliberate steps echoed through the stairwell as he returned to his office.

"What's going on, Chief?" Kelly asked, his voice rough.

Robinson blew on his hands to warm them. The air carried the mingled scent of rain and the sharper tang of coal smoke.

"It's Murphy's wife."

Kelly raised an eyebrow, intrigued.

"She couldn't have picked a better time. Did you tell her you wanted to question her about the tavern brawl?"

"No. I didn't want to frighten her. But since she insists on waiting here for Murphy, we'll have her at hand if we need her. Now, let's get to work."

Morin, shuffling papers with a nervous hand, chimed in.

"Miss Dupuis isn't here?"

"No," Robinson replied curtly. "She ran into trouble Saturday with the photo development—was short on supplies. She's gone to fetch what she needs to finish the job."

Morin folded his arms, frowning.

"So we're not getting the photos of the victim today?"

"We'll likely have them by this morning. Dupuis knows her craft."

Kelly turned his gaze to the window, watching the sleet gently drum against the dulled panes, smothered in soot and grime.

"In any case, we don't need her to know who the victim is: Aidan Walsh," he murmured.

At this, Robinson and Morin exchanged a weighted glance, lowering their heads slightly. Kelly didn't like their silence.

"What? You're not sure it's him?"

The two men remained silent, but their expressions spoke volumes. Kelly clenched his fists and pressed on:

"Well, we've got our killer, at least. How did you manage to catch him, Morin?"

Morin lifted his head and shrugged.

"Easy. I already knew where he lived. We learned yesterday that he'd be back home by evening. It wasn't hard—he sat down to supper with his wife when we arrived."

Kelly's eyes widened.

"He didn't resist arrest?"

Morin let out a short, almost bitter laugh.

"He didn't. But his wife… a real tigress! The constable had to hold her back to stop her from hurting us with her fists and feet. She kept shouting, 'What do you want?'"

"Well, we've got him now, and that's what matters."

Robinson adjusted his cravat with a sharp tug.

"I'll question him with Morin. Kelly, you're going to search Walsh's house."

"You've got his address?" Kelly asked, already reaching for his still-damp coat.

"Yes. I spent part of last evening at the archives and found a file on him. He was convicted two years ago for robbing a shop on Wellington Street."

Kelly frowned.

"Did he serve time?"

Robinson shook his head.

"No. He was young, and the judge was lenient. He got off with a reprimand and a record."

"You're sure the address is correct?"

"At the time, he lived with his widowed mother. She's likely still at the same place."

Kelly hesitated briefly, a shadow of a thought crossing his face.

"Should I tell her about her son's death?"

"Absolutely not. We don't have any certainty yet. Just tell her we're looking for him and want to search his room for clues."

"All right, Chief. I'm on my way," Kelly said, pulling down the brim of his bowler hat.

He left the room with brisk steps, his boots echoing on the worn floorboards. Descending the cold, dim stairwell, he felt a draft seep through a crack in the outer door. When he pushed it open, a blast of icy wind swept in, sending a swirl of sleet through the entryway. The door groaned shut behind him, the sound swallowed by the howl of the wind.

***

Robinson and Morin pushed open the door to the interrogation room, the creak muffled by the thick walls. The room carried the faint scent of stale tobacco and polished wood. At its center stood a heavy oak table, scarred with years of use, and behind it stood a young man, seemingly calm. His brown hair curled into untidy locks, a neatly trimmed mustache adorned his lip, and a fine chinstrap beard framed his jaw. He might have appeared well-kept if it were not for the purple bruises mottling his jaw and forehead and the vivid shiner blooming around his right eye.

"They took my cap," he began without preamble, his voice unexpectedly high-pitched.

Morin stifled a chuckle, but Robinson remained unmoved, his face carved from stone.

"What am I doing here?" Murphy continued, his fingers drumming nervously on the table. "Why'd you throw me in jail? I didn't do anything."

Morin settled into a chair, notebook and pencil in hand, drawing slow, deliberate lines, while Robinson placed a thick dossier on the table. It was a practiced tactic: with an air of gravity, Robinson leafed through the file's pages, scrawled at random, allowing the suspect's imagination to run wild. Yet with Murphy, the ploy seemed ineffective. His gaze betrayed neither fear nor curiosity. Robinson opened the file with a deliberately loud sigh.

"Michael Murphy, is that correct?" Robinson asked, fixing the young man with a steely gaze.

"That's me."

"Twenty-one years old. Married."

"Twenty-two," Murphy corrected, a hint of pride in his tone. "Been married to Margaret for two years."

"No children?"

"Not yet," he replied, his voice hardening slightly.

"You work… let's see… for the Grand Trunk Railway."

Murphy shook his head.

"No, I work on the Lachine Canal."

Robinson paused, slowly flipping through the papers again, letting the silence stretch uncomfortably.

"What do you want with me, anyway?" Murphy finally burst out, his patience thinning.

Robinson straightened slightly.

"Where were you, Murphy, on the evening of March 17?"

Murphy frowned, clearly trying to puzzle out the direction of the questioning.

"Thursday? That was Saint Patrick's Day. I went out celebrating with my wife."

"Where?"

"At Mother Scanlan's tavern."

"Kate Scanlan?"

"That's the one."

Robinson narrowed his eyes as though trying to read Murphy's thoughts.

"You go to that tavern often?"

"It's my favourite place. Yeah, I go there quite a bit," Murphy admitted without hesitation.

Robinson feigned intense focus on the file, flipping through the pages as though each held a crucial secret.

"So, you were at Kate Scanlan's tavern on the evening of March 17?"

"That's what I just told you," Murphy replied, irritation creeping into his tone. "We were celebrating Saint Patrick's.

The place was packed. We had fun—there were musicians, singers, and dancers. It was a good time."

Robinson slowly lifted his gaze, his piercing eyes locking onto Murphy's.

"You didn't just have fun... That's what I'm reading here..."

Murphy's eyes widened, caught off guard.

"What do you mean? Of course, we had a good time all evening."

"Not all evening," Robinson replied, snapping the dossier shut with a loud thud. "At least, that's not what I'm reading here. It seems you got into a fight."

Murphy stayed silent, his gaze flicking between Robinson and the thick file on the table. His jaw tightened, and his fingers tapped nervously on the edge of the rough wooden table. Then, suddenly, a spark of realization lit his face.

"Ah, so that's why I'm here! Because of the fight at the tavern," he said, a hint of defiance in his voice.

Robinson, unflinching, fixed him with a steady gaze.

"But that's nothing!" Murphy continued, shrugging as if the matter were trivial. "Fights in taverns happen all the time. Every week, in every tavern. And you arrested me for that?"

Crossing his arms, Robinson responded in an icy tone:

"I'm not concerned with other fights in other taverns. I'm interested in the one you started on March 17."

Murphy's eyes widened slightly before he shook his head, his expression darkening.

"Started? Me? Come on now, I didn't start it."

"Oh, you didn't?"

"Of course not. It was that damned Walsh," Murphy shot back, slapping his hand on the table, the sound echoing in the small room. "He kept ogling my wife. Damn Walsh!"

"You know Walsh well?"

"Walsh? No, I don't know him well," Murphy said, rolling his eyes. "I just know he's a no-good scoundrel."

Robinson's brow furrowed slightly.

"And your wife?"

Murphy hesitated, caught off guard.

"What about my wife?"

"She didn't mind Walsh's attention?"

Murphy chuckled bitterly, his tone turning sharp.

"Bah, you know women. It doesn't take much to make them swoon over a man."

"So, you got tired of watching Walsh hanging around her?"

Murphy straightened his shoulders, his fists clenching on the table.

"Wouldn't you?"

Robinson remained silent, lowering his head slightly as though deep in thought. He knew from experience that a well-timed silence could be more effective than any question. Murphy finally broke the quiet, his voice tense with barely restrained anger.

"Well, I didn't let him get away with it," he said, almost proudly.

"Was Walsh alone?"

"Of course not," Murphy replied with a bitter smile. "He's never alone. He had his little gang of thugs with him."

"And you still took him on? You weren't afraid?"

Murphy puffed out his chest slightly, lifting his chin.

"It was a matter of honour. Besides, I'm stronger than him."

Indeed, Murphy had a formidable build. Though not particularly tall, his broad chest and massive shoulders spoke of raw strength. Perhaps a bit stout, he was undeniably robust—a labourer built for hard work. His employers no doubt valued such solidity.

"So, you went after him?"

"Of course," Murphy replied with a defiant grin. "I stood up, walked over to him, and told him to leave my wife alone. He laughed at me. I lost it. I pulled him out of his chair and started hitting him."

"Well, he must've hit back, judging by your face," Robinson retorted, glancing at Murphy's black eye and the bruises mottling his face.

Murphy shrugged with a dry laugh.

"You should see his."

A heavy silence filled the room, broken only by the creak of the wooden chair under Murphy's weight. Robinson, unflinching, seemed to be measuring his interlocutor, his fingers tapping lightly on the edge of the file before him. He knew silence was a formidable weapon. Finally, he lifted his head, pretending to peruse his notes.

"It looks like they threw you out, Manu militari," he said in a detached, almost nonchalant tone.

Murphy blinked, visibly confused.

"Manu what…?"

A faint smile played at Robinson's lips.

"The bouncer kicked you out, quite literally."

Murphy grumbled, but a wry grin tugged at his bruised face despite himself.

"That's right. Tom's a big guy. Grabbed me with one hand… and Walsh with the other!"

"You ended up outside together?" Robinson asked, tilting his head slightly.

"Yeah. We were both pretty beat up," Murphy admitted, rubbing his sore jaw absentmindedly.

"And thoroughly drunk as well."

Murphy let out a resigned sigh.

"That's true. I had more to drink than usual. Had a hell of a time getting back on my feet. Lucky Margaret was there."

"And Walsh?" Robinson leaned forward slightly, watching every flicker of emotion.

"He wasn't much of a Samson either," Murphy replied with a short laugh.

"So, you got up and went home, did you?"

"Of course," Murphy said, as if the answer were obvious.

"And Walsh?" Robinson pressed, his eyes narrowing.

Murphy shrugged.

"I don't know. He went his own way."

Robinson straightened, his sharp gaze cutting through the room. It was time to deliver the decisive blow.

"You're good at spinning tales, aren't you, Murphy?"

Murphy looked up, his brows knitting together, though his tone remained steady.

"I'm not spinning any tales. That's what happened."

Robinson fixed him with a steady gaze, letting a palpable tension settle over the room. The pale light of the lamp glinted off the worn wood of the table.

"Well, I've got another story for you," Robinson said coldly, enunciating each word with deliberate precision. "When you left the tavern, you didn't stop with Walsh. You both headed into the alley next door. Then you pulled out a knife and stabbed him."

Murphy jolted like a bucket of ice water had been thrown over him.

"What? Are you mad? Walsh?"

"He's dead. Did you know that?"

The colour drained from Murphy's face.

"Walsh is dead? That's not possible. If he's dead, it wasn't me who killed him. I don't even own a knife. Ask my wife— she was with me the whole time."

"A wife's testimony doesn't hold weight in court."

"In court? You've lost your mind!" Murphy exclaimed, his voice rising. "I've never killed anyone. I'm a good Catholic, you know. Killing is a mortal sin. You don't do that."

"And fighting? Is that a mortal sin, too?"

Murphy frowned and shot back sharply:

"That's not the same thing. You've got to defend yourself, don't you?"

The heavy, oppressive silence fell again, broken only by a sharp knock at the door. Robinson rose with measured movements and went to answer it. Miss Dupuis stood in the doorway, straight-backed and slightly out of breath. She wore a simple, elegant dark wool dress with a fitted bodice accented by a white lace collar. A modest brooch adorned her neckline, and her hands, slightly reddened, bore faint traces of the chemicals used for developing photographs. Her long sleeves ended in neatly buttoned cuffs, and a black twill apron covered the lower half of her skirt, a clear sign she had just come from the darkroom.

"Dupuis, do you have something for me?" Robinson asked, crossing his arms.

"At last," she replied, brushing a stray wisp of hair back into her tightly coiled chignon. "I managed to develop one photo. I hurried to bring it to you. Was that the right thing to do?"

"Yes, yes. You're just in time," Robinson said, taking the envelope eagerly.

He opened it and pulled out a still-damp photograph, faintly hazy from moisture. The victim's face was clearly visible: serene, almost as though he were sleeping—a man who appeared to have found eternal rest.

Robinson returned to the interrogation room, holding the photograph between his fingers.

"I've just received the photograph of Walsh—the man you killed," he announced, holding out the image to Murphy.

Murphy stared at the photo, his eyes widening in shock.

"But... that's not Walsh!"

Sitting quietly in the background, Morin straightened in his chair and leaned forward, resting his forearms on the table.

"What do you mean that's not Walsh?"

"I mean, it's not Walsh."

"Then who is it?"

Murphy shrugged, a mix of confusion and panic flashing across his face.

"I don't know."

"You've never seen him before?"

Murphy leaned closer to the photograph, studying it intently.

"He looks like he's sleeping... Yeah... I think I've seen him before. But it's not Walsh. I don't know him."

"Where do you think you've seen him?"

"At Mother Scanlan's tavern," Murphy answered after a moment. "I must've come across him once or twice."

"And you don't know who he is?"

"Not a clue. But Mother Scanlan might. She knows everyone who comes into her tavern."

Robinson and Morin exchanged glances, a silent yet weighted conversation passing between them.

"Can I go now?" Murphy asked, his voice wavering between hope and irritation.

Robinson replied without breaking eye contact:

"Not yet. I'll be back to speak with you soon."

Robinson left the interrogation room alone, his footsteps echoing heavily on the stone steps as he descended the grand staircase. In the dimly lit corridor, the air carried a mix of mustiness and coal smoke, a scent characteristic of public buildings.

Murphy's wife sprang up from the rickety chair where she had been waiting as if propelled by some invisible force.

"Mrs. Murphy," Robinson said, observing her closely.

"Can he leave?" she asked, her voice tinged with hope and worry, her fingers nervously twisting a ribbon hanging from her hat.

"I have a question for you," he said calmly. "Were you with your husband at the Saint Patrick's Day celebration?"

"Yes, at Mother Scanlan's," she answered immediately, lifting her chin slightly as though the detail alone should suffice.

"Do you often accompany your husband to the tavern?"

She hesitated briefly, her cheeks flushed from the chill outside or perhaps a hint of embarrassment.

"Rarely. Only when there's a celebration."

"On Saint Patrick's night, did your husband get into a fight?"

"Yes, with some man I didn't know," she replied, frowning, clearly irritated by the memory.

"The bouncer threw both men out to stop the fight?"

"Yes. Poor Michael, he was in a bad state," she sighed, her voice trembling slightly. "I helped him get home."

"Nothing else happened outside between your husband and the other man? They didn't continue fighting?"

She shook her head vigorously, the ribbons on her bonnet bouncing with the movement.

"Oh no! They wouldn't have been able to anyway," she said with a mixture of exasperation and thinly veiled reproach. "I've always told Michael not to drink so much."

Robinson withdrew a photograph from a weathered envelope he had tucked into the inner pocket of his coat.

"Was the other man this one?" he asked, holding out the image.

She squinted, scrutinizing the photo carefully, before shaking her head firmly.

"No, it wasn't him."

"Do you know this man?" Robinson pressed, his sharp gaze unrelenting.

"I've never seen him," she replied resolutely, folding her arms as though shielding herself from an invisible accusation.

Robinson turned to the constable stationed nearby, a stocky man with a weary face.

"Bob, fetch the man in the interrogation room and let him go," he ordered crisply.

Mrs. Murphy's eyes widened in surprise at these words, her face lighting up. She looked at Robinson, and a subtle, heartfelt smile softened her tired features.

"Thank you, sir," she murmured, her gratitude unmistakable.

Without delay, the Chief ascended the staircase briskly, his boots striking the steps with purpose. A faint draft, carrying the chill of melting snow and the scent of damp air, seemed to seep into every corner, even within the building.

CHAPTER 8

Monday, March 20, at noon

"Walsh isn't dead!"

Kelly burst into the office like an icy gale, his cheeks reddened by the biting cold. He removed his hat and placed it on the table, then shrugged off his coat, heavy with melting snow. The three other detectives, huddled around their desks piled high with files and papers, looked up, intrigued. Their discussion about the impact of losing their prime suspect abruptly ended, only to dissolve into laughter at Kelly's bewildered expression.

"What's so funny?" he demanded, frowning, visibly annoyed.

"We already know Walsh isn't dead," Robinson replied, folding his arms.

"What do you mean, you know? I just found out!"

Perched on the edge of her chair, Miss Dupuis confidently picked up the victim's photograph and handed it to Kelly, who was already stepping forward to examine it.

"What's this?" he asked, squinting at it.

"A photograph of our victim," she explained.

"But this isn't Walsh… He looks like he's sleeping."

"Precisely," Miss Dupuis replied with a faint smile. "Our victim isn't Walsh."

Clearly taken aback, Kelly sighed, frustrated, before slumping into a chair. His dramatic entrance had fallen flat. The detectives' office, a cramped but practical space with desks arranged in a square to encourage collaboration, echoed with the murmurs of his colleagues' satisfaction. Robinson broke the silence.

"So, Kelly, what happened?"

Kelly straightened his shoulders slightly, regaining some composure, and launched into his story:

"I went to Walsh's address over in Griffintown. I was certain his mother would be the one to answer the door… Well, imagine my surprise when he opened it himself."

As Kelly continued, his account gaining colour, a ripple of interest spread through the room.

"I found Walsh's place without much trouble. A shabby little wooden shack that looked like it could collapse under the weight of a stiff breeze. I knocked on the door, unsure what I would find. A few moments later, a kid opens up. Small fellow, scrawny, with ash-blond hair and blue eyes that stared at you like he was trying to size you up. But what struck me most was his face. Bruises everywhere, marks that screamed he'd taken a beating. He gave me a sharp 'What do you want?' as if I were bothering him. I stared him straight and said, plain as day, 'I'm looking for Aidan Walsh.'

"That little rascal, he snapped, 'Don't know him,' and tried to slam the door in my face. But I was quicker. I stuck my foot in the doorway to stop it from shutting. 'Well, Walsh,' I said, pointing at his bruises, 'haven't you been roughed up?' I knew I'd hit a nerve. But a woman's voice called out from inside before he could speak.

'Who's Aidan?'

"That was it. The kid panicked. He shoved me with everything he had, and I swear, he almost managed to knock me over. Then he bolted. I watched him take off down the street, leaping over puddles like the devil was chasing him. No way I could catch him. That boy ran like his life depended on it."

Kelly paused as if to ensure the weight of his account was fully understood by his audience.

"So, it was Walsh, then?" Robinson asked thoughtfully.

"Absolutely. His mother confirmed it afterward."

"And you couldn't catch him?"

"No. The little devil ran like the wind."

Miss Dupuis, her tone playful, turned a teasing gaze toward Robinson.

"Chief, we've never seen a Newfoundland dog catch a hare," she said, bursting into laughter.

"MISS Dupuis!" Kelly growled, raising a mock-threatening finger, though his smile betrayed his amusement.

Morin watched the exchange silently, slightly taken aback by Kelly's light-hearted reaction. If he had dared to make such a joke, he'd likely have been scolded on the spot.

Kelly, regaining his composure, finally spoke.

"I searched the house after that. Guess what I found in his room?"

Silence fell like a heavy curtain. He waited, savouring the anticipation in the room.

"A pistol, a mask, and money… a lot of money."

The shock was palpable. Robinson slowly nodded his head.

"Well, we've uncovered one of our bank robbers."

"That makes no sense, Chief," Morin protested. "Why would he keep that stuff at home? It's absurd."

"These little scoundrels aren't exactly brilliant," Robinson replied with a shrug. "They think they're untouchable. Either way, good work, Kelly. You've almost solved one case. But there's still the alley murder to deal with."

The Chief settled into his chair, his coat still damp and hanging from a peg, evidence of the light snow falling outside. Crossing his arms, he fixed his gaze on Kelly and summarized the latest developments: Murphy's interrogation about the tavern brawl, confirming that Walsh wasn't the victim. The questioning had cleared Murphy of any involvement.

"We're starting from scratch," he concluded, a trace of weariness in his voice. "We've got no suspect."

Kelly, arms crossed, leaning against the edge of a desk, his boots leaving wet marks on the worn wooden floor.

"I told you, Chief. It's just a grudge match among the Irish, nothing more," he asserted confidently.

"It's a theory we'll keep in mind," the Chief acknowledged with a nod.

"If that's the case, it'll be tough to find the culprit. There's a code of silence in those circles. Even if someone knows something, they'll never tell the police."

The Chief pursed his lips and glanced toward the frost-covered window. Montreal's damp and dirty snow-covered streets seemed to dissolve under a dull grey light.

"We'll see," he said at last, as if to put an end to the discussion.

Morin, seated slightly apart, leaned forward and spoke up:

"You said, Chief, that you don't believe in coincidences. Still, we must admit our victim has some connection to Kate Scanlan's tavern. Murphy claimed to have seen her there several times."

A pensive silence settled over the room. The detectives knew Griffintown, whose shadowy alleys and secrets were buried under the snow, likely held the answers they sought.

"Indeed, Griffintown and Scanlan's tavern appear to be at the heart of this case," the Chief finally said. "We'll need to pay the proprietor another visit. You're coming with me, Kelly."

Kelly nodded, stood, and took his thick wool coat from the rack. March's biting cold was unforgiving.

"And Walsh? What are we doing about him?" he asked.

The Chief turned to Morin.

"Morin, you're in charge of that. If you need assistance, ask Dupuis."

A mischievous smile lit up Miss Dupuis's face as she looked playfully at Morin.

"I'm not sure I'll need her," Morin grumbled.

Raising her eyebrows, a barely concealed grin on her lips, Miss Dupuis replied in a tone of mock innocence:

"I could at least dig up some information to help figure out where he's hiding. What do you think?"

Morin hesitated a moment before conceding.

"Yeah, that's not a bad idea. I'll go talk to his mother's neighbours in the meantime."

The Chief rose, brushing off his sleeves.

"Good. Everyone knows what they have to do."

The detectives dispersed, each pulling on scarves, coats, and hats before heading out. The icy wind rushed in every time the door to the Bonsecours building opened, whipping up swirls of slushy snow. The city, caught between shades of grey and white, echoed with the creak of wagons and voices muffled by the cold.

***

It was nearing noon. The police chaise moved briskly through the muddy streets leading to Wellington Street, its wheels splattering melted snow mixed with dirt. Robinson and Kelly sat somewhat cramped inside, their thick wool coats adding to the tight quarters. Robinson held the reins firmly, steering his favourite piebald horse—a placid creature capable of surprising bursts of energy when called upon. The Chief preferred this mode of transport, quick and nimble, far better suited to the city's chaotic traffic than heavier alternatives.

When they reached Kate Scanlan's tavern, Robinson gently pulled the reins, bringing the rig to a halt. Kelly immediately climbed out, his coat sweeping away some loose dirt across the roadway. He made his way to the nearby alley, where the body had been found. When he returned to Robinson, his expression was grim.

"They've cleaned it all up," he said, shaking his head. "Fresh dirt to cover the blood."

Robinson nodded slowly, clearly not surprised. Together, the two men pushed open the tavern door, immediately enveloped by a mingled smell of beer, warm food, and sweat.

Inside, half the tables were occupied. Labourers in soiled aprons and caps pulled low were eating hastily, taking quick bites between gulps of beer. The hum of conversation and the clatter of cutlery ceased abruptly as they entered, and every head turned their way. An awkward silence fell over the room. The patrons, clearly unaccustomed to strangers—let alone law officers—stared at them warily. Behind the bar, Kate Scanlan froze mid-motion. Her hands, still damp from drying glasses, sent them a look that seemed to ask, What do you want here?

Robinson and Kelly scanned the room, searching for an empty table. They found one near the wall, slightly removed from the others. As they approached to sit down, a tall man at a nearby table spoke up in a sharp tone:

"That spot's taken."

Kelly shot him a dark glare, a flicker of defiance in his eyes. Ignoring the remark, the two detectives took their seats, removed their hats, and laid their coats over an empty chair. A tense silence lingered for a moment.

The staff seemed reluctant to approach, and Kelly finally waved over a young waitress in a broad white apron with a tired face. She approached slowly, avoiding eye contact, and asked in a dull voice if they wanted to order.

"Pork and beans for me," Kelly said.

"Calf's head," Robinson replied, adding, "And two pitchers of beer."

The waitress walked away without another word, and the two men lapsed into a contemplative silence, observing the room's happenings. The patrons' curious or hostile gazes still lingered like embers waiting to flare at the slightest provocation.

After finishing their meal and polishing off a slice of custard pie, the detectives stood and made their way to the bar. Scanlan was still there, watching their movements with a mask of feigned neutrality.

Robinson pulled out his wallet, his gaze fixed on her.

"How much do we owe you?"

"It's on the house for you," she replied, an enigmatic smile on her lips.

Robinson held her gaze, squinting slightly.

"Bribing officers, Mrs. Scanlan?"

"I've never seen a constable turn down a free meal," she countered with a sarcastic pout.

"We're the exception that proves the rule," Robinson said, pulling out the money to pay.

After settling the bill, he reached into his pocket and placed a photograph on the counter before her.

"Do you know this man?"

Scanlan leaned forward to examine the image. After a moment, she shrugged.

"Looks like he's sleeping."

Robinson muttered through gritted teeth, "For heaven's sake!"

Beside him, Kelly leaned over and quipped with a wry grin, "Next time, we'll ask Miss Dupuis to ensure the corpse's eyes are open before snapping the picture."

A fleeting smile crossed Robinson's face before he turned back to Scanlan, his tone becoming firmer.

"Do you know this man?" he repeated.

Scanlan avoided his gaze, hesitating as she picked up the photo with visibly reluctant fingers. Her hands reddened slightly from the cold, betraying an unease she struggled to conceal.

"I don't think so," she said, shaking her head lightly.

Robinson's expression remained impassive as he pointed to the photo.

"Look carefully, Mrs. Scanlan. This is important."

She narrowed her eyes, her guarded expression revealing an inner conflict between caution and memory.

"Who is he?" she asked, her tone verging on defensive.

"The body found in YOUR alley," Robinson replied, deliberately emphasizing "your" to drive home the gravity of the situation.

Scanlan stared at the image again, her brow furrowing slightly. After a pause, she murmured, "Maybe."

Robinson didn't relent.

"Maybe what?"

She shrugged, feigning indifference, though her tone hinted at unease.

"Maybe I've seen him here before."

"Have you seen him, or haven't you?" Robinson barked, his patience wearing thin.

Scanlan sighed before finally admitting, "Yes, he's been here a few times, but he wasn't a regular."

Robinson furrowed his brow.

"Was he here during the St. Patrick's Day celebration?"

Scanlan made an irritated face.

"Now you're asking too much. There were so many people," she said, raising her hands as if to dismiss the question.

"When he came here, was he always alone?"

"Always," she admitted. "He'd sit at a table in the corner. He'd order a beer and nurse it for a good while. He wasn't much of a paying customer."

"What did he do? Did he try to interact with people?"

"No, he stayed by himself and watched."

Robinson raised an eyebrow.

"Watched?"

"Yes, he watched the patrons," she replied, her tone rising slightly as if this were the most obvious thing in the world.

"It seems to me you remember more about him now than you initially let on," he said, his piercing gaze fixed on her.

Scanlan, visibly annoyed, planted her hands on the counter.

"Well, of course, if he ended up dead in my yard, that does change things a bit," she shot back. "Once or twice, he'd sit at the bar when I was serving and not too busy."

"And what did he do then?" Robinson pressed.

"He asked questions."

"What kind of questions?" he asked, his tone growing insistent.

"Just ordinary ones, like someone making conversation," she said with a vague gesture.

"What did he want to know?"

Scanlan sighed exasperated, as if she regretted engaging in the conversation.

"He asked if I was the owner, worked here alone, or knew everybody. He was trying to be nice to me, you see... Not like you lot," she added with a sly smirk.

Kelly, who had been observing silently until now, interjected with a mischievous glint in his eye:

"But we're kind to you, sweetheart! Say, did he ever ask about the Fenians in your tavern?"

Scanlan fixed him with a sharp look, her mouth opening as if to deliver a cutting reply.

"Well, he speaks, does he... I don't know. I don't remember," she said curtly.

"Don't remember, or don't want to remember?" Kelly pressed, his stern gaze locking onto hers.

Scanlan crossed her arms defiantly.

"Either way, I've got nothing to say about that."

Kelly let out a derisive laugh.

"Oh, no?"

"No. What do you take me for? An Irish rebel wench?" she spat, her eyes blazing.

"Isn't that exactly what you are?" Kelly retorted, a provocative smile curling his lips.

Scanlan clenched her fists, her voice trembling with fury as she responded:

"Fuck you, bloody bastard!"

After this heated exchange, the atmosphere around the bar grew heavier, almost stifling. Having just donned his wool coat, Robinson leaned slightly over the counter. His piercing gaze seemed to pin in place anyone who dared to meet it.

"If this patron spoke with you, he might have shared something personal?" he asked in a measured but insistent tone.

Scanlan lifted her head, her face lighting up with an indignant expression.

"Chief Detective, I am not a whore," she retorted, her voice a blend of defiance and scorn.

Unmoved, Robinson raised an eyebrow and replied calmly, "I'm not talking about that kind of confidence. Perhaps he told you his name."

This time, Scanlan seemed to relax slightly, her demeanour shifting toward reluctant cooperation.

"He did, actually," she admitted. "I remember because he had a typical Irish name: Liam."

"Liam, what?" Robinson pressed.

"O'Neil. Liam O'Neil."

Robinson nodded slowly, repeating the name to imprint it in his memory.

"A proper Irish name, indeed. Did he say anything else that struck you?"

Scanlan shook her head, a faint, ironic smile on her lips.

"No. Just the usual trivialities I'm used to hearing when I'm behind the bar."

Robinson didn't seem convinced, his gaze probing for the slightest hesitation in her responses.

"Did he mention where he was from, where he lived?" he continued. "Did he say if he was married, had children?"

Scanlan shrugged with exaggerated weariness, her eyes rolling toward the ceiling.

"Nothing of the sort. Just small talk," she answered curtly.

A brief but weighty silence followed, punctuated by the faint sound of the tavern's front door opening and closing under a gust of wind. The wind whistle seeped through the gaps in the windows, carrying errant snowflakes inside.

Robinson broke the silence, inclining his head slightly.

"Thank you, Mrs. Scanlan, for your time. If anything else comes to mind, please don't hesitate to reach out to us," he said, his tone almost overly polite.

Scanlan narrowed her eyes, her lips twisting into an expression half-mocking, half-defiant.

"Yeah, sure," she murmured, her tone making it clear that this was unlikely to happen.

Robinson and Kelly straightened, setting their hats back in place as the weight of the interrogation seemed to ease. They turned toward the exit without another word.

The two men left the tavern in silence. This time, no one's gaze followed them. The patrons had resumed their conversations and meals as though the detectives' presence had been a mere passing shadow. The door creaked shut behind them, sealing the hum of voices and the stale scent of beer inside.

Outside, the cold March wind swept under their thick wool coats, and a light drizzle added to the damp chill. The filthy snow on the ground mingled with mud, forming a slippery layer that squelched under their leather boots as they climbed into the carriage.

Robinson took his place at the reins, tugging his hat lower to shield himself from the fine droplets falling from the overcast sky. Kelly sat beside him, pulling his coat collar tightly against the biting cold.

"So, Chief, what do you make of it?" Kelly asked, breaking the silence.

Robinson frowned, his gaze fixed straight ahead as the piebald horse trotted slowly along the gas-lit street.

"We have a name," he said at last. "That's something… if it's his real name."

Kelly turned his head, intrigued.

"You think it's not?"

"I don't know. I find his behaviour at the tavern strange. Always alone, watching people, asking questions, interested in everything happening—but no friends."

Kelly squinted as though trying to make sense of the whole.

"What does that tell us?" he murmured.

"I don't know," Robinson replied gravely, his tone betraying his distaste for the uncertainty.

Silence fell again, broken only by the steady clatter of hooves against the muddy road. The streets were nearly deserted; only a few bundled figures hurried past, bracing against the cold and drizzle.

"In any case, finding him won't be easy," Kelly said eventually. "He wasn't a regular at the tavern. None of the patrons seemed to know him. He was a loner. And there's nothing harder to dig up than information on a loner."

Robinson gave a faint, cynical smile.

"True, but we're the best, aren't we, Kelly?"

Kelly shrugged without replying, allowing the silence to settle once more. The horse slowed slightly as it maneuvered around a muddy puddle.

After a moment, Robinson said, "I'll ask Dupuis to make copies of the photograph. We'll distribute them."

"Distribute them?" Kelly raised an eyebrow.

"Yes. I want the three police stations to display the photo prominently on their walls. And every constable in the city should carry a copy in their pocket. They can show it around and see if anyone recognizes him."

Kelly scowled, skeptical.

"That's like looking for a needle in a haystack," he grumbled.

Robinson nodded, his expression hardening.

"We'll have to rely on luck this time. I refuse to believe no one will recognize him. He's not a ghost."

Kelly smirked mockingly.

"Maybe he is now that he's dead," he said with a chuckle.

Robinson didn't respond, though his face betrayed a flicker of irritation.

"In any case," he said after a pause, "until we find someone who knows him, this investigation is at a standstill. And I don't like it. I don't like depending on luck to make progress."

Kelly nodded silently. The carriage trundled on, the muffled sound of wheels on the wet ground merging with the rhythmic clop of the horse's hooves.

Ahead, the police station came into view, its dim lights flickering behind fogged windows—a temporary refuge from the cold of this late winter day.

CHAPTER 9

March 26, Sunday evening

"Good evening, Mr. Robinson," said a woman of a certain age as she opened the door. Her English, heavily accented with French, rolled like a wind over icy steps. "It has been far too long since we last saw you at our Sunday suppers. Good evening, Miss Thérèse," she added in French, with a warmth that felt sincerely genuine. "Come in; the master is expecting you."

"Good evening, Maria," Robinson replied in a steady voice, a faint smile stretching across his lips.

Maria, the devoted housekeeper and an indispensable presence in the household, stepped aside to let them enter. They were immediately enveloped by the welcoming warmth of Thomas Ryan's manor, perched on Côte-à-Baron along the slope of Mount Royal. Though not a château, the place's elegance never failed to impress Robinson. The two-story facade, adorned with sturdy colonnades, stood as a bastion of comfort and refinement. Four chimneys rose confidently above, while a large, well-kept annex complemented the building's imposing silhouette. A stone fence embellished with balustrades encircled the property, where towering maples and elms, their branches still bare of foliage, stretched out like a veined network in the garden.

Underfoot, the snow from the previous day, mingled with patches of grey ice, crunched softly as they crossed the threshold. Maria swiftly welcomed them, taking their coats, heavy with cold, and their hats, still beaded with moisture. She gestured to a mat at the entrance for them to wipe their boots before naturally guiding them toward the library. A comforting warmth emanating from a crackling fire in the center of the room embraced them, chasing away the lingering chill.

"Please, have a seat," Maria said, motioning to two English-style armchairs upholstered in worn but elegant green velvet.

Robinson settled himself, his gaze wandering across the shelves. The imposing bookcases overflowed with leather-bound volumes, a collection that attested to Ryan's erudition and curiosity.

"Dear Silas! Thérèse!" exclaimed Thomas Ryan as he entered, his broad smile lighting up his face.

Ryan approached Thérèse and enveloped her in a paternal embrace, holding her with the same tenderness he might reserve for his daughter. Then, turning to Robinson, he embraced him with equal familiarity—the only man Robinson allowed such closeness to. The two men gave each other hearty pats on the back in camaraderie.

"It was high time we resumed our good old Sunday suppers," Ryan declared, his tone filled with genuine joy. "Rosalie is already in the kitchen helping Erin."

Robinson nodded, amused.

"You still haven't hired a cook?" he asked, raising an eyebrow slightly.

"You know, Erin," Ryan replied with a laugh. "She won't let anyone in her kitchen. 'Too many hands, too much chaos,' she says. And besides, we have modest tastes, as you well know."

A round of laughter filled the room, the jest from one of Montreal's most prosperous businessmen carrying its own irony.

Ryan, an Irish Catholic, and Robinson, an Anglican Briton, made an unlikely but inseparable pair. Their friendship, forged during the hard times when Robinson arrived in Canada penniless, was built on trust and shared interests. Ryan had taken a chance by investing in Robinson's private detective agency, a gamble that had proven highly successful.

From an old family in central Ireland, Ryan arrived in Canada in 1822, armed with an excellent education and comfortable resources. He quickly delved into business, building an extensive and influential network. For years, he had been the principal correspondent for London banks within Montreal's business community, particularly for the Baring office. Now, he sat on the boards of several banks and companies, a true pillar of the city's financial world.

Ryan picked up a small bell on the side table near the armchairs and gave it a gentle ring. The sound had barely resonated before a young maid appeared, wearing a crisp white apron tied neatly at her waist and a perfectly fitted cap over her brown hair.

"Yes, sir?" she asked with a slight curtsy.

Closing his hands together, Ryan turned to Robinson with a mischievous smile.

"A Scotch whisky for our friend," he declared confidently, "and an Irish whisky for me. And…"

He pivoted slightly toward Thérèse, raising an inquiring eyebrow.

"A glass of cognac," she replied with assurance, her smile barely concealed.

Ryan let out a hearty laugh.

"Ah, Thérèse!" he exclaimed. "You'll always be that little girl to whom we served hot chocolate as a feast. Very well, a cognac for the lady."

The maid gave a silent nod before disappearing into the shadowed hallway. Once the silence returned, Robinson pulled out his pocket watch, checked the time, and said in a neutral tone:

"Are we too early? I thought we were running a bit late."

Ryan shook his head with a reassuring smile.

"No, no. We're just waiting for another guest to join us for supper."

"Oh? And who might that be?"

"Thomas D'Arcy McGee," Ryan replied with a note of pride.

"The politician?" Thérèse interjected, visibly surprised.

"And an old friend as well."

Thérèse straightened slightly.

"Quite a character, that one... I've followed his career from a distance. He's unique among the Irish here. He knows how to rally the crowds like no other, but he has an unfortunate habit of changing his political convictions as often as he changes his shirt."

Ryan's face darkened as he cast Thérèse a reproachful look.

"Thérèse!" he said gravely. "I ask that you show more respect for D'Arcy McGee. My friend is a man of principle, even if it's not always obvious at first glance. Above all, he's a true Irishman who protects our community and faith. That's what drives him, what has always driven him."

Sensing the rising tension, Robinson hastened to steer the conversation elsewhere.

"How is Erin?" he asked gently.

Ryan's face softened slightly.

"Ah, you know… She's more unwell every day, but she's a powerful woman. She insisted on preparing tonight's meal herself. Luckily, Rosalie was there to help her."

"And Finn?"

At these words, Ryan lowered his head, his jaw tightening almost imperceptibly. When he raised his eyes, a heart-wrenching sadness was visible in his gaze.

"He's still at the sanatorium in Sainte-Agathe-des-Monts," he murmured. "That cursed consumption… I don't know if he'll pull through."

"He'll recover," Robinson said, trying to inject a little hope.

Ryan slowly nodded, but his expression remained grim.

"I'm not so sure… Not sure at all. A father should never outlive his son."

"And Shannon?" Robinson ventured, hoping to lighten the mood.

Ryan's face instantly brightened.

"Ah, my Shannon!" he replied with a spark of pride. "My ray of sunshine. She'll be joining us tonight."

"And Patrick? How is he doing?"

A tender smile appeared on Ryan's lips.

"Very well, very well. That boy works hard. He's got a real fighting spirit, as they say."

Robinson nodded.

Patrick O'Brien was Ryan's adopted son, a young man Robinson had encountered years ago during an investigation. At the time, Patrick had been a lost teenager, speaking only Gaelic, having lost his mother to typhus during a harrowing voyage from Ireland. Moved by pity, Robinson had entrusted him to Ryan and his wife, who had taken him in with boundless generosity. Though too old for a formal adoption, Patrick had found a home with the family, eventually becoming a trusted partner in Ryan's business ventures.

The maid reappeared silently, carrying a silver tray with three glasses. She placed it on the side table with measured precision, adjusted her apron quickly, and vanished like a shadow. Ryan, Robinson, and Thérèse stepped forward to retrieve their drinks.

"So, Silas, still keeping busy?" Ryan asked, swirling his Irish whisky gently in his glass.

Robinson shrugged with feigned weariness.

"More than ever," he replied vaguely.

Ryan's brows furrowed slightly.

"Another tough case?"

"Yes, very," Robinson admitted, his tone turning sharper. "But it's at a standstill for now. And honestly, I'd rather not discuss it tonight. We're here to enjoy ourselves, aren't we?"

"Absolutely!" Ryan said with a hearty laugh, raising his glass.

Thérèse and Robinson followed suit, and the three crystal glasses chimed softly in the air.

There was a knock at the door, followed by the low murmur of conversation in the entryway and the muffled sound of boots brushing against the carpet. Distinct footsteps soon echoed, heralding the guest's arrival. Finally, the door revealed a man whose stature commanded attention: Thomas D'Arcy McGee.

D'Arcy McGee was not what one would call a handsome man. His face, often considered plain, was nonetheless captivating in many respects. His curly, unruly brown hair appeared as though it had never made the acquaintance of a brush. His large, prominent brown eyes lent him an almost magnetic intensity. Despite his dishevelled appearance, irresistible energy radiated from him. When he entered a room, the atmosphere seemed to shift as though the air became livelier in his presence.

McGee's contemporaries described him as a man of sharp wit and immense charm, brimming with infectious energy. "He is one of the most delightful writers," reported the papers. "An eloquent man, captivating in company, whose every word and subtle reference reveal a rare erudition."

Ryan sprang to his feet, his enthusiasm giving his face a youthful glow.

"Dear Thomas!" he exclaimed, extending his arms.

"Dear Thomas!" McGee replied with a sly grin, continuing their habitual jest born of their shared first name.

The two men embraced heartily, their greetings punctuated by the laughter of old friends.

After a few pleasantries exchanged by the warmth of the hearth, the maid reappeared to announce that supper was ready. They all moved to the dining room, where a simple yet comforting meal awaited them, prepared by Erin with Rosalie's invaluable help.

The table, though pleasant, was not fully attended. Only Shannon, their sixteen-year-old daughter, brightened the evening on the Ryan side. Finn, still unwell, was recovering in the Laurentian mountains, while Patrick, their adopted son, was away conducting business in the North. As for the Robinsons, only Thérèse was present; Aimé was absent on a business trip. D'Arcy McGee, too, apologized for the absence of his wife, who was tending to their youngest daughter, Peggy, bedridden with a nasty bout of influenza.

The meal unfolded in a warm atmosphere, punctuated by laughter and McGee's stories, which kept everyone enthralled. True to his reputation, he dominated the conversation with a mix of humour and insight, sharing memories and political ideas. At one point, he raised his glass to toast the "new Canada," that nascent confederation he had helped shape during the previous year's Charlottetown Conference.

Yet, despite his usual charisma, Ryan seemed to notice something. Leaning discreetly toward Robinson, seated beside him, he murmured:

"He doesn't have his usual spark."

Robinson gave a slight nod, observing McGee with a critical eye. Despite the liveliness he worked hard to project, something weighed on the politician.

Finally, the meal came to an end. Erin and Rosalie helped the maid clear the table and wash the dishes. Erin, an Irishwoman from a modest background, found it unthinkable to leave all the work to the servant while she sat idly knitting.

Thérèse and Shannon went upstairs to Shannon's bedroom, decorated with the keepsakes of her youth. It became their refuge, and the muffled laughter and whispers escaping under the door revealed conversations about the day's news and confidences of budding romances, just as they used to share in earlier times.

The three men returned to the library. Ryan took hold of a crystal decanter of whisky and poured generously into cut-glass tumblers, the golden liquid catching fire's dancing light.

"Thank you, Tom, for agreeing to receive me in your home."

"I couldn't possibly turn you away under the current circumstances."

"Yes. What a misfortune!" said D'Arcy McGee, glancing at Robinson.

"You can speak freely in front of my friend Silas. If anyone can help you in Montreal, it's him."

D'Arcy McGee reached into his satchel, which he had placed nearby, and pulled out a piece of paper with a few words hastily scrawled. He handed it to Robinson, who took it and read aloud:

"'You are not loyal to the Crown of England! There is still time to rectify the situation. We are holding your daughter hostage. You will denounce in the papers the rebels who seek to destroy our great country and harm our Queen. If we do not see a public declaration within a week, you will never see your daughter again.'"

Robinson looked at D'Arcy McGee, waiting for an explanation.

"They've taken Frasa."

"The rebels mentioned in this letter would be the Irish Catholics they call the Fenians?"

D'Arcy McGee merely nodded.

"Mr. D'Arcy McGee..."

"Call me Thomas."

"All right, Thomas. So, you received this letter… when exactly?"

"Last Thursday."

"You knew that Frasa had been abducted."

"No, not until that day. Erin and I thought she had simply run away."

"Run away? Was that something she often did?"

"Things haven't been going well between her and us for some time. She's been moody and defiant. We knew something was troubling her, but she wouldn't tell us what."

"So, you're saying she ran away?"

"This wasn't the first time she disappeared without telling us where she was going… at least not while she lived with us."

"She no longer lives with you?"

"She boards with the Sisters of the Congregation of Notre Dame. She would only visit us on Saturdays and Sundays.

When she was home, she'd sometimes slip away for part of the day without telling us where she went."

"But Thomas, from my perspective, that's not what one would call running away."

"You're right. But we also learned from the nuns that she occasionally played truant from school."

There was a pause in the conversation as Robinson considered his next move.

"So, she has a habit of 'running away,' as you say. How is this time different?"

"This time, she vanished... simply vanished. Usually, Frasa would disappear for a short while. But she never stayed out overnight, neither at home nor the boarding school. This time, it's different..."

"When exactly did she disappear?"

"We learned of it Thursday evening from the nuns. They told us Frasa hadn't attended her classes in the morning. They delayed informing us because it wasn't the first time she had played truant."

D'Arcy McGee, a man Robinson knew to be confident and arrogant, now appeared utterly despondent.

"We are very worried, Mr. Robinson... deeply worried!"

"And why didn't you report this to the police?"

"I believe you're aware of my situation, Mr. Robinson..."

"Call me Silas."

"Very well, Silas... You know that my political position makes me a prime target for my enemies on all sides."

"Meaning?"

"Well, to the Orangemen—Irish Protestants—I'm an Irishman they see as insufficiently loyal to the Crown. They've already tried to physically attack me once in Toronto during a lecture I was giving."

"And the Irish Catholics, the Fenians?"

"Precisely. To the Fenians, I'm a traitor to my Irish brethren because I support the Canadian Confederation project rather than annexation to the United States."

"So, you're caught squarely between two radical factions."

"Not an easy position to hold, as you might imagine. If it became known that my daughter had been kidnapped, the news would go public, with all the consequences you can picture. My adversaries would leap to attack me from every direction."

"In your opinion, which group sent this blackmail letter?"

"The Irish Protestant Orangemen, without a doubt. The Catholic Fenians are their mortal enemies."

"I don't know you well, Thomas, but I do know you were once a fierce advocate for an Irish republic, which, of course, is the primary goal of the Fenians."

"That was long ago, true. But Canada is a land of opportunity for us Irish. That's why I now support the Confederation project. It's also why I've distanced myself from the Irish radicals."

"Then I must ask: why would the Orangemen want you to do more against the Fenians?"

"That, I don't know. In any case, I've decided to meet their demand. I've just written a rather scathing article against the Fenians. It will be published this week, and I hope that, by doing so, those holding my daughter hostage will be satisfied."

"You're giving in to blackmail?"

"I have no choice, Silas… no choice. She's my daughter, you understand?"

"In any case, I'll begin my investigation to learn more about her disappearance and this blackmail letter."

"I would be most grateful, Silas."

CHAPTER 10

March 26, Sunday Evening

At the end of the meal at Thomas Ryan's home that late March Sunday, the guests naturally divided into three groups, as etiquette dictated. The men, shrouded in a light haze of cigar smoke, sipped their whisky in the parlour, where the warm scent of burning wood mingled with the rich aroma of leather from the armchairs. Nearby, in the kitchen, the two women, joined by the maid, busied themselves in a quiet ballet of dishwashing and muffled voices. Meanwhile, the two young girls, Thérèse (Miss Dupuis) and Shannon had slipped away to the latter's upstairs bedroom, far from the commotion of the main floor.

The Ryan and Robinson families had maintained ties for over a decade, cemented by Robinson's marriage to the widow Rosalie Cadrin-Dupuis. Thérèse, Rosalie's daughter, and Shannon, then just a little girl, had struck up an immediate friendship from their first meeting. Thérèse, eleven at the time, had instinctively taken Shannon under her wing despite their lack of blood relation. To Shannon, Thérèse became a kind of elder sister—caring, confiding, and exemplary. Their bond had only deepened during their years at the Congregation of Notre Dame's school, despite their age and academic level differences.

That evening, as was their habit, the two girls had retreated to Shannon's bedroom. Lined with slightly faded floral wallpaper, the room was a warm haven within a manor house struggling against the day's lingering chill. They sat on the bed, its plush red coverlets offering a cozy contrast to the windows, where melting snow gathered in icy ridges. The wind, though gentle, sometimes whistled through the ill-fitted panes. A few flickering candles cast dancing shadows across their faces.

"Sometimes I feel like everything is changing too quickly," Thérèse confessed, tugging at the collar of her dark wool shawl, worn but carefully mended. Her voice was low, carrying a rare weight for a twenty-year-old woman.

Shannon, wrapped in a blue flannel dress with a simple white collar, turned to her with a faint smile. Her blonde hair, swept into a loose chignon, glimmered in the flickering light.

"You say that, but you're already a woman. Me? I'm still just a child in everyone's eyes," she remarked in a teasing and pensive tone.

Their conversations often shifted between levity and heartfelt confidence. They spoke of classes, school friends, and even the young men they saw in town or at church—a subject that always brought a blush to Shannon's cheeks and a knowing smile to Thérèse's lips. Shannon, with her lively manner and bright eyes, naturally drew attention. There was a sunny cheerfulness about her, even on these grey March days.

Their laughter occasionally rose above the wind's murmur, filling the room with a warmth no bedcover alone could provide. Yet beneath this seeming lightness, a specific gravity hung in the air that night as if the outside world had slipped through the manor's thick walls with its tensions and secrets.

"It's been too long, Thérèse," Shannon said, a faint note of reproach in her voice.

"It has. We haven't seen each other since I left school. It has been far too long," Thérèse replied with a soft nod.

"Two years already… You look radiant."

"Thank you, and so do you."

Sitting upright at the edge of the bed, Shannon clasped her hands over her knees. Her thick grey wool dress enhanced the clarity of her eyes. She turned a curious gaze toward Thérèse.

"So, what have you been up to, Thérèse?"

"I'm working for a photographer," Thérèse replied with apparent ease, though a flicker of hesitation crossed her eyes.

"Oh, really! Will you take my photograph, then?" Shannon grinned broadly, her blonde curls framing her radiant face.

"If you'd like," Thérèse replied with a light laugh.

But she refrained from telling her friend the truth about her work with the Montreal police's detective team. She knew Shannon too well—her irrepressible enthusiasm would inevitably lead to a flood of questions, something Thérèse was determined to avoid.

"And what about you, Shannon? How are things at school?" Thérèse asked, deftly steering the conversation.

"Just a few more years to endure," Shannon sighed, distractedly glancing at the misted window.

Outside, the low grey sky threatened a cold drizzle while traces of slushy snow clung stubbornly to the edges of the windowsills.

"But you are happy there, aren't you?" inquired Thérèse, adjusting her dark wool shawl more snugly over her shoulders to ward off the chill that seemed to creep even into the room.

"Oh, of course. I'm enjoying myself, but… I can't wait to find a husband. And that won't happen at the college," Shannon replied with a playful shrug.

"You have time… don't rush it," advised Thérèse in a calm, measured tone, though a faintly amused smile played at her lips.

Shannon laughed lightly, shaking her golden mane with careless grace.

"The Sisters keep us on a tight leash, as you know. It's nearly impossible to meet a boy. You know Sister Marie de la Providence is always watching. She keeps an eye on us like a hawk."

"That dear Cerberus!" Thérèse said, her smile broadening at the teasing nickname.

The girls referred to the disciplinarian prefect as "Cerberus," after the three-headed dog of Greek mythology that guarded the gates of the Underworld, ensuring no soul escaped back to the living.

"She sees everything," Shannon said, crossing her arms over her chest to emphasize her point. "I don't know how she does it."

They broke into peals of laughter, their mirth echoing in the room, momentarily dispelling the chill and gloom from outside.

"The only one who ever managed to elude her is Frasa," Shannon added with a mischievous grin.

"Frasa?" Thérèse repeated, raising her eyebrows slightly.

"Euphrasia, really, but everyone calls her Frasa... Oh, and she's the daughter of Mr. D'Arcy McGee, with whom we dined this evening."

"His daughter? I thought he only had one—Peggy, who stayed home tonight because she was unwell."

"That's Peggy, the younger one. Frasa is the eldest. She attends the same college as me. Even though she's a few years younger, it hasn't stopped us from becoming best friends."

Thérèse raised an intrigued eyebrow.

"Why wasn't she with us tonight, then?"

"That, I don't know. Mr. D'Arcy McGee didn't say anything."

A cold wind seeped faintly through the poorly fitted windowpanes, producing a faint whistling sound. The two young women, comfortably ensconced in the warmth of the bedroom, continued their chatter while adjusting the folds of the plush coverlets. They laughed aloud at anecdotes: mishaps in the chemistry lab or spirited rhetoric competitions where each had tried to outdo the other.

Thérèse, never losing her instinct as an investigator, seized the opportunity to probe further.

"So, your friend Frasa managed to evade Cerberus, did she?" she said with a sly smile.

"Oh, she wasn't the only one. Poor Cerberus might have eyes everywhere, but we were cunning," Shannon replied with a conspiratorial laugh.

Thérèse chuckled softly.

"Oh, I know it well. I still remember the pranks we played on the Sisters… But about Frasa?"

Shannon lowered her voice slightly as if adding an air of intrigue.

"Frasa is a good girl, rather shy, top of her class, and even the Sisters' favourite… Until recently."

Thérèse straightened, her curiosity piqued.

"Oh? Do tell."

"She changed a few weeks ago."

"In what way?" Thérèse asked, pulling her shawl tighter and leaning forward attentively.

"I'm not entirely sure. She was always so kind and cheerful. But then she became… more serious."

"More serious? What do you mean by that?" Thérèse pressed, raising an eyebrow.

"I don't have better words to describe it. She often seemed lost in thought during classes. She would stare out the window, daydreaming, until the Sisters had to snap her out of it."

Thérèse fixed Shannon with a curious gaze, her eyes sparkling.

"And how long had she been like that?"

Shannon hesitated, searching for the right words.

"She used to tell me everything. I could tell she was different. She's my best friend, and I was worried about her. Lately, I had to work hard to get her to open up. She finally shared a little."

Thérèse leaned in slightly.

"She was seeing a boy, wasn't she?" Thérèse guessed, a knowing smile on her lips.

"How did you know?" Shannon exclaimed, startled.

"Oh, come now! I was her age once, too. Boys can throw us into such a whirlwind," Thérèse replied with an amused smile.

Shannon nodded vigorously.

"That's exactly what happened... And it was serious. She confided in me that she was seeing someone. They met at the Mardi Gras masquerade ball at the Victoria Rink. It was love at first sight. You should have heard how she described it to me. She told me about their... striking encounter. She was skating, looking around without attention, and crashed into him at full speed. He went flying, head over heels."

Thérèse burst into laughter.

"That's quite an amusing way to meet someone."

"To say the least! When he got back on his feet, he seemed unhappy and was about to scold her. But when he saw Frasa..."

Shannon let out a crystalline laugh that filled the room.

"Oh, I wish I'd seen it. He looked at her, and his skates slipped out from under him. He ended up flat on his back again. And he was supposed to be an excellent skater! She laughed so much he couldn't help but laugh, too. When he finally got up, he offered her his arm, and they spent the rest of the ball together. It was love at first sight, I tell you."

Thérèse nodded, a faint smile tugging at the corner of her lips.

"It seems it was mutual."

"Oh, it was! Apparently, the boy couldn't take his eyes off her."

Thérèse's brow furrowed slightly.

"Did they see each other again?"

Shannon nodded enthusiastically.

"They looked for every opportunity to meet. Frasa told him where she lived. He would throw small stones at her window when she was at the manor, even though it was still cold and her window was on the second floor. She would bundle up warmly, wrap a shawl around her shoulders, and lean out the window to speak to him, whispering so no one could hear."

"So, they met several times?" Thérèse asked, fixing Shannon with an intense gaze.

"For about a month, at least. As far as I know, they met every Sunday. Frasa even snuck out of the boarding school during the week to see him," Shannon replied, idly toying with the edge of her thick wool sleeve.

"And Cerberus didn't notice?" Thérèse asked with a wry smile, referencing the strict prefect.

"Oh, of course she noticed! But what could she do against a longing so powerful as being with her beloved? Naturally, Frasa received a few punishments, but it didn't stop her. She said she simply had to see him, no matter the cost."

Thérèse crossed her arms and pondered momentarily, letting the silence settle between them. The ever-present sound of the wind seemed to punctuate their words.

"When she sneaked out of the boarding school, do you know what they did together?" she finally asked.

Shannon nodded, her smile turning wistful.

"She was so in love, poor Frasa. She told me everything in the greatest detail. They would walk to Mount Royal, hand in hand, through the woods still bare of leaves. They kissed along the way and whispered sweet nothings to each other. Sometimes, they'd talk about the birds they heard. He would say, 'That's the song of a nightingale.' And she'd reply, 'No, it's a skylark.' You know, the nonsense people say when they're in love."

Shannon paused, her eyes momentarily lost in the flickering movement of the candle flames. Thérèse, on the other hand, studied her friend intently, weighing every word.

"I don't understand why Frasa had to hide like that to meet her sweetheart," she said at last.

Shannon fixed her with a grave look.

"She had good reasons, believe me."

"What reasons?" Thérèse pressed.

"The boy is Protestant."

Thérèse drew a slow breath, her expression hardening slightly.

"Ah, I see… D'Arcy McGee is a staunch Irish Catholic. He would never allow his daughter to court a Protestant."

"Worse… an Irish Protestant."

Thérèse frowned and shook her head slowly.

"I understand even better now. How tragic," she murmured.

"It's no wonder Frasa has been acting the way she has these past few weeks. She's torn between her parents and her love for Rowan," Shannon said, her voice betraying genuine concern.

"Rowan?" Thérèse repeated, slightly surprised.

"That's the name of her sweetheart."

"Rowan... Rowan, what?" Thérèse asked, tilting her head.

"She didn't even know his last name. But that didn't matter to her. You have to understand."

A long silence stretched between them, punctuated by the wind's persistent whistling, which seemed to swell, echoing the turmoil in their thoughts.

"Did you find out what Frasa wanted to do?" Thérèse asked at last.

"I know they had plans," Shannon said, wringing her hands nervously. "They wanted to leave the country, to escape and live their love free from the obstacles they faced here. She dreamed of marrying him, building a life with him, having children, and growing old by his side. She told me so many times... They were so in love."

Thérèse nodded slowly, absorbing Shannon's words.

"So, it's severe."

"I believe it is... And that worries me. I don't see how this can end in anything but tragedy."

Thérèse fixed Shannon with a sharper gaze.

"Tragedy?"

"Yes. They'll never agree to part ways, and the parents on both sides will never allow them to be together. How else could this possibly end?"

"But they're still young. There will be other opportunities for both of them in life," Thérèse offered in a soothing tone.

"Not for Frasa, at least. She only sees him," Shannon replied, her face darkening.

"You mentioned they had plans together. Where do they stand now?"

Shannon drew a deep breath, hesitating before answering.

"That's where it becomes troubling," she finally said, her voice trembling. "I've lost contact with her."

"What do you mean? She doesn't want to see you anymore? Is she upset with you for some reason?" Thérèse asked, her expression tinged with concern.

"No, it's not that," Shannon said, shaking her head. "Since last Thursday, she hasn't been at the college. I don't know where she is."

Her words, tinged with anxiety, were accompanied by a shadow that darkened her face.

"Is that so!" Thérèse exclaimed, taken aback, her breath catching slightly at the revelation.

"I thought I'd see her here tonight with her father," Shannon continued. "But she isn't here, and her father didn't even mention her at supper. I don't know what's happening with her. I'm worried, you know."

A heavy silence settled, broken only by the creaking of the wind, which caused the windows to groan in protest. The two young women exchanged looks, each silently weighing the gravity of the situation.

After their prolonged discussion about D'Arcy McGee's daughter, Thérèse and Shannon shifted to lighter topics, trying to dispel the oppressive atmosphere. They reminisced about school days, shared college gossip, and even laughed over the nuns' occasional awkwardness. Their lighthearted laughter eventually brightened the room, though a shadow lingered, tucked away in the corners of their thoughts.

Outside, the wind howled, rising in gusts that flung wet snowflakes against the panes. Despite the crackling fire in the corner stove, the room seemed suddenly invaded by a creeping chill. Thérèse felt a shiver run down her spine, though she knew it wasn't merely the cold.

This story seemed unsettling, like a discordant note in a melody. She glared at Shannon, who struggled to conceal her worry behind a fragile smile.

"We'll solve this mystery together," Thérèse promised, placing a reassuring hand on Shannon's arm before embracing her.

Adjusting her thick shawl over her shoulders, Thérèse left the room. As she descended the dark wooden staircase, the murmur of conversation and bursts of laughter drifted up from the kitchen. Yet her thoughts remained elsewhere, weighed down by this troubling story that seemed cloaked in shadows.

She ran her hand along the polished banister, her steps echoing softly in the corridor adorned with aged portraits. The air of the main floor, heavy with the scents of burning wood and whisky, offered a measure of warmth but did little to lift the unease that clouded her mind.

Thérèse joined her family in the flickering glow of the oil lamps, carrying with her the promise of uncovering the truth and a foreboding sense that such a discovery would not come without consequences.

CHAPTER 11

Monday Morning, March 27

It was a dull Monday morning, the leaden sky wavering between clouds and sunlight. In the cramped office of the central police station, the four detectives had gathered as they did every week. A stubborn smell of damp paper and cold tobacco hung in the air, mingling with the earthy scent of mud tracked in by their boots. It had been nearly two weeks since a body was discovered in the dark alley beside Kate Scanlan's tavern. They had finally identified the man: Liam O'Neil. But beyond his name, there was almost no information to be found.

"This investigation is frustrating," said Miss Dupuis, the recruit, who appeared less tense than when she had first joined. "Is it always this tedious?"

"Not always this bad," admitted Robinson, leaning back in his chair, which creaked sharply in protest. "But often enough, yes."

Since the previous week, O'Neil's portrait had been circulated to every police station in the city. On-duty constables slipped a copy into their coats or hats. Despite this wide distribution, the incomplete census records offered no leads, and the criminal archives were equally silent. It was as though Liam O'Neil had been a ghost, living beyond the reach of any register.

"We're getting nowhere," grumbled Kelly, his tone biting. "This case belongs on the 'unsolved crimes' pile. We're wasting our time here—there are more urgent investigations."

"Perhaps, but at least the bank robbery case is progressing," Morin interjected.

"You've finally caught Walsh, then?" Kelly asked, raising an eyebrow.

"It wasn't easy, I can tell you," Morin replied. "I scoured dozens of houses trying to find where he was hiding. The moment his name came up, doors slammed shut."

"So, how did you manage to catch him?"

Morin paused dramatically before admitting, "It's Miss Dupuis we have to thank."

Dupuis modestly lowered her gaze at this, though a faint smile betrayed her pride. Morin, initially skeptical about the recruit's arrival, now seemed genuinely pleased with her contributions.

"Oh, it wasn't just me," she protested, visibly uncomfortable with the praise.

"Well, tell us how it happened!" Kelly urged, intrigued.

"Nothing magical," she replied. "Just a lot of hard work and patience. I combed through census records, police archives, and, most importantly… newspapers."

"Newspapers?" Robinson echoed, raising an eyebrow.

"Yes, they often contain forgotten information. I sifted through articles dating back several years. And I found some interesting details."

"Such as?"

"An article from 1862," she said calmly, her eyes glinting excitedly. "It described Walsh as a gang leader in Griffintown."

"A gang leader at 19?" Kelly said, astonished.

"Exactly. The article portrayed him as a precocious ringleader, surrounded by a band of four or five young ruffians his age. They terrorized certain parts of the neighborhood."

"And the police did nothing?"

"I didn't find any information on that. In any case, the journalist wasn't kind to our predecessors," Dupuis said with a shrug.

Morin suddenly sat up, looking pensive.

"Wait... A band of young ruffians... What if..."

"You're thinking what I'm thinking," Kelly interrupted.

"Yeah. What if it was that gang that settled the score with Leclerc? Those blasted hoodlums..."

"Too early to draw conclusions," Robinson said sternly. "Continue, Dupuis. What else did you find?"

"Another article, more recent, reported his arrest for theft."

"The one in his criminal record," Morin clarified.

"Exactly. But the article mentioned a crucial detail: they found his hideout. The loot was stashed in an abandoned warehouse once used during the construction of the Lachine Canal."

A heavy silence followed this revelation. The wind howled against the office windows as if emphasizing the significance of this new lead.

"An abandoned warehouse," Kelly murmured, his expression darkening. "Of course... That's where you found him, isn't it?"

Morin nodded slightly as if recalling the details of his story.

"We'd known he was hiding there for a week, but we couldn't pin him down. It was Miss Dupuis who led us to the right spot. I took two constables with me, and we headed to the warehouse. To maximize our chances, we went at dawn, when he was likely still asleep. The air was freezing, and a thin layer of snow blanketed the ground, muffling our steps. He didn't see us coming. He didn't hear us, either. Within moments, we had him. The poor fellow was in a sorry state—emaciated, likely starving for days."

"And now? Where is he?" Kelly asked, arms crossed, his piercing gaze fixed on Morin.

"In a cell here," Morin replied with a faint smile. "Ironically, he seems relieved. He's been gorging himself at Her Majesty's expense and enjoying a proper bed for two days. Honestly, he almost looks happy."

A silence settled over the room. The morning light barely filtered through the fogged-up panes, and everyone seemed lost in their thoughts. Then Miss Dupuis, seated near the stove that gave off only a timid warmth raised her eyes to Robinson, who gave her a slight nod of encouragement.

"Chief," she said, hesitating for a moment, "what are we doing about the kidnapping of D'Arcy McGee's daughter?"

Morin furrowed his brow.

"What are you talking about, Miss Dupuis?"

It was Robinson who answered.
"D'Arcy McGee's daughter was reportedly kidnapped last Thursday. Her father received a ransom letter. It claims she's being held hostage."

"You say 'reportedly'?" Kelly noted, his tone laced with suspicion.

"Yes, because I'm not convinced it's true. Miss Dupuis, tell them what you learned from Shannon."

Robinson turned to her and added, "Shannon is the daughter of my friend Thomas Ryan. We shared a meal last night."

Miss Dupuis nodded.
"Yes, that's right. After supper, I spent some time with Shannon."

She turned her keen eyes to Morin and Kelly.
"Shannon is like a cousin to me. When we meet, we share all kinds of gossip."

"Ah, women and their chatter," Kelly quipped with a teasing smile. "What could you possibly have to say about us poor men?"

Miss Dupuis shot him a sly look.

"You'd be surprised, Kelly. But don't worry—talking about men is far too dull. We have much more interesting things to discuss."

Her remark drew a round of laughter, even from Kelly, who shook his head with a grin. Encouraged, Dupuis continued.

"We chatted about everything and nothing until Shannon mentioned Frasa, D'Arcy McGee's daughter."

"The one who was kidnapped?" Kelly asked, his smile vanishing.

"Yes, that's her. Shannon and Frasa attend the same school. Although Shannon is a bit older, they're friends. Frasa often confides in her about things she wouldn't tell her parents. And Shannon told me that Frasa had a secret sweetheart."

"A secret sweetheart?" Morin repeated, suddenly attentive.

"Yes. She didn't want her parents to know because they would never approve of the relationship."

"Why not?" Morin asked.

"Because her sweetheart is an Irish Protestant," Dupuis explained. "A scandal for D'Arcy McGee, a staunch Catholic. Frasa would sneak away to meet him whenever she could."

"And this boy—who is he?" Kelly pressed impatiently.

"Shannon only knows his first name: Rowan. She says he's the most handsome boy on earth—strong, intelligent… Frasa was madly in love."

Robinson, arms crossed, spoke again.
"That's why I have doubts about this supposed kidnapping. What if she simply ran away with him? She knew her parents would never approve of their relationship."

"And the ransom letter?" Morin countered sharply.

Robinson shrugged, looking thoughtful.
"That's where things don't add up. A ransom letter doesn't fit with a lovers' escape. There's still something we're missing."

Silence fell again. The concentrated expressions around the room betrayed deep contemplation while the cold wind blew outside.

At that moment, three sharp knocks echoed against the door.

"Come in!" Kelly barked, not lifting his eyes from a document on the table.

The door creaked open slowly, revealing a young constable in a pristine uniform that hung slightly too loose on his narrow shoulders. His youthful face betrayed a nervousness he was struggling to mask.

"Mr. Robinson... A certain Mr.... uh... Hermann is asking for you," he stammered, the words nearly tumbling out of his mouth.

Robinson raised an eyebrow.
"Hermann? Hermann, who?" he asked, his voice laced with curiosity.

The Constable appeared to dig through his memory.
"I think it's... Hermann Tanguay. He says he knows you."

"Ermatinger, you fool. Ermatinger!" Kelly barked, visibly exasperated.

The young man flushed a deep red, stammering a confused, "Ah... I see."

"That's our former Chief of Police," Kelly added, rolling his eyes. "Though back in his day, you were probably still in diapers. Speaking of which, did your mother put you in diapers?"

"Uh... I think so," the Constable replied, clearly flustered.

Robinson stifled a chuckle and stepped in with a calm tone.

"Very well, Constable. Go downstairs and tell the man I'll meet him immediately."

The young man offered an awkward nod before disappearing, closing the door with a dull thud. As soon as Robinson left the room, Morin, lounging back in his chair, turned his head toward Kelly.

"I've heard of Ermatinger. Quite the reputation," he murmured, almost to himself.

"That's putting it mildly," Kelly replied, straightening his seat. "He was quite the figure. Made his mark as a soldier long before joining the police. He handled major disturbances, including those at the Lachine Canal. And do you remember the Gavazzi affair?"

Morin nodded.
"The riots, yes."

"Well, he was injured during those events. A really tough customer. He was Montreal's first proper Chief of Police, back when they still called the position 'Superintendent.' He brought order where there was none and shaped the force into what it is today."

Miss Dupuis, who had been quietly observing, crossed her arms and turned to Kelly.
"So, he knows the Chief, then?"

Kelly shrugged as though the answer was obvious.

"Of course. He was the one who hired him to establish this detective bureau. It was just the Chief, Leclerc, and me."

Miss Dupuis smirked slightly, a hint of teasing in her expression.

"You seem to admire him, Kelly."

"Admire?" Kelly retorted, his voice carrying an unusual intensity. "That man feared nothing. He stood by the Chief even when investigations became politically sensitive. Not everyone would have had the courage."

"Do they still stay in touch?" she asked.

"That, I don't know. But I know they called each other by their first names back then. When you work with someone like Ermatinger, that says it all."

Miss Dupuis pressed her lips together thoughtfully and gave a slight nod.

"Yes… that does say it all," she murmured. "I know the Chief well enough to say he rarely addresses anyone by their first name."

Silence fell again, broken only by the soothing crackle of the stove's flames. Outside, the winter sun finally broke through the clouds, casting golden rays through the soot-streaked, fogged-up windows. A hesitant light filled the office, drawing shifting reflections on the walls and illuminating the tiniest motes of dust floating in the air.

Descending to the ground floor, Robinson spotted a towering man with the build of a lumberjack and an imposing air. His thick beard lent him a rugged appearance, while his long hair framed a face etched by a life fully lived. His slightly almond-shaped eyes, a legacy from his mother, the daughter of a Saulteaux chief, glimmered with an intense light.

Ermatinger approached with a confident stride. Before he could speak, Robinson extended his hand, a genuine smile lighting up his face.

"Dear William, what a pleasure to see you! It's been an age."

Ermatinger, equally delighted, grasped his hand firmly, his grip a testament to their friendship.

"Dear Silas," he replied simply, his tone imbued with rare sincerity.

Robinson, his curiosity piqued, gestured toward the offices.
"So, what brings you back to your old stomping grounds? Are you chasing the ghosts of the past?"

"Oh no, Silas! I'll leave those to you. That said, nothing seems to have changed here, has it?"

"Not entirely," Robinson replied with a smile. "Though the detective bureau has expanded. We've finally secured a new office space. I managed to unlock the funds... something my former Chief of Police stubbornly refused."

They broke into laughter, the sound echoing down the narrow corridor, effortlessly rekindling the camaraderie of years past.

"Come, I'll give you a tour," Robinson offered enthusiastically.

"No, thank you, Silas. I'm not one to chase after nostalgia."

"Then why are you here, William?"

Ermatinger lowered his voice, glancing around the hallway.
"I need to speak with you... but not here."

Robinson's lips curled into an amused smile.
"Still as cryptic as ever! Let's head to the port. With weather like this, it would be criminal to stay indoors."

CHAPTER 12

Monday Morning, March 27

After retrieving his coat and bowler hat from upstairs, Robinson returned swiftly. Ermatinger carefully adjusted his fine fur hat before they stepped out into the brisk air, the dry cold lightly biting their cheeks. The sky was clear, a pale blue lit by a winter sun that barely warmed the air. Ermatinger wore a thick, double-breasted coat with a fur-lined collar that spoke of its quality. Meanwhile, Robinson had wrapped a woollen scarf around his neck, and his worn leather gloves bore signs of frequent use.

The pair rounded the building and descended a gentle slope toward the port. The activity there was in full swing, the clamour of voices and the crash of crates filling the air. The wharf teemed with life.

The bright sun of this spring morning played on the still snow-dusted facades of the buildings lining the quay. Although the temperature hovered around 35 °F, the brisk, clear air exuded energy. Two imposing steamships were moored side by side, releasing heavy plumes of grayish smoke that rose lazily into the sky. Their chimneys spewed clouds that, as they descended, mingled with the bustling activity of the port, where melting snow formed small, glistening puddles on the cobblestones.

On the first ship, many workers bustled about tirelessly, unloading carts overflowing with goods. Clad in worn wool coats and topped with tweed caps or thick woollen hats, they perspired despite the cold. Their jackets, damp with effort, clung to their shirts as they heaved crates marked with exotic destinations, iron-bound barrels, scuffed leather trunks, and bundles tied with coarse ropes. The dockworkers, shouting instructions in a chaotic mix of French and English, often had to raise their voices to be heard over the creaking of carts rolling on the uneven cobblestones.

Not far away, a group of mischievous boys darted about laughing, weaving between stacks of crates. Their boots splashed small sprays of water as they ran through puddles. The foreman, a man with a rough voice and a patched coat, waved his arm to disperse them, though he had little real intention of driving them away.

On the second ship, a narrow and slightly frosted gangplank allowed a crowd of passengers to disembark cautiously. Their heavy coats and woollen scarves betrayed the hardships of a journey under maritime skies. A few uniformed sailors, their faces weathered by the wind, extended helping hands with professional smiles. Once on the quay, the passengers were swept into the bustling activity: Hansom cabs waited in orderly lines, their drivers bundled in long coats, calling out to potential fares with broad gestures and booming voices. Porters, their backs bent under the weight of massive trunks, moved carefully to avoid the remaining patches of snow or the treacherous puddles.

Under the shadow of a shed, a few officers in impeccably buttoned uniforms smoked their pipes at leisure, their relaxed posture starkly contrasting with the incessant commotion around them. Sunlight reflected off their brass buttons, adding a glimmer to their deliberate stillness. Meanwhile, dockworkers exchanged loud banter with travellers, throwing out occasional bold remarks that were always followed by hearty laughter, enough to dispel any tension.

Further down, a woman wrapped in a thick woollen shawl was selling fresh apples from a basket at her feet, calling out to passersby with an insistent and sing-song voice. The cries of seagulls, drawn by scraps of food and freshly unloaded fish, mingled with the tolling of ship bells and the hum of human activity. This vibrant and ever-changing symphony captured the whole morning energy at the port, where the melting snow and bright sun heralded the hesitant arrival of spring.

Robinson paused to take in the scene.

"Quite a spectacle, isn't it? These docks aren't what they used to be."

Ermatinger, his eyes fixed on the bustling port, nodded slightly.

"And that's partly thanks to you," Robinson continued.

"A little, yes," Ermatinger replied with a modest tone. "There was a time when these docks were dangerous—run by thugs and smugglers."

Eventually, they spotted an empty bench and sat, their gaze drifting toward the horizon, where the waters of the St. Lawrence, still speckled with drifting ice, shimmered under the bright winter sun.

After a moment, Ermatinger spoke again, his voice soft, almost wistful:

"I love this city, Silas. It's so full of life, so vibrant."

"And yet, you left it."

"I had to," Ermatinger replied gravely. "New responsibilities awaited me."

"Yes, I know—defending Canada."

"Much was happening along the border at the start of the Civil War. American newspapers called for an invasion of Canada to force Britain to support the Union."

"Fortunately, that's all about to end," Robinson said thoughtfully.

"Not quite yet, but soon," Ermatinger admitted. "Lincoln has offered the Confederates terms for peace."

They sat there for a while, silent, each lost in thought as the port's commotion formed a strangely soothing backdrop.

The quiet was punctuated only by the creak of ropes at the docks and the clamour of activity on the wharves. Ermatinger slowly pulled a cigar from his inner pocket, his deliberate movements revealing years of habit. This small pleasure, he had discovered years earlier during the Carlist Wars in Spain, where he had served as a lieutenant colonel. At the time, the Spaniards imported Cuban cigars, an exotic luxury he had quickly adopted.

He carefully lit the cigar, drew a deep puff, and released a thin stream of smoke into the crisp air. After a moment, he resumed speaking, his expression thoughtful:

"Today, the Union army no longer seeks to invade Canada. But it's not over yet."

"Oh? How so?"

Ermatinger, between puffs, fixed a grave look on his companion.

"I was appointed last year to monitor the borders of Lower Canada. Another threat is emerging—one more insidious."

"You mean the Fenians? Those radical Irishmen?"

"I see you're well-informed. Yes, those damn Fenians. They're dangerous, Silas. Their clear goal is to pressure Britain into granting Ireland independence."

"I thought their fight was limited to Ireland itself."

"Until recently, that was true. But things have changed. In the United States, Irish expatriates are beginning to organize. They believe the best way to liberate their homeland across the Atlantic is to attack Canada."

"Attack Canada? What purpose would that serve?"

Ermatinger exhaled a long puff of smoke, his features hardening.

"Their plan is to invade Canada and provoke a war between the United States and Britain. If the U.S. annexes Canada, it could inspire a revolution in Ireland."

Robinson raised an eyebrow, his tone tinged with sarcasm. "A bold gamble—and a risky one at that."

"Risky indeed. But they believe in it. And they are not without resources. The Fenians have infiltrated several Irish Catholic organizations, particularly in Toronto. In Montreal, they're more discreet but still present."

Robinson shook his head.

"I doubt they'll find much support here. Montreal's Irish community isn't prone to fanaticism."

"Perhaps not," Ermatinger conceded with a nod. "But they are divided. Even if most reject the radical ideals of the Fenians, many share their desire to see British dominance in Ireland come to an end."

As he spoke, Ermatinger took another puff from his cigar, his eyes briefly scanning the bustling docks. The cries of stevedores, the wails of children, and the metallic clatter of cartwheels on cobblestones filled the air. The neighing of horses punctuated the cacophony, creating a vivid tableau of daily life.

"William, you didn't travel all this way just to talk politics," Robinson said, a hint of a smile on his lips.

Ermatinger smirked, a playful glint in his eyes.
"And why not? You know I value your company, Silas."

"I value yours too, William, but you won't win me over so easily."

"Very well. You're as perceptive as ever."

Robinson slipped his hand into the inner pocket of his jacket and pulled out a photograph, which he handed to Robinson.

"Look at this. That's your corpse, isn't it?"

Robinson took the photograph.

"Yes, that's him. Where did you get this?"

"I still have good contacts in Montreal," Ermatinger replied, taking another puff of his cigar.

"And who might those be?"

"No need to be coy," Ermatinger said with a smile. "It's Penton."

Robinson raised his eyebrows, clearly surprised.
"Fred Penton? Our new Chief of Police?"

"The very same."

Ermatinger's gaze grew sharper as he fixed his eyes on Robinson.

"Tell me, Silas, are you still part of a Masonic lodge?"

"And you, William?"

A quick, almost imperceptible exchange passed between them as they shook hands. That discreet yet coded gesture confirmed what they already knew of each other: their shared membership in the secret society whose threads wove silently across nations.

"Penton belongs to the same lodge as I do," Ermatinger explained, tapping the edge of his cigar. "He gave me this photograph last week. He knew of my network and thought I could help."

"And?"

Ermatinger let the silence linger, his eyes fixed on the port below.

"I can help, indeed—and by extension, help you. I knew this man."

"So do we. We identified him as Liam O'Neil."

An enigmatic smile flickered across Ermatinger's lips. "That's his cover name."

"A cover?" Robinson straightened in surprise.

"His real name was John Monahan. He was… one of my spies."

Robinson froze, his thoughts momentarily swirling. Ermatinger, unfazed, continued in a measured tone:

"I was tasked by Macdonald's government to establish a secret service. I'm in charge of it for Lower Canada. Over the past year, we've been building our team. So far, we've gathered valuable intelligence, especially regarding the planned Fenian invasion."

He took a final puff of his cigar before holding it delicately between his fingers as though it were a relic.

"These fanatics form a secret society. They're tough to infiltrate. That's why we relied on Irishmen like Monahan."

Robinson squinted, trying to piece together the implications.
"Monahan was Irish?"

"Yes, but a Protestant Irishman, not Catholic. You know, Silas, how deeply those two communities loathe each other."

"Yes, that's no recent development."

"Precisely. We asked Monahan to infiltrate the Fenians in Montreal by posing as a Catholic. He had been working on this mission for several months."

"That explains a few things," Robinson admitted, furrowing his brow. "We noticed his strange behaviour when he visited Kate Scanlan's tavern."

Ermatinger let out a low chuckle.

"That tavern is a veritable den of Fenians. Monahan was trying to infiltrate the Irish Catholic community in Griffintown."

"And someone uncovered his true intentions, didn't they?"

"That's our assumption. He was discovered and killed. But we don't know by whom. That's precisely why I'm here."

He locked eyes with Robinson, his gaze heavy with meaning.

"I know you, Silas. You always find your man. But you need the right information to start."

"Our investigation had stalled, of course. We were looking for Liam O'Neil…"

"Who never existed," Ermatinger interjected with a nod. "Monahan's cover was excellent, no doubt. But what went wrong? How did they uncover him? And above all, who killed him?"

He paused, allowing his companion to absorb the questions.

"You should direct your inquiries toward the Fenians."

"Understood," Robinson replied.

Ermatinger went on to share a few additional details about John Monahan. Then, with a brusque gesture, he crushed his half-smoked cigar against the cobblestone ground, leaving a dark stain on the thin layer of snow.

The two men walked back up the gentle slope toward the imposing Bonsecours Market. Reaching Saint-Paul Street, Ermatinger hailed a Hansom cab, which halted with a clatter of wheels on the stones.

Turning to Robinson, he extended a firm hand.
"You'll keep me informed?"

"Most certainly, William. But how can I reach you?"

"I'll find you, Silas. It was a pleasure seeing you again."

"The pleasure was mine," Robinson replied with a nod.

Ermatinger climbed into the cab. Moments later, the vehicle trundled away, the snap of reins and the rhythmic clatter of hooves fading into the distance. Robinson lingered, watching the scene before turning away.

He stepped into the building and ascended the worn steps, each footfall echoing softly in the stairwell. Reaching the upper floor, he walked down the familiar corridor toward the detective bureau. A new lead had surfaced, and he had no intention of letting it go cold.

CHAPTER 13

March 27, Monday Morning

When Robinson pushed open the heavy door of the Bonsecours building after he met with Ermatinger, he was immediately stopped by the officer on duty. The young man, his face marked with pock scars, addressed him curtly:

"Chief wants to see you, Mr. Robinson. Right away."

Robinson nodded absentmindedly, unbuttoned his coat without a word, and headed toward the staircase. The steps creaked slightly under his still-damp boots. Cold air had seeped into the building, lending a muffled echo to each footfall.

Reaching the top floor, he knocked on the door of Penton's office. A commanding voice bade him enter.

"Ah, Robinson, finally! Sit down quickly. We need to talk."

"Good morning, sir," Robinson replied, removing his hat with measured politeness.

"Yes, yes, good morning. No time for pleasantries. Sit."

Penton waved impatiently, not even allowing him to remove his thick coat.

The chief's office exuded order and authority. The room, bathed in bright light from tall windows, afforded an impressive view of the bustling docks and the river. A fine mist rose from the waters, where a few sailing ships struggled forward. Everything here contrasted starkly with the grim confines of the detectives' office, perpetually shrouded in shadow.

Seated behind an impeccably organized desk, Penton looked as rigid as his uniform. Gaunt to an extreme, almost skeletal, his angular face seemed carved from marble. His prominent cheekbones and aquiline nose evoked an engraving of a tormented Saint Anthony. But his heterochromatic eyes—one deep brown, the other bluish grey—mesmerized anyone bold enough to meet his gaze.

"So, Robinson, why didn't you tell me about this murder before today?" Penton demanded, fixing him with a nearly unnerving intensity.

"With all due respect, sir, I wasn't obligated to. My predecessors—"

"I don't want to hear about your predecessors," Penton cut him off, slapping his hand on the desk. "A new era begins here, and I have no interest in old habits."

Robinson raised an eyebrow but remained composed. His gloved hands rested calmly on his lap.

"Traditionally, detectives conduct their investigations without... how shall I put it... interference from their superiors."

"Interference, you say?" Penton hissed. "I am your superior, Robinson. I'm the one under pressure from the mayor and the attorney general. I make the decisions here. You answer to me."

A heavy silence settled, broken only by the distant sound of horses' hooves clattering over the snow-covered cobblestones.

"Have you identified the body?" Penton asked, his tone slightly lowered.

"Yes. William Ermatinger came to see me. He mentioned that you showed him the photograph of the corpse. Do you know him?"

"That's none of your concern," Penton snapped. "But he recognized the man. However, he refused to give me his name. He seemed unsettled."

"John Monahan," Robinson said. "An Irish Protestant, apparently linked to the Orangemen."

"Monahan, you say? I'm well acquainted with the Orangemen. If he were active, I'd know. A sympathizer, perhaps... But who could have killed him?"

"That's precisely what I aim to uncover. Ermatinger claims the Fenians may be involved."

Penton's face tightened, and he abruptly stood.

"Those damned Irish Catholics," he muttered. "They despise our Empire. If they had their way, they'd set Britain ablaze."

He fixed his mismatched eyes on Robinson.

"You're British, aren't you? Anglican?"

"I'm Canadian now," Robinson replied calmly. "But I was born in London."

"Then you understand what's at stake. We must preserve our stability."

Robinson remained stoic, offering no response. Penton drew a deep breath before declaring:

"You will keep me informed of every detail. Is that clear?"

"Perfectly," Robinson said, rising to his feet.

He replaced his hat, offered a brief nod, and left the room, his mind already consumed by the riddles of this investigation.

Robinson entered the dim, cramped office he shared with his three detectives. The lingering scent of stale tobacco and old papers hung in the air. Kelly, Morin, and Miss Dupuis were bent over their files, silent, their expressions grave. The silence in the room was heavy and oppressive, like the pall that follows a failure or unanswered questions. Even the creaking of the floorboards beneath their boots seemed amplified.

Robinson hesitated, his coat still draped over his shoulders. Then, instead of succumbing to their gloom, he clapped his gloved hands to draw their attention.

"Come now, we won't let this get the better of us. Dinner's on me."

The detectives looked up, startled, but none protested. The sun shone high in a clear blue sky, dazzling against the pristine snow and making the biting air feel even sharper. Moments later, bundled in their wool coats and scarves wrapped tightly around their necks, they walked the icy streets, their footsteps crunching over snow hardened by the frost. The brisk air stung their cheeks, and their breaths formed faint, white clouds in the brilliant light.

The inn, tucked into a corner of Rue de la Commune, offered a welcoming refuge. As they crossed the threshold, a comforting warmth and the savoury aroma of stewed dishes enveloped them. They made their way to a secluded table in a shadowy corner, away from the clamour of conversation.

Their orders came swiftly. Kelly chose grilled sausages, the smoky scent wafting from nearby plates. Robinson opted for a meat pie, its golden, flaky crust promising a hearty, rustic meal. Morin, ever frugal, settled for a thick, hearty potato soup, while Miss Dupuis requested an oyster stew, a rare treat she savoured in small spoonfuls.

The warmth, the food, and the first pints of beer soon dispelled their gloomy mood. Faces relaxed, shoulders loosened. Morin, ever the brash one, broke the silence.

"So, chief, what did your friend Ermatinger want?" he asked, wiping a drop of soup from the corner of his thin mustache.

Robinson set down his fork, considering his response for a moment.

"First of all, he's not my friend. We were colleagues, that's all. That said, he brought some... surprising news. Our victim's name wasn't Liam O'Neill. His real name was John Monahan."

Kelly's fork clattered loudly onto his plate as Miss Dupuis and Morin's eyes widened.

"What?" Kelly exclaimed. "Not O'Neill? What's this all about?"

"A complicated matter," Robinson replied. "Monahan used O'Neill as a cover. He was a government spy."

A stunned silence fell over the table, broken only by the room's ambient noise. Miss Dupuis finally spoke, her spoon hovering mid-air.

"A spy?" she murmured. "But why would there be a spy here, in Canada?"

"Because we're under threat. Ermatinger explained that he manages an espionage network for the government. Monahan was part of it."

Morin furrowed his brow and set his mug down firmly.

"Threatened by whom, exactly? The Americans?"

"Partly. But mostly by the Fenians," Robinson explained. "Those radical Irish Catholics who dream of toppling the British Empire."

Kelly gritted his teeth, his fists clenching around his fork.

"Those damned radicals… They're behind this, no doubt."

"That's what Ermatinger suspects as well," Robinson added. "They may have discovered Monahan was an Irish Protestant connected to the Orangemen. They would've killed him for it."

Miss Dupuis nodded thoughtfully.

"This changes everything for our investigation," she said. "If it's a political murder, it's no longer just a street quarrel."

Robinson nodded, his gaze distant for a moment.

"Precisely. This complicates matters. Monahan wasn't a saint, but he wasn't an ordinary criminal either. He was an orphan recruited after a riot in Toronto. Ermatinger brought him here to use him as an undercover agent."

Morin nodded.

"What's our next step, chief?"

Robinson straightened.

"We start the investigation over. But first, Kelly and Morin finish up the Walsh case. Dupuis, you're coming with me. We've someone to see."

The detectives nodded. The inn's warmth seemed to fortify them, readying them to face the biting chill of the investigation once more.

Kelly and Morin entered the small interrogation room, where Aidan Walsh sat motionless behind a worn wooden table. The harsh light of a hanging lamp cast sharp shadows across his face, still bearing the fading marks of his recent fight with Murphy. His calm, almost defiant demeanour stood in stark contrast to the seriousness of the charges against him.

Still wrapped in a heavy wool coat, Kelly slowly removed his gloves and tossed them carelessly onto the table. He then shrugged off his jacket with a sharp motion, revealing a fitted dark waistcoat beneath. Beside him, Morin followed suit, placing his belongings down with less flourish. Outside, the brisk air had left their cheeks ruddy, while faint daylight filtered through the dusty, barred windows, casting flickering shadows on the cold floor.

"Good morning, Walsh," Kelly began, his tone a mixture of false cordiality and irony. "They've been treating you well in prison, I trust?"

Walsh lifted his head, his pale eyes locking with Kelly's in a challenging gaze.

"I have no complaints," he replied evenly.

Kelly smirked, leaning slightly against the table.

"I met your mother, you know. Lovely woman."

Walsh's brows knit together, but his face remained otherwise expressionless.

"Leave my mother out of this," he growled, his voice laced with restrained anger.

"Oh, but she was very cooperative," Kelly continued, a mocking glint in his eye. "She even let us have a look at your room. We found some treasures, didn't we, Morin?"

Until then, having stayed in the background, Morin flipped through his notebook with a distracted air before approaching the table and sitting on a chair nonchalantly.

"Yes, treasures," he confirmed lightly. "A pistol, a mask… and quite a bit of money."

Walsh said nothing, his cold stare fixed on Kelly. The detective leaned in slightly, trying to break through the veneer of indifference.

"We showed the pistol and mask to the bank employees. You know what? They recognized them straight away. So tell me… who was with you for that little 'withdrawal'?"

"Do you really think I'm going to tell you?"

"So, you're admitting you were there."

"You've got all the evidence, don't you? Why deny the obvious?"

Kelly straightened up, crossing his arms.

"Quite a stash of money in your room. What were you planning? A fine house to rival the wealthy?"

Walsh's gaze darkened, and his tone turned sharp.

"Do you really think I did this to mimic the bourgeois parasites who exploit us every day?"

"Oh, really! You don't like the… what do you call them again? The 'bourgeois.' And what exactly is the 'bourgeois,' Walsh?"

"They're the rotten ones who own everything. The ones who build fortunes on our misery. They set up their businesses and profit off the backs of workers. 'Property is the root of all evil.'"

Morin glanced up, intrigued.

"That's quite a line. Did you come up with it?"

Walsh shook his head, a flicker of pride in his eyes.

"No, it's Proudhon."

Kelly let out a short, mocking laugh.

"Proudhon? And who's that?"

"A French writer you should read," Walsh replied, his tone laced with condescension.

Kelly turned to Morin, who gave an amused shrug.

"Did you hear that, Morin? We've got ourselves a bookworm here. And a proper one at that!"

"I read a lot," Walsh said simply.

Kelly crossed his arms over his dark waistcoat.

"Well, it didn't stop you from being a thief," he said, his voice laced with disdain.

Walsh lifted his head, his expression cold and indifferent, though his eyes betrayed a hint of defiance.

"That money wasn't for me," he replied calmly.

"Oh, no? And who was it for, then?" Kelly asked, narrowing his eyes slightly.

"We needed it…"

Morin, who had been scribbling notes, stopped and interjected, a wry smile on his lips.

"'We,' huh? Oh, that's right. Word is, you're the big boss of a gang. Supposedly got all of Griffintown shaking in their boots."

"That's just what your bourgeois newspapers say," Walsh retorted. "But we're not a gang of ruffians, no matter what they write."

Kelly tilted his head slightly, intrigued despite himself.

"Then what are you?"

Walsh's voice rose, vibrating with restrained anger.

"Have you ever set foot in one of those rotten factories? Ten hours a day, six days a week, sometimes more. Kids as young as twelve tearing their fingers apart on those damned machines. And for what? Wages that can't even feed a family."

Kelly was silent for a moment, studying Walsh's tense features.

"I see. So you wanted to help the poor folk, is that it?"

"We already have a mutual aid society to help the neediest families," Walsh replied sharply. "But it's not enough. To survive, we need to unite—all the workers. And we have to force these bosses to respect our labour."

Morin furrowed his brow and crossed his arms.

"You're talking about strikes, aren't you? You know that's illegal. Look what happened to the workers on the Lachine Canal."

"They were massacred by the police, I know," Walsh replied bitterly.

"That wasn't me, I assure you," Morin said with a shrug. "I was still playing knucklebones back then."

"The police helped the military crush them," Walsh spat, contempt in his voice. "You're all bought and paid for by the grand capital."

Kelly let out a short, incredulous laugh.

"Well, there's a new one. 'Bought by the capitalists.' Me, Walsh, I don't even know who this 'grand capital' of yours is. But I know one thing: you're going to prison for this theft."

Walsh averted his eyes, slowly lowering his head. The tension in the room was palpable, every movement seeming louder in the silence.

Kelly straightened slightly, his arms still crossed.

"I'm curious, Walsh. What would you do with it if you didn't want the money for yourself?"

Walsh raised his eyes, a fierce determination blazing in them.

"We need money to organize a trade union," he said. "You don't build something like that on goodwill and volunteer work. We decided to use the money from the rich against them. After all, it's what the Confederates did in St. Albans— they robbed three banks to help their cause."

"So, if I understand you, you're not a thief but a hero? A saint, even?"

Walsh remained impassive, deliberately ignoring the remark.

Kelly's tone grew more serious.

"I have another question. During St. Patrick's Day a few weeks ago, one of our officers was attacked on Wellington Street by a gang of thugs. That wasn't you, was it?"

Walsh shook his head slowly.

"Neither me nor my group. I told you, we have nothing against the police as long as they do their job and don't become the watchdogs of the wealthy."

"So, neither you nor your group had anything to do with the assault?"

"Certainly not."

"And you don't know who it might have been?"

"Do you think I'd tell you if I did?"

Kelly sighed and leaned back slightly.

"Well, then, I think we're done here. You have nothing more to add?"

"Nothing more. I'm the only one responsible. You won't get anything else out of me."

Kelly studied Walsh for a moment before shrugging.

"You'll go before the judge. It's a shame, honestly. If your statement is true, I can understand what you're trying to fight for. But did you really have to land yourself in this mess?"

"If you've got a better idea, I'm all ears."

Kelly allowed himself a faint smile for the first time in an interrogation. Morin gathered his notebook and pencil, having jotted down notes throughout. The two detectives stood, donning their coats and hats once more. They gave orders to the constable waiting by the door and returned to their office.

CHAPTER 14

March 28, Tuesday Morning

On this sunny late-March morning, a week and a half had passed since the discovery of the body in the alley behind the tavern. The biting cold, hovering between 30°F and 35°F, compelled every passerby to wrap themselves tightly against the chill. What had initially seemed like a mere quarrel among Irishmen had now revealed far more sinister undertones. This was no simple altercation; it was a premeditated murder laced with political implications. The victim, John Monahan, a government spy tasked with infiltrating the Fenians—a secretive group of Irish Catholics advocating violence as a means of emancipation—had not been chosen at random.

The previous evening, over a modest yet comforting supper, Robinson, Rosalie, and Thérèse—referred to as Miss Dupuis by her colleagues—had shared their meal in the warm intimacy of their home. Thérèse, still living with her parents since finishing her college studies, had taken on the role of Robinson's assistant on the condition that work discussions be kept from the dinner table. Yet that evening, Silas Robinson broke their agreement—for the first time, and likely not the last.

"You know, we've already wasted too much time," Robinson declared, slicing a piece of bread. "We need to understand what motivated this murder."

Thérèse glanced up from her plate, curiosity lighting her eyes.

"Do you really think there's a link between the Fenians and this murder?"

"Thérèse," Robinson replied, leaning back in his chair, "you need to understand one thing: I never assume anything about murder. I deal with facts. And the facts are that my superior, Penton, is convinced, and Ermatinger seems to share his opinion."

"But isn't it risky to make such assumptions without proof?" she asked, tilting her head slightly, doubt flickering in her gaze.

Robinson allowed a faint smile.

"You're learning quickly, Thérèse. Yes, prudence and an open mind are vital. Some cases, like this one, demand that we examine the context more than the potential culprit."

"But isn't it our job to catch the killer?" she countered, her brow furrowing slightly.

"Of course. However, focusing solely on finding a suspect without understanding the motive is dangerous. I've seen too many men wrongly convicted because no one asked the right questions."

"In this case, the motive seems obvious: political crime."

"Perhaps, but that's too simplistic. Listen carefully. Monahan was an Orangeman—a member of that extremist Protestant faction of the Irish. This isn't merely a religious dispute. It's a struggle between two opposing worldviews."

Thérèse lost in thought, gazed for a moment at the dim light of the chandelier.

"Two factions of Irishmen, Catholics and Protestants… It's like two feuding brothers ready to destroy one another, like in the old Greek tragedy The Seven Against Thebes," she murmured.

Robinson, amused, looked at her over his glass.

"Well, that's an interesting reference. Your college years weren't wasted, I see."

"I had a good teacher," she replied, a small smile on her lips as she gestured lightly toward him.

Rosalie, watching them with a tender expression, chimed in.

"You make quite the pair, the two of you. It's almost like watching characters in a novel solving a riddle."

They burst into laughter, but Robinson soon regained his serious tone.

"Tomorrow," he said, "we'll meet Thomas Ryan. He has valuable connections among the Orangemen."

"Uncle Thomas? Why didn't you mention this during our visit to his house last Sunday?"

"We didn't know anything then. And even if we had, it wouldn't have been appropriate to bring it up, not with the D'Arcy McGee situation hanging over us."

A quiet settled over the table as they finished their dessert. Glancing alternately at her husband and daughter, Rosalie finally broke the silence.

"You two seem to enjoy these discussions, don't you?"

Robinson looked at Thérèse with a glimmer of pride.

"That's true. She's talented, the little one."

Thérèse blushed faintly, caught off guard by the compliment, though her lips curled into a modest smile.

***

That morning, a dry cold enveloped Montreal, and the sun's rays played on the hardened snow lining the streets. Robinson and Miss Dupuis exited the police station at Bonsecours Market, their breath mingling with the frosty air. They decided to walk to the Bouthillier warehouses, where Ryan had temporarily set up his office. The distance was short, barely ten minutes, but long enough to feel the bite of winter in full force.

Miss Dupuis walked with a light step despite the uneven sidewalks coated with frost. She wore a gown of deep green, discreetly patterned with floral designs, though it was nearly hidden beneath an elegant anthracite coat with a brown fur collar. A black velvet hat, faintly reminiscent of a man's top hat, framed her delicate face. On another woman, such headgear might have appeared heavy and awkward; it seemed entirely graceful on her. Beside her, Robinson, imposing and impeccably dressed as always, wore a long black coat with brass buttons that reached his calves, firmly in place, topped off with his ever-present bowler hat. Beneath the coat, he wore a brown waistcoat, a matching vest, a crisply buttoned white shirt, and his signature black cravat. Walking side by side, they could have been mistaken for a doting father escorting his daughter to some grand event.

Though bustling with activity, the Rue de la Commune felt tranquil under the clear sky. The Bouthillier warehouses—three gray stone buildings with pitched roofs—soon appeared on the horizon. Passing through the carriage gate, they

247

entered a courtyard where bundled-up workers vigorously unloaded crates. The main entrance to the office lay to the right, at the top of a small staircase worn by years of use.

Inside, a young man with a hurried air dressed in a vest that seemed too large for him glanced up from the counter.

"Yes, what do you want?" he asked, his tone both anxious and condescending.

"We're here to see Thomas Ryan," Robinson replied, calm but firm.

"And who's asking?"

"Tell him it's Silas."

The young man raised an eyebrow, clearly unimpressed.

"Silas?!" he repeated as though the name were entirely foreign.

"Yes, just 'Silas.'"

The clerk hesitated, then stood with an exaggeratedly dramatic expression.

"Mr. Ryan is a very busy man. I'm not sure he'll be able to see you," he drawled, drawing out his words unnecessarily.

Robinson, unperturbed, made a small, sharp gesture with his hand—casual yet commanding—that clearly said, Do as you're told, and quickly. Beside him, Miss Dupuis stifled a laugh behind her gloved hand, her amusement barely concealed.

After a few minutes, the clerk returned, looking disgruntled.

"He'll see you," he said grudgingly.

Ryan's office was at the end of a narrow hallway, where the wooden floor creaked under their steps. The door was slightly ajar, and the two detectives knocked lightly before stepping in.

"Silas, my dear friend!" Ryan exclaimed, springing up from behind his cluttered desk. "Come in! Forgive my clerk; he can be a bit overzealous at times. I've already given him a talking-to."

"That wasn't necessary, Tom," Robinson replied with a faint smile. "Policemen are used to… let's say, less-than-warm welcomes."

"And you've brought Thérèse! What an excellent idea."

Ryan gestured for them to sit in the two chairs facing his desk. The modest room was filled with piles of documents, and a wood stove radiated a welcome warmth.

"What a Sunday evening that was," Ryan said, leaning back in his chair. "Well, pleasant, if one can call it that... Have you learned anything about Frasa's abduction?"

"Not yet..." Robinson replied, hesitation evident in his voice.

"You seem uncertain?" Ryan pressed, his brows knitting together.

"Well, cases like this don't usually fall under our jurisdiction. Disappearances are generally handled by the local police, and—"

Ryan cut him off, his voice rising.

"Not your jurisdiction?" he repeated, incredulous. "Come now, Silas! My friend is in despair, and you're telling me it's not your jurisdiction? Look at what those scoundrels forced him to do."

Ryan grabbed that day's newspaper from the corner of his desk, its pages yellowed by the winter light streaming through the window. With a sharp motion, he opened it and, adjusting his glasses, read aloud an excerpt from D'Arcy McGee's article. His deep voice reverberated through the small room, lending weight to the scathing condemnation of radical Irish Catholics.

"Listen to this," he said, glancing up at Robinson and Miss Dupuis before returning to the text.

"If this root of treason that is the Fenians were to spread among us, no loyal subject of this country, no lover of Canada or its laws, could ever employ or encourage the settlement of another Irishman in our midst. I, therefore, fulfill my highest public duty faithfully and fully when I remain vigilant for symptoms of this malady, which, like cholera or any other plague, might be carried over from Ireland in a bundle of old clothes but, once unleashed, could ravage an entire province."

Ryan paused, the newspaper trembling slightly in his hands, before continuing in a more accusatory tone.

"And here's what he writes further on."

"The great majority of Irish Catholics have nothing in common with the mad progeny of these fools. Seditious societies, like those of the Fenians, are akin to what Irish farmers used to say about Scotch grass: the only way to destroy it was to cut it at the roots, grind it to powder, and scatter the ashes to the four winds. True prudence demands that such conspirators be immediately trampled underfoot."

Ryan carefully folded the newspaper and placed it back on the desk, his face dark with contemplation.

"Do you see what my friend was forced to do because of the blackmail from those bastards? Don't tell me this case isn't your concern."

"Calm down, Tom. You know I'd do anything to help you. But this case is… unusual."

"What do you mean by 'unusual'?"

"I'm not certain Frasa has actually been taken hostage."

Ryan started, his hand dropping onto the desk.

"What do you mean? You read the letter, didn't you?"

"Yes, just as you did. But I have other information that suggests she might have run away."

"Run away?" Ryan repeated, incredulous.

"Yes, run away… with a secret lover."

Ryan let out a short laugh, more nervous than mocking.

"Frasa, with a secret lover? That's news to me."

"That's why it's called 'secret,' Tom. Even D'Arcy McGee has no idea."

Ryan sank back into his chair, his mouth slightly agape.

"This is astounding. Do you think she just ran off like that? And the letter?"

"That's a question we'll have to answer," Robinson replied, his tone more serious.

A heavy silence fell over the room, broken only by the crackling of the woodstove. Ryan seemed to struggle with the revelation. At last, he straightened up, trying to regain his composure.

"Well, in any case, I'm glad you came to see our warehouse—or my son's warehouse."

"Patrick!" Robinson exclaimed. "He's still up north?"

"Yes, still chasing contracts. That's why I'm here, holding the reins in his absence. You know how it is with the young… They still need us old hands to show them the way."

Ryan stood abruptly, throwing his arms wide in a theatrical gesture.

"So, shall we tour the warehouse?"

Robinson hesitated, exchanging a quick glance with Miss Dupuis before responding in a measured tone.

"In truth, Tom… We're here in an official capacity."

"You mean… as a detective?"

At this, Ryan sank back into his chair, crossing his arms over the cluttered desk. His gaze landed on Miss Dupuis, and he squinted slightly as if seeing her for the first time.

"But… Thérèse is with you?" he asked, incredulous.

"That's right! She's working with me now," Robinson replied.

Ryan's eyes widened, his tone laced with genuine surprise.

"Thérèse!… Little Thérèse… No taller than a sapling… She's working with you?"

Miss Dupuis lifted her chin slightly, her expression calm but with a mischievous smile tugging at the corner of her lips.

"I've grown up now, wouldn't you agree, Uncle Thomas?"

Ryan caught off guard, nodded as he tried to mask his astonishment.

"Yes… Of course… You're no longer a little girl… You've become a woman. A very lovely one, I might add."

"And intelligent, too," Miss Dupuis replied, unfazed. "I'm rather skilled at what I do."

Ryan raised an eyebrow, his skepticism evident, though he refrained from commenting. Sensing the tension, Robinson straightened in his chair.

"Tom," he said, steering the conversation back on track, "let's focus on why we're here. We need information on a critical matter."

"What are you investigating?"

"A murder was committed in Griffintown," Robinson explained.

"Ah, Griffintown. An Irishman, I presume."

"That's correct," Robinson confirmed.

"Well, are you surprised that there's been a murder there? You know how they are, those Irish: always bickering and fighting. They carry their feuds like an inheritance."

"Yet you, an Irishman, aren't like that. I'd even say you're one of the most conciliatory men I know."

Ryan chuckled softly, waving a hand dismissively.

"That's because of my trade, Silas. You don't catch flies with vinegar."

Robinson leaned forward, his voice taking on a more serious tone.

"I don't believe this murder is just a simple tavern quarrel, Tom. Everything points to a political assassination."

"A political assassination?"

"Yes. Our victim was an Orangeman."

"An Orangeman, you say? Well... I see..."

"You know the Orangemen well, don't you, Tom?" Robinson continued, his gaze probing Ryan's reaction.

"What are you getting at, Silas?"

"Tom, I know you have connections in some of Montreal's more influential circles."

"And why the Orangemen, specifically?" Ryan asked, his tone growing firmer.

Robinson paused, carefully choosing his words.

"Because our victim was one—or, at the very least, had ties to them."

Ryan stroked his chin, lost in thought. After a moment, he let out a bitter laugh.

"The Orangemen! Yes, this is the great historical tragedy of the Irish community. For generations, Catholic and Protestant Irish have waged an endless war against each other. And, I doubt anyone remembers why anymore between you and me."

Miss Dupuis, who had remained silent until now, spoke in a gentle but confident voice.

"Can you tell me more about this war, Uncle Thomas? It could be useful."

Ryan shot her an amused look tinged with a hint of suspicion.

"You're quite inquisitive, young lady."

Miss Dupuis responded with a professional smile, retrieving a notebook and pencil from her bag.

"You understand, I need to take notes. It's part of my work."

Still unconvinced that Miss Dupuis belonged in this conversation, Ryan looked doubtful at Robinson, who gave him an encouraging nod. With a resigned sigh, Ryan folded his hands on the desk and spoke gravely.

"You have to go back to the seventeenth century, to Northern Ireland—Ulster in particular," he began. "At that time, the British government embarked on a massive colonization effort, sending in Anglo-Scottish Protestants to suppress the Catholic religion among the Irish. This attempt to seize Irish lands for settlers provoked fierce resistance and created secret and often violent organizations. Among them was the Orange Order, modelled after Masonic lodges."

"But that was long ago and in another country," Miss Dupuis interjected.

Ryan tilted his head slightly, a glimmer of amusement in his eyes as if she had stated the obvious.

"Indeed," he conceded. "But the Order made its way here to Canada with the waves of immigration. Today, it has adherents scattered throughout the country, particularly in rural areas but also in the cities. It's estimated there are over fifteen thousand members nationwide."

"You seem well-informed about the Orangemen, Uncle Thomas."

"In my line of work, knowing about them is essential. You can't conduct business in Montreal without crossing paths with their network."

"And yet, you're an Irish Catholic?" she asked, her tone laced with mild provocation.

"And proud of it. But, Thérèse, the Irish community is far from united. And if you only knew how much that pains me... We were just talking about my friend D'Arcy McGee. That poor man devotes all his energy to trying to reconcile the irreconcilable factions among the Irish. Unfortunately, by walking the tightrope between two sides, he's received death threats from both—the Catholic Fenians and the Protestant Orangemen."

Robinson interjected, his expression thoughtful.

"Tom, no community is truly homogenous. Even French Canadians have their internal divisions. Why would the Irish be any different?"

"It's probably worse with us," Ryan admitted. "Do you know that several of the most successful businessmen here in Montreal are Irish? The McCords, the Clendinnengs... and what about Thomas Workman?"

"The president of the Molson Bank?" Robinson asked, surprised.

"Himself," Ryan confirmed. "He started with nothing and now runs Canada's largest wholesale hardware business."

"Everyone knows about these successes," Robinson replied. "But what's the connection?"

"Few people realize they're Protestant Irish, Silas. And that makes all the difference. The Protestant Irish in Montreal has little in common with the Catholic Irish in Griffintown, apart from owning businesses there. Otherwise, they're far more aligned with the Anglo-Scots, sharing networks and resources that propel them to the top of the economic elite."

"And what about you, Tom? Where do you fit into all this?"

"Me? I'm a Catholic Irishman who succeeded thanks to my London connections. But I'll never be 'one of them.' Never."

Miss Dupuis, who had been scribbling notes fervently, looked up.

"Are there Orange Lodges in Montreal?"

Ryan cast a hesitant glance at the young woman, still visibly uneasy with her active role in the conversation. At last, he answered, almost reluctantly.

"Yes, here in Montreal, the Grand Orange Lodge has a unique characteristic: it's not made up exclusively of Protestant Irish. You'll also find Englishmen, Scots, Germans... even Indians."

"So, mostly Protestants?"

"Not all. For instance, I've never heard of Anglicans among their ranks. Which is strange, given that those Queen's

Papists adore our Sovereign, as everyone knows," Ryan said, casting a sly glance at Robinson.

Robinson raised an eyebrow, amused by the jibe. Ryan knew his friend well: the son of a pastor and a former theology student, Robinson had deep ties to Anglicanism. But he was no zealot, far from it—especially after marrying a Catholic like Rosalie. This camaraderie allowed Ryan to jest without fear of offending his old friend.

A silence settled over the room, broken only by the crackling of the woodstove. Outside, the bright winter sun illuminated the icy street while the conversation took darker turns.

"Are the Orangemen in Montreal powerful?" Robinson asked.

Ryan crossed his arms, leaning slightly against the back of his chair.

"In a sense, yes, but not as much as they like to think. They're less sectarian—or at least appear to be—than in places like Toronto. Here in Montreal, they're part of the commercial and financial elite. But with the predominance of Catholics, whether French, Canadian, or Irish, they know they can't openly display intolerance. That said, they're not entirely closed off. Look at the Saint Patrick's Society. It was founded to celebrate a saint revered by Irish Catholics, yet the Orangemen joined in."

Robinson lowered his gaze to the floor, distractedly studying the worn wooden boards. He seemed deep in thought, his index finger tapping lightly against the arm of his chair.

"I wonder, Thomas if the Orangemen in Canada could be as violent as those in Ulster," he said at last. "For instance, could they go so far as to assassinate a political opponent?"

Ryan shrugged, his gaze drifting momentarily to the window where pale winter light seeped through.

"I don't know... Perhaps. After all, they're the ones who burned down the Parliament here in Montreal, aren't they? In Toronto, they've often resorted to violence against Catholics. It's funny you should ask that, Silas. Didn't you tell me the victim was an Orangeman?"

"That's right," Robinson said, lifting his head.

"Then why not look to their enemies? Those Fenians... Those Catholic fanatics are capable of anything, believe me."

"Yes, you're right. The Fenians have caught our attention. What can you tell me about them?" Robinson asked, his tone sharpening.

"Honestly, I'm not the best person to ask. They don't concern themselves with me, and I don't concern myself with them. If you want to dig deeper, see Bernard Devlin, the president of the Saint Patrick's Society."

Miss Dupuis, who had been dutifully taking notes, looked up curiously.

"Why him?" she asked, her pencil poised above her notebook.

"Devlin likely knows more about that world than I do. My friend D'Arcy McGee even believes he's a Fenian sympathizer."

Another silence fell, broken only by the faint creak of the floorboards beneath Ryan's shoes. Robinson eventually straightened, adjusting the lapel of his coat.

"Well, we've bothered you long enough, Tom. Let's pack up, Dupuis, and be on our way," he said firmly.

"Yes, sir," she replied, slipping her notebook and pencil into her bag.

Ryan sat upright, visibly surprised by their abrupt departure.

"Finished already? We didn't even have time to tour the warehouse," he protested.

"We'll do that another time, Tom. For now, we have a murder to solve."

Robinson and Miss Dupuis stood in unison, their movements almost military in precision, leaving Ryan no opportunity to rise and escort them out. After a quick round of goodbyes, they left the office, retracing their steps down the narrow hallway. A draft seeped through a poorly sealed window, reminding them of the winter chill outside.

Passing the counter, they politely nodded to the young clerk, still buried in his paperwork. He briefly looked up and acknowledged them with a hesitant wave.

Outside, the sun gleamed on the frozen streets, making the frost sparkle on the uneven cobblestones. Miss Dupuis pulled her coat tighter around her as Robinson adjusted his bowler hat, ready to continue their investigation.

CHAPTER 15

March 29, Wednesday Morning

Heavy snow fell that morning, its large, wet flakes settling gently on the sodden cobblestones, cloaking the streets in a fleeting mantle. The low, uniformly grey sky seemed to press upon the city as a cold wind whistled through the alleys. Robinson, bundled in a heavy dark wool coat, had chosen a Brougham. This type of carriage, both luxurious and well-insulated, offered better protection against the piercing cold and persistent dampness than the more exposed Hansom Cab.

Inside the vehicle, Kelly, his companion, adjusted the collar of his overcoat to guard against the occasional drafts that seeped in.

"Penton's going to pull quite the face when he sees the bill," Kelly muttered with a smirk. "These days, all he dreams of are budget cuts."

Robinson, arms crossed, shot him an amused look.
"Penton can go straight to the devil."

The sharp, cutting retort drew a hearty laugh from Kelly, his mirth echoing in the upholstered interior.

But Robinson's thoughts were elsewhere. His mind circled the murder of Monahan, a Protestant Orangeman found in a frozen alley off Wellington Street. He was convinced the case was far from a simple isolated act. The chief detective sensed the crime was rooted in the broader, enduring conflict between Montreal's Catholic and Protestant Irish communities.

The previous day, he had spent several hours with Thomas Ryan, a trusted friend who had outlined the structure of Montreal's Orangemen. This group of Protestant Irishmen, firmly established in the city, operated through a complex network. However, to balance his understanding, Robinson needed to delve into the other camp: the Fenians, radical Catholic Irish nationalists dreaming of liberation and revolution.

Bernard Devlin, a pivotal figure within Montreal's Irish community, was the man for the job. Ryan had been unequivocal: if anyone could shed light on the Fenians without being compromised, it was Devlin. As president of the St. Patrick Society, Devlin played a delicate role mediating between moderates and radicals. Robinson hoped their meeting would help untangle the complex web of this investigation.

The detective's frustration was palpable. It had been fifteen days since Monahan's body had been discovered, his face frozen in the grim cold of that dismal alley. Fifteen days chasing promising leads that proved as fleeting as smoke.

Every hour lost wore down his patience. Progress was imperative—and swiftly so.

Devlin enjoyed an enviable reputation: one of Canada's foremost criminal lawyers. His office was housed in the prestigious St. Lawrence Hall, a hotel of legendary elegance in Montreal. A factual nexus of power, the venue regularly hosted eminent figures like Governor Monk and John A. Macdonald, Canada's prime minister. Among its most celebrated visitors were the Prince of Wales and Charles Dickens, whose tour had captivated Montreal's high society.

When Robinson informed Miss Dupuis that he would meet Devlin accompanied by Kelly, she immediately protested, tightening her woollen shawl around her shoulders.
"But Chief, I could come with you."

He shook his head slowly, his expression serious.
"I'd rather not," he replied in a tone that brooked no argument. "Devlin is Irish to the core, a staunch nationalist. It's bad enough that a British bastard like me will hardly inspire his trust—imagine what he'd think if I showed up with a French Canadian."

Miss Dupuis raised an eyebrow.
"What grudge could the Irish possibly have against French Canadians?"

Robinson managed a weary smile, though his eyes betrayed a hint of impatience.

"You know the answer as well as I do. The relationship between our two communities is… let's say, complicated. As Catholics, the Irish and French Canadians should, in theory, get along. But the Irish speak English. And that complicates everything. French Canadians distrust them, seeing them as natural allies of the Anglo-Scots. And the Irish return the favour without hesitation."

"That's not always the case, though."

"No, you're right. But in politics, as in life, perceptions often outweigh the facts."

She opened her mouth to argue, but Robinson fixed her with a pointed look. Realizing the discussion was over, Miss Dupuis let out a resigned sigh.

The Brougham moved slowly through the heavy, wet snow. Large flakes splattered against the windows, forming a glistening veil that obscured the view of the sidewalk. The horses, shod with iron shoes, struggled to head on the slippery road, now coated with a thin layer of packed snow. The challenge was compounded by the tracks of the horse-drawn tramway, which they followed at a cautious distance. Bundled in a heavy wool coat, Robinson used the time to refine his interrogation strategy.

"Listen, Kelly, we'll need to stroke Devlin's ego. It's the only way to get what we want. And I'm counting on you for that."

Kelly, startled, looked up, his battered hat sitting askew.

"Mc? You must be joking, Chief. You know that's not my style."

"Precisely. I've known you for years, Kelly. A real Irish mule: hot-headed, sharp-tongued…"

"You have a fine way of paying compliments, Chief."

"And it serves you well, in most cases. But this time, I need you to take a different approach."

Kelly regarded him with a skeptical frown.

"You're asking me to go easy on him?"

"I'm asking you to win his trust. If anyone needs to press him hard, that'll fall to me."

"You're asking the impossible, Chief. It won't feel natural, that's certain."

"Make an effort. If we want to make headway in this case, we must adapt."

After a brief silence, Kelly nodded reluctantly.

"Fine, I'll try. But I'm not making any promises."

The Brougham finally came to a stop in front of St. Lawrence Hall. The classical-style building rose in perfect symmetry over four stories, each window on the second floor adorned with sculpted arches resting on delicate capitals. Lined with panoramic windows, the ground floor revealed warm, welcoming lights within—a promise of comfort for drenched travellers. Stone columns flanked the main entrance, which was unnecessary from a structural standpoint but added an understated elegance.

Under the wet snow, Robinson glanced at his companion, then adjusted the brim of his bowler hat to keep the melting flakes from sliding down his face.

"Ready, Kelly?"

"As ready as one can be in this cursed weather."

They stepped down from the carriage, determined to face Devlin and, perhaps, finally break open this infernal case.

Robinson and Kelly pushed through the heavy glass-panelled doors of the St. Lawrence Hall Hotel, leaving behind the damp and chilled air of Saint-Jacques Street. Inside, the establishment stood in stark contrast to the dreary scene outdoors. The richly panelled walls and glossy ceramic-tiled floors reflected the warm glow of gas chandeliers, enveloping the space in a hushed elegance. Gentlemen in frock coats, some puffing on cigars, crossed the lobby with the air of men accustomed to prosperity.

The two detectives approached the reception desk, where an attendant in impeccable livery greeted them with a professional, albeit slightly distant, smile.

"We are looking for Bernard Devlin's office," Robinson said confidently.

The man gestured toward a staircase carpeted with thick red plush.

"Mr. Devlin's office is on the first floor, gentlemen. Take the corridor to your left at the top of the stairs. His name is engraved on a brass plaque on the door—you can't miss it."

Climbing the stairs, their boots muffled by the plush carpet, they reached a hallway lined with heavy, dark wooden doors. Each step elicited a faint creak from the floorboards. The air carried a mingled scent of paper, ink, and tobacco— clearly indicating where business was conducted in words and documents.

Arriving at a door with a plaque that read *Bernard Devlin—Barrister*, Robinson glanced at Kelly before turning the handle. The door opened with a soft creak, revealing an office both practical and bustling with life.

Tall arched windows, partially obscured by olive-green damask curtains, admitted a pale, wintry light. The massive mahogany desk was cluttered with stacks of documents, ink pens, and a crystal inkwell. A porcelain cup, most likely containing the remnants of cold tea, sat beside an open file.

A few carved wooden chairs were arranged before the desk, ready to receive clients or colleagues. The cream-coloured walls bore framed engravings, certificates, and a large map of the United Province of Canada. In the corner, a cast-iron stove hummed softly, radiating a warmth that made the room pleasant despite the winter's chill. A small pile of logs and a poker lay nearby, evidence of careful attention to the room's comfort.

Robinson allowed himself a faint smile as his eyes landed on a top hat casually perched on a coat stand by the door.

"Here's a man who dislikes disorder… except on his desk," he murmured as he gently shut the door behind them.

Bernard Devlin had risen to greet them. Tall and solidly built, he wore a well-tailored black frock coat, only slightly creased, over an impeccably buttoned shirt—a testament to his meticulous nature. His short, curly brown hair lent him an air of distinction and authority, further emphasized by his sharp, almost piercing gaze, which seemed to take in every detail of his visitors. Yet his luxuriant and perfectly groomed moustache drew the most attention, framing his chin so precisely that it almost gave the impression of a goatee.

A note slipped into his box informed Devlin of their visit, and he offered them an affable smile. He gestured to two brown leather armchairs near the cast-iron stove, where a dying fire still radiated a welcome warmth.

"What brings the head of the Montreal Police Detectives to my office?" he asked in a playful tone. "Are you here to arrest me, perhaps?"

Robinson replied with a wry smile.

"Would I have a reason to do so, Mr. Devlin?"

The lawyer's laughter broke the tension, easing the atmosphere weighed down by the damp chill outside.

Bernard Devlin, a prominent lawyer and influential advisor, had built a formidable reputation. In addition to representing the Corporation of Montreal, he had made his mark prosecuting the infamous Confederate raiders responsible for the St. Albans Raid—men whose aim was to provoke a war between Great Britain and Lincoln's government. This blend of audacity and political calculation had only enhanced his standing, especially among Montreal's Irish Catholic community, where he was revered.

Kelly was the next to speak, clearing his throat as he addressed Devlin with respect and warmth.

"Mr. Devlin, it's truly a pleasure to meet you. As a police officer, I probably shouldn't say this—neutrality and all—but I must express my admiration for what you've done for our community."

As Robinson turned his head slightly, amused by his colleague's almost ceremonial tone, Devlin fixed his gaze on Kelly, a look of keen curiosity crossing his face.

"You're Irish, aren't you?"

"Born in the fair city of Cork," Kelly replied with a hint of pride.

"Cork? That's quite far from Roscommon, where my parents hailed from," Devlin retorted, a subtle smile on his lips.

"A fine region as well," Kelly admitted, then added, "Jack Kelly, at your service."

"A true Irish name, Mr. Kelly... But tell me, why exactly did you wish to see me?"

Robinson, who had maintained a strategic silence until then, nodded to prompt his colleague to continue. Kelly took the cue, his tone growing more serious.

"Your reputation precedes you, Mr. Devlin. You're one of the most influential figures in our community. Your role as president of the St. Patrick's Society attests to that. If I'm not mistaken, it's under your leadership that the society became exclusively Catholic, is it not?"

Devlin crossed his arms, his gaze turning sharper.

"Indeed. Protestants no longer have a place in our society. We needed to preserve our values."

"Precisely," Kelly replied. "That's why we believe you might be an invaluable ally in helping us with our investigation."

Devlin, his expression growing more guarded, sank into his armchair. His gaze shifted alternately between Kelly and Robinson.

"An investigation, you say? And what kind of investigation might that be?"

Robinson took over, crossing his arms as he leaned slightly against the back of his chair.

"You may not be aware, but a murder was committed in Griffintown a few weeks ago. An Irishman was killed."

Devlin narrowed his eyes, a mix of surprise and gravity crossing his face.

"Ah! In Griffintown! The poorest Irish community in Canada… My compatriots there lead such wretched lives. The cold, mud, and epidemics… suffer greatly from their circumstances. I feel deeply for them."

"Forgive me for saying so, Mr. Devlin," Robinson interjected, "but I've spoken with many prominent Irish figures. You're the first to express such compassion for the residents of Griffintown. Usually, they're blamed for every ill."

Devlin leaned back in his chair, crossing his legs. His hands came together in a contemplative gesture.

"I'm well aware," he replied in a measured tone. "I often find myself defending them to my wealthier compatriots. Money, you see, has a troublesome way of clouding memory. People forget too quickly where they came from. We weren't poor when I was growing up, but my father, a just and humble man, taught me to respect those who work hard to make a living. 'Never forget, Bernard,' he said, 'those people who put food on your plate daily.' Those words have never left me."

A brief silence settled, punctuated only by the crackling of the fire in the stove. The flickering light cast shifting shadows across the room, lending their conversation a sense of weight. Kelly, listening intently, straightened slightly in his chair.

"You deeply love your people; that is clear, Mr. Devlin. And, indeed, life in Ireland has never been easy."

Devlin offered a sad smile, his gaze fixed on the worn carpet covering the floor.

"That's putting it mildly," he sighed. "Great Britain has never done us any favours, especially since what little autonomy we had was stripped away by the Act of Union and handed to Westminster. In our own country, we're treated as second-class citizens."

Kelly nodded, his face betraying a simmering anger.

"I couldn't agree more. And the Great Famines—what a disgrace! Honestly, I sometimes wonder why the Irish haven't risen up."

Devlin lifted his eyes to Kelly, his expression a mix of thoughtfulness and caution. For a moment, he seemed to weigh his words, his gaze drifting toward the fogged-up window, where the contrast between the warmth inside and the icy wind outside blurred the glass.

Finally, he said, "I believe the time for Ireland's liberation is drawing near," his tone measured.

Kelly leaned forward slightly.

"Do you truly believe that?"

Devlin raised an eyebrow, his eyes glinting with a newfound intensity.

"You must be aware of the unrest shaking Ireland and the following brutal repression."

"Yes," Kelly replied gravely. "You're speaking of the Fenians, aren't you?"

A faint smile touched Devlin's lips as though he were fully aware of the word's weight. He straightened in his armchair, his arms resting on the padded sides, ready to delve into what promised to be a delicate yet compelling conversation.

Robinson spoke up, his eyes fixed on Devlin, his tone calm but incisive.

"Yes, the Fenians. That radical group of Irish Catholics. It's primarily why we're here. We've heard you might have information about the Fenians in Montreal."

At this, Devlin leaned back slightly in his chair. His expression, warm and cordial until now, hardened abruptly, his features shutting down like a door slammed shut.

"Ah, I see! You've been speaking with my 'friend' D'Arcy McGee," he said, heavily emphasizing the word "friend."

Robinson's brow furrowed slightly, intrigued by the reaction.

"No, not at all. Should we have?"

Devlin let out a bitter smile.

"And yet, D'Arcy McGee loudly proclaims to anyone who will listen that I'm a sympathizer of the Fenians. What an unpleasant man!"

"And... are you a Fenian, Mr. Devlin?" Robinson interjected, his tone growing more direct.

Devlin lifted his chin slightly, his gaze defiant.

"I have never hidden the fact that I am an Irish nationalist. Yes, I want freedom for my compatriots in Ireland. Does that make me a Fenian in your eyes?"

"But that is precisely what the Fenians want, right?"

"In Ireland, I can understand their determination to seek freedom by any means, even through violence," Devlin conceded. "I understand… but that doesn't mean I approve of their methods."

Kelly sat slightly back, straightened, and spoke up.

"And what about the Fenians here, Mr. Devlin?"

Devlin averted his eyes momentarily, staring at the window where cold rain mixed with melting snow slid lazily down the glass. His tone grew graver.

"I am entirely opposed to their efforts to bring their war to Canada. We are not Great Britain."

"Yet," Robinson said, leaning forward slightly, "isn't it said that they've been organizing for years in the United States to invade Canada? Their plan, as I hear it, is to destabilize the British Empire by provoking a war. If Canada were annexed by the United States, it could inspire revolution in Ireland."

Devlin fixed him with an intense stare, his fingers drumming nervously on the arm of his chair.

"You seem better informed than I am about their intentions, Inspector."

"You know more than you're letting on," Robinson countered. "I have reliable sources claiming that the St. Patrick Society has been infiltrated by Fenians."

Devlin let out a short, bitter laugh.

"More rumours spread by my dear D'Arcy McGee. Yes, we have Fenians in our ranks; that's undeniable. Yes, they'd like our actions to be more radical. But to believe that the St. Patrick Society is their stronghold? That's absurd."

"So many Irish support their cause?" Kelly asked, his tone more conciliatory.

Devlin shook his head, a sigh escaping his lips.

"No, far from it. The majority of the Irish share their patriotism and opposition to British rule, but very few support the radicalism of the Fenians."

Kelly nodded slowly, as if in agreement, before continuing in a more personal tone.

"I understand, Mr. Devlin. I don't usually talk about my private life, but my wife, Nora, is an Irish Catholic. She comes from a family in Derry."

Devlin straightened, surprised.

"A Catholic from Derry, in Ulster? That must not have been easy. Orangemen are everywhere in that region."

"No, it wasn't," Kelly replied gravely. "She doesn't talk about it much, but I know it was tough. In Derry, Catholics were constantly targeted. Parades were attacked, the streets became battlegrounds, and there were injuries, sometimes deaths. That's what drove her parents to leave Ireland for Canada. But even here, in Montreal, we face similar tensions."

Devlin nodded, his expression marked by a sombre understanding.

"It is certain that Protestant and Catholic Irish live in separate worlds."

"They call us papists, slaves to Rome…" Kelly added with restrained bitterness.

"…and they see themselves as more loyal to the Crown than the Queen herself," Devlin finished, a brief, ironic smile crossing his face.

Kelly fixed him with a serious look.

"You understand why I wouldn't hold it against you if you told me you were part of the Fenians. After all, they are the mortal enemies of the Orangemen."

Devlin, his irritation suddenly rising, lightly tapped the arm of his chair.

"Listen to me, Inspector! I have just formed a volunteer militia to fight the Fenians at the border. Do you seriously think I could condone their actions after that?"

A heavy silence followed his declaration, broken only by the crackling of the stove's fire. Outside, the wind whistled softly, carrying stray snowflakes, as if to underline the fragility of peace on this cold March day.

Robinson resumed in a calmer tone, raising a hand as if to temper the exchange.

"Forgive my colleague, Mr. Devlin. That's not what he meant. We are dealing with a particularly complex investigation, and we are severely lacking in information. We need your help to identify the most radical elements among the Fenians, those who might even resort to murder."

Devlin leaned forward slightly, his elbows resting on the desk. Silence fell again, punctuated only by the scratch of the wind against the windows. Finally, he lifted his head, his brow furrowed.

"It's that serious? You believe a Fenian might have wanted another Irishman dead?"

"That is exactly what we believe," Robinson replied gravely.

Devlin shook his head slowly, visibly troubled.

"Unacceptable, of course. It is one thing to kill enemy soldiers in the fight for freedom and quite another to assassinate one of our own. That is betrayal. I am willing to provide you with a list of names… but understand this: I'm not saying that any one of them could be a murderer."

Robinson straightened slightly in his chair, crossing his arms, his gaze growing more direct.

"You don't know me yet, Mr. Devlin. Rest assured, I conduct my investigations with the utmost rigour and caution. Never, I repeat, never have I wrongfully condemned an innocent man."

A flash of defiance shone in Devlin's eyes, but he finally inclined his head.

"Very well," he said at last. "I will trust you."

He opened a drawer of dark wood, drew out a blank sheet of paper, and, after a brief hesitation, began to write a list of names. His pen scratched against the paper, the sound echoing faintly in the quiet room. Once finished, he handed the document to Robinson.

"Here. These are the most radical Fenians I know. Some openly advocate violence in their writings. Do with this what you will, but tread carefully."

Robinson took the paper and slipped it into the inner pocket of his thick wool coat. He nodded in acknowledgment.

"Thank you for your help, Mr. Devlin," Kelly said warmly. "Keep up your excellent work. And if I may say so, the St. Patrick's Day procession you organized was remarkable—a true show of solidarity!"

Devlin allowed himself a faint smile, pride softening his features.

"Thank you. It's good to hear that."

After a firm handshake, the two detectives bid Devlin farewell and left the room. They descended the wooden staircase, their footsteps echoing faintly in the cold, dim hallway.

Outside, a fine, almost slushy snow continued to fall from the leaden sky, quickly clinging to their thick coats. Their boots sank into the typical spring mixture of slush and mud-lined Montreal's streets.

Robinson turned to Kelly, a smirk on his face.

"You overdid it a bit back there, Kelly. Don't you think?"

Kelly shrugged, his mischievous grin lighting up his face, reddened by the cold.

"Oh, really? Do you think so? I may be softening up. My Nora would be pleased to hear that."

Robinson chuckled quietly, pulling his coat tighter against the cold.

"I'll be sure to let her know."

"Don't you dare!" Kelly replied with a burst of laughter. "She loves me just as I am."

The two detectives left St. Lawrence Hall as the snow began to ease. Knowing it would be futile to hail a Brougham at this hour, they paused briefly to watch a horse-drawn tramway laboriously inch forward, nearly at a snail's pace. A simple exchange of glances was enough to decide that walking back to the police station would be faster. Around them, the city seemed frozen in an oppressive stillness, and the biting cold, amplified by a light breeze, reminded them with every step of the relentless harshness of their time.

CHAPTER 16

March 29, Wednesday Evening

Thérèse, or Miss Dupuis as her colleagues called her, was sharing a simple yet heartwarming meal with her parents that evening. Outside, a bitter wind swept through Montreal's deserted streets, stirring snow flurries that danced in the dim light of the street lamps. The modest row house, humble yet inviting, was a haven against the harshness of winter. The soft crackle of wood in the hearth warmed the room while the savoury aromas of simmering stew and freshly baked bread filled the air, enveloping the family in a cocoon of comfort.

The dining room, unpretentious and functional in design, bore a few personal touches. A hand-embroidered tablecloth adorned the sturdy wooden table, and a narrow shelf laden with enamelled dishes stood against the wall. Small engravings of pastoral scenes, clad in simple wallpaper, decorated the walls, offering a quiet nod to a love of nature and simplicity. Candles, arranged at the table's centre and atop the furnishings, cast flickering light that played gentle shadows across the room.

Thérèse's mother, Rosalie, wore a dark grey woollen dress, cinched at the waist with a pristine white apron. Her hair, streaked with silver, was gathered into a simple bun, and she exuded a calmness tinged with maternal pride. She poured a steaming cup of tea for her daughter, the amber liquid releasing a delicate fragrance of bergamot.

"How is the move coming along?" she asked, her soft voice breaking the peaceful quiet.

Thérèse set her tin-plated spoon down with a faint clink against her faience plate. She wore a practical brown wool dress paired with a shawl draped over her shoulders to ward off the lingering chill of the room. Her cheeks were still faintly flushed, a trace of the cold she had braved earlier.

"It's coming along well," she replied with a smile. "There's hardly anything left to bring over."

Rosalie nodded thoughtfully, her hands instinctively smoothing the corner of her apron—a gesture she often made when lost in thought.

"And do you like it there?" she asked, her eyes sincere with curiosity.

"I've found a small apartment in the Mile End," Thérèse answered, sitting up slightly straighter. "It's not much, but it's enough for me. I don't need more."

Rosalie's smile, tinged with nostalgia, reflected both tenderness and a hint of concern.

"You know, this house will always be yours," she murmured after a moment, as though reluctant to disturb the tranquil moment.

Thérèse, her fingers idly tracing the rim of her cup, looked up and returned a smile—small but resolute.

"I know, Mama. But it's time for me to spread my wings. And with my new job…"

Thérèse sat upright on her wooden chair, her voice a mix of determination and enthusiasm. Her shawl, loosely draped over her shoulders, revealed the simple yet refined collar of her wool dress. She placed her spoon on the edge of her plate, her eyes bright in the soft candlelight.

"—Temporary," interrupted Silas, her stepfather, raising a finger as though to underscore his point. "Don't forget."

Silas, dressed in a dark waistcoat and neatly buttoned white shirt, leaned back against his chair. Though laced with mild reproach, his voice was softened by a wry smile. The firelight at the centre of the room played across his weathered features, revealing a blend of experience and affection.

Thérèse couldn't help but smile at his remark, her cheeks warming slightly from the ambient heat and her stepfather's kind attention.

"Temporary! Perhaps for now," she replied, her eyes glinting with spirit. "But I know how to make myself indispensable."

Silas chuckled, shaking his head lightly.

"That, my dear, I do not doubt," he said, sipping tea, the steam curling gently above his favourite, slightly chipped porcelain cup.

Thérèse, folding her hands on the table, continued with quiet confidence.

"With my salary and a few small jobs at my photographer's studio, I'm managing just fine."

After a moment, Rosalie fixed her gaze on her daughter with curiosity and amusement, her eyes sparkling beneath her greying curls. The flickering light of a candle resting atop a small commode illuminated her face softly, casting a dancing shadow on the wallpapered wall behind her. Around them, the air seemed filled with the whispers of memories—the furniture's polished surfaces, worn by years of care, and the lingering scent of warm wood imbued the house with its history. Near the hearth stood a slightly worn wicker chair adorned with a hand-embroidered cushion, a testament to their simple pursuit of true comfort. The atmosphere, though tranquil, held the soothing warmth of a home where every object told a story.

"There's a man involved, without a doubt," Rosalie said, narrowing her eyes slightly, her smile betraying a playful affection.

Thérèse blushed despite herself, glancing away momentarily before shaking her head gently.

"Not at all!" she replied, her voice rising slightly under the weight of emotion. "I enjoy my freedom. That doesn't mean I don't love you, of course."

Rosalie, still smiling, set her teacup down and tilted her head slightly, her hands folded on the table as if restraining a comment. The room's ambiance, cradled by the warmth and flickering candlelight, remained intimate and comforting—a perfect setting for this tender family conversation. She took her daughter's hand with a rekindled tenderness, her fingers roughened by years of household work pressing gently against Thérèse's.

"That, I know well, my Pouponette," Rosalie murmured with a smile.

The old nickname drew a soft laugh from Thérèse, her cheeks flushing faintly. It had been so long since her mother had called her that! The endearment, drawn from her childhood, conjured memories of a round, innocent face Rosalie had so often kissed. In the dim light of the candles and hearth, a shadow of nostalgia flickered in Thérèse's eyes.

She squeezed her mother's hand briefly to prolong the moment of closeness before sitting up slightly. Then, releasing her hand, she took her teacup with the grace of a bourgeois lady.

"By the way, Silas," she said, breaking the stillness, "I have news of Frasa. I ran into Shannon at the market yesterday, quite by chance. She was with a Sister. They were shopping for her sick mother, and that's how I learned where Frasa is."

Sitting at the other end of the table, Silas set his teacup down with a soft clink against the saucer. His furrowed brows betrayed growing curiosity.

"Well then. So Frasa is alive and well, I presume?" he said, a trace of irony softening his words.

Thérèse nodded gently, a faint smile on her lips, before responding.

"She wrote Shannon a long letter. It seems she and Rowan are staying with his aunt in the village of Saint-Laurent."

Silas's brow furrowed slightly, a mixture of interest and suspicion crossing his features.

"Rowan's aunt?" he asked, tilting his head slightly.

"Yes," Thérèse continued, her tone now serious. "They took refuge there after Rowan had a violent falling out with his father. He left the house and went to fetch Frasa from the boarding school. They ran away together."

Rosalie, who had been listening attentively while adjusting the collar of her apron, glanced at Silas. The hearth murmured softly in the background, its warmth wrapping around the room as snow continued to fall outside.

"And the aunt took them in without question?" Silas asked, setting his teacup down carefully.

Thérèse nodded, her eyes glinting with a hint of amusement.

"Apparently so. Her uncle is a farmer in the village. Rowan claimed he needed help on the farm to justify staying with them."

Silas leaned back against his chair, which creaked softly under his weight. His gaze wandered to a framed engraving on the wall—a pastoral scene, perhaps reminiscent of the fields where Rowan now worked.

"And they're safe?" he asked at last.

Thérèse nodded, her hands clasped together on the table.

"Yes," she replied with confidence. "But Shannon told me Mr. D'Arcy McGee is very distressed about his daughter's disappearance."

A silence followed her words, broken only by the faint whistling of the wind slipping through the cracks of the window. Rosalie straightened slightly, her silhouette illuminated by the glow of the hearth.

"I understand his concern," said Silas gravely. "But for now, there's no crime. They're just two young people in love. Nothing more."

Rosalie, crossing her arms around herself as if to keep warm, murmured with a hint of unease, "Still, it's troubling, this whole affair."

Silas raised his shoulders slightly, deep in thought. His gaze turned to Thérèse, studying her face as though searching for a hidden emotion. A faint shadow crossed the young woman's features, but she quickly regained her composure and offered a small smile.

"It affects you, doesn't it?" Silas asked gently, his voice softened by genuine curiosity.

Thérèse, absently staring at her porcelain teacup, lifted her eyes to meet his.

"Yes, I suppose," she admitted, accompanied by an almost imperceptible sigh. "With everything happening in the world, seeing two young people love each other so deeply, it…"

She let her sentence trail off, a melancholy smile brushing her lips. Sitting back against his chair, Silas gazed at his stepdaughter with a profound and affectionate look.

"… It reminds us of the better side of human nature," he finished softly, his fingers tapping lightly on the wooden armrest.

Thérèse nodded, though her expression was tinged with hesitation, which she made no effort to conceal.

"Perhaps," she conceded after a moment. "But I'm not sure their story will endure."

A comfortable silence followed, interrupted only by the soft crackling of the fire in the hearth. The gentle yet insistent warmth filled the room, a stark contrast to the icy gusts of wind that occasionally seeped under the front door. On the walls, framed engravings of snowy landscapes mirrored the winter beyond, while the clock's steady ticking punctuated the dining room's calm.

The meal concluded in thoughtful quiet, each lost in their own reflections. Rosalie quietly cleared the table, her precise movements honed by years of habit. Once the dishes were neatly placed in the polished wooden sideboard, Rosalie and

Silas retired to the adjacent parlour. Seated near the parlour hearth, they immersed themselves in their evening routine. Rosalie read a French novel, her lips moving soundlessly. At the same time, Silas turned the newspaper pages leisurely, his round glasses occasionally slipping to the tip of his nose.

A few minutes later, Thérèse reappeared, returning from what had once been her bedroom. Her arms were laden with canvas bags, brimming with her belongings. The sturdy leather soles of her boots creaked slightly against the well-maintained floorboards, drawing Rosalie's gaze.

"Do you want help?" Rosalie asked gently, though the answer was already apparent.

Thérèse shook her head with a smile.

"No, no. I'll hail a Hansom cab. Thank you, Mama. I still have some unpacking to do."

Setting her bags down briefly, she kissed Rosalie and Silas, a gesture of tenderness and respect. Then, opening the front door, she was met with a blast of icy air that swept into the house, causing the flames in the hearth to flicker.

The night was calm and deep, the ground blanketed with a fine layer of fresh snow that crunched beneath her feet. Her breath formed soft plumes in the frosty air, and the wavering light of a streetlamp timidly lit her path. Her boots left crisp prints in the powdery snow, a fleeting trail that the next gust of wind would erase.

Soon, the steady clatter of a horse's hooves broke the stillness of the street. A cab pulled up in front of her, and Thérèse climbed aboard, offering the driver a brief greeting. The carriage rolled away, vanishing into the shadows.

Rosalie, who had risen and drawn back the curtain, stood at the misted window, watching the carriage lanterns disappear around the corner of the street.

CHAPTER 17

March 30, Thursday Afternoon

Fred Penton's office was bathed in a pale light filtered through frosted windowpanes. An oil lamp cast an unsteady flame.

In the corridors of the police station, Robinson's footsteps echoed heavily on the worn wooden floor, amplified by the place's austere silence. When he pushed open the office door, a wave of stifling heat greeted him, thick with the metallic tang of a glowing wood stove. The room, oppressively warm, was steeped in a peculiar dampness, where the ambient humidity mingled with the acrid scent of fresh ink.

"Close the door!" barked a sharp, authoritative voice.

Fred Penton, the police chief, was bent over his meticulously organized desk, where every file, quill, and inkwell seemed to have been arranged with painstaking precision. He barely glanced up, his ascetic face etched with severe lines, sharply outlined in the flickering shadows of the oil lamp.

Robinson, dressed in a thick brown coat layered over a well-fitted jacket and an impeccably white shirt, discreetly adjusted a scarf draped loosely around his neck before shutting the door with measured care.

"I instructed you to update me daily on the progress of your investigation," Penton growled, tapping his desk impatiently with his long fingers.

"I hadn't understood that you required a report every day," Robinson replied with apparent calm, his hands folded neatly on his lap.

Penton abruptly scowled and struck the table, sending a quill rolling to the floor.

"Why don't you follow my orders? What part of my instructions do you not understand? What have you done this week, hmm?"

"Well, that is to say—"

"Not a single visit. Not a word is written! Have you been working or taking a holiday?"

Robinson straightened his posture slightly, meeting Penton's glare with steady determination.

"Chief, I understand your frustration. But that doesn't give you the right to disrespect me or my team."

Penton clenched his jaw and bent to pick up the fallen quill. His fingers, trembling slightly, carefully returned it to its place on the desk as though seeking to reassert his composure. After a moment of silence, he nodded.

"You're right. I went too far," he conceded in a quieter tone. "But you must understand, Robinson, this case weighs heavily on me. Monahan was no ordinary man—a fellow Protestant and an Orangeman at that…"

Robinson raised an eyebrow.

"You're an Orangeman as well?"

"Of course! I'm proud to belong to the Grand Orange Lodge of Montreal. Do you have a problem with that?"

Robinson folded his arms with measured nonchalance, leaning back in the chair, which creaked in protest. Fixing his gaze on Penton, he posed a question to which he already knew the answer.

"But isn't it true that Orangemen are exclusively Irish Protestants? You're British, after all," Robinson added.

"Exactly. Born in Southampton. And that makes me a proud supporter of the Queen and the British Empire… of which we are a colony, Robinson. Don't forget that!"

A tense silence settled between them. Penton picked up a quill and began scribbling something, but his erratic and jittery handwriting betrayed his pent-up tension.

"Do you know what the greatest threat to Canada is?" he finally asked without lifting his eyes.

"You're going to tell me, I assume."

"The Romish Church, Robinson. The Catholic Church and its leader, Pope Pius IX."

Robinson shrugged slightly, a wry smile playing at the corner of his lips.

"Oh, really? That's terrible, is it? How many soldiers does he command?"

Penton slammed the quill down, his piercing eyes locking onto Robinson's.

"You jest, but it's serious. The papists conspire wherever they have numbers. Here, in Lower Canada, they are the majority. And with those cursed Catholic Irish flooding over the past twenty years, the threat is growing. Yes, Robinson, we are in danger."

Robinson drew a deep breath.

"Perhaps. But that should not distract us from our mission. Catholic or Protestant, our job remains the same: to catch those who break the law."

Penton straightened abruptly.

"Very well! But don't lose sight of the fact that, in this particular case, it's a Protestant Orangeman who's been murdered. And quite likely by a Catholic. Find me the culprit, Robinson. And quickly."

"That's precisely what we're doing."

"You have leads, at least?"

"A few."

"It's those Fenians, I'm certain of it! Those radical Irish Catholics…"

"We're exploring that angle, yes."

"Do you have suspects?"

"We do," Robinson replied, his face expressionless.

"Then give me their names."

Robinson hesitated, studying his superior's tense features. After deliberation, he pulled out a crumpled list of suspects, hastily scrawled by Bernard Devlin. Penton nearly snatched it from his hands and began reading, his eyebrows rising as he deciphered the names.

"Who is their leader?"

"Francis Brennan. A Montreal businessman, an importer of wool."

Penton, silent, copied the names onto a sheet of paper. Robinson frowned, watching the scene with growing unease.

"If I may, Chief... This list should remain with the investigators until we have stronger evidence."

Penton set his pen down with a sharp click.

"Do you think I am some petty scribbler ready to divulge information recklessly?"

"Of course not. But caution is always advisable."

"I understand. Now, get back to work. And don't leave me in the dark for so long again."

"Understood, Chief," Robinson replied as he rose, loosening his scarf slightly before stepping out of the office, leaving behind the oppressive and overheated atmosphere of the room.

Robinson entered the detectives' office, shutting the door sharply behind him. The air was heavy with the stale smell of cold tobacco and yellowed paper, deepening the tension already hanging in the room. His three deputies were huddled around a table, casting furtive glances at their Chief. Robinson's expression was grim, his lips set in a bitter line.

"Something wrong, Chief?" asked Miss Dupuis, tucking a stray strand of hair back into her carefully arranged bun.

Robinson folded his arms and leaned against the wall.

"No, it's not fine. Penton just gave me an earful. That man is an utter incompetent. Doesn't know the first thing about police work. God, how I sometimes miss Ermatinger! But enough about him. Where do we stand?"

Morin rubbed the back of his neck, hesitating.

"We're not making much progress, Chief. Two weeks have passed since Monahan's murder, and after dropping the lead about the argument between Murphy and Walsh, we've got next to nothing."

Miss Dupuis, ever attentive, chimed in:

"By the way, what's happening with Walsh?"

Kelly, balancing precariously on his chair, which seemed on the verge of collapse, answered in a weary tone:

"They brought him before a judge. He'll stand trial for the bank robbery."

"Well, at least that's one case solved," she remarked with a shrug.

"Yeah," Kelly muttered, staring at the table.

"You don't seem too pleased, Kelly," Miss Dupuis pressed.

Kelly sighed and let his chair thud back onto all four legs.

"Bah! That guy didn't rob a bank for himself but to help his community. It's still a shame he's ending up in prison."

"What do you mean?"

"He was trying to set up a trade union for the Grand Trunk workers. Poor devils are underpaid and can barely feed their families."

Morin, who had been silent until now, responded with a hint of suspicion:

"Since when do you care about those people, Kelly?"

"Since always," Kelly shot back, bristling. "Don't forget I'm Irish. Us Irish have never had the best slice of the pie in this country."

Morin crossed his arms, his expression darkening.

"And you think the French Canadians are better off? Maybe we don't live in Griffintown, but our neighborhoods are just as wretched. We built this country, and look where we are after the English conquest."

Kelly let out a short, almost mocking laugh.

"Well, would you look at that! Seems we've got ourselves a rebel Patriote in the room!"

Robinson raised his hand, commanding silence.

"Enough. These political discussions won't get us anywhere. What matters is our investigation. Who killed Monahan, and more importantly, why?"

Miss Dupuis, ever pragmatic, suggested, "We could go back to your initial intuition, Chief. A quarrel between Irish Catholics and Protestants."

Morin, skeptical, shook his head. "That's a pretty vague lead. How are we supposed to find a killer with so little to go on?"

Robinson fixed him with a piercing gaze. "You know, Morin, sometimes you must take a detour to reach your goal. The most direct path isn't always the best one in criminal investigations. You can know the facts, the circumstances, but without the motive, it all falls apart."

Morin shrugged, still unconvinced. "But time is running out, Chief. And you're always saying every minute counts."

Robinson nodded, but his expression remained grave. "True, time is precious. But in the end, only the result matters. Let me tell you a story."

He perched on the table's edge, his voice taking on a more narrative tone.

"Once, I worked a case where a woman had been poisoned. It wasn't an accident; we were certain of that. All the evidence pointed to her husband: no alibi, access to rat poison, opportunity to slip it into her tea. But there was no motive. Everything suggested he loved his wife. Naturally, we had to believe it."

Morin frowned, intrigued. "And then?"

"At the time, autopsies were rudimentary. Just before we brought him to trial, we discovered the woman had been pregnant. She hadn't told her husband and had tried to abort the child. A quack gave her a deadly concoction. If we had relied solely on circumstantial evidence, the husband would have ended up on the gallows. Everything was against him…"

Morin nodded, deep in thought. "…Except the motive," he concluded. "I see your point. The motive is crucial. In this case, what would the motive be for killing Monahan?"

"That's precisely what we're trying to uncover. Miss Dupuis gave me an intriguing idea: what if we're dealing with a ruthless fratricidal struggle?"

"Enemies among brothers?" Morin repeated, frowning.

Robinson nodded and elaborated, "Between Irish Catholics and Irish Protestants."

Morin straightened slightly in his chair, crossing his arms. "I know a bit about those two groups. Do you really think they'd go as far as murder? Those bloody clashes were in the past and another place, weren't they?"

"And what if those conflicts had crossed time and the Atlantic, continuing here and now in our city?" Robinson replied gravely.

"You think that's possible?"

"Not only possible but certain, based on the information we've gathered recently."

The Chief paused, letting his deputies absorb his words, before continuing:

"The Orangemen, those Irish Protestants—of which Monahan was one—are engaged in a constant struggle against Irish Catholics, whom they call 'papists.' Their fanaticism for the Queen, the British Empire, and the Protestant religion makes them particularly aggressive. Opposing them are the Fenians, those radical Irish Catholics gaining influence. In the United States, their movement is growing at an alarming rate, and here in Montreal, they're beginning to make waves."

Miss Dupuis, attentive, fixed her gaze on Robinson.

"Why would the Fenians specifically target the Orangemen?"

"It's not just the Orangemen they oppose but everything they represent. To the Fenians, the Orangemen embody British oppression, the force crushing Ireland. They believe there will be no salvation for their people as long as the current political system in Britain endures."

A heavy silence settled over the room, each person's thoughts drifting in the smoky air. The sunlight, still cold and pale despite the arrival of spring, filtered through the grimy windows, casting shadows on the gray walls.

Morin finally broke the pause.

"All this is good in theory, but it doesn't bring us much closer to solving the murder."

Robinson turned toward him.

"You're right. It's time to focus on solid evidence. Let us review what we know."

He raised his thumb.

"First: Monahan, a Protestant Orangeman, was stabbed in Griffintown, a neighborhood densely populated by Irish Catholics in Montreal. That can't be a mere coincidence."

Then, he raised his index finger.

"Second: He was a spy hired by the government to infiltrate the Fenians. Someone must have uncovered his double-dealing."

His middle finger joined the count.

"Third: Monahan was being watched. Whoever killed him knew he would be at Ann Scanlan's tavern on St. Patrick's night."

Finally, he raised his ring finger, his piercing gaze sweeping the room.

"Fourth: The murder happened that night for a reason. A rowdy St. Patrick's celebration in a crowded neighborhood was the perfect opportunity to strike unnoticed. This crime was premeditated."

Morin nodded slowly, then remarked, "So, we must focus on Montreal's Fenians. That won't be easy. There are a lot of them."

"Not as many as you think," Robinson replied. "According to our informant Bernard Devlin, their ranks are smaller than they let on. And among them, those capable of committing a murder are even fewer. That's why the list Devlin provided us is critical."

Miss Dupuis spoke up, her tone more determined.

"So, we have a lead to follow. These names could bring us closer to the truth."

"Exactly," Robinson concluded, tapping the table with his fingertips. "But we must proceed cautiously. This murder is a tangled knot of politics, religion, and revenge. Every mistake could cost us dearly."

"There's still one question," Miss Dupuis said, crossing her arms and fixing Robinson with a piercing look. "How did the Fenians discover Monahan's true identity? After all, he blended in well among the Irish."

"Excellent question, Dupuis. Do you happen to have an answer?" Robinson asked, raising an eyebrow.

"Not exactly… Just a theory, perhaps. What if he was careless enough to confide his secret to someone? And that person betrayed him?"

"To someone… or some woman," Kelly added, leaning casually against the table.

"Pillow talk?" Miss Dupuis murmured with a sly smile. "Yes, that would make sense."

"Oh, Miss Dupuis, you scandalize me!" Kelly exclaimed, a broad grin spreading across his face. "A young lady like you shouldn't have such thoughts!"

Miss Dupuis only smiled a mischievous glint in her eyes before replying, "Perhaps. But it's worth investigating. It's not improbable. There's bound to be a woman involved."

She paused briefly as if gathering her thoughts, then continued, "Do you know what I've learned about the Fenians? As we know, these people form a secret society, with every member sworn to keep the group's secrets, which makes infiltrating them difficult. But here's something interesting: they debated whether to allow women into their ranks during one of their founding congresses."

Kelly straightened, intrigued.

"Well, well… Women in a secret society? Now that's an unusual idea."

"Exactly!" Miss Dupuis said, pointing a finger at him. "They thought so, too. But do you know why they ultimately decided against it?"

"I bet it's because they thought women weren't strong enough to fight!"

"No, wrong answer, Kelly." Miss Dupuis paused theatrically, then quoted, "Because of their inability to keep a secret."

A burst of laughter erupted in the room, with Miss Dupuis laughing the loudest. Even Robinson allowed himself a faint smile.

"That may explain quite a bit," Robinson said, regaining his serious demeanor. "If Monahan confided in a woman from Griffintown, it wouldn't be surprising if she revealed his secret to the Fenians."

Kelly nodded thoughtfully.

"Griffintown, always Griffintown! Everything leads back to that neighborhood. If that's the case, what kind of woman could she be? A prostitute, perhaps? There's no shortage of them there."

Robinson nodded slowly.

"It's a possibility. Whoever she is, we'll need to find her."

Morin frowned, skeptical.

"Finding this woman, Chief, won't get us much closer to solving Monahan's murder."

"That's true, but it would at least tell us how the Fenians discovered he was a spy. And it would confirm that the crime was premeditated and likely coordinated."

Kelly chimed in.

"You think they might have hired someone to do the job?"

"Perhaps," Robinson replied, rubbing his chin. "But it's more likely that one of the Fenians carried it out themselves. In the meantime, let's focus on the names from their list. Dupuis, I want you to discreetly investigate these men."

Miss Dupuis nodded, though a wry smile touched her lips.

"That may take some time, Chief. Several days, perhaps. I can't just walk up to any Irishman on Wellington Street and ask, 'Do you know a Fenian who wants to destroy our country?'"

"You could always use your legendary charm, Dupuis," Kelly quipped, giving her a wink.

She let out a small laugh, shrugging.

"Alas, my charm doesn't work on everyone. If it did, this job would be far easier."

Robinson nodded.

"Do your best. For now, we'll take this one step at a time."

With a biting tone, Kelly added, "Monahan's corpse isn't going anywhere, after all."

"Carry on with your regular tasks, and we'll regroup on Monday," Robinson ordered, gathering the papers on his desk. "Dupuis, I trust you'll have some information by then."

"You can count on me, Chief."

Robinson paused momentarily, observing his team with satisfaction at their resolve, then concluded, "I have no doubt, Dupuis. No doubt at all."

CHAPTER 18

April 3, Monday Morning

This April morning, the biting wind whistled through the streets of Montreal, slipping through every crack and crevice and carrying with it the damp scent of spring mixed with the soot of chimney smoke. Beneath a low sky heavy with grey clouds, the city still seemed drowsy, reluctant to shed the grip of winter. A meagre warmth emanated from the room's lone stove inside the cramped detective's office. Oil lamps cast flickering light upon the worn walls.

Rickety and overburdened shelves brimmed with crumpled files and old newspapers—silent witnesses to past investigations. The air was steeped in the scent of aged wood and yellowed paper, broken only by the occasional creak of a chair or the faint rustle of paper, the sole disturbances to the studious calm.

Miss Dupuis stood at her worktable, draped in a thick shawl that hung from her shoulders. She held a dark leather-bound notebook, worn by hours spent meticulously recording her observations. Behind her, the frosted panes of a small window let in a dim, grey light, heightening the austerity of the scene.

The assistant to Robinson, methodical and focused, had devoted the past days to combing through dusty ledgers, questioning discreet sources, and connecting seemingly unrelated clues. Today, she finally held the information needed to initiate their operation. Absentmindedly tucking a stray lock of hair behind her ear, she raised her head and declared:

"We have five Fenian names. Their leader in Montreal is Francis Brennan. He runs a small Scottish wool import business near the Lachine Canal. His accountant is William Mansfield."

Robinson, who had been standing slightly apart, nodded slowly before replying in a measured tone:
"Miss Dupuis and I will take care of them."

Miss Dupuis inclined her head and continued in a calm but resolute voice:
"Next, we have William Linehan, a tailor whose shop is in Griffintown. As for Daniel Lyons, a cobbler, he has a stall next to Linehan's."

She produced two neatly folded papers from her notebook.

Seated at his worktable, Morin listened intently. Of medium height and still youthful—not yet thirty—his slightly boyish face was framed by neatly combed brown hair. His brown eyes were fixed on the documents Miss Dupuis held while his fingers tapped lightly on the table's edge, betraying a restrained impatience. Clean-shaven except for a carefully trimmed moustache—an affectation adopted to resemble his superior, though the effort was only moderately successful—he nodded resolutely as he took the papers.

"I'll handle these two," he said, his voice steady.

Miss Dupuis, brushing another strand of hair back into place, continued:
"That leaves Patrick O'Meara, a foreman at the Lachine Canal."

"Does he also live in Griffintown?" Kelly asked, looking up from his notebook where he was absentmindedly jotting notes.

"Yes, here's his address," she replied, handing him a third paper.

Kelly took it, the look of a man already lost in his calculations.
"I'll take that," he said. "And while I'm at it, I'll try to track down the Fenian informant—she won't be hard to find."

"You're certain the informant is a woman?" Morin asked.

"Almost sure," Kelly replied, a mischievous glint in his eye. "I'd wager it's a prostitute."

Miss Dupuis frowned, clearly skeptical.
"And how do you plan to find her?"

Kelly, unruffled, responded with a playful wink, his confidence tinged with mischief.

"That's my secret, Miss Dupuis."

Robinson, who had been silent until then, straightened, cutting the exchange short.

"Right. Everyone knows what they're to do?"

The others nodded gravely, the weight of their task settling over them.

"Then, to work," Robinson concluded.

They left the room individually, donning their heavy coats and hats. Behind them, the door closed with a low creak, leaving a faint scent of damp wool and stale tobacco lingering in the air.

***

Robinson and Miss Dupuis took their places in a police chaise, the clatter of the horses' hooves echoing on the damp cobblestones as they reached Brennan and Mansfield's address. Robinson had deliberately assigned himself the delicate task of meeting Francis Brennan, the Fenian leader in Montreal. This confrontation could prove decisive, and he would also take the opportunity to question William Mansfield, the business accountant.

As they approached Griffintown, the urban landscape changed dramatically. The buildings grew larger but were blackened with soot, and the air carried a sharp, acrid smell. The district buzzed with industrial activity. Chimneys everywhere belched grey smoke, further obscuring the sky already heavy with clouds. The neighbourhood housed a variety of enterprises: metallurgy workshops, sugar and flour refineries, chemical factories, and textile mills. The proximity of the Lachine Canal, with its dark, restless waters, had spurred this industrial boom. Built in 1821 and expanded in 1848, the canal allowed ships to bypass the Lachine Rapids to reach the Great Lakes. Yet now, this grand structure scarcely seemed sufficient for the unrelenting stream of vessels laden to the brim.

Robinson and Miss Dupuis halted before the Scottish Wool Import warehouse. The building was starkly unattractive—a three-story rectangle with small windows, some shattered. Its red brick walls showed advanced signs of decay: here and there, dislodged bricks revealed gaping holes. The warehouse stored raw wool, which was then delivered to nearby textile mills to be fashioned into garments.

The façade, facing a bustling street filled with carts and labourers at work, was in disrepair. The rear of the building opened directly onto the canal, facilitating the unloading of boats. The smell of raw wool mingled with the stagnant odour of the canal water, creating an oppressive and unpleasant atmosphere.

Robinson and Miss Dupuis stepped down from the police chaise, adjusting their coats against the biting wind that found its way into their collars. They approached the front door, its warped wood and rusted hinges attesting to years of neglect. Inside, the atmosphere was no more welcoming: the paint on the walls, yellowed and peeling, hung in tatters, revealing plaster patches beneath. A rancid odour of dust hung heavily in the air.

A woman of middling years stood behind a rickety counter. Her dark brown hair, verging on black, was severely pulled back from the sides of her head and tied into a simple braid at the nape of her neck. Her long, angular face—almost masculine—was marked by a straight nose and thin lips, which she kept stubbornly pressed together. Her sombre, plain clothing seemed to mirror her disposition.

"Yes. What is it about?" she asked curtly, raising one eyebrow slightly, her displeasure thinly veiled.

Robinson, unflinching, stepped forward slightly and spoke in a calm but firm voice:
"Silas Robinson, a detective with the Montreal police. This is my assistant, Miss Dupuis."

The woman fixed her gaze on Miss Dupuis, scrutinizing her as if assessing her presence. Yet she betrayed no sign of curiosity or particular interest.

"We'd like to speak with Mr. Francis Brennan," Robinson continued.

"He isn't here," she replied sharply, her tone leaving little room for negotiation.

"And when will he return?"

"I don't know."

"You've no idea?" he pressed, his tone slightly more insistent.

"No."

Robinson sensed that he would get no further about Brennan. Adjusting his approach, he studied the woman with a calculating glance.

"Is Mr. William Mansfield here?"

"Yes," she replied tersely.

"Could we see him?"

She gave a faint shrug, clearly weary of the questioning.
"Second door on the left," she said, punctuating her words with a brief wave.

Robinson and Miss Dupuis exchanged a fleeting glance, equally perplexed and determined. Without another word, they moved toward the indicated door, their footsteps echoing on the worn wooden floor. Upon reaching the door, Robinson knocked twice, the sound sharp in the quiet. They waited for a voice to grant them entry before pushing it open.

"What's this about?" barked the man behind the desk, his voice as sharp as the wan light in the room. Conciseness was the house motto.

Robinson stepped forward and introduced himself, then presented Miss Dupuis. Mansfield, a middle-aged man with angular features and a piercing gaze, scrutinized the young woman intently. A flicker of sarcasm lit his eyes before he remarked:
"I didn't realize detectives needed a girl to take notes."

"Miss Dupuis is not my secretary. She is my assistant," Robinson replied with a firmness that brooked no argument.

"If you say so! Now, what do you want, detective?"

Mansfield, visibly disinclined to courtesy, did not invite them to sit. Robinson and Miss Dupuis, however, took the liberty of occupying the two straight-backed chairs positioned before the desk, their measured movements conveying an air of ostentatious politeness. While Miss Dupuis calmly retrieved her notebook and pencil, Robinson began the conversation:

"You're one of Mr. Brennan's men, are you?"

"I'm the company's accountant," Mansfield corrected sharply. "I am not a mere employee."

A faint, ironic smile flickered across Robinson's lips.

"If you say so," he replied, returning the jab with disarming calm.

Mansfield frowned, clearly annoyed.
"What do you want?"

"We're investigating a murder that took place nearby, on Wellington Street," Robinson explained.

"And?"

Reaching into the inner pocket of his coat, Robinson produced a photograph and handed it to Mansfield.
"Do you know this man?"

Mansfield took the photo, gave it a cursory glance, and returned it with a brusque gesture.
"No. I've never seen him."

"Really? Take a proper look," Robinson insisted, his words carrying a subtle weight.

"Unnecessary. I told you—I've never seen him," Mansfield repeated, his tone tinged with impatience.

Robinson let a calculated silence hang in the air, his eyes keenly observing the accountant's every nervous tic. Then, as was his habit, he shifted gears, his tone becoming almost detached.

"Your business doesn't seem particularly prosperous, Mr. Mansfield."

A flicker of sarcasm crossed Mansfield's face.
"Ah, you noticed. We barely manage to break even."

"Wool isn't selling well?"

"That's not the issue. Our stock moves easily enough. But we struggle to cover expenses—chartering ships, purchasing in Scotland, covering overhead. It all requires significant investment."

"And you don't have reliable backers to support the business?"

Mansfield shrugged, a glimmer of bitterness in his eyes.
"We Irish aren't trusted in Montreal. The English control all the good business. Not a single English bank will lend us a penny."

He paused briefly, then added with an acrid tone:

"The only one who will lend at extortionate rates."

"And who might that be?"

"Thomas Workman, from Molson Bank."

Robinson and Miss Dupuis exchanged a subtle glance. The name was not unfamiliar—Thomas Ryan had mentioned it the previous week, referring to those privileged Protestant Irishmen with close ties to the Anglo-Scots.

"Workman?" Robinson asked, feigning innocent curiosity. "Isn't he Irish himself? Shouldn't he be supporting members of his community?"

A bitter smile twisted Mansfield's lips.
"Yes, he is. But he's a Protestant Irishman and an Orangeman. He despises us Catholic Irish. He strangles us with his usurious interest rates."

Robinson nodded lightly as if filing the information away. After a few seconds, he changed the subject.

"Where do you live, Mr. Mansfield?"

"In Griffintown," the man replied after a brief hesitation.

At Robinson's prolonged silence, he seemed compelled to add:
"… Near Sainte-Anne's Church."

Robinson knew this church well. It was one of the places of worship frequented by his colleague Leclerc, and he had visited it several times himself, either on business or for celebrations. Unlike the rest of Griffintown, often regarded as grim and disreputable, the area around Sainte-Anne's Church seemed somewhat more respectable—almost peaceful by comparison.

The detective fixed Mansfield with a piercing gaze while leaning forward slightly.

"Do you know Kate Scanlan's tavern?" he asked, his tone neutral, bordering on nonchalance.

Mansfield raised an eyebrow, a faint, mocking smile curling his lips.
"Who doesn't know that tavern?"

"Do you go there often?"

"No, not often. I prefer other taverns. The food's better than what Mother Scanlan serves," he replied, his voice laced with disdain.

Robinson gave a slight nod, maintaining his calm demeanour.

"I'm asking about that tavern because it's near where we found this man's body," he said, pulling out the photograph of John Monahan and placing it squarely in front of Mansfield.

Mansfield glanced at the image briefly before leaning back in his chair with an expression of thinly veiled boredom. His look seemed to say, "Why are you still here?"

"He was stabbed to death," Robinson added, watching Mansfield's reaction closely.

Mansfield shrugged.
"So what? What does that have to do with me?"

"I don't know yet, Mr. Mansfield. But we think you might be able to help us shed light on the circumstances of his murder."

"I don't even know this man!" Mansfield retorted irritably. "What do you expect me to tell you?"

Robinson narrowed his eyes slightly, letting a tense silence hang in the air before speaking again, his tone turning more incisive:
"Your reaction is… odd. Normally, when people hear about a murder, they're curious. They ask questions about what happened and when it happened. Aren't you curious, Mr. Mansfield?"

"Why should I be? That murder has nothing to do with me," Mansfield replied curtly.

Suddenly, Robinson shifted the topic, his tone abrupt.

"Where were you during the Saint Patrick's Day celebrations?"

Mansfield frowned, startled by the question.

"During Saint Patrick's Day? That was nearly three weeks ago. Why do you want to know that?"

"I thought all Irishmen knew exactly where they were on that day. It's an important celebration, isn't it?"

A nervous smile flickered across Mansfield's face.

"Of course, I know. I wasn't in Montreal."

"Oh? You weren't in Montreal? And where were you?"

"I was in the United States, in Cincinnati, for a meeting."

Robinson nodded slowly.

"A meeting? You went alone?"

"No, Francis... Mr. Brennan was with me," he replied, pausing to correct his familiarity.

"A conference, I imagine?"

"A meeting," Mansfield corrected. "There were about thirty of us. You can verify it if you like."

"In Cincinnati," Robinson repeated. "Isn't that where the Fenian congresses are held? Are you a Fenian, Mr. Mansfield?"

At this, Mansfield straightened slightly, folding his arms, his gaze hardening.

"Because you are a Fenian, Mr. Mansfield. Don't deny it; we know," Robinson added, his voice growing firmer.

Mansfield hesitated briefly, then retorted defiantly:
"So what? What of it? I don't believe being a Fenian is against the law in this country."

"No, not at the moment," Robinson conceded with a sly smile. "What is illegal, however, is organizing an invasion of Canada."

Mansfield's face darkened further, his jaw tightening. Robinson pressed on without easing the tension.

"So, you were in Cincinnati to plan the invasion of Canada?"

"I don't have to answer that question," Mansfield declared coldly. "We are patriots, sir, who want what's best for Ireland. Nothing more."

"By assassinating your political opponents, for example?" Robinson countered, his gaze sharp as a blade.

"We assassinate no one," Mansfield replied angrily.

"And yet our victim, John Monahan, was a known opponent of the Fenians. He was a prominent Orangeman."

"I wouldn't know. I don't know him," Mansfield insisted.

Robinson shifted tactics because he would get no further on this front.

"Mr. Brennan, your employer, isn't here?"

"No."

"Do you know where he is?"

"No."

"Would you know someone who might?"

"His wife, probably."

"And where might we find Mrs. Brennan?"

"She's at the front. She's the company's secretary."

The two detectives rose, nodded briefly to Mansfield without another word, and left his office.

Robinson and Miss Dupuis returned to the front of the establishment, where Mrs. Brennan was still standing behind the counter, a weary expression on her face. Seeing them return, she raised an eyebrow slightly, expecting them to leave for good. Instead, they stopped in front of her.

"Mrs. Brennan, I presume?" Miss Dupuis asked, a polite smile lighting her face.

"Yes, that's me," the woman replied, her tone neutral, almost cold.

"I'm pleased to make your acquaintance, madam," Miss Dupuis added, extending her hand.

Mrs. Brennan hesitated, uncertainty crossing her features, but she finally extended her right hand for a quick, distant handshake.

"It's not often one sees a wife so involved in her husband's business," Miss Dupuis remarked, attempting to ease the tension.

Mrs. Brennan regarded her silently, her expression wavering as if deciding whether to engage.

"I gather you don't limit yourself to front-desk duties here," Miss Dupuis continued gently.

After a moment's thought, Mrs. Brennan seemed to relax slightly.

"No, of course not. I handle everything in this business. If I had to rely on my husband, we'd have been bankrupt long ago," she said with a trace of bitterness.

"Oh? And why is that?" Robinson asked, crossing his arms and fixing her with an attentive gaze.

"Francis isn't a bad man," she sighed. "But he has no head for business. Distracted, disorganized—he forgets to pay the bills, lets the mail pile up... You know the type."

"He prefers politics, I suppose?" Robinson interjected.

"Exactly. Those damned Irish and their politics..."

Robinson noted her distinct accent and remarked in an even tone:
"You're not Irish, are you, Mrs. Brennan?"

"No. I'm French Canadian. My maiden name is Boucher—Étiennette Boucher. Everyone calls me Nénette," she said, her tone softening slightly.

"And I suppose you don't share your husband's political opinions?"

"I don't understand them… nor do I want to. Politics isn't for me. I know that Francis spends more time on it than on his business. Luckily, I'm here to manage everything else," she said, straightening her shoulders defiantly.

Miss Dupuis picked up the conversation:
"We'd like to meet him. He isn't here today?"

At this, Mrs. Brennan cast her eyes downward, visibly hesitating.
"No, he's not in the office this morning."

"Does he often step out like this?" Robinson asked.

"Certainly not," she replied after a moment. "He usually spends his days here and sometimes comes home late…"

She fixed her gaze on Miss Dupuis, frustration and resignation mingling in her expression.

"I know what you're thinking: if he spends so much time here, why is the business failing? What does he really do all day? Isn't that what you're wondering?"

"Not at all, madam," Miss Dupuis replied calmly.

"My husband is a faithful man," she continued, insistent. "He's never cheated on me. And believe me, if he had, I'd know. When he's here, it's all about his politics—his meetings with his friends… or ruffians, I should say."

"These ruffians—are they the Fenians?" Robinson asked.

"Yes. That's what they call themselves."

"What do you know about them?"

"Nothing at all. I've told you—I'm not interested in politics. Francis holds his meetings here because I won't allow him to invite them to the house."

A short silence followed before Robinson resumed: "Do you know why he isn't here this morning?"

This time, Mrs. Brennan lifted her head. Her previously guarded features showed a shadow of concern.

"I haven't seen him in two days," she said quietly.

"Since when?"

"He didn't come home Friday night, and I've had no news since."

"Does this happen often?"

"Never without letting me know. For him, Saturdays and Sundays are sacred—family days," she explained.

"You have children?"

"Yes, two. Where could he have gone? I'm so worried," she murmured, tears welling in her eyes.

"Why do you think something's happened to him?" Miss Dupuis asked gently.

"Because of his cursed politics. He often receives threatening letters."

"From whom?"

"I don't know. He refused to talk to me about it, but I could see it weighed on him some days. As if his mind was elsewhere…"

She looked Robinson in the eye.

"I know the police don't care about missing adults, but… do you think…"

"We'll see what we can do, Mrs. Brennan," Robinson replied. "Can you describe your husband to me?"

She took a deep breath before answering:
"He's a small man, shorter than average. Five foot three."

"You're taller than he is?"

"Yes, but it's never bothered him. He's energetic and quite handsome, with brown eyes."

"And his hair?"

"He doesn't have any. He's bald. He suffers from complete baldness, no eyebrows either."

"Alopecia! Does he wear a wig?"

"Yes, but he hates it. He often takes it off at the office."

Robinson jotted down these details in his notebook.

"Very well, Mrs. Brennan. We'll contact you if we hear anything."

They took their leave, leaving the woman alone behind her counter, her eyes red with worry.

CHAPTER 19

April 3, Monday afternoon

This Monday afternoon, grey, diffuse light filtered through the police station's windows, casting ghostly shadows upon the peeling walls. The air was heavy and damp, still steeped in the lingering smell of stale tobacco and musty paper. Outside, a biting wind whistled through the streets, a stark reminder that winter had not yet fully retreated.

A wood stove installed in one corner warmed the modest but functional office. Its heat slowly spread through the room, creating a convivial and, at times, slightly smoky atmosphere. The detectives sat at their desks, arranged in an imperfect circle to facilitate discussion.

Robinson, the Chief, occupied a separate seat, sitting upright in a chair with a worn backrest. Clad in a dark woollen jacket, a tightly buttoned black waistcoat, and a sombre cravat, he projected a natural authority. His commanding gaze swept over his subordinates in turn.

Kelly, at his desk, appeared far more relaxed. His unbuttoned jacket revealed a white shirt with sleeves slightly rolled up and its collar undone—a hallmark of his usual nonchalance. He lounged in his chair, one hand holding a document while the other idly rested on his stubbled chin.

With an air more youthful than he would have liked, Morin wore a neatly buttoned shirt beneath a fitted grey waistcoat paired with subtly striped trousers. Ever immaculate, he absentmindedly stroked his carefully groomed moustache as if to assert a maturity he sought to project.

Nearby, Miss Dupuis, ever elegant and composed, wore a navy-blue merino dress, cinched at the waist with a bodice adorned with fabric-covered buttons. Its long sleeves, slightly puffed at the shoulders, ended in delicately embroidered cuffs. The ample skirt, accented by neatly pressed pleats, brushed the floor, hinting at the polished sheen of her black leather boots. A fine, off-white lace collar lent a touch of refinement to her attire.

Open files, crumpled sheets, and a few cold teacups on the detectives' desks testified to the intensity of their labours.

Robinson glanced at Miss Dupuis, accompanying the look with a slight nod, inviting her to speak.

"We spoke to Mansfield," Miss Dupuis began in a clear voice, "the accountant from Brennan's firm. We also questioned the latter's wife."

"And?" asked Kelly, his gaze still fixed on the document he pretended to be reading.

"The Chief and I have ruled out the possibility that either Mansfield or Brennan killed Monahan. Both have solid alibis. They were not in Canada at the time of his death."

Morin furrowed his brow, his keen gaze fixed on Miss Dupuis.

"Solid, you say? Can they be verified?"

"That remains to be done, but we believe they had no part in it," she replied, consulting her notes.

Kelly raised his eyes to Miss Kelly and stated, "Not directly, perhaps. But could they have orchestrated it?"

"A possibility, yes," she admitted. "But directly involved? It seems unlikely."

Robinson, who had thus far been content to listen, interlaced his fingers and added gravely, "There is one troubling detail, however. Brennan has disappeared."

The statement elicited a reaction from everyone. Kelly let out a small, sardonic laugh.

"Brennan has disappeared! Now that's intriguing. Since when?"

"For several days," Robinson replied.

"Smells of guilt, plain as day." declared Morin.

"Or," Kelly added with a sly grin, "He's simply had enough of his shrew and thought, 'Bah! A new life awaits me elsewhere.'"

Miss Dupuis shook her head, clearly unconvinced.

"No, from what we know, that seems unlikely. He has vanished. Quite simply."

"And what does that signify, in your view?" Morin asked.

"I do not know yet," Robinson answered after a brief silence.

Then, turning to Morin, he continued:

"And you, Morin? How are things progressing with those two fellows of yours?"

Morin cleared his throat before replying, a mischievous glint in his eyes:

"I saw both of them this morning. Linehan and Lyons have their shops right next to each other. Hard to miss."

"And?" Kelly asked, drumming his fingers nervously on the table.

"Well, honestly, they don't strike me as murderers, believe me. Both of them are in their sixties. One walks with a cane, and the other resembles a hair's breadth from the grave."

Robinson, as impassive as ever, allowed a flicker of irony to cross his gaze. Kelly, however, appeared unimpressed.

"And what did you learn?" he asked.

"They were quite cooperative, which surprised me, to be honest. Perhaps it's because I'm French Canadian?"

Miss Dupuis nodded, adding seriously:

"That's plausible. The Fenians are trying to rally French Canadians to their cause, appealing to their shared faith and the sympathies of the Société Saint-Jean-Baptiste. After all, many would rather see annexation to the United States than creating a Canadian Confederation."

Morin resumed, visibly pleased with his investigation:

"At any rate, they weren't at Kate Scanlan's tavern on St. Patrick's Day. The two families were celebrating together at Linehan's. They told me that noisy tavern evenings are no longer their style."

Kelly let out a scoff.

"And you believe them?"

"Yes," Morin replied without hesitation. "It should be easy to confirm with their wives and children."

A heavy silence fell over the four detectives, broken only by the scratching of a pen as Miss Dupuis took notes. Their gazes met, each weighing the others in the palpable tension, until Robinson, ever unflappable, finally spoke.

"We've just significantly narrowed down our list of suspects. Only yours remains, Kelly," said Robinson, fixing him with a calm gaze.

Kelly nodded with a slight smirk.

"It's possible I may have a bit more luck than the rest of you... if we can call it that."

"Oh? Let's hear it," Robinson replied, his tone neutral though his eyes betrayed curiosity.

Kelly leaned against the edge of his desk, pretending to relish the attention.

"I managed to contact my source this morning."

Miss Dupuis, ever focused, looked up from her notebook, one eyebrow slightly raised.

"Your source? What kind of source?" she asked.

"A business acquaintance… An informant, if you prefer," Kelly replied, clearly pleased with himself.

"And who is she, this informant?" she pressed, unconvinced.

Kelly shook his head, a crooked smile on his lips.

"She's someone I've worked with before," he said, emphasizing the pronoun. "You've still much to learn about our trade, Miss Dupuis. Let me enlighten you: the identity of a police informant is known only to their handler."

"Not even your colleagues?"

"Not even the chief," Kelly said, glancing at Robinson.

Robinson gave a slight nod of approval, his expression unchanged.

"In the past, I had to pull my informant out of a few tight spots. Ever since she owes me favours."

Morin, who had been observing Kelly with interest, leaned forward slightly.

"So, you've received information?"

"I learned about a young Irishwoman who mingles with the men of Griffintown. A prostitute. She frequently takes her clients to Kate Scanlan's tavern."

"You think she might have crossed paths with Monahan?" Morin asked.

"Not just crossed paths," Kelly replied with a knowing smile. "If you catch my drift."

Miss Dupuis frowned slightly.

"No need to spell it out, Kelly, nor to coddle me," she added curtly.

Kelly raised his hands in mock surrender.

"All right! Monahan was a regular client. At first, this girl—she goes by the name Stella (an alias, of course)—was his way of infiltrating the Irish community in Griffintown. What he didn't realize, however, was that Stella also had clients among the Fenians."

Morin nodded slowly.

"That's fairly common in that area," he said. "Many of Griffintown's prostitutes likely had clients on both sides. It doesn't prove she revealed Monahan's identity to the Fenians."

"You're right, Morin. But here's the thing: I managed to track down Stella."

For the first time, a flicker of approval crossed Robinson's gaze.

"That's progress," he said.

Kelly straightened slightly, folding his arms.

"Poor girl. I pity her. She's only fifteen or sixteen. She could be my daughter if I had one."

Miss Dupuis didn't hide her skepticism.

"Yes, fine! She's pitiable, I'll give you that. But she's still a prostitute."

"An orphan," Kelly corrected sharply. "She had no choice but to take up this line of work. She might have worked as a maid for the Anglos without an education, but they won't hire Irish girls. And the businesses in Griffintown won't hire women at all. What else was she supposed to do? She must eat."

Robinson, his tone authoritative, steered the conversation back on track.

"So, did you learn anything?"

"Yes. I earned her trust. That's how I discovered she had known Monahan for several months. He visited her regularly, and, according to her, he found her 'very likable.' 'I often inspire sympathy,' she told me."

Miss Dupuis pursed her lips, impatient.

"Go on, Kelly."

"Well… Monahan grew attached to her to the point where he revealed his real name and why he was in Griffintown. He believed she would keep it to herself. A mistake."

"He confided in her on the pillow," Miss Dupuis remarked sharply.

Kelly nodded.

"Exactly. Stella, however, was too young and naive to grasp the importance of what he'd shared."

"Naive? That's quite the claim, Kelly," said Miss Dupuis with a touch of irony.

"Listen, she didn't know Monahan was a government spy. He simply told her he wanted to better understand the Irishmen who frequented Scanlan's tavern so he could become a Fenian himself. She didn't see how that could be dangerous."

Morin furrowed his brow.

"How did the Fenians discover the truth about Monahan?"

Kelly sighed.

"She told her pimp. And he, well, he immediately understood who he was dealing with."

Miss Dupuis appeared shocked.

"She had a pimp?"

"Of course," Kelly replied with a trace of irritation. "In that line of work, Miss Dupuis, a woman doesn't survive without a man to protect her."

Robinson, ever pragmatic, interjected.

"Do you have a name for this pimp?"

Kelly answered confidently:

"I certainly do…"

He stopped speaking, his gaze moving slowly from one face to the next. A mischievous glint in his eyes, he finally broke the silence.

"That's when a drumroll would be fitting," Kelly said, miming the exaggerated gestures of a drum major.

After a theatrical pause, he declared:

"His name is Patrick O'Meara."

Miss Dupuis started, her notebook nearly slipping from her hands.

"O'Meara!" she exclaimed. "But he's one of the suspects on our list of Fenians!"

"You've got it, princess," Kelly replied with a sly grin. "So, I went straight away to look for O'Meara. First stop, his residence. His wife told me he was at work. But at work… no one had seen him."

"Oh, what a fine suspect we've got here!" Morin quipped, a smirk on his lips.

"Indeed," Kelly agreed, nodding with a satisfied air. "I believe we've found our killer."

Robinson, ever composed, regarded him steadily before raising his voice slightly.

"Not so fast, Kelly. Not so fast. We need to find him and question him first."

Kelly shrugged, a nonchalant smile playing on his face.

"True enough, Chief, I'm getting ahead of myself... I'm getting ahead of myself..."

At that moment, a knock at the office door interrupted their exchange. The door opened slowly, and two constables entered, their expressions grave and sombre. Their outer coats, still damp from the heavy humidity, carried the distinct scent of wet wool mingled with the chill of the air.

"What's going on?" Robinson asked, his brow furrowing.

One of the constables cleared his throat before responding:

"We've just found a body."

Robinson straightened abruptly, everyone in the room focusing on the two men.

"What? Where?" he demanded, his tone sharp.

"By the riverbank, near the entrance to the Lachine Canal," the constable replied, his voice steady but tense.

"Did he drown?" Morin asked.

The second constable, a broad-shouldered man, shook his head.

"Sean and I don't think so. He'd been struck in the face, and his neck was broken. Perhaps from falling into the water... or before he went in."

"Were you able to identify him?" Robinson asked, his tone cutting.

"No, Chief. He had no papers on him," the first constable replied.

"What does he look like?" Robinson pressed.

The constable hesitated momentarily as if searching for the right words.

"He's rather small... tiny, actually. And there's something odd: he has no hair or eyebrows."

Miss Dupuis suddenly turned pale, pressing a hand to her mouth.

"Brennan!" she gasped, almost breathless.

Robinson's face, already tense, darkened further as the details mounted. His jaw clenched, and he nearly growled through gritted teeth, anger rumbling in his voice:

"Damn, Penton!"

A heavy silence descended over the room. After a moment that seemed interminable, Robinson suddenly stood, his chair scraping loudly against the floor. Red with fury, he stormed toward the door, his shoulders rigid, and shouted:

"The bloody bastard!"

CHAPTER 20

April 3, Monday afternoon

Robinson had just learned of Brennan's death under troubling circumstances. He connected it to the list he had handed to his superior the previous week. His set jaw and hardened expression betrayed a simmering anger poised to erupt.

He grabbed the handle of the detectives' office door with a sharp motion and flung it open so forcefully that it slammed against the wall. Without a word, he strode down the corridor, his boots striking the wooden floor with a grim, resounding echo that reverberated through the tense atmosphere.

At the foot of the staircase, he gripped the banister firmly and ascended the steps two at a time, his breath quick and measured, mirroring his agitation. At each landing, the flickering gaslight cast his shadow on the walls—a shadow of a man brimming with determination and fury.

Arriving at the door to Penton's office, Robinson paused briefly, instinctively smoothing his jacket as though attempting to contain the storm raging within. Then, without so much as a knock, he pushed the door open swiftly and decisively and stepped into the room with an energy that left no doubt about his state of mind.

The door crashed open, the impact of the panel against the wall echoing like a gunshot. Robinson entered like a tempest. His face was a mask of restrained rage, and each step on the worn floorboards thudded with purpose. The air in the room grew heavier, thick with tension, like the moments before a thunderstorm.

Penton's office was spacious and impeccably organized. The large windows behind him overlooked the Saint Lawrence River, whose gray, restless waters mirrored the cloudy April sky. A hearth burned in one corner, radiating a welcome warmth and the comforting scent of dry wood being consumed. Near the fireplace, a small coffee table was flanked by two dark leather armchairs, starkly contrasting the oak-panelled walls.

Strategically placed kerosene lamps bathed the room in a warm, flickering light, casting shifting shadows that heightened the tense atmosphere. Police Chief Penton, a man in his forties, stood behind his desk. Dressed in a pristine uniform, he wore a dark blue jacket adorned with gold cuffs and epaulets. His stiff collar was complemented by a carefully knotted black cravat, and his perfectly polished boots gleamed in the lamplight.

"What… what is the meaning of this, Robinson?" Penton stammered, startled, his composure shattered as he looked up from behind his impeccably organized desk.

"Is it you, Penton?" Robinson demanded, his voice icy, his gaze like lightning striking.

It was rare to see Robinson lose his composure in such a manner. When he did, even his closest colleagues could not help but shudder. Penton, for his part, scrambled to recover his bearings.

"Who gave you permission to enter?" Penton asked, his tone feigning authority.

Robinson ignored the question and approached the desk with the slow, deliberate movements of a predator closing in on its prey. He halted abruptly, his fists clenched, his eyes fixed. After a weighty silence, he suddenly leaned forward, his gaze searing.

"Look me in the eye, Penton, and tell me it wasn't you!"

Penton instinctively recoiled in his chair, his left hand fumbling for the edge of the desk as though seeking support. He blinked, visibly rattled.

"W-what are you talking about?" he stammered.

Relentless, Robinson moved closer, then sat heavily in the chair opposite the desk, his piercing gaze locked onto Penton.

"I warned you," he roared. "The list was not to be circulated! And yet, you made it known. To whom? Who got their hands on it?"

"The list! What list?" Penton replied, feigning ignorance, though his trembling voice betrayed him.

With such force, Robinson slammed his palm down on the desk that Penton flinched.

"Don't play innocent with me," he spat. "No one in my team could have leaked the names on that list. It had to be you."

Penton straightened slightly in his chair to regain his composure and tried deflecting.

"Ah! You mean the Fenians?" he said with a forced smile. "Robinson, come now. Let's discuss this calmly. After all, I am your superior."

Robinson let out a harsh, joyless laugh, his tone razor-sharp.

"Superior, my ass! Do you even realize what you've done? Do you?"

Penton raised a brow, attempting to reassert control.

"Bah," he said with a slight shrug. "I simply shared the names of those Fenian rebels with my Orangemen associates. We had a meeting that evening. What harm could it possibly have done?"

Robinson straightened, his features twisted with barely contained fury.

"What difference does it make?" Penton repeated, his voice rising in the room.

"It makes you utterly irresponsible, Penton!" Robinson thundered. "One of the men on that list has been found murdered."

Penton opened his mouth, but no sound came. Finally, he murmured:

"Murdered? A man from the list? But... how?"

"They just found his body on the riverbank," Robinson replied, his voice cold and sharp.

Penton furrowed his brow, perplexed.

"What does that have to do with the list?" he asked, confusion clouding his features.

Robinson locked eyes with him, each word landing like a sledgehammer.

"His name was Francis Brennan. The leader of the Fenians in Montreal."

Penton's eyes widened, surprise mingling with unease.

"Brennan… Brennan… Oh yes, I remember! Francis Brennan. A damned Fenian," he muttered.

"Now you remember, do you?" Robinson growled, his voice dripping with contempt.

"Yes… Yes…"

"And you gave his name to your gang of Orangemen scoundrels," Robinson pressed relentlessly.

Penton tried to defend himself.

"I won't have you…"

"Oh, you won't have me, will you?" Robinson cut him off, raising his voice. "And what gave you the right to do that? They were the only suspects, Penton! Suspects! We had no proof they were connected to Monahan's murder."

Cornered, Penton attempted a feeble justification.

"It must have been one of them who killed him…"

Robinson shook his head slowly, a sneer of disdain twisting his lips.

"Fool!" he spat, leaning back in his chair.

He turned slightly as if to master his anger, but his gaze soon snapped back to Penton, who remained frozen, unable to respond. The silence that followed was almost tangible, heavy with reproach and tension.

"The worst of it all," Robinson resumed, his voice biting, "is that Brennan was innocent. He had a solid alibi for the night Monahan was murdered. He wasn't even in Canada."

Penton, already pale, seemed to collapse further into his chair as though the weight of Robinson's words had crushed him.

"What... what are you saying?" he stammered, his eyes widening in shock.

"I'm saying he was innocent, Penton," Robinson snapped, emphasizing each word. "What part of that don't you understand?"

Another oppressive silence fell over the room. Robinson drew a deep breath, his piercing gaze never leaving Penton's.

"Now," he said sharply, "what can you tell me about that infamous evening with your pack of Orangemen scoundrels?"

Penton, visibly uncomfortable, shook his head slightly.

"But I can't... Those are secret meetings."

Robinson, feigning to rise, fixed Penton with an icy stare, pinning him in place.

"All right... All right," Penton finally relented, his voice trembling. "I see the situation is exceptional. At first, I was furious to learn that one of our Protestant countrymen had been so brutally murdered by Catholic Fenians. Everyone in our group was riled up. We decided we had to act."

"And that's when you decided to share the names," Robinson cut in, his lips pressed into a thin line.

Penton nodded weakly, avoiding his gaze.

"It had to be done. Among us, we don't hide much... I gave the five names. But I didn't know, at the time..."

"You didn't know they'd kill Brennan?" Robinson interrupted, his tone dripping with icy sarcasm.

"That's not it," Penton replied, squirming slightly in his chair. "I didn't know just how involved one of our members was... in Monahan's murder."

Robinson leaned forward, his anger radiating from every movement.

"Involved? Explain yourself, Penton."

The other swallowed hard before answering.

"John Monahan was the son of one of our most prestigious members: Thomas Workman."

Robinson raised his eyebrows, visibly surprised.

"Monahan, the son of Workman? The director of the Molson Bank?"

"The very same," Penton confirmed with a slight nod.

Robinson furrowed his brow, his mind racing.

"Why is his son named Monahan?" he asked, suspicion lacing his tone.

"Workman never had any biological children," Penton explained, his voice regaining composure. "Years ago, he adopted two Irish immigrant children—orphans whose parents died of typhus. Monahan's biological father promised Workman before passing that he would preserve the family name if he took the boy in. That's why the son kept the name Monahan."

Robinson stared pensively at an invisible spot on the desk, piecing together the information.

"You mentioned two children?" he asked suddenly, looking up.

"Yes," Penton replied. "Rowan... Rowan Workman. But I know nothing about him."

Robinson exhaled softly, the sound barely audible. Those who knew him recognized the combination of silence and his fixed gaze on the floor as signs of intense deliberation. Rowan. According to Miss Dupuis's information, the same name as Frasa's suitor. Frasa had been involved with an Irish Protestant: Rowan. A coincidence? Perhaps. But it is too significant a coincidence to ignore.

At last, Robinson raised his eyes, fixing Penton with a piercing, icy stare.

"So, you handed Brennan's name to a grieving father, desperate to avenge his son's death. Brilliant! Truly brilliant."

Penton stammered, searching for a defence.

"But... but I didn't know... Anyway, I warned them. I told my colleagues they were only suspects."

Robinson clicked his tongue, a sneer of disdain curling his lips.

"Oh, really? Did you know?"

Penton nodded almost sheepishly.

"They were so riled up..." he offered weakly.

"And you told them Brennan was their leader?" Robinson pressed.

"Well... yes... of course," Penton replied as if trying to downplay his actions.

Robinson leaned in slightly, his voice low but cutting.

"And now Brennan is dead. Murdered."

Penton lowered his head, his shoulders slumping under an invisible weight. His voice dropped to a murmur.

"It's as though I killed him myself."

"As you say," Robinson replied, his tone ice-cold.

A heavy silence fell over the room, so thick one could hear a pin drop. The air, charged with reproach and tension, felt almost suffocating.

Finally, Robinson broke the silence, his voice sharp as a blade.

"What you've done is unforgivable, Penton. I could report you to the authorities. I know Attorney General Cartier well. If he were to learn of this, your tenure here would be short-lived… and any other career aspirations, too. Farewell to your political ambitions."

The words fell like a guillotine. Penton, already defeated, seemed to shrink further into his chair. He raised pleading eyes to Robinson, fear etched across his face.

"You… you wouldn't do that, would you?" he whispered, barely audible.

Robinson remained still for a moment, savouring the impact of his threat. Then, at last, he replied in a cutting tone:

"You'll stop pestering me with your requests and demands for information. You'll let us conduct our investigations in peace. And most importantly, stop slandering my team."

Penton nodded frantically.

"Yes, of course… Agreed," he said in a trembling voice.

But Robinson wasn't finished.

"As for your budget cuts, you can shove them where I think they belong."

Penton stammered, "Yes... yes... I understand. Anything else?"

Robinson rose slowly, a sarcastic smile forming on his lips.

"Not for the moment, 'boss,'" he said, emphasizing the word with biting disdain.

Without waiting for a response, Robinson turned on his heel and left the room, slamming the door behind him and leaving Penton in an even more oppressive silence.

CHAPTER 21

April 4, Tuesday Morning

Robinson strode with measured steps along Saint-Jacques Street. His imposing figure cut through the brisk wind, funnelling between the buildings like a rock defying the gusts. The leaden sky seemed to press down upon his shoulders, intensifying the tension that had gripped him since the previous day. He had just left the Jacques-Cartier Market, where a few frostbitten merchants were arranging their wares on the stalls, their numb fingers struggling to escape the biting cold.

The Detective had been coming from the police station housed in the grand Bonsecours building. His night had been restless, haunted by the memory of his acrimonious exchange with Penton, his superior. Penton had admitted, with no small measure of nonchalance, that he had handed over a list of Fenian suspects to the Orangemen the previous week. Among those named was Francis Brennan, now dead under troubling circumstances. A coincidence? Of course not.

The evening before, Robinson had dined tête-à-tête with Rosalie. The atmosphere had grown sombre since Thérèse left their home to settle in her apartment. Rosalie had quickly noticed his silence, heavier than usual. She knew her husband well enough to sense that something weighed on his mind. Yet she confined herself to observing him quietly, respecting the space he sometimes withdrew into.

Robinson settled into the drawing room library, as was his custom after the meal. This warm sanctuary, adorned with dark woodwork and shelves lined with books, was illuminated by the flickering glow of an oil lamp and the flame in the hearth. While the biting cold remained at bay behind the heavy curtains, Rosalie seated herself near the fire with a French novel. For his part, Silas had chosen a Greek tragedy, which he read in its original text. A long silence stretched between them, broken only by the crackle of the firewood and the rustling of turned pages.

Finally, Rosalie broke the silence, lifting her eyes from her book to ask, "What are you reading, Silas?"

He half-closed his yellowed copy and replied softly, "Oedipus at Colonus."

"Oh, yes!" she exclaimed, a spark of curiosity in her gaze. "That's the play where Oedipus is old and blind, isn't it?"

"That's right. He lives in exile, just across from his former kingdom, Thebes, where he was banished. His two sons are fighting over the throne, and each sends a messenger to persuade him to take their side. But he refuses."

Rosalie raised her eyebrows slightly, thoughtful.

"Well, now! Doesn't that remind you of something? I'm thinking of Thomas D'Arcy McGee."

"How so?" Silas asked, intrigued.

"Well," she replied, placing her book on her lap, "the Irish Catholic Fenians and the Irish Protestant Orangemen, those feuding brothers, both want to win him over because of his influence. But he, like Oedipus, refuses to take sides."

"Quite true. Strange, isn't it? How is there nothing new under the sun? Those old Greeks understood everything already."

Rosalie, her smile tinged with slight unease, continued, "What happens to Oedipus in the end?"

Silas answered with mock gravity.

"Oh! It's a tragedy. Everyone dies."

"I hope that's not a bad omen for D'Arcy McGee."

A heavy silence settled between them again as each, lost in their thoughts, returned to their reading. Outside, the wind made a window creak to remind them that the shadow of tragedies, whether Greek or modern, was always lurking nearby.

Robinson was now approaching the imposing Molson Bank building, overseen by Thomas Workman. The streets of Montreal bustled despite the biting cold of the morning. Carriages laboured over the damp cobblestones while a few passersby, bundled in heavy woollen coats, walked briskly, their shoulders hunched against the icy wind. Robinson, for his part, advanced with a steady gait, his boots crunching faintly against the wet wooden sidewalks. He scarcely felt the sting of the air, accustomed as he was to these late-winter temperatures. His expression betrayed preoccupation, likely spurred by Penton's troubling revelation the previous evening: John Monahan was Thomas Workman's adopted son. This disclosure raised questions that Robinson was determined to unravel.

He halted before the bank, taking in the sight of the brand-new edifice. A true architectural feat. The symmetrical façade commanded respect, with its central projection and three levels, each bearing distinct stylistic elements. The rusticated ground floor and the elegant windows of the first floor evoked the palaces of the Italian Renaissance. At the same time, the upper section, adorned with paired granite columns and a mansard roof, reflected the influence of the French Second Empire. This blend of architectural styles, imported from London, exemplified the emerging tastes of Canada's burgeoning metropolis.

Robinson ascended the few steps to the portico, framed by massive columns with smooth surfaces still gleaming with condensation. The interior, however, betrayed the fervour of ongoing construction. Workmen, clad in worn aprons and frayed caps, bustled about, installing mouldings and adjusting gilded details on walls that rivalled the exterior's splendour.

A young clerk, dressed in a dark jacket slightly too large for his frame, escorted Robinson upstairs to Workman's office. There, the bank's director greeted him with grave politeness. Thomas Workman was an imposing man, though his figure was slightly stooped. His balding head and long, dark brown beard framed a stern visage, yet his almond-shaped eyes, nearly closed, struck Robinson most. They seemed to conceal a profound sadness.

"Detective Robinson?" Workman said, extending a firm hand. "I have been expecting you."

He invited Robinson to sit in a small parlour tucked into a corner bathed in morning light. The armchairs, upholstered in burgundy velvet, stood in contrast to the walls, still bare of paintings. A crystal decanter presided over a small table, surrounded by elegantly engraved glasses. Workman offered a glass of whisky, but Robinson declined with a brief motion.

Workman then rose, his gaze drifting through the large arched window that provided an unobstructed view of the bustling street. He remained silent for a moment, then murmured, almost to himself:

"What a beautiful city, don't you think? So lively… so vibrant… The city of endless possibilities."

He finally turned to Robinson, a touch of melancholy in his eyes.

"The American continent offers opportunities my homeland, Ireland, could never provide. Too old, too burdened by despair. Emigrating to Canada was the best decision my family ever made. Here, everything is yet to be built."

Robinson, after a calculated pause, replied with feigned interest:

"You were born in Ulster if I'm not mistaken?"

"Yes, in Lisburn, Northern Ireland."

"Protestant, I presume?"

"A former Presbyterian," he said with detachment. "But I am now a Unitarian."

"What prompted your father to leave Ireland for Canada?"

Workman gave a faint, distant smile.

"My father was a dreamer. Never content with what he had, always seeking something new. When he was on the brink of ruin, he left everything behind and embarked on an adventure, taking the entire family with him."

"An adventure that seems to have served you well," Robinson remarked, gesturing around the opulent office. "A prosperous businessman, bank director..."

"Yes, but not without struggle. My brother and I worked tirelessly to build all of this."

Robinson nodded slowly.

"Your hardware store is the most successful in Canada. And I hear you also own several businesses in Griffintown."

Robinson had a habit of approaching interrogations with the advantage of foresight. He had carefully researched Thomas Workman, preferring to know the answers to his questions before even posing them. This allowed him to gauge the honesty of his interlocutor. For his part, Workman seemed intrigued and almost amused by the situation.

"I see you've done your homework, Detective Robinson," he remarked with a hint of respect. "Ermatinger was right when he said you're the best detective in Canada."

"Oh! You know Ermatinger?"

"Of course," Workman replied, adjusting his dark jacket. "He also mentioned that you're a Freemason. As am I. Ermatinger and I belong to the same lodge."

Robinson did not respond immediately, maintaining his usual calm. He knew a well-placed silence could sometimes reveal more than a direct question. But Workman did not continue. The Detective finally broke the pause.

"Was it he who told you about the death of your son, John Monahan?"

Workman flinched almost imperceptibly.

"So, you know about that too…"

He averted his gaze, and his face darkened. Swaying slightly, he sank into his chair like an invisible weight had crushed his shoulders.

"John, my beloved son…" he murmured, his voice trembling. "Ermatinger came to see me when he received the police photograph two weeks ago. It was you who photographed his… body, wasn't it?"

"Yes. We didn't know who he was, and it seemed the most reliable way to identify him."

Workman rested his elbows on the armrests and clasped his hands together, searching for words.

"Ermatinger was deeply saddened… He also told me that John was working for the government. He said he was a hero. A hero, yes… dead!"

"You didn't know he worked for the government?"

"Not until Ermatinger told me," Workman admitted. "John was… discreet. He didn't always tell us where he was going or what he was doing."

A silence fell, heavy with palpable tension. Robinson drew a short breath, indicating that he was about to broach a delicate subject.

"Was John an Orangeman? Ermatinger told me he was part of a volunteer militia targeting Catholics."

Workman frowned slightly, a shadow of pain crossing his face.

"He sympathized, yes. But he did not belong to any Orange lodge. That said, we often discussed the plight of Irish Protestants in Canada. He despised Catholics, it's true."

Workman sank deeper into his chair, crossing his arms as if shielding himself from the harshness of his own words.

"Were you close to him?" Robinson asked, his voice softening.

"Close in heart, but not in body," Workman replied after hesitating. "We knew he was in Montreal these past months, but he refused to tell us where he lived. He sometimes telegrams to Annie… my wife… just to reassure us that he was fine."

Robinson straightened slightly in his chair.

"So, one could say that John was following in his father's footsteps?"

"If you like..." murmured Workman, his hesitant tone betraying a mixture of pride and guilt.

"Are you a staunch Orangeman, Mr. Workman?"

Workman lifted his head this time, his piercing gaze meeting the Detective's.

"I was... once," he replied, his voice lower. "You know, we are a British colony. We must constantly defend our place within the Empire. You, as a Briton, understand that, don't you?"

"We are not here to speak of me, Mr. Workman."

A tense silence stretched between them, finally broken by Robinson:

"You said you were an Orangeman in your youth?"

Workman nodded slowly, his face marked by the weight of distant memories.

"Yes. I was proud to belong to the Doric Club. We fought the Sons of Liberty, those French-Canadian Catholic rebels who called themselves Patriots. They sought independence for Canada, as the United States had achieved."

"I wasn't around in those days, but I understand the Doric Club often resorted to violence—looting, arson, even murder…"

"That's true. We were young and impetuous. But what else could we do? We had to defend our country."

"You mean your vision of the country, of course."

"If you prefer," Workman replied, averting his gaze.

After a pause, Robinson continued:

"You say you've changed now?"

"I've mellowed, yes… The years have changed us, Detective. Even the deepest convictions erode over time."

The Detective studied Workman, slumped in his chair like a man crushed by life. If he had ever been a figure of energy and resolve, there was now minor left but a shadow, weary and disillusioned. Breaking the silence, Robinson lightened the moment.

"I'll take that drink now, Mr. Workman."

Workman raised his head as if surprised by the request, then nodded slowly. He picked up the decanter from the low table, removed the stopper, and poured a generous measure of whisky into two glasses. His movements were precise but mechanical, his gaze distant. He extended one glass to Robinson, who rose to take it.

Instead of sitting down, the Detective stood before the large window, the same one where Workman had paused earlier. Daylight flooded the room, and the sky, now clear and radiant, stood in stark contrast to the heavy mood of their conversation. Robinson took a moment to contemplate the bustling city below.

"It truly is a beautiful city," Robinson said softly, almost to himself.

After a moment, he turned to Workman, glass in hand.

"You have another son, don't you?"

"Yes, that's correct. Rowan."

"Rowan Monahan?"

"No. Rowan Workman. He isn't John's biological brother. The Monahan family took him on a voyage across the Atlantic. His mother died at the start of the journey. He was only four or five, barely that. He spoke so little… He was never able to tell us his surname. All he kept saying was 'wowan.' We understood that his name was Rowan."

"So, Rowan is John's younger half-brother?"

"Three or four years younger, yes… We were never certain. John was… was nineteen, and Rowan sixteen. At least, that's the age we assigned him. Yet, looking at him now, he seems older. He's very tall for his age."

"How did he take his brother's death?"

The question struck Workman visibly, and he took a deep breath before answering, his voice trembling slightly.

"He was devastated… So utterly devastated… John was everything to him. From the time he was a child, John looked after him like a parent. Rowan followed him everywhere. Absolutely everywhere."

Robinson leaned in slightly, scrutinizing Workman's expressions.

"Was he also an Orangeman sympathizer?"

Workman straightened in his chair, a flash of indignation in his eyes.

"Oh no! Far from it."

"Yet you say he followed his brother in all things."

"Not in politics," Workman retorted, shaking his head firmly. "Rowan didn't understand these conflicts between Protestant and Catholic Irish. In fact..."

He hesitated as if weighing the gravity of the words he was about to utter.

"In fact, what?" Robinson pressed, his voice sharper.

Workman averted his eyes, fixing an invisible point on the wall ahead.

"In fact... when he learned of John's death, he didn't blame the Fenians who killed him. No. He turned on me. He shouted, 'You and your damned politics, see what you've done!'"

Robinson regarded Workman for a moment, noting the pain in his voice. Then, with measured steps, he returned to his seat. He sat, took a sip of whisky, and savoured the warmth of the liquid, a stark contrast to the chill of the atmosphere between them.

"You knew, then, that it was the Fenians who killed him?" Robinson asked, his tone deliberately neutral.

"Of course, it was them. Who else?" Workman replied, his voice tight. "Ermatinger confided to me that John wanted to infiltrate them. They found out and..."

"You're very angry with them," Robinson observed, his eyes fixed intently on Workman.

"What do you think?" growled Workman, his voice rising slightly. "Wouldn't you be in my place?"

The Detective let the silence settle, a heavy, calculated pause. He took a discreet breath, ready to strike.

"That's why you wanted the Fenians to pay... by blackmailing D'Arcy McGee to denounce them."

Workman's eyes widened briefly before a flash of anger lit them. For the first time, his austere façade cracked, revealing a simmering rage.

"Those bastards..." he muttered through clenched teeth, his fists tightening. "Something had to be done."

"Why D'Arcy McGee?"

Workman averted his gaze slightly, hesitating before answering.

"Because I knew how to reach him."

Robinson's eyes gleamed with sudden understanding.

"Through his daughter, Frasa," he said calmly.

Workman almost flinched, astonished.

"That's right. How do you know?"

"I learned that Frasa was in love with a Protestant Irishman. It was Rowan, wasn't it?"

"Yes, that's correct."

"Rowan told you about it?"

"Never!" Workman exclaimed, frowning deeply. "He knew what I thought. I would never have agreed to him courting a Papist girl. I would never have tolerated it. But... he spoke to my wife, Annie."

"And your wife told you," Robinson concluded confidently.

"Women can't keep a secret," Workman muttered bitterly. "She was worried about Rowan, especially after he left home. She thought he was with Frasa. And that's when the idea came to me... to blackmail D'Arcy McGee by making him believe his daughter had been kidnapped."

"And it worked," Robinson stated, not asking a question.

"Yes... It seems it did. He published an article in several city newspapers."

Robinson rose slowly as if holding back a surge of inner tension. He began pacing back and forth across the office, the glass in his hand catching glints of the morning light.

"You know what you did was illegal," he said, his voice sharp and cold. "Not only that, but you plunged an entire family into unbearable pain."

Workman lifted his head, his face conflicted with remorse and defiance.

"Yes, I know," he replied in a hoarse voice. "And I regret it now. But at the time… I was so angry. So utterly lost…"

A tense silence filled the room, Workman's words hanging heavy in the air like a confession fraught with consequences. Robinson stopped before Workman's chair, his tall figure casting a shadow over the slumped man. He set his half-empty whisky glass on the dark wooden table and fixed Workman with a piercing stare. His voice, calm yet cutting, broke the silence:

"Did you kill Brennan, Mr. Workman?"

Workman nearly leapt from his chair, surprise etched across his face.

"Brennan… Brennan… The Fenian?" he stammered, his tone thick with disbelief.

"That's correct," Robinson confirmed coldly. "One of the Fenians on the list you received Thursday from our police chief, Penton."

"He's dead?"

"Yes. Murdered."

"Murdered!" Workman repeated, almost in shock. "That's impossible!"

"Did you kill him?" Robinson pressed, relentless.

"No, of course not. I'm no murderer!"

"And yet, you've killed men before."

Workman swallowed hard, his gaze shifting slightly away.

"It's true," he admitted, "that I've been involved in violent acts during certain protests... Men died, yes. But cold-blooded murder? Never! I wouldn't be capable of it. Just the thought of it..."

"Then what happened?" Robinson demanded, his tone stern. "Did your Orangemen colleagues take care of it?"

"Absolutely not," Workman replied, shaking his head vehemently. "That's not how we operate. We don't assassinate people."

"But it was your son," Robinson countered. "You had to avenge him somehow."

"Yes, he was my son," Workman replied bitterly. "And I avenged him… by using that blackmail letter against D'Arcy McGee."

"If it wasn't you or one of your Orangemen, who could it have been? Who else did you tell about Brennan?"

"I'm certain it never left our inner circle of Orangemen. Don't forget, we're a secret society."

"And you? Did you mention it to anyone outside the circle?"

"No, of course not…"

He stopped abruptly, a flicker of realization crossing his face.

"I may have mentioned Brennan's name to Annie," he admitted. "I told her he was the leader of the Fenians, nothing more."

"Nothing more?" Robinson repeated, raising an eyebrow. "You wouldn't have happened to add that he was the prime suspect in your son John's death, would you?"

"I... I don't know if I put it that way," Workman murmured, visibly uneasy.

"So, your wife knew Brennan's name and that he was suspected of murdering John. And as you said: a woman can't keep a secret..."

"This makes no sense," Workman muttered.

After a brief silence, Robinson abruptly changed the subject:

"Where is your son Rowan right now?"

"I don't know... I don't know," Workman stammered, a trembling hand rising to his forehead.

"What do you mean you don't know where he is?"

"Since he ran off with Frasa, I haven't heard from him."

"How long has it been?"

"Two weeks, maybe."

"He may not have written to his father, but to his mother? I'd wager he has."

"It's possible. I'll ask her."

"Let me do that," Robinson interjected firmly.

"All right. She'll be back on Friday. She's spending the week at her sister's in the village of Saint-Laurent."

Workman scribbled an address on a scrap of paper and handed it to the Detective.

"What's going to happen to me?" he finally asked, his voice weary.

Robinson took the paper, slid it into the inner pocket of his coat, and replied:

"For now, there are no criminal charges against you for your attempt at blackmail. However, I'll inform D'Arcy McGee of your actions, and it will be up to him to decide whether to pursue you in civil court."

Without another word, Robinson grabbed his bowler hat from the low table and, with a sharp motion, placed it on his head. He turned away without offering his hand to Workman and left the room, leaving the man alone in the heavy silence of his regrets.

CHAPTER 22

April 6, Thursday Morning

Robinson and Kelly bent over their desks and scrutinized some report, their faces set in nearly identical expressions of deep concentration. A pale light filtered through the room's windows, illuminating the dust suspended in this early April morning's cold, dry air. They were waiting for the two other detectives to join them for their daily briefing, but nearly an hour had passed, and their patience was wearing thin. Neither of them liked wasting time, especially with tasks awaiting their attention.

At last, hurried footsteps echoed on the wooden staircase. Miss Dupuis burst into the room, slightly out of breath, her cheeks flushed from the biting cold outside and the exertion of the climb. A tailored charcoal wool coat hugged her figure, and a gray felt bonnet, set slightly askew, allowed a few unruly chestnut strands to escape. She removed her black leather gloves, blowing on her hands to warm them, then tucked them into her coat pockets before unbuttoning them.

Until the previous week, she had lived with her stepfather, which had made her commute far simpler. But since moving into a small apartment in the Mile End, north of the city, her daily journeys had become an adventure in themselves. This morning, again, she had struggled to find a Hansom cab in that outlying district. Drivers preferred to stay in the more central areas at such an early hour, and she had been forced to walk a good part of the way on foot.

The nearly hour-long walk in the icy air had brought a healthy glow to her complexion, but she couldn't deny her fatigue. Even though she was young and in excellent shape, long treks through streets still partially frozen, bundled in a heavy coat with a wind that found its way through nonetheless, were no small effort. Once in the room, she cast an apologetic smile at Robinson and Kelly, who barely looked up from their report.

"Apologies for my tardiness; no luck finding a cab this morning…"

Miss Dupuis crossed the threshold quickly, still wrapped in her thick wool coat, and delivered her explanation in a hurried tone. She removed her bonnet with a sigh, then ran her fingers absentmindedly through a few stray chestnut strands that had slipped from her bun.

"A fine excuse, Miss Dupuis," Kelly said with a mocking smile, folding his arms in front of him. "You didn't oversleep by chance, did you? Though I suppose the good doctor might have kept you occupied."

Miss Dupuis's face, already pink from the biting cold, turned a deeper crimson at Kelly's remark.

"What are you implying, Kelly?" she protested, furrowing her brow.

She turned an accusing gaze toward Robinson.

"Don't look at me like that, Dupuis," Robinson replied, raising his hands in mock innocence. "I didn't say a word."

"You know, Miss Dupuis," Kelly continued, clearly amused, "I have the best informants in town. They had to replace the candles twice; the dinner lasted so long."

"First of all, he's not a doctor… Not yet, at least. Secondly, mind your own business, Kelly," she said, shrugging with irritation. "Did I miss something?"

"We were waiting…"

The door opened abruptly, letting in a gust of fresh air. Two figures appeared in the doorway. Morin stepped in first, his quick stride contrasting with the hesitant gait of Leclerc, who leaned heavily on a cane.

The others rose almost in unison, smiling, though none dared approach too hastily. Leclerc moved forward with a slowness that betrayed his pain. His figure, thinned by weeks of convalescence, appeared frail beneath the thick dark coat he struggled to wear.

"Leclerc," said Robinson, taking a step forward. "What are you doing here?"

"I came to see you," replied Leclerc, his voice weak yet tinged with a trace of humour. "I know you can't do without me."

It had been three weeks since Leclerc's assault in Griffintown had shaken the team. Four thugs had set upon him, breaking his left arm—still encased in a cast—and cracking several of his ribs. A violent blow to the head had left him unconscious for hours, and it had taken him days to piece the events back together. The bruises on his face were beginning to fade, yet they still marked his skin like painful reminders.

Morin gently took his arm to help him sit on a chair near the stove, where the muted warmth of the fire lent a cozy touch to the room.

"I've settled him into his new apartment in the Hochelaga district," explained Morin.

"Griffintown's done for me," murmured Leclerc with a timid laugh, his fingers nervously gripping the head of his cane.

"We're all happy to see you again," Robinson replied with a sincere smile. "But you shouldn't be here, Leclerc."

"I know… I know… I'll leave right away, Chief. I just wanted to say hello."

Robinson observed him for a moment, then gave a slow nod.

"We were just about to review the situation. Very well, for this time, I'll allow you to sit in on our meeting. But right after, you're to head back home."

A tired smile lit Leclerc's face.

"All right. Thank you, Chief. It'll be a nice change from hospital conversations."

Robinson began his summary in a clear, steady voice, his words resonating in the austere room, where the chill from outside seemed to linger despite the stove's warmth. He started from the beginning: the discovery of the body in the alley adjacent to Scanlan's tavern. The detectives had initially believed the case to be tied to a brawl in the establishment and had wasted several days pursuing a fruitless lead.

"A false lead?" Leclerc said with a doubtful air.

The Chief continued, explaining how an entire week had been spent chasing a pseudonym. Only through determined efforts did they finally uncover the victim's true identity: John Monahan.

"An agent in the service of the government," Robinson specified, pausing to let the information sink in.

Monahan, a Protestant Irishman active in Orangemen circles, had been tasked with infiltrating the Fenians, radical Catholic Irishmen stirring unrest across Canada. Monahan's mission had complicated the case, muddling the already tangled political tensions between Protestant and Catholic Irish factions.

To this was added the mysterious disappearance of D'Arcy McGee's daughter.

"An unrelated case at first glance," continued Robinson, leafing distractedly through a few pages of his dossier, "until we uncovered the reasons behind this supposed abduction."

D'Arcy McGee, an influential figure in the Irish community, had fallen victim to blackmail. He had been coerced into publicly denouncing the Fenians, which he did under pressure, publishing a scathing editorial in several newspapers.

Robinson paused, his tone growing graver.

"And as if that weren't enough," he said, "the recent death of Francis Brennan, that wig-wearing Fenian, has further muddied the waters. A key figure in the Fenian movement in Montreal found dead—murdered."

Leclerc slumped in his chair and nodded slowly.

"I see the case is rather tangled," he said thoughtfully. "Where do things stand now? Have you found the killers?"

"As for John Monahan, we have a suspect," Robinson replied, his tone betraying a faint glimmer of satisfaction.

Kelly spoke up, leaning his back against the edge of the desk.

"After several days of searching, I tracked down the main suspect in Monahan's murder—a Fenian named Patrick O'Meara. We'll be questioning him this morning."

"Oh, really! And the other one… Brennan, was it?"

"As for him, we're still looking," Robinson said, closing his dossier. "But I have a strong lead, thanks to my interrogation of Thomas Workman."

Leclerc furrowed his brow slightly.

"Workman… Of Frothingham & Workman, the wholesale hardware business?"

"The very same. He's a prominent Orangeman in Montreal. And wouldn't you know it, John Monahan, our government spy, was his adopted son. Workman would have ample reason to hold a grudge against Brennan."

A silence fell, each man digesting the revelation. Then Leclerc, visibly weary, rose slowly, leaning on his cane.

"Well, I'll not trouble you any longer. I'm off home to unpack my trunks."

Standing near the window where the winter light cast a pale glow, Morin turned toward him with concern.

"Will you be all right, Émile? Can you manage on your own? I can help you settle in after work if necessary."

"I'll be fine, thank you, Morin. I can manage."

Leclerc took a few slow steps toward the door, his hunched shoulders still betraying the lingering effects of his assault.

"Poor Leclerc," murmured Morin once the door closed behind him. "He's not in great shape."

Then, turning toward Miss Dupuis with a mischievous smile, he added, "We're not rid of you yet, Miss Dupuis."

Robinson and Kelly also left the office, heading toward the interrogation room. Robinson still held his thick dossier under his arm, focusing on the task ahead. He had a method all his own: the dossier often had nothing to do with the witness in question, but the psychological effect was undeniable. By conspicuously flipping through the documents, he sowed doubt in his subjects' minds, making them believe the police knew far more than they let on.

***

The two detectives entered the interrogation room. The air was heavy, thick with palpable tension, despite the harsh light spilling from the lamp suspended above. A man whose broad frame barely fit the narrow chair was seated before them. Robinson and Kelly, skilled at sizing up a man even while seated, could see he was massive—a mountain ready to rise if provoked.

His long red hair framed an angular face, made more striking by robust sideburns. Beneath his prominent brow, his cold, almost inhuman blue eyes shone unsettlingly. A broken nose and a scatter of scars across his round head spoke of a violent past—perhaps a boxer, a brawler, or both.

The man's gaze shifted between them, silent, his arms crossed over his imposing chest, much like a caged animal scrutinizing its keepers.

Robinson and Kelly pulled out their chairs simultaneously, the wood's creak amplifying the room's stillness. Robinson placed his thick dossier on the table with a resounding "thud," shattering the oppressive quiet, while Kelly retrieved a notebook and pencil, poised to take notes.

"Well now, Patrick, we've been looking for you for quite some time," Kelly began, his tone light, almost mocking.

No reaction. The man's gaze remained fixed, cold and unyielding.

"You're a hard man to get hold of. You may need a secretary, old boy. Where have you been?"

Still no response. The silence was almost insolent.

"Mind you, it's none of my business. But you know, I paid your wife a visit. Lovely brunette!"

This time, a flicker: Patrick tilted his head slightly, his eyes hardening.

"You'd best keep away from my wife, you bloody bastard," he growled, his rough voice finally breaking the silence.

Kelly glanced at Robinson, a satisfied smile curling his lips.

"Well, he speaks after all... though not very politely. So, were you on holiday, Patrick? Because I also stopped by where you work. They told me you hadn't been seen in a while. Quite the time to take a leave, isn't it?"

The man's expression returned to its stony impassiveness as he fixed Kelly with the same icy stare.

"Anyway, we've found you, and that's what matters," Kelly feigned indifference. "I hear you gave the constables a bit of a fight when they came to bring you in. Not very clever, that. Resisting the law rarely ends well."

Robinson, who had remained silent thus far, now stepped in. It was a dance the two detectives knew well—Kelly provoked, Robinson steadied.

Robinson opened his notebook slowly, carefully leafing through it as though it held the most vital of secrets.

"Patrick O'Meara," he began calmly, "thirty-five years old, married, three children, resident of Griffintown. Is that correct?"

The man turned his head toward Robinson, his expression unchanging. He did not reply immediately.

"Look, O'Meara, I'm asking something simple. I understand you don't like policemen, but even so."

"That's right."

Robinson raised an eyebrow, intrigued.

"That's right, what? What's your name?"

"Yes, that's my name," O'Meara replied, his gravelly voice carrying a hint of weariness.

"You work on the Lachine Canal project. Foreman, is that correct?"

The man nodded brusquely, confirming.

"Foreman. That's a respectable job," Robinson continued, his tone taking on a sharper edge. "I can't imagine you're too popular with your men. And if you're still in the position, your employers must be fond of you."

"I do my job, that's all… and I do it well," O'Meara replied with an air of detachment.

Robinson smirked slightly, his piercing eyes fixed on the man as if probing his thoughts.

"Of course, among the Irish, you understand one another. Don't you, O'Meara?"

"Yes, sir," he answered curtly, his tone carrying a faint trace of mistrust.

Robinson remained silent, slowly leafing through the pages of the dossier before him. The rustle of paper echoed in the tense stillness of the interrogation room. After a moment, he stopped on a page, narrowing his eyes slightly as though focusing on a crucial detail.

"I see here that you're still quite attached to your homeland," he said calmly, lifting his gaze to O'Meara. "And I don't mean Canada... I'm talking about Ireland."

The red-haired man's expression darkened instantly, but he held Robinson's gaze without flinching.

"And what would you know about what I like or don't like?" he growled, his voice betraying a barely contained anger.

Robinson straightened slightly, a faint, almost imperceptible smile on his lips.

"You know, O'Meara," he said in a calm but menacing tone, "we're quite good at what we do, too. Isn't that right, Kelly?"

Leaning against the back of his chair, Kelly nodded, a subtle smile flickering on his lips, though he remained silent.

"We manage to learn a great deal about people... a great deal," Robinson continued, turning another page, his fingers lightly tapping the edge of the dossier. "I see here that you're part of an organization... let's see..."

He pretended to read the document carefully.

"The Fenians. That's right, isn't it? You're a Fenian, my friend?"

At those words, O'Meara flinched ever so slightly. A flicker of unease crossed his eyes, though he quickly masked it by squaring his shoulders.

"Who told you that?" he asked, his voice tighter than intended.

"I told you," Robinson replied, fixing him steadily. "We know a great many things."

He turned another page, taking his time, before pausing again.

"The Fenians," he resumed thoughtfully, "from what I read here, they're no saints. Capable of just about anything. It's even said they want to invade Canada."

Robinson raised his head, his piercing eyes locking onto O'Meara.

"And yet, we've welcomed you Irish folk with open arms. Isn't that right, Kelly?"

He turned slightly toward his partner.

"You're Irish too, Kelly. Weren't you welcomed when you came to Canada?"

Kelly nodded slowly, his eyes fixed on O'Meara with measured intensity.

"Canada hasn't treated you well, O'Meara?" Robinson pressed, his voice growing more insistent. "Tell me, why do you resent us so much?"

A heavy silence hung in the air, broken suddenly by an outburst of anger.

"British bastards!" O'Meara shouted, his voice filled with rage, his fists clenching on the table.

Robinson, unperturbed, glanced at Kelly before turning back to O'Meara, a cold smile curling his lips.

"Ah yes, of course. We're the wicked British oppressors keeping Ireland in chains," Robinson said with a tone of near-dismissiveness, his eyes boring into O'Meara with icy precision.

He let the silence linger as though gauging the impact of his words before continuing in a calmer voice:

"That might be true in Ireland. But here, Patrick, what have we ever done to you?"

O'Meara, though seething with anger, remained stubbornly silent. He seemed to hesitate as if wary of stepping onto dangerous ground. Kelly chose that moment to step in.

"Say, Patrick," he began, straightening slightly in his chair, "I ran into your lady friend. You know… and I don't mean your pretty brunette wife. I'm talking about your other friend… Stella, isn't it?"

The effect was immediate: O'Meara stiffened, and a flicker of unease returned to his eyes. He shrugged mechanically, feigning ignorance.

"Come now, Patrick. Don't spin me a tale. The Chief just told you—we know everything. You make a bit of pocket money with her, don't you? Ring a bell now?"

"Ah, yes, little Stella…" he said in a neutral tone. "She's a friend."

"A profitable friend, eh?" Kelly shot back, a sly smile curling his lips. "Because she does things for you—interesting things. And she's not just friends with you. She often has Irishmen over at her place. Seems like half of Griffintown knows her."

O'Meara shrugged again, attempting to downplay his words.

"That's true. She has a lot of friends."

"Don't I know it!" Kelly leaned forward slightly, his tone turning almost conspiratorial. "I've even become one of her friends recently. We've had quite a few exchanges. She's very friendly, little Stella... quite talkative, too. She also told me plenty about you and other friends of hers."

The silence in the room deepened. O'Meara maintained an outward calm, though his worried eyes betrayed his thoughts.

"What could that little whore have told you?"

"Ah, so she's not really a friend, then? She's a prostitute, is that it?"

"She always talks nonsense. She loves spinning tall tales."

"Ah, of course!" Kelly smiled as if in agreement. "I thought as much... She told me some hard-to-believe things, but that's true. Must be another one of her inventions."

Another heavy silence fell over the room. Kelly resumed speaking, this time with deliberate slowness.

"She told me about a client. An Irishman, but not like the others. She said he wasn't who he claimed to be. She brought him several times to Mother Scanlan's tavern. He wanted to know all sorts of things about the Fenians. And Lord knows there are plenty of Fenians at Mother Scanlan's. What do you think of that, Patrick?"

"She worked with many men," O'Meara replied, his voice weaker than he had intended.

"Maybe so, but she didn't tell me about all of them. Just this one. He caught her attention. She said..." Kelly pretended to search for the words. "You took a great interest in knowing about the men she worked with."

"She's the one who talked to me about them," O'Meara snapped sharply. "I never asked. That chatterbox can't keep her mouth shut."

"Fair enough," Kelly replied, crossing his arms. "But she talked to you about this particular man. A man who wasn't what he claimed to be."

"Maybe. I don't remember."

"Oh, but you do, Patrick. Let me refresh your memory. She told me his real name was John Monahan. He said that he was very interested in the Fenians. He mentioned that it was for his work. She didn't understand everything, but you did, Patrick. You understood."

For the first time since the interrogation began, O'Meara turned his head, fixing his gaze on an invisible point to his left.

Robinson, who had remained in the background, spoke again, his deep voice breaking the silence:

"You realized Monahan was a government spy. You and your little band of Fenians were warned it was possible. Your compatriots in the United States had already rooted out a few of them."

O'Meara stayed silent, his head still turned, his jaw muscles visibly tense.

Robinson paused, letting the tension peak, before delivering the fatal blow.

"That's why you killed him."

O'Meara snapped his head toward Robinson, panic flashing in his eyes for the first time.

"What are you saying? He's dead?"

The glint in his eyes made it clear he was feigning innocence. A sliver of light, cutting through a dusty window, barely illuminated the interrogation room, where the chill in the air rivalled the frostiness of their gazes.

"Don't pretend to be surprised. You killed him on St. Patrick's night. You were at Scanlan's tavern that evening."

Kelly leaned back against his chair, arms crossed. His relaxed posture contrasted with the icy sharpness of his words.

"St. Patrick's night? No, I wasn't at Scanlan's tavern."

"Then where were you?" Robinson asked, his piercing gaze dull into the accused.

"I don't know. I don't remember."

"So, you have no alibi for this murder."

A tense silence followed. O'Meara averted his gaze, staring at a knot in the table's wood as if that insignificant detail might save him.

"I'll tell you what happened," Robinson continued, flipping through his notebook with a swift gesture. "You already knew who Monahan was from little Stella. Maybe you even mentioned him to your gang of Fenian ruffians. You planned the deed, and you were chosen to carry it out. You'd been watching him, perhaps following him, waiting for the right moment. St. Patrick's night gave you the perfect excuse. The chaos of the evening made it the ideal time for a crime. Am I getting close to the truth?"

O'Meara shook his head silently, his lips pressed tightly together, as a bead of cold sweat trickled down his temple despite the chill in the room.

"You knew Monahan was at Scanlan's that night. So, you waited for him outside the tavern. It was late—Monahan was one of the last to leave. You lured him into the alley under some pretense. Perhaps you dangled the idea that the Fenians wanted him to join. Then, without warning, you stabbed him with your knife. What do you think of that story?"

O'Meara finally lifted his eyes to Robinson. His breathing had steadied.

"That's a fine story," he said with a forced smile. "Sounds like the same sort of nonsense that little whore likes to tell."

Kelly stiffened at the word, but Robinson remained impassive.

"A fine story? But this one happens to be true," Robinson retorted, snapping his notebook shut with a decisive motion.

"But you've got nothing on me. Did anyone see me do it? Did anyone see me kill that scum?"

Robinson didn't respond, his face as unreadable as a stone wall.

"And what about the knife? Where's the knife I supposedly used to kill the man? Did you find the knife?… That's what I thought—you didn't find the knife. You've got no witnesses."

"We'll find them, don't worry," Kelly interjected, his gaze fixed on the floor, his jaw clenched with resolute determination.

"Are you sure about that?"

"And you've got no alibi," Robinson reminded him.

"I said I don't remember," O'Meara muttered, his shoulders slumping. "But it'll come to me if you give me some time."

Robinson closed his notebook with authority.

"Either way, we have enough circumstantial evidence to bring you before a judge. Let's see what he has to say."

"We'll see," O'Meara replied, an enigmatic smile curling his lips.

Robinson and Kelly left the room, their boots echoing sharply on the cold, tiled floor of the corridor. The moment they stepped through the door, Kelly's anger erupted.

"It's him! It's definitely him!"

"It's him, indeed," Robinson replied wearily. "But he'll likely walk free. We don't have enough evidence."

"Bastard," Kelly spat. "Bloody bastard. All this for nothing!"

Robinson shrugged with measured indifference, adjusting his coat with a precise gesture before brushing away some invisible dust.

"We can't win them all, Kelly."

CHAPTER 23

Friday, April 7, Afternoon and Evening

A piebald horse, Robinson's favourite, struggled to pull the police chaise up the icy slope of Sherbrooke Hill. Its shod hooves hammered the frozen road with an almost hypnotic regularity, creating a dull echo in the crisp morning air. At the close of the 18th century, Sherbrooke Street wound along a natural terrace overlooking the city. This unique geological feature of Montreal disrupted the rigid orthogonal grid below, offering a striking view to those who ventured upon it. Sherbrooke had since become the city's most prestigious thoroughfare, home to the grand estates of Anglo-Scottish industrialists, whose opulent mansions bore witness to their wealth and ambition.

Inside the chaise, Robinson adjusted his heavy wool coat and pulled the fur collar close to his neck, reddened by the biting cold. He had left the police station to pay a visit to Annie Workman, the wife of Thomas Workman, an influential merchant still under suspicion in the death of Francis Brennan. The latter had reported his wife's return after a week spent with her sister in Saint-Laurent, a village north of the Island of Montreal. Cautious as ever, Robinson had decided to bring Miss Dupuis along. Wrapped in a thick knitted shawl over her wool coat and a lined bonnet, she had a natural gift for soothing tempers—a priceless asset when questioning the ladies of high society.

At last, they arrived in front of the Workman mansion, which was notably situated. To the front, one could glimpse a sweeping view of the city and, beyond it, the St. Lawrence River shimmering under the pale winter sun. Behind, Mount Royal unfurled its snowy charms, its frost-laden pines glittering like jewels.

The mansion itself, nestled at the end of a sizeable tree-lined courtyard, was hardly impressive in its architecture. A wrought-iron fence enclosed the property, with a stone-pillared gate granting access to a straight path leading to the house. Utilitarian in style, the building resembled a square, two-storey box. Two rectangular windows flanked the ground floor, while three smaller ones gazed out from the austere façade above. A classical columned portico marked the entrance, topped by a terrace rendered inaccessible in this season. To the side, a smaller structure and a carriage door hinted at the stable and outbuildings.

After waiting in the extraordinary, faintly wax-scented entryway for ten minutes, Robinson and Miss Dupuis, relieved of their heavy coats and hats by the butler, watched as a woman descended the grand, carved wooden staircase. She was dressed in a silk house gown, delicately draped with a cashmere shawl to shield herself from the lingering chill of the mansion. Her fluid gait betrayed the confidence of a grande bourgeoise well accustomed to social graces. Reaching their level, she offered a polite smile and said simply:

"I am Annie Workman. Welcome to our home," she said simply, in a soft, slightly lilting voice.

The mistress of the house, diminutive in stature, had a delicate, slightly oblong face framed by carefully coiffed auburn hair. Her bright green eyes, sparkling with a lively gleam, unmistakably betrayed her Scottish heritage. Delicate freckles scattered across her cheeks lent her appearance a youthful freshness that softened her otherwise formal elegance.

She led them to the parlour, opening the French doors with an almost mechanical delicacy. Like most mansions of this calibre, this one featured a parlour near the entrance, serving at times as a boudoir and at others as a library. Here, however, the room gave an impression of clutter. Armchairs, low tables, and objects crowded the space without true harmony. A Persian carpet, rich but worn, covered the wooden floor, and the walls were lined with framed paintings, most of them second-rate works. Above a modest fire crackling in the room's centre, the marble mantelpiece was cluttered with a profusion of trivial knick-knacks, betraying a questionable taste in decoration.

Robinson and Miss Dupuis exchanged a discreet glance. The opulence of the setting could not mask its awkward and tasteless aesthetic. The Workmans, it seemed, favoured quantity over quality, a failing often seen in those with more money than refinement.

As she invited Robinson and Miss Dupuis to sit in faux Louis XV armchairs with worn armrests, Mrs. Workman, a faint smile on her lips, asked in her gentle voice:

"Would you like some tea?"

"Gladly," replied Miss Dupuis lightly, lifting her gloves.

"Please excuse me; I shall inform my maid to prepare it," said Mrs. Workman, rising gracefully, her silk gown rustling softly with her movements.

She departed the parlour with elegance, leaving a subtle scent of lavender. Miss Dupuis, ever attentive, observed their hostess with quiet interest, noting every detail of her manner and appearance. Evidently, beneath her outward refinement, Annie Workman bore something weightier than a silk gown. Her observations could prove to be of great significance.

A few minutes later, Mrs. Workman returned to the parlour. She resumed her seat with measured elegance, crossing her finely shod ankles and resting her legs in a studied pose.

"When I arrived last night, my husband informed me that you would be coming," said Mrs. Workman, folding her delicate hands on her lap.

"Did he explain why we wished to speak with you?" Robinson asked in a measured tone, attempting to catch her gaze.

"No. Indeed, Thomas is not much of a talker, but I confess it intrigued me nonetheless," she replied, a faintly melancholic smile gracing her lips.

Miss Dupuis then intervened, her voice soft, almost maternal:

"Mrs. Workman…"

"Call me Annie," she interrupted with a slight inclination of her head.

"Very well, Annie," Miss Dupuis said warmly. "We have learned that you recently lost a son… Please accept our heartfelt condolences for your terrible ordeal."

Annie's features froze momentarily. Her green eyes, glistening with restrained tears, stared into the void.

"Yes… A true tragedy," she murmured. "Like a hammer blow. We were all devastated."

Miss Dupuis nodded gently, her expression sombre.

"We truly understand your pain, believe me."

"Thank you, Miss…"

"Dupuis."

"Miss Dupuis… I hope I do not seem indiscreet, but I am surprised to see a young woman like you working with the constabulary," said Mrs. Workman, a faint smile breaking through her sorrow.

Miss Dupuis let out a small laugh, light as a breath:

"Oh, I am an assistant on the detective team. I am not a member of the police, heaven forbid!"

Miss Dupuis's candour elicited a more sincere smile from Mrs. Workman, who nodded slightly before continuing:

"It was an immense loss for us. John was so… vibrant, so full of life…"

At that moment, a maid entered quietly, carrying a tray with a porcelain teapot and three matching cups. She placed the tray on the low table in perfect silence and poured the tea with precise movements. She handed a cup to her mistress, then one to Robinson, and finally to Miss Dupuis before disappearing almost like a shadow.

For a moment, they each focused on the comforting warmth of the amber liquid. Robinson, after setting his cup back on the table, broke the silence:

"Your husband spoke to me about your son John. He also mentioned that your other son… Rowan, is that correct?… seems even more shaken by this tragedy."

Annie nodded, placing her cup down with care.

"That is entirely true. John was his elder, and he admired him greatly. We adopted them both at the same time, you know."

"Your husband mentioned as much," Robinson replied, tilting his head slightly. "Rowan was younger than John?"

"Yes, by three years… At least, as far as we believe. When we adopted him, he was so frail, so lost. He could barely say his own name."

Miss Dupuis exchanged a glance with Robinson before asking:

"Is Rowan here? Could we meet him?"

A veil of hesitation passed over Annie's face before she replied:

"No. He is at my sister's in the village of Saint-Laurent."

"Oh? And he's not attending college?" Robinson asked, intrigued.

Annie averted her gaze slightly, her expression shadowed by sadness.

"No… Not anymore…"

Mrs. Workman's face darkened further if such a thing were possible. A heavy melancholy filled the room, and the silence stretched, broken only by the soft crackling of the wood in the hearth. Robinson resumed, his voice calm but firm:

"You say your son is with his aunt?"

"Yes," she answered, absentmindedly adjusting a fold of her dress. "They needed him on the farm. My brother-in-law is a farmer, and he has no hired help. The livestock require constant care, and the planting season is about to begin."

"You spent the week there?"

"Yes, my sister Allison also needed assistance," she added, lowering her eyes to avoid a painful topic.

"Rowan must have been glad to see you. Was he alone there?"

A slight tremor crossed Mrs. Workman's lips.

"Yes… yes, he was alone," she replied hesitantly.

Robinson fixed her with a piercing gaze that seemed to say: Don't lie to me. She looked away, then buckled under the pressure.

"In truth, he wasn't alone. He was with a young woman."

"Frasa?"

Mrs. Workman raised her eyebrows slightly, visibly surprised.

"Ah! I see you are already aware. Yes, Frasa. Rowan is madly in love with her. Madly."

"Have they been seeing each other for long?"

"Some time... I couldn't say precisely."

"You're not certain?"

She hesitated, fiddling with the folds of her dress.

"It's because Rowan kept it from us."

"Why? Why would he hide such a thing?"

Mrs. Workman lifted her head, feigning surprise.

"Why would he hide it?" she repeated, pretending not to understand.

Miss Dupuis interjected at that moment, her voice soft and full of compassion.

"Annie, I know what it's like to be in love. It turns your world upside down; you lose your bearings. Sometimes, you want to keep that love a secret, like a private garden, just for yourself."

A faint smile briefly lit Annie's face.

"Yes, that must be it. It was only recently that we learned he was seeing Frasa."

"The daughter of an Irish Catholic," Robinson added in a neutral tone. "That must not have pleased your husband."

Annie's smile faded. She nodded gravely.

"I am certain that's why they kept it hidden for so long. In our family… My husband would never have accepted such a relationship. We are Protestants, you see. The idea of our son marrying a Catholic was utterly out of the question for him."

"Frasa's father, D'Arcy McGee, must have been just as opposed to the union," Robinson added.

Annie nodded again.

"Certainly. D'Arcy McGee is a staunch advocate for Irish Catholics. I wouldn't be surprised if he forbade his daughter from marrying a Protestant."

Miss Dupuis, pensive, spoke up.

"So, we have two lovers, Frasa and Rowan, aware that insurmountable obstacles stand between them. An impossible love…"

Silence settled once more. Each seemed lost in thought, absorbed by the weight of this family tragedy. Finally, Robinson broke the quiet.

"How long has Rowan been at your sister's?"

"It must be over two weeks," Annie replied.

"What made him leave home?"

Annie drew a deep breath as though mustering her courage.

"When he learned of his brother's death, he was… devastated. He lashed out at his father. He said it was his fault John was dead."

"And why would he say that?"

"He shouted that it was Thomas who had drawn John into his political battles, that he had put him in harm's way. Rowan was so angry…"

"And then he left. Did you know he was with Frasa?"

"Yes."

"And your husband?"

Annie hesitated before answering, her voice quivering slightly.

"I told him. He was furious."

"Furious that Rowan had left?"

"No… Furious that he had run off with Frasa. He rejected Rowan. He said he was no longer his son. Do you understand? After John's death, Thomas was no longer himself…"

Robinson nodded, his gaze dark.

"So, Frasa and Rowan fled to the village of Saint-Laurent. You were aware of this?"

"Not immediately. Allison wrote to me a few days later to say they were with her and that I needn't worry. But I worried all the same."

"That's why you decided to visit your sister," Robinson observed. "When was this?"

Annie raised her eyes, her expression fixed.

"Last week. Last Friday. I will remember it for the rest of my life."

"Why? What was so particular about that day?"

She clasped her hands tightly, her knuckles white with emotion.

"That was the day I learned who killed our son John."

Mrs. Workman's voice trembled slightly at these words as if each syllable tore a fragment from her soul. Her gaze fixed on one of the paintings before her. She seemed lost in a whirlwind of pain and fury while a heavy silence settled, amplifying the gravity of her revelation.

Miss Dupuis, meanwhile, had halted her writing, her eyes wide with astonishment. Robinson pressed on, his tone incisive:

"So, you knew who killed your son?"

Mrs. Workman nodded slowly, her trembling hands gripping the edge of her dress.

"My husband had learned it the day before. He was so distraught... Normally, he would never tell me such things. But that time, he gave me the killer's name. You know, I am a gentle, kind woman... But at that moment, I felt hatred rise, a rage I had never known."

Robinson tilted his head slightly, fixing his interlocutor with a piercing gaze.

"So, you wasted no time in telling Rowan."

"Of course! It was his right to know who had killed his brother."

"What was his reaction?"

Mrs. Workman closed her eyes momentarily as if trying to push away the memory.

"What do you think? He was beside himself. I had never seen him in such a state. He paced around the house like a caged animal. He fumed, completely out of control."

"And then? What happened?"

"I asked my sister Allison to let me stay for a few days. It might do him some good that I could help calm him. And he did calm down… or so it seemed. That afternoon, he suddenly announced he needed to go into town to run some errands."

"He went alone?"

"Yes, he took Paul's best horse—my brother-in-law's—and rode off. Frasa stayed with us. She was worried. Rowan always told her where he was going, but not this time. She couldn't believe he didn't want to take her along."

"What time did he return?"

"Late in the evening. He was exhausted."

"And had he brought back any purchases?"

"No, not that I know of," she replied, shaking her head with a trace of worry.

Robinson frowned slightly, lost in thought.

"And for the rest of the week? What happened then?"

Mrs. Workman offered a faint, almost wistful smile.

"Nothing out of the ordinary. Rowan kept working with Paul on the farm, and Frasa helped Allison. Those two…" She sighed. "They were so in love. Always close to one another, exchanging knowing glances. If you had seen them…"

"Allow me to ask a delicate question, Annie, though necessary," said Miss Dupuis with calculated gentleness. "Did they share the same room?"

Mrs. Workman raised her head sharply, visibly indignant.

"Never! Absolutely not! My sister would never have allowed it, and they wouldn't have wanted it either. Rowan and Frasa had vowed not to know one another until after the wedding."

Robinson, impassive, nodded.

"Could you give us your sister's address? We would like to speak with your son."

A shadow of embarrassment crossed Annie's face.

"It would do no good…"

"Why not?"

"They're no longer with Allison. They left yesterday. That's why I returned to Montreal. I thought Rowan might have come back here."

"You don't know where he is, then?"

Mrs. Workman shook her head slowly, her expression marked by sincere worry.

"No… I have no idea."

Robinson glanced briefly with Miss Dupuis, who slid her notebook and pencil into her satchel.

"Thank you for receiving us, Mrs. Workman," Robinson said, rising to his feet.

Miss Dupuis followed him to the front door.

A butler, exhibiting exemplary discretion, entered the hall carrying their carefully folded coats and hats on his arm. He stopped a few steps away and, with a faint clearing of his throat, signalled his presence without disrupting the solemnity of the moment. "Madam, gentlemen, here are your coats," he murmured composedly.

Slowly, they began donning their coats. The rustling of fabric timidly broke the oppressive silence, though it did little to dispel its weight entirely. Robinson adjusted his collar quickly, his broad shoulders making the garment appear almost too snug. Meanwhile, Miss Dupuis fastened her coat meticulously, her gaze shifting between Mrs. Workman and the butler as if seeking distraction in these mundane gestures from the moment's intensity.

As they were about to leave, Robinson paused and turned back, his gaze fixed on Mrs. Workman.

"One last thing, Mrs. Workman. You didn't tell me the name of the man who murdered your son John."

Mrs. Workman blinked, surprised.

"But I did tell you…"

"I don't believe so," he replied calmly. "Could you remind me?"

She lifted her chin slightly, her voice trembling with emotion.

"Francis Brennan. I will remember it for the rest of my life."

At the mention of the name, Miss Dupuis started, turning sharply toward Robinson. Her eyes, glistening with emotion and surprise, seemed to spark. Robinson, however, remained expressionless, his demeanour unchanged.

Mrs. Workman added, almost pleadingly:

"Will you find my Rowan, Detective?"

"We will do everything we can, Madam," he replied gravely before closing the door softly behind him.

***

The end of a beautiful, sunlit day bathed Montreal in a golden glow. The last rays of sunlight reflected off the snow-covered rooftops, creating a gentle impression of warmth despite the biting cold in the air. Evening descended softly; a penetrating chill crept into every corner, even past the thick curtains struggling to keep the warmth inside.

Robinson was sharing a meal with Rosalie at the table in a warmly lit dining room. The lingering aroma of the stew they had enjoyed earlier and the sweet notes of apple pie filled the air, adding to the cozy atmosphere.

The front door opened abruptly as they were finishing dessert, letting in a rush of cold air. Thérèse appeared in the dining room doorway, her face alight with palpable urgency.

"Well, Thérèse!" exclaimed Rosalie, setting down her fork. "We weren't expecting you. I'll set another place."

"I've already had supper, Mama," Thérèse replied, removing her shawl and coat.

"Would you like some dessert? I made apple pie."

"I'd love some, thank you," she said, taking a seat.

After settling herself, she focused on Robinson, serious and intense.

"I've just heard some startling news, Silas."

Robinson regarded her with curiosity, his eyebrows slightly furrowed.

"Shannon came knocking at my door this evening. I was in the middle of eating a bowl of soup."

Shannon, the daughter of Thomas Ryan, was like a cousin to Thérèse, though they shared no actual kinship. Thérèse continued:

"Shannon and Frasa are as close as two peas in a pod, as you know. They both attend the same college."

"Yes, I know all that. Where are you going with this?" Robinson asked.

Thérèse took a bite of pie, savouring the sweetness of the apples and spices before responding.

"Mmm! Always delicious, Mama! Well… Shannon hadn't seen Frasa at the boarding school for several weeks. But this afternoon, as she was leaving college to head back to her parents, Frasa was waiting for her at the entrance."

"Frasa! So she's in Montreal?" Robinson asked, his tone suddenly sharper.

"That's right, she's been in Montreal since this morning."

"Is she with Rowan?"

Thérèse paused as if to heighten the suspense. Then she set down her fork and declared:

"She's shopping for her wedding."

Robinson slowly placed his own utensil down, his eyes narrowing in surprise.

"Well! That's the last thing I expected."

"Quite the news, isn't it?" Thérèse added with a sly smile. "Shannon told me Frasa was overjoyed, absolutely elated. She said she would marry her true love, that they'd have many children, and that they'd be happy until the end of their days. Everything a young girl might say on the eve of her wedding, really."

"And when is this grand event supposed to take place?" Robinson asked, sitting up slightly in his chair.

"Tomorrow."

"Tomorrow? This Saturday?"

"Of course," Thérèse replied with an air of obviousness. "Catholics always marry on a Saturday. Surely you know that."

Robinson furrowed his brow, the news unleashing a whirlwind of thoughts. Earlier that day, he had resolved to find Rowan at all costs. Now, this wedding added a layer of complexity to his investigation.

"They're getting married in a Catholic church?"

"It seems so, yes."

"Are their parents aware?"

"Of course not. Both families would disapprove of the marriage. They'd do everything in their power to stop it."

"So, they've found a priest willing to marry them," Robinson observed skeptically.

"It looks that way," Thérèse replied with a shrug. "And I'd wager the church won't be hard to find. They're both Irish, after all."

"True, but don't underestimate the fact that one is Protestant and the other Catholic," Robinson countered. "Priests and ministers alike are rarely eager to perform mixed marriages. We know that well enough, don't we, Rosalie?"

Rosalie, calmly enjoying her dessert, smiled softly at the remark. Their own marriage had been a trial due to their differing confessions.

"I can think of only two possibilities," Thérèse interjected. "It's either St. Anne's Church or St. Patrick's. Those are the two Irish churches in Montreal."

"You're probably right," Robinson admitted. "Tomorrow, we'll visit both churches."

Thérèse looked at him, intrigued.

"You don't mean to interrupt their wedding, do you?"

"Come now, Thérèse! That's not my intention. I have no desire to separate those who love one another. But I need to speak with Rowan. I also feel a responsibility for Tom Ryan. I promised him I would find Frasa."

Thérèse finished her pie with a satisfied sigh, and the conversation drifted to lighter topics. Meanwhile, Robinson remaine

CHAPTER 24

April 8, Saturday Morning

Robinson and Miss Dupuis were returning from Sainte-Anne parish, nestled in the heart of rain-soaked Griffintown on this grey and cheerless Saturday morning. They had spoken with the Sulpician overseeing the parish, an elderly man with a stern countenance, but he had no knowledge of any wedding scheduled at his church. Disheartened yet unsurprised, the two detectives resolved to continue their investigation and set their sights on Saint Patrick's Church.

The journey was interminable, marked by the relentless drumming of rain against the worn leather of the police carriage. Their horse, an aged and visibly weary creature, plodded with a stubborn indifference. The carriage followed Wellington Street to McGill Street before laboriously climbing the slope of Beaver Hall Hill. The icy rain, driven by a sharp wind, found its way into every crevice, clinging to their garments like a promise of misery.

Miss Dupuis, vainly adjusting the collar of her soaked coat, seized the moment of sluggish travel to question Robinson.

"Silas, I have a question for you. Yesterday, as we were leaving Annie Workman, you asked her for the name of her son John Monahan's murderer."

"Yes, Thérèse," he replied, shaking his head, his gaze fixed on the misty horizon. "I remember it clearly."

"When she mentioned Francis Brennan—that Fenian whose body was found on Monday—you didn't even flinch."

"That's because I expected it," he said with a trace of gravity. "I am convinced Brennan's murder is connected, in some way, to the Workman family. As soon as Chief Penton informed me last Monday that John Monahan was the son of Thomas Workman, I sensed there was a link."

"Do you think Monahan's father could have killed Brennan?"

"I'm not certain, but he's likely involved somehow. Perhaps he confided in other Orangemen. Perhaps they decided to deal with it collectively. But the idea that Thomas Workman killed him with his own hands… That's a theory I still find hard to swallow."

Miss Dupuis nodded, her expression betraying deep thought.

"Why would the Orangemen have wanted to target Brennan?" she asked. "After all, no one knew he might be

Monahan's killer. Even we only considered him a suspect among many."

"The Orangemen wouldn't have concerned themselves with such details," Robinson replied with a sigh of frustration. "This is where Penton made a monumental mistake—he gave them a list of suspects without sufficient precautions. We, as detectives, understand the weight of our words when dealing with suspect names."

"And they picked the first name on the list," Miss Dupuis concluded, her tone tinged with anger. "Brennan. Their leader."

"Precisely. They decided he would pay for the rest."

The horse slowed even further as though intent on halting altogether. The rain continued its assault, seeping through Miss Dupuis's dress and Robinson's trousers despite their efforts to shield themselves.

"In that case, who could have killed Brennan?"

"I'm not sure yet," Robinson admitted. "But it's precisely why we need to speak with the one member of the Workman family we haven't yet met—Rowan."

"And what about Frasa?" asked Miss Dupuis, her eyes searching her colleague's.

"Frasa is a victim," he replied without hesitation. "A puppet manipulated by the Protestant Irish Orangemen. She played along with Thomas Workman's schemes in blackmailing D'Arcy McGee. Her blind love for Rowan made her vulnerable, unable to grasp the consequences of her actions."

"Then, if we find Rowan and Frasa, what do we do with them?"

"Rowan must be brought to the station for questioning. He's a suspect in Brennan's death. As for Frasa, I'll leave her to you. In any case, this carriage cannot carry four people."

"Very well," Miss Dupuis answered with confidence. "I'll take care of her."

"The best course would be for you to question her and return her to her father. D'Arcy McGee needs reassurance. He's worried about her and doesn't want to remain uncertain about his upcoming departure for Ireland."

Robinson sat slightly in his seat while Miss Dupuis pulled the soaked folds of her dress tighter around her. Their mission still lay ahead, down a long road strewn with doubt and icy rain.

After half an hour of travel at a sluggish pace that might have rivalled that of a tortoise, Robinson and Miss Dupuis finally arrived at Saint Patrick's Church. The building loomed majestically in the damp grey morning, its dark stones glistening under the relentless rain.

Yet, nothing in its appearance or the immediate surroundings suggested a celebration. There was no jubilant crowd clad in their Sunday best, no festive peal of bells, no laughter or scattered grains of rice heralding a newlywed couple. All was calm—oppressively so—as the persistent drizzle completed the scene's desolation.

Robinson raised an eyebrow, skeptically brushing the droplets streaming from the lapels of his coat. Her heavy dress clinging to her legs, Miss Dupuis gazed at the dimmed stained glass windows and sighed softly.

"There's no one here," she murmured. "This bodes ill."

Despite their misgivings, they stepped inside. The solemn silence within seemed to absorb the sounds of the outside world, leaving only the muffled echo of their footsteps on the smooth, cold stone tiles. The nave stretched out before them, vast and imposing, its towering dark stone pillars seeming to reach up to the intricately adorned Gothic ceilings. The flickering light of brass chandeliers, placed along the walls and upon the altar, cast shifting shadows over the still statues of saints, lending the space an almost otherworldly air. Wooden pews, worn smooth by time and the silent prayers of the faithful, stood in neat rows, adding to the austerity of the place.

At first glance, the church appeared deserted. Yet, at the far end of the nave, near a finely carved marble balustrade, an unexpected scene drew their attention amid the sacred emptiness.

A celebrant, draped in resplendent liturgical vestments embroidered with gold and purple, stood facing a young man and a young woman.

The young woman's simplicity enhanced her natural grace. She wore a plain white linen dress adorned only with delicate lace trim at the collar and cuffs. A light grey wool shawl, worn but clean, rested on her shoulders, speaking of modest means, while a white bonnet, slightly faded with age, concealed her neatly arranged dark hair.

The young man beside her was equally modestly attired: a black frock coat with subtly worn elbows over a crisp white cotton shirt. A narrow black cravat, tied with care, lent an air of dignity to his appearance. Though polished to a shine, his boots bore the marks of daily use.

Two older men stood nearby, clad in thick, dark overcoats. They lingered slightly apart, observing the scene with solemn expressions under the softened glow of the chandeliers.

The priest's steady and solemn voice echoed through the quiet church, filling the space with reverence.

"You may kiss the bride."

Robinson and Miss Dupuis exchanged a stunned glance before striding purposefully toward the small group. The priest looked up at their approach, his expression immediately clouding with displeasure.

"What are you doing here?" he demanded, his voice ringing with authority. "This is a private ceremony."

Miss Dupuis, whose knowledge of Catholic rites surpassed her colleagues, stepped forward with a disarming poise.

"Father, is it not true that marriages must be celebrated before the community and, therefore, publicly?" she asked, her tone a careful balance of gentleness and authority.

Her gaze swept the nave, where the empty pews only underscored the clandestine nature of the occasion. She continued, her eyes glinting with quiet defiance:

"I see no community here."

The faces of the other four participants had already turned toward them. The young man and woman, radiant, seemed to float in the euphoria of their recent union. Rowan and Frasa, for it was indeed them, could not conceal their joy.

Robinson observed the scene with heightened scrutiny. The two older men, by contrast, adopted a markedly different demeanour. Their wary eyes fixed on the detectives with palpable intensity as if bracing for an imminent confrontation.

Rowan placed a protective hand over Frasa's while the silence hung heavy, like a judgment passed over the peculiar ceremony.

"Do you recognize me, Father Dowd?" Robinson asked, taking a step forward, his rain-specked coat glistening in the dim light.

The priest, an austere figure draped in his chasuble, regarded him briefly before responding with measured reserve:

"Of course, Detective Robinson. But that still does not explain your presence here."

Robinson, his hands clasped behind his back, studied the group before him, his gaze lingering on Rowan and Frasa.

"Where are the bride and groom's parents, Father Dowd?"

The priest hesitated.

"They couldn't attend," he finally replied, his voice quieter.

"They are not here because they didn't know their children were to be married."

The priest inclined his head slightly.

"Perhaps…" he murmured at last.

Miss Dupuis, who had been observing the exchange with a cold concentration, spoke up in a clear and assured voice:

"You are aware this marriage could be declared invalid, aren't you, Father? You didn't publish the banns. You didn't ask the community if they had objections. And, in any case, to whom would you have posed the question? Your two sacristans, who know neither of them from Adam?"

A heavy silence filled the church. The statues of saints, motionless in their niches, seemed to stand as silent witnesses to the confrontation. As if turned to stone, the ceremony participants remained at the foot of the balustrade.

The priest pressed his lips together, then said softly:

"These children love each other with a devotion I have seldom seen."

"You know them?" Miss Dupuis pressed, stepping forward.

"I have known Frasa since she was a child," Father Dowd replied with a hint of nostalgia. "D'Arcy McGee is a good Catholic who attends Mass regularly in Montreal."

"And him? Do you know him as well?"

Father Dowd lowered his eyes to Rowan and Frasa before lifting his head again. A visible emotion darkened his features.

"I know Rowan is a Protestant. Yesterday, he told me everything. How he lost his mother at a young age, how he was adopted by the Workman family. He even admitted he doesn't know whether he is truly of Protestant or Catholic origins."

Robinson, folding his arms, replied in a neutral tone:

"Since he was adopted by Protestants, he takes on their religion. That's the custom."

Father Dowd straightened slightly, a flicker of defiance lighting his eyes.

"Perhaps the custom of men, but not the custom of God. God is love. That is God's golden rule: 'Love the Lord your God with all your heart and your neighbour as yourself.'"

A tense silence followed the declaration. Robinson, unflinching, stepped forward again, his tone growing more direct.

"I regret interrupting such a lovely ceremony, but Rowan must accompany me. I need to question him."

The priest opened his mouth, but before he could speak, Frasa suddenly burst out:

"You're arresting him? But he's done nothing wrong! No… no… you can't! He's my husband!"

Her voice trembled as much as her hands clung to Rowan like a castaway clutching a lifeline.

Robinson, softening his tone, tried to quell the outburst.

"I'm not arresting Rowan. I just want to ask him a few questions."

But Frasa, overtaken by fear and anger, erupted again.

"He's done nothing wrong…" she cried, tears streaming down her face.

The tension in the church was palpable. The chandeliers cast flickering shadows on the stone walls, heightening the dramatic atmosphere. Rowan, who had remained silent until then, placed a calming hand over Frasa's, but his dark and resigned gaze remained fixed on Robinson.

While Robinson spoke with Father Dowd, Miss Dupuis moved slowly toward the couple, her steps barely audible on the marble floor of the chancel. With a gentle gesture, she laid her gloved hand on Frasa's trembling shoulder.

"Frasa… Frasa…" she murmured soothingly. "Let him go. You'll see him again soon."

Frasa slowly turned her tear-streaked face toward Miss Dupuis. Her red, swollen eyes conveyed an almost tangible distress. Without a word, she allowed herself to be guided, her trembling lips whispering:

"We're married… nothing can separate us."

Miss Dupuis, her face calm and composed, approached Father Dowd.

"May we use your sacristy?" she asked, her tone firm but respectful.

The priest shrugged and gestured vaguely, indicating she might do as she pleased.

"Could you send someone to fetch a Hansom cab?" she added.

Father Dowd sighed.

"It will be difficult on a Saturday morning, but I'll send one of my sacristans. What do you intend to do with her?" he asked, glancing at Frasa worriedly.

"Don't worry," Miss Dupuis replied confidently. "I'll take care of her."

Holding Frasa by the shoulders, Miss Dupuis gently guided her toward the sacristy door. But as they moved forward, Frasa suddenly stopped and turned back to Rowan. Her cry pierced the sacred silence of the church:

"I love you… forever, my love!"

Rowan, who had remained stoic until now, broke down at her words. Tears streaming down his face, he turned as well and called out, his heart shattered:

"My little bird, I love you. I can't live without you!"

The tension was almost unbearable, every word echoing through the empty church like a desperate prayer. Robinson, suppressing a sigh, finally stepped out of the church, leaving behind the poignant scene.

Miss Dupuis led Frasa into the sacristy, a small, solemn space imbued with the mingled scents of beeswax and faded incense. The walls, lined with polished dark wooden cabinets, seemed to hold years of secrets and whispered confidences. The aged wood gleamed faintly under the light of an oil lamp on a small table cluttered with prayer books and ornate candlesticks. A large mullioned window, slightly fogged by the cold outside, admitted a pale, grey light that softened the sharp lines of the furnishings.

Two straight-backed chairs with cracked leather seats stood near the window, offering a partial view of the damp courtyard where puddles had gathered. Frasa collapsed into one of them, her frail body giving way under the weight of her emotions, her ample dress pooling in disordered folds around her. Miss Dupuis, carefully pulling the other chair closer so as not to disturb the heavy silence of the room, sat beside her and rested a comforting hand on the young girl's shoulder.

"Frasa," she said softly. "I'm Shannon's cousin. You know Shannon, don't you?"

Frasa lifted her tear-streaked face, her despairing eyes meeting Miss Dupuis's. She nodded faintly, unable to speak.

"Shannon cares for you deeply, you know," Miss Dupuis said encouragingly. "And so do your parents."

After a brief silence, Frasa murmured in a barely audible voice:

"You know my parents?"

"Yes," Miss Dupuis replied. "I met your father a few weeks ago. He's very worried about you, Frasa."

The young girl shrugged, her expression defeated.

"He thought you'd been kidnapped," Miss Dupuis added calmly.

Frasa tilted her head slightly, incredulity washing over her features.

"Kidnapped? What sort of story is that?"

"Your father received a letter saying Rowan had abducted you."

Frasa shook her head vehemently, her dark curls bouncing around her face.

"That's not true! It's a lie! Rowan is my great love!"

"So, you went with him of your own free will?"

"Of course," she said passionately. "I was the one who asked him. I wanted to live with him and leave for the United States. We wanted to escape far away from here."

"And your father knew this?"

Frasa averted her gaze, a flush creeping into her cheeks.

"He would never have accepted it," she murmured after a moment.

"He didn't want you to be with Rowan?"

"Certainly not with a Protestant Irishman," she replied bitterly. "He would never have tolerated it."

"Even knowing you loved him?"

"You can't reason with my father when it comes to Protestant Irishmen," she said, shaking her head.

Miss Dupuis paused in thought before speaking again, her tone gentle:

"I suppose it was the same with Rowan's parents regarding Catholics."

"Of course. They would never have accepted Rowan marrying a Catholic."

Miss Dupuis regarded Frasa thoughtfully before asking:

"And Rowan, what does he think of all this?"

A faint smile crossed Frasa's face.

"Rowan doesn't care about those feuds. He doesn't understand why Catholic and Protestant Irish hate each other so much. All he wants is to be with me."

"Look at my wedding ring," she murmured, her eyes glimmering melancholic.

Frasa lifted her trembling hand to show the golden ring she wore on her finger. It was a simple band, plain and unadorned, without engraving. It held no monetary value, but for Frasa, it was the treasure of her love—a promise eternal.

Miss Dupuis, seated opposite her, regarded the dull glint of the ring for a moment before continuing, her voice gentle but insistent:

"You said, Frasa, that you wanted to flee to the United States with Rowan. Why didn't you?"

Frasa lowered her gaze to her hands, which she twisted nervously, before answering:

"We didn't have enough money… How could we make such a journey with nothing? Rowan said he'd work to earn some."

"Is that why you ended up at Rowan's aunt's place in the village of Saint-Laurent?"

"Yes, that's right. His uncle gave him a small wage for helping out. It wasn't much… not enough."

"Was it then that Rowan learned of his brother John's death?"

"No," Frasa replied, gently shaking her head, her dark curls falling untidily around her face. "He had learned about it before going to his aunt's. That's why he left home in the first place. When we talked about going to the United States, we didn't mean to leave immediately. He wanted to save enough money to go in a few months."

Miss Dupuis let the silence stretch, watching the young girl wrestle with her memories.

"What happened?"

Frasa drew a deep breath, her fingers intertwining further, betraying her unease.

"He argued with his father... terribly. That's what he told me. After that, we left home and went to his aunt's."

The tension in the small room was nearly palpable. Frasa's words seemed to drain her, each one weighing heavier on her already burdened heart.

"So, you'd been there for more than two weeks?"

"Yes... that's right."

"You were always together?"

Frasa lifted her head slightly, a soft glow of tenderness brightening her tearful gaze.

"Always. We never left each other. I helped his aunt with the cooking and cleaning. Rowan took care of the animals and the farm work. You know, there's so much work to do on a farm."

A silence settled again, broken only by the faint creak of a chair. Finally, Frasa whispered, almost to herself:

"What's going to happen now?"

Miss Dupuis, who had not ceased watching her, felt her heart tighten at the sight of this fragile young girl, scarcely more than a child. Her dress, far too large, hung awkwardly from her narrow shoulders, and her face, still marked by innocence, bore the signs of a love too heavy for someone her age to carry.

"I think you should see your parents," she said softly.

"Do you think so?" Frasa asked, anxiety edging her voice. "And Rowan?"

Miss Dupuis placed a comforting hand on the young girl's.

"You'll see him again now that you're married," she said with a conviction that was kind but subtly feigned. "But for now, it's important to ease your parents' worries. Don't you think?"

Frasa nodded, brushing away a tear that trailed down her cheek.

"Yes… you're right."

At that moment, a gentle knock sounded at the door. Father Dowd entered, his kindly eyes immediately settling on Frasa.

"Are you all right, my dear Frasa?" he asked warmly.

"Yes, Father… I'm all right," she replied, though her voice betrayed the emotion welling within her.

But no sooner had she spoken than her shoulders began to shake, and she burst into tears again. Without a word, Miss Dupuis pulled a clean handkerchief from her purse and offered it to her.

Father Dowd, visibly moved, approached gently.

"We've found a Hansom cab. It's waiting for you at the entrance," he announced.

Miss Dupuis rose, placing a firm yet gentle hand on Frasa's trembling shoulder.

"Thank you, Father. Shall we, Frasa?"

Still shaken by her tears, Frasa struggled to her feet. Without a word, she followed Miss Dupuis, her slow, dragging steps echoing faintly in the hushed sacristy.

CHAPTER 25

April 8, Saturday afternoon

The rain fell upon Montreal with a chilling persistence, draping the streets and sidewalks in glistening puddles. The irregular patter of the rain against the frosted panes of the police station heightened the pervasive cold. The fire, confined within a stove blackened by years of use, struggled to warm the cramped room where Robinson, Morin, and Kelly conversed. Their coats were still beaded with rain and draped over chairs, while the air was thick with the damp smell of wet leather. The feeble, grey daylight barely seeped into the room, deepening the sombre and oppressive atmosphere marked by expectant silence. Miss Dupuis, usually punctual, had not yet arrived.

As for O'Meara, the Fenian accused of murdering Monahan, the evidence seemed both damning and elusive. Locked behind bars, he awaited his appearance before a judge. The detectives were sure of his guilt. Too many converging clues pointed in his direction, yet none sufficiently convinced a court. No witnesses, no murder weapon.

To make matters worse, O'Meara had meticulously constructed an alibi. According to his account, he had spent St. Patrick's evening drinking and spinning yarns with his fellow Fenians, far from Kate Scanlan's tavern, where

Monahan had last been seen. Interrogating his friends had only reinforced his story. Each of them swore, hand over heart, that he had not left their sight.

"It's hopeless," grumbled Morin, shaking his head bitterly. "He won't be convicted."

"Quite possible," Robinson replied in an even tone, his gaze fixed on a map before him.

Kelly, ever quick with his comments, glanced up.

"In any case, John Monahan brought it on himself with all he's done."

Robinson lifted his head, his features hardening with a shadow of disapproval.

"No man, Kelly, deserves to end up in the back of a filthy alley, stabbed to death."

Caught off guard, Kelly avoided a direct reply. Instead, he shrugged and shifted the conversation.

"Do we have any more information about our other murder—the one involving Francis Brennan?"

Robinson gave a slight nod, absently smoothing his moustache.

"Some, but nothing decisive."

He continued slowly, weighing each word as though handling fragile objects. After he met with Thomas Workman, he was convinced that Brennan's murder was intimately tied to the Workman family. John Monahan, Workman's adopted son, had been killed by a Fenian—this was certain for the Orangemen. Brennan, the leader of the Fenians, was their ideal culprit. A perfect syllogism for their fervent minds.

Yet everything grew more complicated regarding Rowan Workman, the younger son. Unlike his father and brother, staunch Orangemen, Rowan vehemently opposed their views. Robinson found himself doubting that Rowan could have been involved in a plot so bloody.

"Where is Dupuis, then?" Robinson asked, breaking the silence.

Morin frowned, arms crossed tightly.
"Why isn't she here with the girl for questioning? Rowan might well be a murderer, and she his accomplice."

Robinson placed his hands on the table, his fingers tapping lightly.
"I don't believe Frasa is his accomplice. She strikes me more as a victim in all this. I asked Dupuis to question her and take her back to her parents."

Outside, the rain hammered down with increasing fervour as though Montreal bore the weight of these dark intrigues. The scattered oil lamps cast a flickering light that danced on the walls, animating the shadows like silent spectres. The wait dragged on, as did the doubts gnawing at the detectives' minds.

At that moment, Miss Dupuis entered, bringing a subtle, almost luminous energy tinged with the dampness of the outdoors. She shrugged off her rain-soaked coat and carefully hung her hat on a hook near the door. Despite the mud outside, her well-polished boots tapped softly on the worn floorboards. Dressed in a dark woollen gown, elegantly fitted and complemented by a black velvet shawl, she seemed to have stepped straight out of a Rembrandt painting.

"Are you sure you had time to change, Dupuis?" Robinson asked, raising his eyes.

"But Chief, a lady must always present herself at her best," she replied with a mock curtsy.

Kelly laughed heartily, his face lighting up for the first time that day. Morin, however, raised his eyebrows and remained unmoved, his surly expression unchanged.

"What do you have to tell us about Frasa?" Morin demanded brusquely, arms still crossed.

After shaking the water from her oilcloth umbrella, scattering shimmering droplets in every direction, Miss

Dupuis carefully folded it. She set it near the stove, where the warmth could dry the remaining dampness. She naturally took her place at her work table, retrieving a weathered leather notebook from her bag and carefully flipping through its pages.

"Poor girl! She's utterly wretched. You should see her."

Morin grunted, tilting his head slightly.
"Utterly wretched, is she? She's likely the accomplice to a murder. Of course, she's wretched."

Miss Dupuis met his gaze, her expression steady and unyielding.
"I'm not so sure of that. I took the time to question her about her stay in the village of Saint-Laurent at Rowan's aunt's house. First of all, those two are madly in love. They can't bear to be apart; they're practically inseparable."

Kelly, leaning back in his chair, whistled through his teeth.
"That'll wear off after a year of marriage."

Robinson, in a more measured tone, interjected:
"Do you remember, Dupuis, what Annie Workman—Rowan's mother—said? She mentioned the same thing. They're inseparable."

Miss Dupuis nodded, her eyes fixed on her notes.
"Except for a short period," she added. "Rowan supposedly left to run errands in town."

Robinson murmured in response, "Except for that short period..."

A silence settled over the room, broken only by the relentless drumming of the rain. Morin, thoughtful, repeated the Chief's words slowly:
"Except for that short period..."

Robinson broke the heavy atmosphere.
"Were you able to take Frasa back to her parents?"

Miss Dupuis hesitated briefly before answering:
"Yes, but it was strange. The entire way, she was reluctant. She kept saying she didn't want to face her father."

"And then?" Kelly asked, his brows knitting together.

Miss Dupuis drew a breath before continuing:
"She was right. When we arrived at the D'Arcy McGee house, her mother and little sister were overjoyed, rushing to embrace her. But the father... He was cold. He simply said he was relieved to see her, and that was it. Not a smile, not a hug. Nothing. I knew at once that he already knew."

Morin squinted slightly and sat up straighter.
"He knew about Rowan?"

"Yes," Miss Dupuis replied. "He had found out, though I don't know how. D'Arcy McGee has connections everywhere."

"And did he know they were married?" Robinson asked gravely.

Miss Dupuis shook her head.
"No. When he found out, his anger erupted. He's a passionate man, you know. He berated her, saying what she had done was unthinkable."

"And how did she react?"

"It was surprising. Frasa composed herself. Not a tear, not a word. She let him speak, completely unfazed. Ultimately, she said, 'I love Rowan with all my heart. You should be happy for me.'"

Kelly grimaced, shaking his head.
"Yeah, not exactly a joyful reunion."

Miss Dupuis nodded, her voice tinged with a sigh.
"No, it was painful—truly."

Morin leaned forward slightly.
"And now? What's to become of Frasa?"

"For now, she's staying with her parents. Her father is leaving for Ireland in a few days. That may ease some of the tension.

"Good. Let's go question our suspect," Robinson said.

The Chief rose with a resolute gesture, his expression sombre yet determined. Beside him, Kelly mirrored the motion, ready to follow without hesitation.

"I'll question him with Dupuis," Robinson declared, calm but firm.

Morin, leaning against the edge of his desk, reacted at once, crossing his arms in a defensive posture.
"Dupuis? But she's not ready…"

Adjusting her shawl, Miss Dupuis slowly turned her head toward him, her lips curving into an ironic smile—a mixture of amusement and disappointment. Her eyes sparkled with defiance as they locked onto Morin's.
"And when will I be ready, Morin?" she retorted, faintly provocative.

Morin frowned, searching for his words.
"I don't know… He might be a murderer. You're not used to this… And it's been barely three weeks since you joined us."

Robinson, who had been observing in silence, finally intervened. His voice, though measured, carried undeniable authority.

"It was a month after you joined the team, Morin when you conducted your first interrogation."

Morin, visibly stung, shook his head.
"That was different…"

Before he could elaborate, Miss Dupuis crossed her arms and, in a sharp tone, added:
"Ah yes, that's right. I tend to forget sometimes—I'm a woman."

Morin straightened up, looking somewhat unsettled.
"No, that's not it. I was a constable for several years before joining the team. I'd already dealt with all sorts of criminals."

Robinson cut the exchange short, his voice hardening slightly.
"Enough! This discussion is over. Dupuis is coming with me because she knows this case better than anyone else. She'll do just fine, Morin."

Robinson and Miss Dupuis left the room without waiting for a response. The latter briefly glanced at Morin—half amused, half triumphant—before following the Chief. Morin remained motionless, his arms still crossed, an expression of evident dissatisfaction etched on his face.

In the silence that followed their departure, Kelly, still seated at his desk, allowed himself a faint smirk. With a casual gesture, he picked up a quill and returned to his paperwork, clearly entertained by the scene that had just unfolded. Outside, the rain continued to pound against the windows, underscoring the unspoken intensity of the exchange.

CHAPTER 26

April 8, Saturday afternoon

Rowan sat behind the worn wooden table in the interrogation room. The flickering light of an oil lamp cast shifting shadows on the walls, making the atmosphere even more oppressive. Despite his youth, he exuded a solid presence. Relatively tall and well-built, his youthful features contrasted with his dark gaze, which was both wary and vacant. His hair, an unremarkable brown, framed a face untouched by the faintest trace of a beard.

Miss Dupuis sat opposite him, calmly placing a notebook on the table before her. Dressed in a dark, modest gown, her measured demeanour softened the severity of the room.

"Good afternoon, Rowan," she said with a gentle smile. "I'm pleased to meet you."

The young man raised his eyes, his face blank, betraying no hint of emotion.
"Who are you?" he asked, his monotone voice tinged with weariness.

"My name is Thérèse," she replied quietly. "I'm a friend of Shannon."

He furrowed his brow slightly.

"Who's Shannon?"

"I thought Frasa might have mentioned her to you. Shannon is her closest friend," Miss Dupuis explained, tilting her head slightly.

Rowan turned away, ignoring Miss Dupuis to fix his gaze on Robinson, who stood near the door with his arms crossed.

"I'm Silas Robinson, Chief Detective with the Montreal police," Robinson stated gravely, his piercing gaze locked on the young man.

"What do you want from me, Detective?" Rowan asked, his voice carrying an air of almost provocative indifference.

"Miss Dupuis and I have some questions for you to clarify certain aspects of our investigation," Robinson replied.

Robinson, silently observing the exchange, stepped forward with a deliberate air. He pulled out a chair and sat across from Rowan, his piercing eyes never leaving the young man's.

Rowan held his gaze for a moment before looking away again. The apathy he displayed seemed almost like a defensive wall. After a moment of silence, he murmured:

"Where's Frasa?"

Miss Dupuis answered gently:

"She's safe. I took her back to her parents."

A bitter smirk twisted Rowan's lips.

"Back to her parents? Pfft! They won't want to see her."

"And why is that?"

"Her parents rejected her," he said, his tone hardening. "They don't approve of our marriage."

"Nor do yours, I suppose?"

For the first time, Rowan lowered his head, his eyes falling to the dull wood of the table. A heavy silence filled the room, finally broken by Robinson.

"Is that why you moved to your aunt's house—because your parents opposed the marriage?"

Rowan lifted his head, a flicker of hesitation passing through his eyes. He seemed to weigh his words before answering.

"No. That's not why I left."

Robinson narrowed his eyes, scrutinizing every nuance in the young man's demeanour.

"Then why did you leave?"

Rowan's voice suddenly rose, trembling with restrained anger.

"My father is a bastard!"

"Your father—he's Thomas Workman, isn't he? I've met him, you know," Robinson said, his tone calm and almost measured, the weight of his words hanging heavily in the air.

Rowan froze, his fists clenching on the table. A faint tremor rippled along his jaw, but he said nothing. The tension in the interrogation room was palpable. The flickering light of the oil lamp deepened the shadows beneath Rowan's eyes, making him appear both furious and burdened. Sitting across from him, Robinson rested his forearms on the table, his intense gaze nearly hypnotic. To his right, Miss Dupuis watched Rowan with a gentleness that starkly contrasted to the moment's gravity.

"It seemed to me he was a good man who loves his children," Robinson began in a calm, almost neutral tone.

Rowan suddenly exploded, his voice shattering the oppressive silence.

"Loves his children!" he shouted. "Is that how you see him? Well, it's the exact opposite. He hates his children!"

"But—"

"He had my brother killed!" Rowan spat, his eyes blazing with fury.

Robinson feigned surprise, his expression darkening.

"What? He had your brother killed? Your brother is John Monahan, isn't he?"

"Of course! He dragged John into his gang of Orangemen thugs. John went along like a puppet. That's why he's dead!"

Robinson nodded slowly as if encouraging Rowan to continue.

"The Orangemen—they're Irish Protestants, correct?"

"That's right," Rowan replied, his tone laced with bitterness.

"I don't understand," Robinson said, his voice carrying a tone of genuine curiosity. "You're an Irish Protestant, too. Why didn't you follow your brother?"

Rowan clenched his jaw and planted his elbows on the table as though holding back a storm of anger.

"Those Orangemen! They're nothing but thugs! They hate Irish Catholics for reasons I can't even comprehend. I'm sure they don't understand them either!"

While taking notes without raising her head, Miss Dupuis spoke soothingly.

"I understand why you feel that way. The one you love, Frasa—she's an Irish Catholic, right?"

Rowan nodded sharply, the words seeming to choke in his throat.

"It makes no sense—these feuds that have lasted for centuries, as if all Catholics were corrupt traitors to the Pope. It's ridiculous! And yes, Frasa is Catholic. That's all it takes for my father to see her as wicked. I hate him!"

A silence fell over the room, broken only by the faint creak of Rowan's boots against the floor. Robinson let the silence stretch before speaking again.

"Your father told me you were close to your brother John."

"Very close," Rowan murmured. "He wasn't just a big brother. He has helped me ever since I was a child. He always protected me. I adored my brother."

"You must have been devastated when you learned of his death."

Rowan, still bowed, began wringing his hands, his agitation revealing a deep pain.

"Devastated, yes… Very devastated… But it's my father's fault he's dead," he said at last. "He dragged John into his political fights. That's why John died. My father killed John."

Miss Dupuis spoke softly, her gaze fixed on Rowan with a sincerity almost maternal.

"I have a big brother, too, Rowan. And I often wonder what I'd do if someone harmed him."

Rowan raised his head, his eyes glistening with tears. He stared at Miss Dupuis with an almost unbearable intensity.

"In any case," she continued, "if someone had killed my brother, I would want revenge."

The young man stared at her, his lips trembling slightly. Miss Dupuis pressed on, her tone growing even warmer.

"Annie… your mother… Oh, I didn't tell you. I met her. She's a very kind woman, your mother."

"Yes," Rowan whispered. "She's kind. She's not like my father."

"That's clear," Miss Dupuis agreed. "Annie told me she came to see you last week."

"She did. She spent the whole week with us… to help us," he murmured.

"She knew you were seeing Frasa, then? And your mother approved?"

Rowan frowned, hesitating.
"Not really. She wanted to talk sense into me, to convince me to break things off with Frasa.

"Didn't work, I see," Miss Dupuis said with a sly smile.

"No, it certainly didn't," he replied more firmly. "Frasa is the love of my life… she is my life…"

Miss Dupuis looked at him tenderly, but Robinson chose that moment to steer the conversation back on track.

"Your mother told us she had something important to tell you last week," Robinson began, calm yet deliberate. "She had learned the name of the man who killed your brother."

At these words, Rowan stiffened, his demeanour shifting abruptly. He began fidgeting in his chair, his left leg bouncing nervously.

"Your mother told you the name Francis Brennan," Robinson continued, his voice growing firmer.

Rowan kept fidgeting, avoiding Robinson's gaze.

"Do you know Francis Brennan?"

"No," Rowan said hastily, almost too quickly.

"But you do know him," Robinson pressed, his tone more insistent. "He's the leader of the Fenians in Montreal. You know who the Fenians are, don't you?"

"They're a gang of Irish Catholic thugs," Rowan growled. "No better than the Orangemen."

"So, your mother told you that Francis Brennan killed John, your brother."

Rowan, flushed with anger, finally burst out:
"Yes, that's what she told me. That bastard killed my brother John."

Robinson's expression grew grave as he fixed Rowan with an intense stare.
"And after learning that, you decided to go and confront Brennan in Montreal, didn't you?"

A heavy silence fell, broken only by raindrops beating against the windows. Rowan, still agitated, remained silent as though carefully weighing his following words. Then, abruptly, he stilled, his movements ceasing as suddenly as the branches of a tree after a gust of wind. His previously darting eyes fixed on the worn wooden table before him, and in a steadier voice, he said:
"Yes, that's right. I wanted to meet him."

Robinson leaned forward slightly, resting his elbows on the table, scrutinizing every word.
"You knew where he worked. Your mother told you. You took your uncle's best horse and rode to his business near the Lachine Canal."

"It wasn't hard to find," Rowan murmured, almost under his breath.

"And you met him?"

"It was late, a Friday. He was still working," Rowan replied, his voice firmer now. "There was no one else there but him."

"So, you wanted to confront him?"

"I asked him why he did it. Why he killed my brother," Rowan said, his anger resurfacing in his tone.

"And what did he say?"

"He pretended not to understand what I was talking about," Rowan said through gritted teeth. "He told me he didn't know anything about it. He lied to me."

Miss Dupuis, seated slightly back, continued taking notes methodically. Though composed, her features softened with an unmistakable compassion each time she glanced at Rowan. Robinson, however, maintained his pressure.

"What happened next?"

Rowan took a deep breath, his shoulders rising and falling in a nervous rhythm.
"He told me to leave. I refused, so I pushed him a little. He got scared. But all I wanted was for him to tell me the truth," he explained, his voice tinged with frustration and regret.

"And then?"

"He pushed me back and ran into the warehouse," Rowan continued, his eyes fixed on some invisible point on the wall. "I chased him. He ended up at the big loading doors. They were open. He didn't know where to go… He was trapped."

Robinson leaned in further, his voice low and measured. "What did you do then?"

Rowan turned his eyes away, the weight of his memories visibly bearing down on him.

"I approached him to talk, but he hit me," he admitted. "It didn't hurt much. He was small, not strong. So… I defended myself… I hit him in the face."

He paused, his face hardening with emotion.

"That's when he lost his balance and fell into the canal. I couldn't do anything to catch him," he added in a broken whisper, his voice cracking under the weight of his confession.

An unusual, almost disorienting silence filled the room, as heavy as the leaden rain clouds outside. Rowan's confession, delivered with disarming candour, starkly contrasted the usual tension of such interrogations. The rain striking the windows seemed suddenly louder, accentuating the strangeness of the moment. Miss Dupuis, visibly moved, was the first to break the silence.

"But Rowan," she said gently, "couldn't you have gone to the police to have Brennan arrested? If he was a murderer, he would have been punished."

Rowan slowly shook his head, his eyes clouded with anger and sorrow.

"I was so angry... So angry... I wanted him to admit to his crime."

Another silence fell, heavier than the last. Finally, Rowan lifted his head slightly, his eyes glistening but resolute.

"It was an accident," he whispered at last. "I didn't mean to kill him."

Robinson and Miss Dupuis exchanged glances. The young man suddenly seemed so vulnerable, like a child crushed beneath the weight of his own actions. The relentless rain continued to drum against the windows as if the city mourned the tragic turn of events.

With a subtle signal from Robinson, Miss Dupuis methodically closed her notebook, tucked her pencil away, and stood with measured deliberation. The Chief Detective fixed his gaze on Rowan before speaking in a grave, steady tone.

"We'll have to charge you for this crime, Rowan."

The young man turned ashen, his already pale complexion draining of all colour. His body stiffened, and his lips trembled as he stammered,

"It was an accident... What will happen now? And Frasa...?"

Robinson remained composed, though his tone softened slightly, each word carefully weighed.

"I believe you can plead manslaughter. With a good lawyer, you'll serve prison time instead of being hanged."

As still as a statue, Rowan furrowed his brow, panic flickering in his eyes.

"Prison? How long?"

"I don't know," Robinson replied, his voice neutral, almost apologetic. "That depends on the judge. Maybe ten years."

"Ten years! No... No... I can't... I'll never see Frasa again... I'll never see her... No, it's not possible. I can't live without her," Rowan murmured, his voice breaking under the weight of despair.

He slowly lowered his head, his forehead nearly touching the wooden table, as though his emotions were physically pressing him down. A silence stretched, interrupted only by the steady drum of rain on the windows.

Robinson crossed his arms, his gaze resting on the young man with a hint of compassion. Then, breaking the tense quiet, he spoke, his voice cutting through the atmosphere.

"There's something you need to know, Rowan. Francis Brennan wasn't your brother's killer. We found the man who was."

The words struck Rowan like a slap. He jerked his head up, his wide eyes brimming with shock. He seemed to wrestle with understanding momentarily, as though the words hadn't yet fully registered. Then, suddenly, his shoulders collapsed, and he broke into deep, wrenching sobs, the cries of a soul overwhelmed by unbearable grief.

Standing a little apart, Miss Dupuis clutched her notebook to her chest, watching the scene with sadness and helplessness. Still standing before Rowan, Robinson remained silent, giving the young man space to release his anguish.

Outside, the rain continued hammering against the windows, amplifying the moment's drama as if even the heavens shared the weight of the day's revelations.

***

On the evening of Rowan Workman's interrogation, Thérèse, known as Miss Dupuis to her colleagues, visited her mother and stepfather for supper. As always, the atmosphere in their stone-terraced house was warm and inviting, the fire in the hearth casting a soft, flickering glow. The rain, still drumming against the windows, heightened the sense of refuge and intimacy the home provided.

During dessert— a farlouche pie served with steaming tea—Thérèse could no longer keep to herself the thoughts weighing on her since the interrogation. She set her cup down delicately and, after a contemplative silence, said.

"You'll find me sentimental, Silas, but I was deeply moved by the love between Rowan and Frasa."

She paused, her gaze wandering to the flickering flames in the fireplace.

"I feel such sorrow for them. Their love was doomed by the senseless rivalries between two groups of Irishmen. It's like Romeo and Juliet trapped between the Capulets and the Montagues. Don't you think?"

Sitting across from her, Robinson stared at his cup momentarily, his features marked by a weariness he made no effort to conceal. At last, he raised his head, his face touched by a shadow of reflection, and replied simply:

"Shakespeare is eternal."

***

On the third day of Rowan's imprisonment, the morning was grey, saturated with a chilling dampness that seemed to seep into one's soul. A guard paced through the dismal corridors of the prison. Heavy with shifting shadows, the damp walls exuded the acrid scent of cold stone and nearly palpable despair. Each step he took echoed like a funeral toll, deepening the oppressive silence over the place.

When he reached Rowan's cell, an unsettling sensation gripped him, a foreboding that stole his breath and slowed his steps. He froze momentarily as though some unseen force warned him not to proceed. At last, yielding to an inexplicable unease, he stepped forward—and the sight before him left him rooted in place.

Rowan hung there, his young body suspended in poignant stillness, slightly leaning forward. Sheets crudely knotted around the bars of the small window had formed a makeshift noose, weighted with a crushing symbolism. The bars, worn and flaking, seemed to bow under the burden of the body and all the sorrow in the world. The pale, grey morning light filtered through the opening, illuminating the scene with a harsh, icy clarity as though the light itself were a dispassionate witness to a human tragedy.

The faint swaying of the body in the draft made the fibres of the fabric creak, each sound rising like a haunting lament in the cell's oppressive silence. It was not merely an end—it was the silent cry of a soul shattered by an impossible love.

The guard clutched his ring of keys, their clinking echoing ominously down the corridor. With trembling hands, he inserted the key into the rusted lock, which gave way with a prolonged, almost plaintive groan. As he entered, his eyes were immediately drawn to a note carefully pinned to Rowan's shirt, like a final confession.

He removed the note, his fingers hesitant, as though afraid of the truth it held. With a near-ceremonial slowness, he brought the paper closer to his face and, in a broken voice, murmured the words scrawled in feverish handwriting:

"I cannot live without her…"

These simple yet heartrending words hung in the cold air of the cell, resonating like a plea to a deaf universe. The guard stood motionless, his eyes fixed on the note, searching desperately within those few words for an explanation, a justification, a glimmer of solace that was not there to be found.

Outside, the sky, heavy with dark clouds, seemed to whisper a silent requiem for Rowan and Frasa's tragic love. This pure and achingly intense love had been extinguished in a world incapable of understanding. It left behind only a fragile, dazzling imprint—like a shooting star cutting through an endless night—obliterated by the hatred of a world that does not know how to love.

.